LANCE OF EARTH AND SKY

The Chaos Knight

BOOK TWO

ERIN HOFFMAN

an imprint of Prometheus Books
Amherst, NY

Published 2012 by Pyr®, an imprint of Prometheus Books

Cover illustration © Dehong He
Cover design by Jacqueline Nasso Cooke
Alorean and Qui Empires map by Kristin Jett

Inquiries should be addressed to

Pyr
59 John Glenn Drive
Amherst, New York 14228–2119
VOICE: 716–691–0133
FAX: 716–691–0137
WWW.PYRSF.COM

16 15 14 13 12   5 4 3 2 1

Library of Congress Cataloging-in-Publication Data

Hoffman, Erin, 1981–
     Lance of earth and sky / by Erin Hoffman.
          p. cm. — (The Chaos Knight ; bk. 2)
     ISBN 978–1–61614–615–3 (pbk.)
     ISBN 978–1–61614–616–0 (ebook)
     I. Title.
PS3608.O47768L36 2012
813'.6—dc23

                                                                                    2011050625

Printed in the United States of America

for my grandparents—
epic heroes
from an epic time

ALOREAN AND QUI EMPIRES

VELIN

Val Hatlon

A Sier'Azar

Val Imris

ALOREA

Western Reaches

Windstooth Mountains

Lehria

Isrinvale

Skywall Mountains

ISHMANTI

DISPUTED TERRITORY

QUI
EMPIRE

RIKAN

Shen Ti

THE
SOUTHERN
CONTINENT

Mai Steppe

CONTENTS

Part Three: Eagles Ascend

"Ethos anthropos daimon."
—Heraklitus

PART ONE
WOLVES WITHIN

CHAPTER ONE

MANAGING THE THREAT

The blast of gale-force wind knocked Vidarian into the brush. He crumpled instinctively, protecting his torso with his arms and knees, leaving his back exposed to the reaching dry branches and rocks that littered the forest floor. With a snarl he leapt back to his feet, using momentum and fury to unleash an arc of fire energy. It sizzled through the brush, leaving smoke and char where it passed. A high-pitched yelp at the end of the sear told him he'd found his target.

Close thunder rattled the sky, and with it the first hissing drops of a cold rain fell through the trees. Tiny candleflames that dotted the brush with fire from his attack crackled their complaints before expiring into steam. Thunder called again, and with it Vidarian heard distant laughter. *Her* laughter.

It would have been easier if the laugh had been wicked or cruel. Instead it was joyous, the laugh of a little girl riding a horse for the first time, of lovers reunited. The Starhunter's storm was vast, his water sense told him, wrapping Andovar from pole to pole in a dangerous embrace. Her laugh reminded him, as the Starhunter always would, painfully of Ariadel, a searing memory that stopped him in his tracks. She hadn't spoken to him since the gate had opened.

The seridi came hurtling through the charred branches with a shriek, heedless of rain or fire. Her eyes, too large in a feathered but human face, were all pupil and full of hell and madness. Fingers that were elegant on a sane creature were warped into claws, and her wings were a tattered ruin. Worse still were the chaotic thoughts she radiated to anyone within a hundred feet—mad ravings and images of impossible machines, liquids that burned, a terrible light that flashed and devoured whole cities.

// *Polyalphabetic substitution,* // the creature said, barraging him with incoherent urgency. // *Wehrmacht—Tirpitz, model T. Specification is appended!* //

It was always more difficult when they talked. The words were mad, poisonously so—but Vidarian always had the disturbing feeling that to the seridi they made perfect sense. Like the others, this one reached out desperately with magic, grasping with elemental hands when words failed her. The rush of wind pulled fire from Vidarian's chest; his own ability wanted to dive into hers and combust, consume the air that gave fire life. It hungered.

But Vidarian had something besides hungry fire. Even as his own soul reached back toward the air, driven to grow, the water in him growled back at it, primally angry, mindlessly intent: water suppresses fire. Vidarian turned the water's smothering force onto the seridi, flinging out an arm. The rain spiraled at his command, making a cyclone of the seridi's energy, then wreathing itself around her throat.

He *pushed*, setting free more of the water's fury, and the seridi crashed against the oak behind her with a keen like a terrified rabbit, always just shy of human. Vidarian tightened his grip, and her keen stuttered into a choke.

For these creatures he had thrown away everything—his ship, his oldest friend, the only woman he had truly ever loved—and all they were good for was containment. For the past two months he had hunted these mad ones, risking life and limb and sanity to catch them before they could rage through the land spreading senseless destruction. But he had never killed one.

Who was this creature, to demand so much of the world? Of him? Vidarian looked into the seridi's eyes and tightened his grip again.

Branches cracked behind him as something large hurtled through the brush. Altair's presence struck Vidarian seconds before the gryphon appeared, crashing through the space around his mind that he only now realized gryphons always respected as personal. He was so startled that his grip on the seridi loosened, and she sprung free, lashing out with claw and magic—

But Altair was there, reaching out with his own formidable wind mastery and turning the creature's raw assault back against her. With one smooth movement she was suddenly contained, and as the sphere of air that spun around her took sound with it, silence fell in the woods, leaving only the patter of steady rain.

Vidarian almost jumped as Altair's massive foreclaw settled gently on his shoulder. Talons longer than Vidarian's fingers and three times as thick brushed his chest and shoulder blade, and he knew from the gryphon's wash of emotion that they were meant to reassure.

// *It isn't her fault, my friend.* // The white-feathered face was gentle, pensive. // *Two thousand years locked in an abyss with the Starhunter and it's a wonder she functions at all.* //

"And what about me?" Vidarian said quietly, releasing his elemental hold on the seridi with as close to kindness as he could summon. "A turn with her in my head and the loss of everything I loved—" a memory: Ariadel, near death, summoning the strength to turn her head away from him. Words died on his tongue, and he fought to summon them again. "How am I to be affected?"

Another rustle from behind them spared Altair from having to answer. Isri climbed over branches and fallen debris, materializing through the rain, her dark spotted feathers the perfect camouflage in the shadowed forest. Guilt flushed through Vidarian as soon as he saw her; her sanity, and the pain that radiated from her whenever they found another of her brethren, whether lost or sane. When her people had come through the gate, half had been insane, lost beyond even her powerful abilities to heal. And yet she had never wavered in their task. He hoped desperately that she had not been near enough, even with her formidable telepathic ability, to witness the weakness in his heart.

But Isri had eyes only for the captured creature. Altair thinned the sphere of his control, allowing her to approach. "She is Alar seridi," Isri said, "storm clan. Their people were among the first to succumb." She closed her eyes, and the wave of peace that spilled out from her, intended for the captured seridi, touched Vidarian as well, chasing away the last of his fury.

It left the guilt untouched. "Am I becoming a monster, Altair?" Vidarian asked quietly.

The gryphon's head tilted toward him, beak parted, but he did not answer.

Frustration welled in him again, threatening to ignite into anger, and Vidarian turned and strode into the forest.

He thrashed his way through low-hanging branches for twenty paces toward their rough camp before realizing there were few places he would rather not be in that moment, alone with the two other mindless seridi awaiting escort back to the gate site.

The *Destiny* was anchored at a clearing beyond the camp, but Altair would expect him to head there, and so he turned in the opposite direction. It happened to be uphill, and so for the next several minutes he vented his anger by striding upward, kicking rocks behind him as he went.

He made it to the top of the hill exhausted, soul-weary, and, finally, silent of mind. And so the spectacular sunset that spread itself before him struck him dumb, a sky stained red with clouds that had just deigned to part, molten light pouring into the valleys that descended all the way to the sea in the west. Something stirred within his fire sense—it reached out to the sun, recognizing something. It was as if, and so Isri had told him the seridi believed, there were not only five elements, but many arrayed beneath them, storm and sun and river and flame. This, too, was a punishment; the fire within him had come from Ariadel, and the cruelty it turned on him was a constant reminder of her absence.

This strange, hilly country was as beautiful as any he'd ever seen, incongruous with his dark thoughts. It ran through him like a river, but where it should have washed peace, instead it laid bare the desert inside him. Now it seemed as though the chaos behind the gate had hollowed him out, eaten his very will to live. The bounty of the world unfurled before him, but he felt only emptiness.

Heat brushed his thigh, and he looked down—a rounded oval glowed red through the pocket of his trousers. The stone was even warmer to the touch, and it flared as he removed it into the fast-fading light of the sun.

As he slid the sun ruby through his fingers, the pang of another memory echoed through the well of his tired mind: Ruby, smiling, trusting him with their destiny. The gate, opening onto madness, twisting the world. The slightest suggestion would bring all of it echoing back again—the empty space between worlds; Ruby's body, stained with her namesake, dying, one of the greatest captains he had ever known. And one of the truest friends.

No sentiment, she'd said. His hand clenched tight around the hot stone.
Then a voice. A familiar voice.
* *Is it really all that bad?* *
"Ruby?" Vidarian whispered.

Chapter Two

Thornwolf

Vidarian fell, landing with a jaw-rattling thump on his back-side. His heart was pounding, his hands suddenly numb, and he almost dropped the stone. "How—" he began to ask, then amended, "This isn't possible." Heat flushed through him again at the memory of his elemental "hand" around the seridi's throat. He'd been ready to kill her, to end a person's—if even a feathered one's—life with his own hands. And now his thoughts strayed beyond reality. He searched the tree line below with his eyes, looking for something stable, dreading that he would find it melting before him.

* You're going to hurt my feelings. * Ruby's sharp humor was there, soaring into the emptiness he still hadn't fully accepted with her death. It was too good to be true, and he knew it.

A darker possibility loomed then and hardened his thoughts. Someone had captured Ruby's voice somehow, or the stone played off of his own memories.

"126 degrees east by 37 degrees north," he said.

* The gateway to the Last Cove, theoretically, * she replied promptly. * And you're not supposed to be talking about it. *

"When I sailed with the Viere that first summer, we hit a squall off of the Imerian Coast—"

* And the winds knocked open that silly cage of songbirds Vell bought in Astera. He was hysterical for three days and never did forgive my mother for making him keep them abovedecks. *

Only a handful of people would have known the answers to either of those, and only Ruby would know both. The Starhunter had been inside his head, but had never pulled or answered his own deep memories. That didn't necessarily mean she couldn't...

"I saw you die," he said, finally. In his mind he saw the small honor guard of gryphons carrying her silk-swathed body off for transport to her family's ship.

* *It's strange,* * she said, her already-remote voice for a moment more distant, * *I don't remember dying. I remember giving you the prism key, then . . . falling asleep? And then waking up to the sunlight here on this ridge.* *

"Giving me the what?" The strange phrase jolted him momentarily out of his melancholy.

* *The prism key.* * Hazily, an image of the sun ruby brushed his mind, and suddenly Ruby's voice grew hazy also. * *Wait . . . we never called it that. A . . . sun ruby? Why would we call the prism key a sun ruby? An evocative name, to be sure, but inaccurate . . .* *

The change in her tone raised the hair on the back of Vidarian's neck. Meanwhile, the gem—a "prism key"?—seemed to glow brighter. Vidarian stared into it, trying to divine its nature as he had never quite done before. Almost, he could see threads of light deep within the stone, crisscrossing into an infinite fabric. Was this what Ruby had seen, looking into the gem on those cold nights across the mountains? Had it pulled at her mind the way it now pulled at his?

Now the ruby seemed to be glowing brightly indeed, and it took him several long moments to notice that it was the sky growing darker. With a jolt he realized he should be getting back to the camp—and the memory of how he'd stormed off, and why, brought a fresh flush of guilt creeping through his veins.

* *Oh, come now. You need to stone up,* * Ruby said, and the vulgar image that came with it raised his ire, as surely it was meant to. When Vidarian grudgingly showed her what he'd done with his mind—something he could now do, as he once had with Ariadel, and always with the gryphons—he expected the memory to quiet her. Instead, she still simmered with impatience. * *And if you had killed her—what then? Perhaps it would have been mercy.* *

Her logic—a pirate logic, one that sealed her identity for him at last—both chilled and reassured him. There was no escaping the weakness he felt at having lost control over *himself*, but it was Altair's reaction that brought on the guilt full-force and sent him spiraling into dark thoughts.

Vidarian sensed Ruby preparing another poignant image and so preemptively levered himself to his feet, shaking out limbs that had grown cold on the damp ridge.

But there was still one thing.

"Ruby, I'm—"

* Save it, * she cut him off crisply. * To apologize is to tell me I was not in control of my own decisions and fate. You wouldn't want to do that, would you? *

He tried and failed three times to reply, then finally said: "So there's nothing . . . ?"

* I didn't say that. *

The strangeness of the conversation settled on his shoulders again, but there was only one possible answer he could give and retain any honor. "I'm in your debt. Anything I can create for you is yours."

* I don't . . . like . . . being in here. *

Vidarian looked around in the waning light, then back at the glowing stone. "In the . . . prism key?"

* It doesn't feel like . . . myself. *

Ruby had never in her life hesitated, and here, as he could feel her mind brushing up against something that was not itself, Vidarian felt that strange feeling crawling up his spine again. And what she said next didn't help.

* I want you to get my body back. *

Vidarian felt his mouth open, then close. "I . . . it's . . ." Wordlessly he called up the memories again, showing her: first, their grief, then Vidarian's pledge to return her body to her ship, where it would surely be commended to a sea burial—and finally, the gryphon flight craft, carrying her away. His heart ached as he lived through those moments again.

* So you're saying it's with Nistra now, ten thousand fathoms. Is that a problem? * As she spoke, Ruby's water sense stirred from within the stone, calling to Vidarian's own. Surprised, he quashed his natural urge to reach back. Whatever of Ruby the "prism key" had absorbed, it had taken her elemental ability with it—and, like Vidarian's, hers had been magnified.

* There's not much I can do from in here, * she said, answering his thought.

*I can feel it . . . bumping up against a wall . . . * And indeed, her magic seemed restrained, as if there were something there it couldn't break through. * That's why you've got to get me out of here. *

"But your body," he said, breaking through his own blockade of denial at last, "how would we even . . . put you back inside it?"

* You're the Tesseract, * she said, lacing the title with friendly acidity. * You'll figure it out. *

It was now full dark, and the red light of the prism key cast the promontory in a bloody false sunset. Vidarian wanted to find any other request she could make of him, but knew there was none. "If that is what you ask of me, I am bound to it," he said at last.

* Thank you. *

Fat drops of cold rain struck Vidarian's face and shoulders, calling his attention back to the fast-descended night. He raised his arms instinctively to protect his face, and Ruby's laughter echoed in his head. More drops splashed against his face, blurring his vision, as he stared down at the stone in irritation. Was it his permanent fate to have a woman laughing at him in his head?

* The world's eminent elementalist, and he covers his face with his hands in the rain? *

Well. Grumpily he extended his water sense, wrapping the raindrops into a glassy shield that absorbed or deflected their fellows. The balance was tricky, and the constant growling complaint of his fire sense was no help at all. "It feels wasteful to use it for such small purposes," he temporized.

Ruby wasn't fooled. * The practice is good for you. *

"And since when are you the authority on magical instruction?"

He'd meant the quip lightly, but Ruby grew quiet, and a memory bubbled up out of the stone: white wings over the sea, a great talon raised in instruction, waves that responded to its command—and Ruby, just a girl, swallowed in awe and a terrible sadness.

"I . . ." Vidarian began.

* It's nothing, * Ruby cut him off. * I don't know what came over me. * And indeed she seemed disturbed by the sudden disclosure of memory. * I guess I'm not used to being a telepathic rock. *

He didn't press further, instead foraying into the forest, downhill toward the camp.

Just to prove he had a handle on his own abilities, Vidarian summoned a sphere of fire energy, a ball of orange light and warmth that lit his path and evaporated the remaining rain from his skin and clothing. For good measure he gave it its own separate water shield, and the overall effect was rather pretty. Ruby did not comment, lost in her own strange gem-encased thoughts, and so he made the hike back toward the camp in silence.

Soon the camp torches glowed through the screen of trees, and when he stepped into the camp at last—dispelling his shields and light, for Altair had protected the entire area with a sphere of rain-repelling air—Isri and Altair looked up at him with relief. The welcome in their eyes assuaged some of his guilt, but the sudden inarticulate outburst of the latest captured seridi—storm clan, Isri had said—brought it rumbling back again.

Isri's own wings flared in response to the cry of her brethren, and she turned immediately, radiating reassurance.

* *Jumpy, aren't they?* * Ruby observed, and both Isri and Altair turned sharply back to Vidarian, answering his unspoken question of whether they would be able to hear her.

// *Ruby?* // Altair asked, startled incredulity wreathing his thought with a sharp scent like broken pine needles. // *It can't be. . .* // Vidarian felt a sudden warmth and reassurance that the tightly disciplined gryphon could react with his same disbelief.

Isri looked between them, not understanding.

Vidarian tried to explain, but found himself once again overwhelmed with an upwelling of frustrating emotion. "She . . . when the gate opened . . ."

Isri gasped in sudden comprehension. "Your friend—with the hair like fire—" And with understanding dawned emotion, also; Vidarian, not for the first time, did not envy her receptiveness to the states of those around her. The feathers around her face lifted with sadness, and her eyes filled with water. It was not the first time Vidarian had seen a seridi weep, but it reached him deeply.

* You all look like— *

"Don't say it," Vidarian warned, recovering some sternness.

* Fair enough. *

Vidarian pulled the sun ruby from his pocket and lifted it to the gryphon and seridi. Isri reached out to take it from him. "She was—caught—within the stone," he said.

Isri's large eyes were dark with thought as she gently turned the stone between her hands. "This is well beyond my expertise," she confessed. "The seridi resisted the use of magical artifacts embraced by gryphons and humans in the Twilight." Like birds, seridi seemed to pass information at lightning speed, owing to their telepathically mediated nightly connections—and as an elder mindspeaker, Isri was even more linked to their seeming-constant conversations. Only within the last few days had they begun referring to the time immediately preceding the sealing of the Great Gate as the "Twilight," but he had to admit it seemed appropriate.

"Gryphons and humans seem to share a delight in the dangerous," Vidarian said.

Altair's head shot upward, his neck straightening to its full intimidating height. His feather-tufted ears flattened against his skull.

"If I've offended—" Vidarian said uncertainly.

The tall gryphon's wordless hiss stopped the words on Vidarian's tongue, and as he listened in the silence that followed, a low growl emanated out of the forest.

// Thornwolves! // Altair cried, and Vidarian had half a breath to imagine the creatures of frightening bedtime stories, and then the pack was upon them.

Three wolves came stalking out of the darkness beyond the torch-line, their movements gracefully coordinated. Easily twice as large as the sight-wolves that had ambushed them at the Windsmouth's edge, these were clearly king predators, even more terrifying than their fairy tales depicted.

* An honest-to-Nistra thornwolf! I thought they were imaginary! *

"Not helpful!" Vidarian grunted, drawing his sword and willing his unruly magics into it.

// *Don't let the spines touch you!* // the gryphon warned, Vidarian thought unnecessarily. Sprouting from the creatures' necks were fearsome weapons that looked like they belonged to a giant sea urchin. Like the wolves' fur, they were striped, each contrasting the individual wolf's color, which ranged from deep red to blue-violet—but the spines were tipped in a lurid green that screamed "I am poisonous!"

Two of the wolves closed immediately on Altair while the third launched itself fearlessly at Vidarian's blade. The gryphon had moved to the center of the clearing, mantling his wings and screaming a deafening battle challenge. Alone, either Altair or Isri could easily have fled to the air, but they dared not abandon either Vidarian or the two captured seridi.

Lashing out with his blade to keep the wolf at bay, Vidarian slowly moved sideways, giving Altair more room to fight and placing himself between the wolves and the bound seridi. Perhaps he could redeem himself, if only in part, by protecting them now.

The advancing wolf suddenly leapt, fangs bared, neck-ruff splayed, and Vidarian danced backwards while letting loose with a wild blast of fire energy. The wolf twisted in midair, avoiding the flames, and leapt again with astonishing agility as soon as its paws touched the ground. This time Vidarian met it with his blade, but again the wolf twisted, leaning low against the ground and mantling its ruff into a deadly armored wreath. The longest spines were half an arm's length longer than his sword, pressing him to the defensive.

* *Here!* * Ruby cried, and a rush of water energy, acrid with the salt of the ocean, flooded into Vidarian's awareness.

Vidarian let the energy roar straight through him, as though Ruby was guiding his hand. The torrent of water struck the wolf full in the chest, driving it backward. He pressed the attack with another sharpened blast of fire energy, but its effect was dampened by the water that coated the wolf in an accidental shield.

Beside them, a screech of pain indicated that Altair had found a mark on one of his wolves. When Vidarian dared look across, he saw the gryphon leap into the air for three short wingbeats, then dive sideways, beak outstretched, to snap at the injured wolf's hindquarters.

Then Ruby was flooding Vidarian with water energy again, reveling in her newly discovered ability, and Vidarian released it into the face of the thornwolf as it leapt to attack. It dodged to the side, but not enough, and was knocked even further by the lash of water. This time Vidarian followed with his sword, sinking the tip of the blade deep into the wolf's side to pierce the heart. It thrashed wildly as it died, and it was all Vidarian could do to pull his blade free and keep clear of the flailing spines.

Altair had just dispatched the wolf he'd injured when two more came leaping from the forest to join the one remaining. This one was the largest and angriest—the two other wolves closed from either side of the clearing to support it, demonstrating a frightening cooperative hunting intelligence.

Vidarian and Altair each closed on a wolf, having little other choice—and the third leapt hungrily for Isri.

Ruby, Altair, and Vidarian all cried a simultaneous warning—

And the tree beside Isri started to move.

At first the tree seemed to melt, its needle-covered branches dropping to the ground, but then they leveled and spread. Dark skin and moss-green hair flashed beneath the splintering wood, and then a spinning warrior was there, beating the wolf back with a pair of sticks tipped with long, white animal teeth. For its part, the wolf seemed to recognize its opponent, and danced back warily.

Vidarian and Altair could only concentrate on their own attackers, and so they did, fighting with sword and talon and magic. Vidarian quickly learned to coordinate his attacks, lashing out with fire to burn and blind his opponent, and only then following it with Ruby's punishing storm of water energy. Drenched, the wolf was less able to lift its spines, and Vidarian moved in with his sword to more easily dispatch this one with a precise blow to its throat.

Altair had dealt with his second wolf as well, and with it dead, turned with Vidarian to the dark-skinned stranger, who had also dispatched a wolf with a thorned noose made from a length of dried vine.

"Thornwolves," the woman said breathlessly. "Terribly vicious. My name is Calphille. Who are you, who shelter in my father's forest?"

CHAPTER THREE
ALL HE HAS

A s silence descended again on the forest, the rain dwindling to a drifting mist beyond the camp's shield, Isri moved to soothe the agitated seridi. Their behavior was so unpredictable that Vidarian often found it difficult to tell when they were actually more agitated than usual, but Isri, her mind brushing constantly with theirs, was much more sensitive.

// *We are passing through,* // Altair said, while he delicately set about the grisly work of dragging the dead wolves away from their camp. Vidarian moved to assist him, but the gryphon waved him off with a talon. He reneged only out of practicality: Altair could seize the wolves by the root of their neck-spines, his large beak impervious to the barbules that would have sliced Vidarian's hands open. Now that they were still, Vidarian could see that nearly every other protruding surface—paws, knees, tails—were dressed with smaller versions of the wicked neck barbs.

"He speaks only mind-to-mind," Calphille observed quietly when Altair had disappeared between the trees, though Vidarian was fairly sure the gryphon's sharp ears would catch the sound. "Did he lose his voice by some misfortune?"

"Gryphons . . . have not spoken with physical voices for hundreds of years, I'm given to understand," Vidarian said carefully, trying to piece together when she might have last spoken with either gryphon or man. If his body and mind weren't still pounding with a battle fervor, he'd certainly be reeling still over the memory of how recently she had been a tree.

Her thoughts must have run parallel to his. A pensive frown shadowed her bark-colored face and she turned slowly, taking in the ring of trees one angle at a time. Suddenly she gasped and hurried over to one, bird-quick and equally as silent, and ducked beneath its low-hanging branches to examine its trunk. Crouching, she looked back at Vidarian, one palm on the tree, a strange expression on her face. "My people have slept a very long time. What—year is it?"

A rustle announced Altair's return. He clacked his beak, a sound unsettlingly like bones cracking, and a backbite of coppery distaste colored his thoughts as he answered. // *1,652 in the Ascendancy, by western human reckoning. 5,008 gryphon reckoning since the First Crossing.* // Then he wiped his beak on the grass. On the one hand, Vidarian was relieved his distaste seemed to be from wolf funk rather than mention of the Ascendancy, but on the other, how had none of the gryphons mentioned that there was any such thing as a "gryphon reckoning"? Much less one going back five thousand years? In his mind he ceded a little bit more credence to the creatures' long-suffering attitude toward humans.

When Calphille didn't answer, Vidarian turned back and found the color washed from her face. "What's wrong?"

"If friend gryphon is correct," she said, barely above a whisper, "my people have slept for eight hundred years."

* *Those trees are pretty long-lived,* * Ruby observed, "showing" Vidarian a page from an ancient book with a watercolored painting indeed similar to the spruce.

"How can that be—" Vidarian began.

A high-pitched yip from the nearby trees thrust them all into tense silence.

Altair stalked immediately toward the sound, waking in Vidarian an incredulous objection to a creature of his size moving so silently. Despite his fruitless denial, he felt worse, not better, when the gryphon quickly found himself blocked by fallen logs and a long, sprawling thicket two lengths into the forest.

// *I can fly a circuit—* //

"I'll go," Vidarian said, drawing his sword. "With a yip like that, and in the thicket, it's a small one." A whisper of thought, and the longsword's blade lit with water energy to his inner eye.

* *Better,* * Ruby said, so caustic he was sure she didn't mean it.

I'd appreciate some respect for risking my skin, he thought acidly at her.

* *Somehow the sting of mortal threat has lost its bite,* * she replied. * *Can't imagine why.* *

Vidarian sent a thin line of fire energy out beneath the water. The two energies snapped at each other, but the fire clung hungrily to the blade while the water was repelled by it, and so they achieved an uneasy balance. He slashed at the thicket, and the fire sprang ahead of his strokes to sear the vegetation away. Even without the blade physically touching the branches, it was slowgoing; it took three slices to clear a space tall and wide enough for his body, and with every lash the water and fire energies squabbled like jealous children.

The creature kept up a steady stream of eerie, high-pitched yips, helping him to cut straight to it—and when he finally broke through the last thicket wall, he saw why.

A terrified thornwolf pup, charcoal-furred with electric blue eyes, sat yipping in a small, low clearing. It yowled when it saw him and scrambled backwards, but was blocked from escaping down its den tunnel by a fallen log. It dug furiously—and ineffectually—in the mud around the log, whining.

* *Kill it,* * Ruby said.

"This is why they attacked us," Vidarian said, letting his sword tip drop toward the ground. "We made camp right against their den."

* *Then we did the larger camp a favor,* * Ruby said. * *Now they won't have to deal with them.* *

"Are you truly so cold? It's practically helpless, and we killed its parents."

* *Are* you *truly considering* not *killing it? It won't be helpless in a couple of months, and besides that, it won't survive out here alone. If you let it live now you're just punishing it with starvation.* *

Vidarian didn't answer, but the longer the wolf scrabbled pathetically at the log, the guiltier he felt.

* *Thornwolves are vicious, destructive predators,* * Ruby insisted. * *You want this one to grow up into what you just saw?* *

"You're right, damn it. But you're not the one having to actually do this."

He only realized that she'd been radiating anxiety at him when it melted into relief and sympathy. When they got back to the camp, he was going to have to talk to Isri about blocking at least some of her out.

Wearily, he lifted the sword again, and now let go of the water energy, letting it fall back inside him. He stoked the fire, but kept it close, willing the blade to be hot and sharp. If the magic was strong enough, he should be able to make this fast enough that the pup would feel almost nothing.

He started toward the blocked den, keeping a tight rein on the fire energy, forcing it down into a tight, white-hot band. The pup looked up, and for a moment he feared it would dash across the clearing or even under the thicket, but it turned immediately back to the mud and dug even faster.

Now he was close enough to get a better look at the creature. Like its parents, it was dark grey over most of its coat, with black stripes on its ruff, feet, and nose. The very tip of its tail was a shock of white, as were the tops of its ears. Unlike its parents, it didn't have any traces of lurid green or dark red; a couple of patches might have been deep blue, but under the soak of the rain it was hard to tell. Of spines it had only nubs—undeveloped, perhaps? He had no idea when they grew the poisonous barbs, but it seemed merciful they weren't born with them.

When he was close enough to touch it, the wolf turned, and he raised his sword, expecting it to growl or attack. Instead it hung its head, exhausted, its bright blue eyes gone dull and vacant. It sat and leaned against the log, panting.

* *Quickly now,* * Ruby whispered gently.

Carefully Vidarian turned his wrist, aiming the point of his sword at the top of the pup's head. From this angle it would be difficult to strike the top of the spine as he'd hoped, so the blow must be sure. He lifted the sword, hand tightening around the hilt as he wound the fire energy tighter one last time.

The pup looked up, mournful and tired, and his eyes flashed white, reflecting a burst of lightning that crashed through the forest behind them. The light seemed to strike right to Vidarian's soul, seeking out his every thought and memory. For that moment it was as if those eyes belonged not to an animal, but to another being, a soul that knew Vidarian's like no other.

Rain hissed down around them, renewed, in waves that drifted across the clearing. Vidarian's arm didn't move, stayed locked until it ached with the weight of the sword.

Finally, he lowered his arm, then reflexively returned the blade to its sheath. He knelt.

* You're not serious, * Ruby burst, revealing that, however close her mind was to his, she hadn't experienced what Vidarian just had. He wasn't sure whether to be reassured or worried.

"A wild creature like this," Vidarian said, leaning back on his heels and slowly raising his hand toward the wolf pup. "Never seen humans, he's wet and miserable and cornered. What do you think he'll do?"

* He'll bite you and you'll get a disease. *

He stopped his hand, which the pup was looking at with curiosity, but not fear. "I'll take that bet. If he bites me, I'll kill him." The words were even difficult to say. "But if he doesn't, I'm bringing him back with us. Agreed?"

* What's there to agree to? It's not as if I have any leverage here. * Her acidity was back.

"Good enough."

Vidarian reached again, palm flat, to the wolf. It stretched its nose to him, then carefully, gently, licked his hand. Just as the pink tongue brushed his skin, a jolt of electricity shot through his fingers, and he yanked them back with a yelp.

The pup's ears drooped sadly and it whined, while Ruby crowed, * There! You see! *

"He didn't . . ." Vidarian slowly clenched and unclenched his hand, wincing. "He didn't bite me. He shocked me."

* Like there's a difference? *

"Of course there is. He didn't mean to." Ruby filled his mind with a disgusted noise, but he ignored her, reaching out to the pup again. This time it put its head under his palm, and he petted it, carefully.

* You have gone completely soft in the head. *

"The gate's magic mutated him," Vidarian said, now understanding the nubs that ringed the pup's neck and paws instead of spines. "It's a wonder the other wolves didn't kill him themselves."

* A wonder, * Ruby echoed flatly.

The pup stood, looked up again for permission, then, with a low wave of his tail, ambled closer to Vidarian, pressing close to his legs for warmth. He trembled in bursts. Vidarian picked him up, and, when he didn't resist, tucked him into his shirt.

The frustrated stream of invective Ruby directed at him was in neither High Alorean nor trade-tongue. He thought it was some sort of southwest islander language but wasn't sure. "You know I don't understand any of that."

* H'salu nikkti kreshaluk. Kreshaluk. *

"I didn't even know you knew one of those languages. That's not Malu, is it?" Much as he wouldn't like to admit it, arguing with Ruby was shaking loose the hold of the dark thoughts on his mind, of Ariadel's rejection. The pup shifted, curling himself up against Vidarian's chest, and despite the rain and his aching muscles, Vidarian felt something close to contentment for the first time in a long time. He even enjoyed Ruby's frustration, if a little guiltily.

Halfway back to the camp, * What's its name? * she said finally, after her vocabulary in that tongue had worn out. At least she hadn't switched to another one he couldn't understand.

"Haven't decided yet. I take it you're not mad at me anymore?"

* I've decided he's your problem. If he zaps you—and he will—or he bites someone, or he eats one of the seridi, it's your hide, not mine. I'm just along for the ride— *

"I appreciate that—"

* —Even if you do any number of things that are totally, completely, ridiculously inadvisable. I am deciding to be entertained. *

They broke then into the clearing and the camp, where Altair had again erected his shield of air to block out the rain. The droplets formed a silver ceiling that magnified the pale moonlight above them.

Altair and Isri both stood from where they'd been warming themselves near a freshly crackling fire, and Vidarian strode straight to it, thinking more of the still-shivering pup than himself. The dead thornwolves, thankfully, were all gone.

Isri radiated relief at him. "I sensed a commotion, intense worry—oh!" She cut off in a squeak as Vidarian pulled the pup from beneath his shirt.

Altair reared back, the feathers around his neck flaring. The pup yipped, terrified, then immediately growled, stiffening the fur along his spine. A crackle of electricity radiated out from the lifted proto-spines, but Vidarian managed to hold onto him.

// *That creature is dangerous,* // Altair said, and he returned his formidable talons to the ground, but the roused feathers of his neck and head still made him seem twice his actual size. // *Thornwolves are—* //

"Vicious and destructive—"

* *I tried to tell him.* *

"—I know."

// *Why did you not destroy this one, then?* // The gryphon's large, sapphire eyes were flared wide, and all-pupil with alarm.

"Because he's not a thornwolf. At least, not entirely." He soothed the pup with a murmur, then lifted him, squirming, toward Altair. As the pup's alarm peaked again, he discharged another crackle of electricity, but the pulses seemed to be getting weaker the more he used them. "But mainly," Vidarian added, "we're the reason he's on his own. I'm all he has."

Altair eyed the pup, about to argue, but a figure came hurtling down through the ceiling of rain overhead.

The dark-feathered shape landed lightly beside the fire, too small to be a gryphon. As she stood, revealing herself to be a seridi, she bowed to Isri, and then to Vidarian and Altair.

The seridi ruffled her feathers, shaking free droplets of water. She either did not recognize the pup for what he was, or was too preoccupied with her mission, or both. "Lord Tesseract," she began, and Vidarian squelched his still-irate reaction to the title, "a messenger waits for you at the foothills."

"Who could send a messenger this far?"

"He claims to be from your human emperor, my lord. We were told you would wish to know of his arrival." She read Vidarian's startlement as affront and her facial feathers lifted with embarrassment. "I apologize if our assumption was incorrect."

"No, no, you're quite correct," Vidarian said, managing to summon back some of his diplomacy. "I'll be along as soon as I can." He looked at Isri. "Can they manage a ride in the ship?" he indicated the two sedated seridi with a nod.

"I believe so," she replied, closing her eyes for a few moments and then opening them again. "If we travel by night they'll take the journey easier."

"I'll convey your response," the messenger said, and Vidarian realized he didn't even know her name. But she was bowing again, and taking off, before her feathers had even dried.

The pup was squirming, the fire and warmth giving him new energy, and so Vidarian set him down to amble around the camp. As he looked around, he realized for the first time that one of their recent number was missing.

"Where is Calphille?" he asked.

CHAPTER FOUR

SUMMONED

He found her sitting alone in the forest at the feet of a great spruce. Her eyes were distant, and she spoke as soon as she heard his footsteps, without turning.

"I do not know why I was awakened even as my kin slumber," she said quietly. "I fear they may never wake." She placed a hand on one of the spruce's massive roots. "This is my father."

Vidarian had never been introduced to a tree, but tried to put that aside. He bowed, and Calphille smiled. "I can see the resemblance," he said. And indeed he could. With her moss-green hair, skin like chocolate, and eyes rich and golden as fresh pine sap, Calphille could have belonged in no other forest—and yet the thought of leaving her here unsettled him. Before he had quite thought it through, he said, "You should come with us."

* What? * Ruby said, with the echoey tone that meant she spoke to him alone.

To his momentary relief, Calphille's smile widened, warmed.

There's no reason for her to stay here, Vidarian thought at Ruby. These trees aren't waking up with her.

* Well, aren't you just a collector of oddities. *

He forced his eyes steady against an instinct to glare. You have no idea. I have this talking rock, you see. . .

"Your presence awakened me," Calphille said, and Vidarian found himself obscurely grateful for his practice at carrying on parallel conversations with the Starhunter. "I thought I should stay with you, but would not have imposed."

There, you see? Vidarian thought.

* She's clingy. *

"It's no imposition at all," he said, rather than answering Ruby, "I must admit to a great deal of curiosity about your people."

At this her aspect darkened glumly again, and he wished he could recall his words. "When last I slept," she said, looking out into the forest—tracing, he knew, lines of greenery that had grown up during her slumber, "the human cities knew this forest, knew of my father and his domain. We were allies." She turned back to him, dread in her eyes, and he wondered again how she could be so trusting, so transparent. Then he thought himself cynical, and wondered again what he was becoming. "You said that your encampment is the only habitation here for many miles? There are no human cities?"

"Not living ones, I'm afraid," he said, unhappy to distress her again but unable to lie. "There are ruins—the people are gone, moved on long ago . . ."

*. . . Or worse, more like. *

Ruby spoke only to him, but Calphille heard his implication. Her eyes filled with tears and she looked away, up into the branches of the tree that she called her father. She blinked, then visibly hardened herself. "How . . ." she began, then cleared her throat. "How shall we travel . . . to your camp?"

Relieved, he turned and pointed back the way he'd come. "I have a ship that can take us—if you'll follow me."

* You'd better hurry, * Ruby said. * That wolf is surely running amok. Either it's eaten Isri or Altair's eaten it. My bet and hopes are on the latter. *

He forced himself to smile reassuringly at Calphille, while what he thought back at Ruby was not nearly so charitable.

When she stood, Calphille bowed low to the spruce, resting her hands against its trunk as if in supplication. She murmured words Vidarian couldn't understand, but, moved by her devotion—and obvious sadness at parting from her family—Vidarian bowed to the tree as well. When he straightened, he lifted his hand and pressed it to the rough bark. To his surprise, it was warm, though no sunlight could possibly reach it down here. He looked up into the vaulting branches, overcome at the thought of the tree's age, and how it housed another creature like Calphille. He wondered what the forest king would look like, in human form. "Sleep well, sir," he said, then turned to lead Calphille back to the camp.

Contrary to Ruby's dire warnings, the camp and wolf pup were both fine, though Altair did look as if he would rather clean his beak with the small creature's pelt than tolerate its curious sniffing about the camp. With the resilience of all young things, the wolf seemed to have adapted to his new "family" well, though with clear partiality for Vidarian. His long, feathery tail fanned the air gently as soon as Vidarian and Calphille crossed into the clearing.

Vidarian crouched and held out his hand, and the pup's tail waved again, this time faster. He ambled toward them, still weak and wary, and stopped about an arm's length away, stretching his neck to sniff Vidarian's hand.

Some lupine decision logic flipped over in the pup's mind, and he walked forward, turning easily and sitting between Vidarian's bent knees. Carefully, Vidarian placed his hand on top of the pup's head. Far from objecting, the pup thumped his tail up and down again on the ground, and panted.

Before thinking better of it, Vidarian slid his fingers downward to pet the pup's neck. A long ruff-spine brushed his hand and pain swept through it, melting his grip into a claw. A stream of invective poured out of his mouth before he quite realized what he was saying.

* I'm impressed! *

Isri's cheek-feathers lifted. "Anatomically—"

"It's a figure of speech," he said quickly. He shook his hand, willing sensation back into it, mostly without success.

The pup was looking up at him, ears drooped and eyes big. In spite of the pain, Vidarian forced himself to pat the creature gently on the head lest it think him angry.

Sorry, the emotion brushed his mind just as he made contact with the soft fur of the pup's head. Vidarian froze, sure he'd imagined it. He'd lifted his hand as if burned, and now settled it down again on the pup. Sorry, sorry the feeling rushed back into him again, a wordless regret. The pup licked his hand.

"Are you all right?" Isri asked, placing a hand on his shoulder. He started, then looked up at her. Her golden eyes were opaque, curious. Vidarian had known Isri to make mental contact with another of her kind several leagues away—he wondered if it was etiquette or ability that masked his own thoughts from her now.

"Just a bit of a shock," he said, carefully petting the pup again. "My own fault. It's fine." He put extra force into his words, hoping the sentiment would transfer to the pup as well. It seemed to; the tail thumped again, gently. "Are we prepared for the return flight?"

"Altair helped me carry our two friends into the craft," Isri said. "I imposed a sleep on them that should last two hours."

"How easy is that, making someone sleep?"

She smiled, sensing the caution behind his question, but her voice was colored with sadness. "For them, not difficult, so little is left of their minds. Far more difficult for someone like you." Her eyes twinkled.

// We thank you for allowing us the refuge of your father's forest, // Altair said to Calphille, who also seemed rather nonplussed both by the wolf pup's shock and Vidarian's invective.

"Calphille will be joining us," Vidarian said, hoping she wouldn't change her mind.

"My family is not yet awake," she explained, "and it would be my duty to ensure our alliances are activated as soon as possible, for their safety." The way she leaned on duty to steer herself through sadness struck deep with Vidarian.

// We are pleased to have you, then, // Altair said, and Vidarian experienced a surge of gratitude for the welcome that radiated out from the gryphon in a feathery embrace.

Calphille smiled, and performed a peculiar little bow Vidarian had never seen before, with the fingertips of both hands together. He was sure her flush of gratitude was unfeigned, and felt another wave of guilty sympathy for her waking alone.

* Don't start that again. *

It's only right that she comes with us, that's all, he thought back testily.

* It's no concern of mine. You're the one'll be crammed in that little boat with a full house. *

Gloomily he realized she was right. He wasn't sure how many the craft was meant to hold, but surely they'd be near its capacity. Carefully he picked up the pup, who didn't know quite what to make of being lifted off the ground, but didn't object. *Only one way to find out.*

~~~

With the two captured seridi sleeping soundly and tucked tight with blankets at the rear of the craft, quarters were tight, but by no means unbearable. Isri took to the sky with Altair while Vidarian guided the craft upward. The glowing gems set into the hull provided not only activation indicators but a gentle blue light that illuminated their path up through the trees. Calphille, perched at the bow, watched them with appreciation, but not surprise.

"You've been aboard one of these before," Vidarian said.

"It's been . . ." she started to calculate, then laughed. " . . . A very long time, of course." Her eyes followed the edge of the trees as they ascended from the clearing, saying a final wordless good-bye, but to his relief, her spirits seemed to lighten the farther they passed from her family's grove. The wolf pup was not nearly so comfortable, and clung to the deck, radiating displeasure despite Vidarian's reassurances.

A prevailing night wind filled the sails as soon as they lifted above the tree line, and they made good time. Soon the fires of the encampment glittered along the coastline before them, and Vidarian directed the craft lightly down for a landing.

Thalnarra's pride had taken up temporary residence along a narrow cliff bordering a great and temperate sea. Here, south of the Dragonspine, the waters were gentle, practically tropical, and the ocean winds that swept up the cliffs were quite pleasing to the gryphons. Thalnarra groused about them growing gentle and fat on the giant, pink-fleshed fish that filled the bay, but she seemed obscurely pleased to have laired there nonetheless.

The Alorean messenger was immediately obvious as they landed, having made his own camp as far away from the gryphons as he could manage without leaving the safety of the pride. "With your pardon, I'd like to get this settled as fast as possible," Vidarian apologized to Calphille, who waved him away. She seemed heartened to see so many gryphons at the cliff.

"Bloody creatures," the messenger was muttering. Vidarian strode up to him, unsure whether he was cursing the gryphons or his own unruly mount. The winged horse, like those of the Sky Knights they'd battled to gain access to the gate, certainly had no love of gryphons, being essentially "prey"—but it also seemed less than enthusiastic about its rider. It pawed the ground nervously, ears flattened against its skull, eyes round and rolling when the messenger made any move toward it.

The messenger, an older man in imperial colors, nodded briskly to Vidarian as he approached. His high forehead, paler skin, and aquiline nose reminded Vidarian of his mother's family, landholding Alorean for ten generations back.

"They've gone all jittery these past months," the man said, offering a slice of dried apple to the horse, who accepted it warily. Vidarian reevaluated his assumption about their relationship—the beast was spooked for sure, but seemed to trust the old man. "Can't blame 'em. Everything's gone jittery, you might say. Half the riders can't even get their beasts to carry them, or they wouldn't've pulled an old git like me out of retirement."

Vidarian smiled in spite of himself, liking the old man even if he was bringing bad news. "My name is Vidarian Rulorat," he said. "I believe you were looking for me?"

"Well," the old man said, eyebrows lifting as he turned and extended his hand. "I am indeed. Alain Malkor, messenger for His Majesty. It's an honor to meet you, I'm to understand."

Vidarian clasped the man's hand in both of his own briefly, but shook his head. "I don't know about that. But you've been a long way from the Imperial City to do it." He didn't quite let an edge creep into his voice. "The last representatives of the emperor I met were—not quite so friendly."

"That's the way of it, isn't it?" Alain said, his voice so light Vidarian was sure he had no idea that his own fellow Sky Knights had attacked Vidarian and the gryphons. "But strange times are about, and stranger rumors. Half the Court of Directors dropping dead, beasts changing their shapes."

"What?" Vidarian asked, his heart gone cold. "The court—of the Alorean Import Company?"

"You haven't heard," the old man said, voice rough with compassion, and maybe a touch of rebuke. "This far out, I suppose it makes sense. But yes, damndest thing. Those old men were held together by their healing magic, you ken? Without it they keeled right over. Happened to a lot of people, but the gossip's about the rich ones, you know."

Vidarian felt as though his heart had turned to lead in his chest.

* Huh, * Ruby said. * Hadn't thought of that. Makes sense, though. Always knew something bad was going to come of using magic that way. * Her tone had the edge of Sea Kingdom superstition, but Vidarian was in no condition to correct her.

"Shows the imperial family's wisdom, never going in for that stuff," Alain said. "A man living six hundred years—hardly right. Maybe that's why he wants to speak with you."

"The emperor?" Vidarian barely managed to tame his voice down from a squeak.

"Yes indeed," Alain smiled, reaching up to pet the velvety nose of his steed, which seemed to have calmed down a bit. "I come with an imperial summons, didn't they tell you?"

"They didn't," he said numbly, thoughts racing.

* What are you going to do? * For once Ruby didn't have a quick remark.

"I'll—leave in the morning, of course."

* My ship, and my body, * Ruby growled, * are in the other direction. *

Would you have me ignore the summons, and have us all cut down by Sky Knights halfway there? Perhaps you think you'd have better luck asking one of them after we're all dead. He hid the heat of his thoughts behind a false mask and gratitude for the messenger.

Alain smiled again and extended his hand, which Vidarian shook out of reflex. Then he mumbled an excuse, something about needing to pack.

Ruby hadn't answered, and so as he retreated, Vidarian continued, guiltily, *The emperor can't want much, or he'd've sent more than a broken-down old warhorse to fetch us. We'll send word to the* Viere *as soon as we reach the city.* He turned to go find Thalnarra and Altair.

But just as he reached the edge of the campfires, someone else found him.

When he turned and saw her approaching, Vidarian froze. She was moving determinedly toward him, and still he found himself paralyzed. What were they, now?

"We should talk," Ariadel said. Her face and body were still wan from illness, but there in the camp, speaking to him after so long a silence, it seemed she had never been more beautiful. Or more alive. He fought against his own reaction, but what welled up in place of that wordless gratitude was something less productive.

"I'm not going to apologize." The words poured out before he could stop them. And once they were out, even with Ariadel's face flushing with anger, he couldn't take them back.

"What?" The question was pointed, absent any confusion, an invitation back from the brink. Part of him ached to seize it.

"I'm not going to apologize," he ground out the words again, though the thunderous look she gave him warned him not to, "for opening the gate. For saving you."

"That's not—" she began, then flushed again, too angry to speak. He nearly quailed; in spite of everything, he had never seen her this angry. "There's something else."

He waited.

"I—" she looked up again, into his eyes, and for a moment they were themselves again, and whatever she was about to say was the most important thing he'd ever heard.

And then her face clouded over with the mysterious expression she'd had for the last two weeks, since the gate, and she was gone behind it. "I'm going with Thalnarra."

He recognized a tack when he saw one, but knew that asking her wasn't going to get the answer now. And with that realization all the rest came crashing down on him again, the mess that he'd made of things.

// *What's this?* // Thalnarra's voice, all hearth-warmth and sweet spices, filled his mind. // *You're going with me? But I'm going with him.* //

"You are?" they said together, then exchanged another awkward look.

// *If he's going into the lion's den, he can't go with only the guardianship of this air-addled lightweight,* // she indicated Altair with a flick of her beak, who crouched near one of the campfires with a copious pile of huge fish. Altair didn't look up from his meal, but made what Vidarian assumed to be a rather rude gesture with the feathered tip of his tail. // *Besides,* // she added, her voice like a waft of cinnamon, // *we look better in pairs.* //

"That settles that, then," Vidarian sighed, not unhappily. "If she's going with me . . . ?"

"I'm staying here," Ariadel said. "With the rest of the pride."

"If I may—" Calphille said shyly, and Vidarian noticed her for the first time, framed against one of the fires. She was holding the wolf pup, to his surprise. "I'd like to come with you as well."

Ariadel shot him a look that was half fury and half disbelief, then stalked off without a word.

He started to follow her, then stopped, three separate times before he gave it up. Calphille lowered the pup to the ground and it scrambled over to him, staying low and nervous. Vidarian held back a sigh. "We'll leave first thing in the morning."

CHAPTER FIVE
LIGHTNING

The next morning Ariadel was nowhere to be found. The camp was large, and the surrounding area even larger, more accommodating to a person who did not want to be found than to the one searching. His companions knew not to press him as Vidarian let the minutes of the morning slip away, but when the sun crested even the tallest trees surrounding the camp, and he had checked their supplies five times, he motioned for them to depart.

* *I'm sorry, old friend,* * Ruby said, with a quiet hollowness that reassured Vidarian in spite of his sadness. Her sympathy felt deep and real, less fractured than her earlier thoughts. He thanked her wordlessly as he headed for the skyship.

Alain, the messenger, had left at first light, aiming to get as far ahead of them as he could. "So they don't misinterpret the gryphons back home," he'd said, giving Vidarian a chill, but certainly the old man and his horse would be glad enough to get some distance between themselves and the pride of giant predators.

Somewhat to his surprise, Isri had packed her own bag and was loading it into the *Destiny*.

"I hadn't thought to ask you to leave your people," Vidarian said.

"And so you did not," she replied, the tiny feathers around her beak lifting with mirth. When they settled again, her eyes were bright. "They are well equipped to attend to those still lost. With your help, we have already subdued the most dangerous of my brethren who remained within a day's flight. I do my people a greater service by meeting your emperor—if you will have me."

"I am honored by your company, of course," Vidarian said, with genuine relief. He insisted to himself that he had not come to rely on Isri, but the thought of her calming presence made the coming journey substantially more bearable.

At a fast pace it would take three and a half days by air, the gryphons said, to reach the Imperial City. It would be the farthest from the western sea Vidarian had been in all his adult life. Once, as a boy, he'd traveled with his mother to her family's holdings south of the capital, and so he had a dim memory of that rolling country nestled against the great walled city. Then, he had thought it a place of culture and excitement, of intrigue and luxury—but as the taxes grew and he took on the burdens of adulthood, it seemed only a far-away place that caused more problems than it solved.

Word of their departure had traveled around the camp, and the steady trickle of gifts, more than anything else, drove Vidarian at last to loose the *Destiny* from its moorings. The seridi had been extremely, if typically, thoughtful: travel rations for humans harvested out of the forest (he wondered, belatedly, what Calphille ate), dried venison bound in strips like firewood for the gryphons, a collection of medicines also distilled from the forest by way of their ancient knowledge, and even leaf-wrapped packets of meat softened with root vegetable mash and wild chestnut milk for the pup. The longer they stayed, the more elaborate the gifts became, which was as good a reason as any to be leaving.

The gryphons took off first, followed by Isri; only Calphille and the pup would ride with him in the small ship. Stuffed with one of his special meals from the seridi, the pup was dozing on the floor of the craft even before they'd taken off, and Calphille, for her part, seemed content to leave Vidarian to his morose thoughts, at least for the beginning of the journey.

Thalnarra, however, was not so inclined, and set upon him nearly as soon as they passed above the first cloud layer and leveled out into a gliding pace. He'd been unable to pull his mind from obsessive mulling about the conse-quences of his recent actions, and was hard-pressed to pretend objection.

// *Your elements,* // she began. // *They fight inside you.* //

It wasn't a question, but she seemed to want an answer. "They do." They'd done so every moment since he rescued Ariadel and kindled himself on her lost fire, but the opening of the Great Gate had more than tripled their ferocity.

// You were never trained in the proper control, // she said, and the iron rust of her assessment was not unkind.

"I fared all right against you," he couldn't resist reminding her. "And against Isri's mad brethren."

// Brute force, // she replied, without sympathy or malice. *// And everyone for leagues senses your thrashing. //*

He kept a tight rein on a sharp retort, lest he prove her point for her. And clung to the reminder that the gryphons might be rough, but they were unfailingly true, more than his own people had been. That, too, stung. But he said instead: "Where should I begin?"

// How does a fire start? // Her tone was gentle, neutral. Too neutral.

He started to answer, but before the words passed his lips he realized the uncomfortable truth: he had no earthly idea, not where it counted.

// There is an art to fire, and a logic. Contain it; think of it mathematically, but not by your simple sailing-merchant reckoning. // She touched his mind more closely then, enough that he could suddenly feel the warmth of her wing muscles as they beat the air. Striking as that was, more so was the image she pressed on him—a formula, a garble of numbers and letters of the kind treasured by scholars. It meant nothing to him, and so she said, *// Think how a tree grows, how an avalanche begins. //*

Vidarian realized with a flush of sharp humility that he did not deeply understand either of those things. Thalnarra read the discomfiture in his thoughts and tried again.

// Think how love kindles. //

That, at the moment, he knew all too well. It began out of nothing. Troubadours sang of a "spark," of mystical connection, but he knew it to be alchemical even without the learning of alchemy. It was potential, which was nothingness, and from that nothingness a curl of possibility, thin beyond realizing. Up it climbed while you were busy not realizing, until suddenly you were aflame, all at once, a burst of spectacular and devastating light, undeniable as rain or stone. In that moment it was as if it came from nowhere, but then the subtle and inevitable path revealed itself before you, right down to the beginning of all things.

// *That's it,* // her voice was a whisper, a thread of woodsmoke. // *Hold that in your mind. Understand it. Summon your power only when you have it carved into your bones. Practice.* //

Vidarian cupped his hands, then dwelt for several long moments on what she had said. He thought of his own acid emotions, his regret and longing. He stepped back from them, saw the avalanche, saw the tree growing. He did not breathe, but let the energy roll out from him, the barest possibility tipped only just into being.

A small, clear, bright flame flickered just above his palms. Unlike any other that he'd summoned, it wasn't torn from him all barbs and anguish. It simply was, a breath of possibility unfolding. And what was more, in that clean place of possibility and action, the weight of all his decisions seemed a little less heavy.

// *There,* // Thalnarra said, and warmth like fresh toasted bread radiated from her. // *You see there the heart of ephemeral magics. All is a process. A change of state from one to the next. Love and spirit, fire and wind. One thing always becomes another, and it does so in its own time. You merely suggest to it what it may become.* //

"Thank you, Thalnarra," Vidarian said, cupping his hands around the warmth of the tiny flame. Then something else welled up within him, forceful and immutable. It pushed the tiny flame out of being, filling him with dread and dissonance. "What was that?" he gasped.

Now Thalnarra's voice was wavering hickory smoke. // *Your water sense. I have never seen one's element seem to have a will so outside of its wielder's control. But I had never met a Tesseract before you.* //

"What can I do?"

// *Only a far older gryphon than I might be able to tell you, and perhaps not even they. Practice.* //

Vidarian set his teeth, placing his fingertips together, calling back the memory of warmth. He began to practice.

~~~

The first fat drops of a cold rain broke him out of his reverie, the first real solace he'd had in days. A dull headache clung to the back of his skull and his eyes would focus only with deliberate effort. But where his mind faltered with exhaustion, his spirit rested for the first time in weeks, perhaps months. Still, exhausted as he was, he had no reserves with which to fend off the deep chill of the rain.

When he looked up over the bow, coal-black clouds rolled along the sky's edge, dampening Vidarian's spirits further. As if acknowledging his attention, an icy storm wind swept over the craft, flattening the gryphons' feathers and finding every nook and cranny in the small ship. Lightning flickered, echoing through the distant thunderheads, and from Vidarian's side, the pup lifted his head and let loose an eerie howl.

Was it the everstorm, the perpetual blizzard that hung over the Windsmouth? But no—they'd passed over those spectacular mountains not long after leaving the gate site, and the everstorm itself had dissipated (for esoteric elemental reasons the gryphons had argued over at length) with the gate's opening.

In moments the storm was upon them, flying with unnatural speed. As it drew closer, it raised the hair on the back of Vidarian's neck, and not out of merely electricity or fear. There was an elemental force behind the storm.

And that wasn't all. The storm did "fly"—it had a shape: a giant hawk with outspread wings, lightning crackling from its "feathers."

The craft rocked suddenly, and behind him Calphille yelped as she grabbed for a handhold. Vidarian turned to assist her, clinging to his own seat, and saw the source of the impact: Isri had landed, not gracefully, on the port quarter.

"There is an elementalist at the center of this storm!" She shook water out of her eyes and arched her wings over her head to block the rain.

// *We noticed,* // Altair called, and Vidarian lifted himself slightly to look for either or both of the gryphons. At first they were nowhere to be found—then he saw the flash of a white wing, signaling Altair's presence several ship-lengths away. He and Thalnarra had given the *Destiny* a wider berth when the storm hit, almost certainly to avoid being driven into the sails, or worse, by a blast of wind.

But how could there be an elementalist this high up? A gryphon?

"They are seridi, but my mind cannot reach them! Their defenses are formidable!" Isri answered his unasked question, an unnerving habit she had. More disturbing still was the thought of a seridi that could block her out, *and* create or control the storm at the same time.

Humans were rarely gifted with either telepathy or elemental magic, but Vidarian knew now that both the seridi and gryphons could carry them at independent levels of strength. Still, even for their kind, someone with Isri's mind-strength and Altair's elemental ability was extremely rare.

// *She is an electricity mage,* // Altair offered. // *A lightning-wielder.* //

"How do you know it's a she?" Vidarian yelled, in between bursts of thunder.

// *Electricity is a specialization within air magic,* // he said, tearing through a bank of cloud and coming into view only for a moment. // *And her energy has a female signature.* //

"Is she sane?" He clung again to the seat as the *Destiny* pitched. Calphille, pressed to the deck, cried out again, but held herself steady even with one arm wrapped around the wolf pup, who continued to bark at the sky.

"I cannot tell . . ." Isri began, then closed her eyes, head-feathers rousing. "She is Alar, storm clan!" Isri cried over the storm.

"Like the last one we captured!" Vidarian shouted back, and Isri nodded emphatically. "You said they were dangerous!"

Just then, the wolf pup ceased his barking but wriggled free of Calphille's grip and scuttled to the forward bow. He put his paws up on the rail and howled.

Three arcs of lightning shot down out of the thunderhead above them, striking the pup, who howled even louder. Vidarian was knocked back off his seat and into Calphille, blinded and senseless.

Vidarian thrashed, unthinking, on the deck, and this time Calphille reached to steady him. When the stun wore off, he straightened, anxiety and grief hitting him like a wall from the wolf pup.

As his vision slowly returned, punctuated by more blasts of lightning off the bow, he saw a shape still standing at the forward rail, and wondered if the pup had been burned standing up, seared in place.

But then the shape moved. A howl split the air, muffled to Vidarian's still-impaired hearing, but distinct.

* *Impossible!* * Ruby had kept her thoughts to herself throughout the whole journey so far, but now radiated astonishment.

// *Control that creature!* // Altair thundered, his voice bitter and sharp like lightning-struck wood. // *It's calling down the storm!* //

Lightning flashed again, mercifully distant, and the pup barked joyously at it again. Altair was right—the pup was *calling* the lightning. And it was answering!

That wasn't all. Another shape within the storm was bearing down on the craft, too small to be one of the gryphons.

Her feathers were black, nearly invisible against the dark clouds, except for streaks of white around her eyes and at the tips of her primaries. Clawed feet, large and strong, caught the forward rail easily, and she perched there like a gargoyle, haloed with a blue aura of electricity.

Mad as it was, Vidarian prepared for a fight, for a stream of insane babbling followed by an elemental attack. But the strange seridi only looked down at the pup and laughed, reaching out to ruffle his fur.

At this Vidarian called out a warning, which, too, was unnecessary. An arc of electricity flashed out from the pup's spines, strong this time, but the seridi's aura absorbed it harmlessly.

"He has a good spirit!" the new visitor cried, her beak parted in a seridi smile at Vidarian.

"Glad to hear it!" he shouted. "Could you—ah—"

"Oh! Of course!" Her feathers slicked down in what would have been sheepishness in a gryphon and he guessed was the same for seridi. Then she made a strange twisting motion with her hands and the storm tamed instantly: lightning vanished, thunder grumbled into silence, the sky itself around them lightened. By the time she pulled her fingers apart again, shafts of sunlight were breaking through the clouds.

* Such quickness! *

Living or . . . whatever it was she was now . . . Ruby had never impressed easily, but in this case Vidarian could hardly disagree. Not only was this seridi equipped with a level of elemental ability yet unseen in this age, she was *accustomed* to it, used it as easily as touch or speech.

Altair and Thalnarra glided closer to the craft, exchanging greetings with their new guest. Isri, who must have fallen from the craft at the lightning strike, performed an interesting full-body shake in midair that sent water droplets flying from her feathers, then came to a delicate landing on the aft rail.

"I am Alikai, of the Alar seridi," the newcomer said to Vidarian, and then added, to Isri, "first storm-wielder, second speaker to Sia'kalia."

// *You call the goddess by her ancient name,* // Altair said.

She parted her beak slightly in a smile: // *I did not know she had taken a new one, sky-brother. But the wind has always worn many names.* //

"They call her Siane now," Isri said gently. "Have you spoken with your clansfolk, since coming through the gate?"

* *She doesn't know!* * Ruby said, exactly as Vidarian realized the same thing. Now the seridi's facial feathers were roused with nervousness.

"I have not, mindspeaker." Her crest, black striped with thin lines of white, lifted as she bowed her head in embarrassment. "I must confess my relief at escaping the gate was so great that I flew aimlessly with the wind, then created this storm, and have ridden it since."

"You should go to your people, who remain at the gate," Isri said, stepping down from the rail and carefully crossing the craft to take Alikai's hands in her own. "Much needs to be done. Many did not emerge from the gate whole."

The black-plumaged seridi nodded, her head still lowered, droplets clinging to her long eyelashes. "I have been foolish, indulging in storm-play out here."

// *We all emerged from the gate changed, and owe no apologies for tending first to our own recovery,* // Isri said. Rarely did she use her formidable telepathic ability to project speech, but when she did, the warm light of her spirit engulfed all who listened with strength and compassion.

Alikai nodded, and lifted her head, dashing tears away with a fingertip. "I will return. Thank you for calling to me." She smiled again at Vidarian, and held her hands out to the wolf pup, who eagerly trotted to them. "Take care of this one," she said, rubbing his eye-ridges. "I haven't seen his like in quite some time!"

~~~

The next three days of flying went smoothly, without unnatural storm or mishap. By night they landed and the gryphons hunted, and they rose to the air again with dawn's light. When they could see the ground, Calphille kept Vidarian occupied with questions as to which people lived where, what villages lay below them, and the names of rivers that had shifted in their beds since last she saw them. He tried not to be grateful for the distraction, but her curiosity was infectious.

Inhabited territories grew more numerous the farther northeast they traveled, and on the fourth morning, thick banks of fog obscured much of the ground below. When they finally peeled away toward midmorning, revealing strips of heavily developed land, Vidarian confessed himself stumped.

"I don't remember this city," he admitted. "It must have been a village when I was a child, now far grown."

But as the fog cleared further beneath them, it did not reveal the rolling green hills he remembered from boyhood. The same tightly packed buildings ranged over height and valley alike, spreading from horizon to horizon. With a sudden shock he realized that there would be no separation—this strange sea of never-ending structures *was* Val Imris, the Imperial City.

CHAPTER SIX
THE IMPERIAL CITY

By noon they drew within sight of the tall walls of the city proper, and three pairs of familiar black-and-white wings launched from a guardpost below, rising to meet them. Vidarian signaled the gryphons and Isri to keep to their course; the steady wingbeats of the Sky Knights indicated they were in no hurry. It took the better part of an hour before they drew within hailing distance.

In truth, Vidarian had expected some form of escort long before they came within the outer boundaries of Val Imris, and at the sight of the three "knights" the emperor had sent, he began to wonder if his anxiety about the summons was entirely misplaced. Of the three riders, one was properly equipped and old enough to have earned some of his scars honestly. The other two were striplings: a thin girl whose ferocious expression could not make up for her small size, and a boy several sizes too small for the battered armor he wore. The emperor must not be too concerned about them if he sent children to escort them to the palace.

He braced himself for a confrontation, but the salute that the lead knight gave them was, if anything, more deferential than etiquette required. He brought his horse, a handsome tricolor with gleaming black wings, up alongside the craft. Without being asked, Isri and the gryphons had given them a wide berth as they hovered to talk. "Captain Rulorat?" the knight called, and when Vidarian answered in the affirmative, he introduced himself as "Caladan Orrin-Smyth, Master Handler of the Imperial Ironhart Wing."

The "captain" was not lost on Vidarian. "Caladan Orrin-Smyth, of the Nirea Orrin-Smyths? Are you a fourth son, sir?" The Orrin-Smyths were an old merchant family—the alliance of two even older ones, in fact—and their loyalty to the imperial family was legendary. The fourth son of every generation was given to the emperor's protection by way of the imperial Sky Knights.

The man smiled and touched his visor with a gauntleted hand. "I am, Captain. My father, Pavel Orrin-Smyth, spoke well of his trading with Rulorats, and with your mother's family, also."

"I had not counted on finding friends at the capital," Vidarian admitted. "I appreciate your volunteering to escort us?" He trusted Caladan's diplomatic upbringing to interpret his tone as: why are a Master Handler and two apprentices sent to greet us, rather than a wingleader?

Caladan's friendliness faded and his mouth hardened to a thin line, only for a moment, but long enough for Vidarian to realize he had misstepped. "You've not heard the news," he began. "There is much—"

A whisper of wings from above them, and Isri, looking tired, landed on the edge of the *Destiny*, swaying it enough that Vidarian stepped back from the rail to avoid being pitched out. Calphille offered her arm to Isri, but they all turned at the soft cry that one of the apprentices let loose at the sight of her.

The girl rode a royal, if a young one, its pelt still mottled with yearling gray but distinctly giving way to iridescent black. Vidarian thought at first she was simply surprised, as he had been, to see a seridi for the first time. But the girl's reaction wasn't simple shock—it was fear.

// *I'm sorry,* // Isri said, speaking telepathically out of uncertainty at the knights' reactions, // *my kind are not so equipped to hover as gryphons are.* //

"This is Isri, Elder Mindspeaker to the Treune seridi—" Vidarian began, but stopped at the look in Caladan's eyes, even darker than before.

"Winged demon," the boy apprentice muttered, and though Caladan raised a hand to silence him, the rebuke Vidarian expected never came, which started a slow flush of anger creeping up his neck.

"She is an envoy from a people that have suffered much," Vidarian said slowly, reining in his temper with each word. For her part, Isri was silent, watching.

// *What's gotten into them?* // Thalnarra growled, sharp eyes reading the knights' discomfort from her far circling distance.

Caladan kept greater mastery over himself than his young charge, but he, too, eyed Isri with fear and suspicion. "Not long after all the . . . changes . . .

began, these creatures started to appear. Word is that they caused the Court of Directors to fall dead."

"Where have you heard such things?" Vidarian demanded, command coming back to him from many a tossing storm deck. Inside he still reeled: was it true? The Court of Directors—all dead?

* Where do you think they heard them? * Ruby said, soft but arch. * The emperor must blame someone to keep a grip on the throne, and it seems he doesn't want to blame you. *

Caladan wavered before Vidarian's determined outrage, but said nothing, letting silence stretch between them. Ruby radiated smugness.

"Perhaps you had better escort us to the emperor," Vidarian said, dragging them back into the safer realms of protocol.

The knight's relief was palpable, but incomplete. "We're instructed to bring you to the palace," he agreed. "His majesty's attendants await you there."

There was something he wasn't saying, but better to take it up with someone in charge, Vidarian decided, and so he nodded, to Caladan's further relief. "Please lead the way, sir knight."

◠◠◠

The promised attendants were waiting in a courtyard just within the palace walls. Caladan and his apprentices led the way, and as they came closer to the ground, citizens and palace folk alike turned their heads to follow their passing, but upon sight of the *Destiny* and the gryphons, lifted their hands and whispered or shouted.

The knights were only too happy to pass them into the palace's care, and had taken back to the sky even before Vidarian could help Calphille, her legs stiff from the long flight, out of the ship.

A steward wearing a sash clasped with the imperial seal stepped forward to welcome them as the shadows of the departing knights passed over their heads. "We welcome you on behalf of his imperial majesty," he began, and Vidarian moved to clasp his hand.

"We've traveled far at the emperor's request," Vidarian said, "and are of course anxious to know how we can be of service."

He'd summoned all of his available diplomacy, but the steward still seemed taken aback. "Of course—Captain," he said, relaxing slightly when Vidarian nodded approval at the title. "We are charged to see to your comfort at the palace, beginning with your rooms and—" his gaze dropped in flickering assessment of Vidarian's clothing, "fresh attire."

With their months of travel, of life-and-death struggle, Vidarian abruptly realized it had been more than a season since he had last thought about what he looked like. In the steward's delicate discomfort he saw himself in the eyes of a courtier: battered, stained, carefully wrought manners worn away by the destruction of all that had been familiar to him. To survive this—the imperial palace!—he would have to do more than summon a little diplomacy. "We would be most grateful for your hospitality and assistance," Vidarian said, letting genuine embarrassment creep into his voice. Long ago, his father had trained him on the value of sincerity, especially where it was least expected.

The steward relaxed further, enough for a rueful smile. He snapped his fingers at one of the three assistants. "Marcelle, if you will see to stabling the captain's—" his eyes roamed across the gryphons "—creatures in the guest barn—"

// If by 'barn' you mean 'guest quarters stocked with live game for guests to consume,' please by all means lead the way. We have flown more than three days at the emperor's pleasure and are quite famished. //

The steward's eyes bulged at every other word, and he gasped aloud when he realized that the "creature," Thalnarra, was in fact speaking to him. By the end he had broken out in a cold sweat and was stammering incoherently.

One of his assistants, a boy—no more than ten winters, or Vidarian would eat his shoe—instead stared at the gryphons with a wild sort of joy, his eyes shining. "They—they could quarter in the old empress's garden?" he said, voice high and shoulders tense, awaiting reprimand.

The steward spun, a look halfway between relief and consternation washing over his wrinkled features. He turned from the boy, eyes narrowed, to Vidarian, and relief won out when Vidarian nodded. He had no idea if the garden was appropriate, but they must have been referring to the late Dowager Empress Celaine. She had died a decade ago, and with the emperor not having taken an empress, the garden was likely shuttered.

"It will be quite overgrown," the steward warned, but hope lingered beneath his beleaguered grasp at authority.

// *All the better,* // Thalnarra replied, her mind-voice cultured and genteel, exuding cinnamon and myrrh. // *We may cut our beds from the vegetation.* //

The steward winced, doubtless imagining the destruction of imperial roses, but the squeak of his young assistant drew all eyes again: "And the hunters have just returned with a spate of venison. I heard Itara complaining she didn't know what to do with all of it."

// *Perhaps this bright lad could escort us and see to our accommodations,* // Thalnarra pushed, and this time her voice carried a hint of carnivorous urgency that sent the steward blanching again. The boy, however, practically hopped with delight.

"Yes, yes," the steward said finally, wiping sweat from his pate, "Brannon, see to them, and—whatever they need."

"Yes, sir!" Brannon chirped, and dashed toward Thalnarra, surprising a yelp out of one of the other assistants, an older girl close enough in features to be his older sister. She grasped at him, too late, and blushed.

"They won't hurt him," Vidarian said, taking pity on her. His reassurance only earned him a daggerlike *they'd better not* glance before she remembered herself and stared at her feet, turning red again.

// *If he behaves,* // Thalnarra said, all carnivore gone from her tone, which had turned grandmotherly. // *Please lead the way, Brannon.* // The boy bowed with the meticulousness of much practice, then turned without a second glance at the rest of them. Thalnarra and Altair—who had watched with silent amusement—followed.

"And if you'll be so kind as to follow me," the steward said in a rush, picking up the shreds of his dignity.

The steward—whose name Vidarian never got—shepherded Vidarian, Calphille, Isri, and the pup (permitted with a token grumble—Isri he seemed not to "see" at all) through several open-air corridors. They came at length to a salon with floor-to-ceiling windows that looked out on a carefully cultivated garden and pond. Once there, he quickly waved his assistants out the door and fled.

"Talrick, a model of gentility as usual, I see."

Vidarian turned toward the voice, which came from a tall, thin man in an elegantly trimmed coat. Before he could introduce himself, the man spoke again.

"You are Vidarian Rulorat, captain of I know not what. I am Renard, and this fitting never happened." The man advanced, a heavy velvet cloak draped across his left forearm, and looked Vidarian up and down. "Reports of your size were apparently overestimated," he sighed, pursing his lips. "I accounted for some exaggeration, but clearly not enough."

"I do apologize for the state of my clothes. Anything you can do will be greatly appreciated."

Renard seemed not to hear him. "I have another coat and trousers in the back that *may* work, quickly stitched. Appalling as it is to consider you going before the emperor in such a state," he said. "I told them I'd have nothing to do with it, but they went and got a bloody decree. I made Emiran swear my name would never be connected with this debacle or I'd ensure the tailors' guild blacklisted him for life." His birdlike eyes turned to Calphille and he gasped dramatically. "And they said absolutely nothing about you, my dear." He didn't wait for her to answer, but clapped his hands and shouted, "Giselle!"

A harried face poked into the colonnaded doorway at the rear of the salon just as Renard drew breath to shout again. He took Calphille gently by the elbow and steered her toward the face. "Take miss—" a look, and Calphille gave her name, "Calphille to the arbor room and fit her up with a gown from the Countess Bel'Maritai's collection." He tilted his head conspiratorially toward Vidarian. "Silly waif won't know it's gone, and anyway she's on 'holiday' what with all the commotion." Calphille shot a startled glance at Vidarian, but let herself be escorted down the hallway.

When Renard turned back to Vidarian, it was not unlike meeting the eyes of one of the elemental goddesses. "First—a bath, a thorough one. It's prepared in the water chamber, just up the hall." He turned immediately to Isri without waiting to see if Vidarian would comply, and opened the velvet cloak with long, clever fingers. "A terrible shame to hide such beautiful plumage," he murmured, brushing one of Isri's primaries when she nodded permission to his proffered hand. Vidarian revised his estimation of the man at the look of kindness and apology he now directed at her. "But the common folk can be barbarians."

Ruby gave a venomous mutter about "uncommon" folk, the first she'd spoken since their landing. Vidarian couldn't help but agree, though he snuck off to the ordered bath before he could risk Renard's attention again.

∿∿∿

Two hours later, Vidarian, Calphille, and Isri were ensconced in separate chambers. Renard had moved like a whirlwind and left Vidarian with three of the best-fitting sets of clothing he'd ever owned, and yet another warning that they had never met. Vidarian had assured him of total secrecy, and another under-steward had come to direct him to his chambers.

The rooms were, of course, palatial, with the water chamber alone easily twice the size of his cabin on the lost *Empress Quest*. In the sleeping room, the velvet-curtained bed was the largest he had ever seen, and the dark, heavy furniture, resplendent with silver-work, was surely worth more than the *Quest* herself had been at the market's height a decade ago.

All of this washed over Vidarian, barely noticed. He was here to see the emperor, and his door was unguarded. The under-steward had left him in the room, wary of the pup, whose spines still emitted the odd spark of electricity, without any instruction. And the pup, in the way of young things, had promptly curled up on the cool stone floor of the water chamber and fallen asleep.

Vidarian eased out into the marble-tiled corridor and closed the door behind him as quietly as he could. He listened for any sign that the pup had awakened, but there was only silence. Quietly he turned, rehearsing a story about searching for the kitchens in hunger—not entirely untrue—in case he should meet a servant.

But after nearly an hour of wandering through hallways—some indoor, some open to the outside and the balmy, flower-scented evening air—he realized that suspicious servants were the least of his problems. The palace was massive, sprawling, and utterly indecipherable.

He was about to turn back to his chambers—assuming he could even find them, which was a big assumption—when Ruby spoke again, after more hours of silence.

* Left, left, right. *

"What?" he said, startled into answering her aloud. He looked around, relieved that they were alone.

* Left around this corner, left again at the end of the hallway, then right, across the courtyard. *

"Are you just guessing?" Vidarian was genuinely hungry now, and on the edge of irritation. Ruby offered no answer, so he followed the directions. He was sure he'd been down these corridors before—but the courtyard she directed him to was a new one.

* Down the stairs, third door, down the hallway. *

"How do you know this?" he said quietly, looking around again for observers.

* I don't know. * A hint of real worry colored her voice, but beneath it the strange tone he'd heard from her before, distant and diffuse.

She continued to direct him, only once leading them astray—* Strange, that wall wasn't there . . . *

Finally they came to an underground room deep in the heart of the palace. This one *was* guarded, and Vidarian offered a hasty and mostly true explanation of his imperial summons to the two pikemen who flanked the plain stone door.

The two guards exchanged looks, and the one on the right opened the door and disappeared inside. Vidarian barely had time to prepare another explanation when he reappeared again. To his surprise, he beckoned Vidarian inside.

A low ceiling in the next hallway forced the guard to angle his pike, and he bore it carefully down a series of mazelike passages. Just when Vidarian was sure he was being escorted out of the building by some other exit, the guard stopped before a final door, flanked by two more guards.

One of the guards opened the door—this one wooden and heavily carved—and the bluish light that spilled from the chamber beyond blinded Vidarian for several long moments.

When his eyes adjusted, it took him another long interval to make sense of what he was seeing.

Nine men and women sat evenly spaced around a circular table of heavy polished stone. The blue light came from thick glass lenses that they all wore. All but one of them were murmuring continuously, though none of them, as far as he could tell, were saying the same thing. In the center of the table was a glittering sphere, a glass orb larger than a gryphon's head, also glowing with blue light and worked all over with holes laid out in geometric patterns. It reminded him of the amplifier, the glass device he'd used to magnify his fledgling elemental abilities against the Vkortha, so long ago.

The ninth figure, a young man sitting closest to the glowing sphere, wore a simple gold circlet at his brow.

"Welcome, Captain," the emperor said, standing and pulling the blue lenses from his eyes with weary hands, "to Val Imris—and the Relay Room."

CHAPTER SEVEN

INVAEL

At the emperor's words, a murmuring echo passed around the table. The remaining eight people continued to stare into the sphere at its center through their glowing lenses. Though they responded to speech, they didn't seem to realize anyone else was in the room— each still kept up a steady flow of words, all different, all indistinguishable to Vidarian's ears. The emperor smiled ruefully and lifted a finger to his lips, then approached Vidarian from the far side of the table.

Color and light, despite the dim hall, gleamed off of the emperor's embroidered silk robe as he drew closer to the doorway. Vidarian worked to keep his feet under him—the long journey, hunger, and now facing a man to whom his family had owed loyalty for generations. The young, chiseled face and dark eyes held authority weightlessly, and some distant, surreal part of Vidarian observed that his likeness on the coin of the realm was quite true to life.

A moment of panic surged through Vidarian's veins as he flailed after words, but to his surprise, the emperor's eyes went up over his shoulder, focused somewhere behind him.

Vidarian turned and recognized the shining black coiffure and grey eyes that looked back at him. He only just caught an eruption of hate and fury before they submerged beneath a portrait-perfect smile. Her eyes were now so welcoming, her greeting to the emperor so warm, that he wondered if hunger and shock had made him hallucinate. The light here *was* so damnably dim . . .

"Ah, Oneira," the emperor was greeting her with equal satisfaction and warmth, "you're just in time. Captain Rulorat has arrived. You must dine with us."

Vidarian fought between relief at the idea of a meal and distaste at sharing it with Oneira, whom, when last they met, was pursuing him and Ariadel through the dead of night with capture orders from the Alorean Import Company.

"Your majesty knows I would love nothing more," Oneira said, her diction cultured to perfection, "but I had come to relieve you at the table." In clasping the emperor's hands in greeting, she had accepted the blue glass lenses from him.

The emperor waved delicate hands, the flurry of his fingers light and controlled at the same time, like a sparrow's wings. "Easily remedied," he said, and waved at one of the guards. "We'll fetch Alandrus. He'll not mind, and should gain practice besides."

Oneira searched the emperor's eyes for a long moment, doubtless gauging whether she could risk resisting him again, but in the end she smiled, all lightness. "Of course, your majesty. As you wish."

~~~

By all accounts the emperor had decided on that moment's whim to dine with Vidarian and Oneira, but in the short time it took them to adjourn to the dining room—the "sable room," his majesty had mentioned offhandedly, one of fifteen imperial dining rooms in the palace—an elegantly dressed table for four awaited them.

Vidarian waited for the emperor and Oneira to take their seats, then placed himself to the left of the emperor, resting a hand on the chair and looking for his majesty's subtle nod of approval before setting himself down.

All four places at the table—sable oak, matching the frame of a huge hunt scene in oils on the north wall, and the pedestals in lit alcoves bearing massive floral arrangements that filled the small room with fragrance—were set. Confirming that they would await another guest, the liveried servant who came bearing an effervescent pale wine filled four glasses, not three.

"To departed friends," Oneira said, lifting her glass, and dropping an obscure look on Vidarian just before she did so.

"Indeed," the emperor replied, lifting his own and then sipping from it. "To those who cannot join us—our poor Justinian included." At that last, the look he gave Oneira was brotherly with sympathy.

"So it's true, then," Vidarian said softly, more to himself than the table. Two faces turned toward him. "The Court of Directors," he said, still absorbing the truth himself—realizing he had not wanted to believe. "We heard . . ." The words failed him.

"That they fell dead," Oneira finished for him, and for the briefest of moments her eyes filled with water, but again she mastered herself so quickly as to make it seem an illusion. "The moment you opened the gate, according to the calculations of our scouts."

Vidarian's head swam, and not just from the surprisingly potent wine. Had they known they would die? Is that why they tried to stop him from making it to the gate? But no—surely if Justinian himself had known the gate's opening would strike him down, he'd have killed Vidarian at the first opportunity, and there had been many such . . .

As he looked across the table, searching for an adequate reply, he realized three things in quick succession:

One: The same shift in healing magics that had caused Ruby's death must have disrupted the longevity magics of the directors.

Two: With the entire Court gone all at once, the Company must be in total chaos—

And three: Oneira had not just been Justinian's second. She had loved him, and likely he her.

It would explain how a director would be so foolish as to insist on a female second, Ruby said, soft with emotion, all trace of her usual cynicism gone.

Oneira's head jerked toward him, suspicion and confusion warring on her face.

Ruby's stone went so cold Vidarian could feel it through the leather pouch at his side. *She can hear me?* Vidarian was equally baffled. Ruby's "voice" had been pitched for him alone.

Before he could find a way to learn what Oneira had or hadn't heard, the door behind him opened. And before he could turn to discover the mysterious fourth guest, the emperor stood, a look of total stricken astonishment on his face. So trained were his features ordinarily that it took Vidarian several moments to recognize the expression for what it was: awe.

Remembering himself, Vidarian stood, and turned toward the door.

It was Calphille. But what a spell Renard had cast over her! The gown was green and black silk, tightly laced in the latest fashion, its shimmering skirts floating on voluminous petticoats. Her hair, which had been dark as shadowed leaves, now had a luster that took it from rich pine to spring bud, accented by tiny jeweled flowers that winked red and gold in the candlelight. The gown bared her shoulders, showing the chocolate smoothness of her skin dramatically, and powdered gold dust brought out the rich amber of her eyes. But eclipsing all of this was her wildness, which no cosseting could mask. If you were to wrap a tiger in finest silk, you would not notice the drape of the fabric; this was how Calphille shone through the countess's finery.

The emperor had shaken off his reverie, and now crossed the floor quickly to offer Calphille his arm. Her eyes widened as he approached, but Renard must have also briefly schooled her in etiquette, for she dropped a graceful curtsey that spoke more of a doe in flight than a courtier. As he walked her to her chair, the emperor's eyes never left her, nor indeed when he took his own place opposite her.

* He's smitten! * Ruby chirped, all of her sullenness lifted like evaporating fog. Vidarian hardly dared breathe; his obligation to Ruby, their macabre task, weighed all too heavily on his mind, and her long silences punctuated by dark moods he attributed solely to his failure thus far. But he could feel her attention now, oddly joyous, utterly on the emperor and Calphille—who, for her part, seemed equally in the emperor's thrall. She might drop her eyes demurely, but whenever the emperor spoke, her whole body oriented toward him like a leaf toward sunlight. * An intriguing development! *

Again, when Ruby spoke, Oneira looked around surreptitiously, a crease of confusion subtle between her eyebrows. There was no doubt in Vidarian's mind that she could hear Ruby—but why, or what it meant, he had no idea. She, too, seemed intrigued with the energy that crackled between Calphille and the emperor, and, to Vidarian's intense relief, utterly without jealousy. He could feel the iron claws of court politics closing around them: the emperor and Calphille, transfixed with each other, while Vidarian, Oneira—and Ruby!—thought only of what this new power dynamic would do to their own schemes.

More liveried servants entered the dining room, bearing glass cylinders of a frothy exotic fruit aperitif that did little to wash the unpleasant taste of politics from his tongue. Delicate cakes of fried shredded root vegetable followed, swimming in a pale cream redolent with far island spice. Though Vidarian prided himself on esoteric knowledge of foodstuffs from across the five seas, he could recognize only the basics of what came before them.

Over a larger plate of poached tigerfish with tiny succulent tomatoes and an exquisite brown-butter eldergrass sauté, the emperor at last yielded Vidarian a polite opening. "In these strange times, I can only summon the empire's wisest, and hope that their counsel can see us through."

"I had wondered, your majesty, what counsel or service I might provide you." Vidarian forced his words into a genteel slowness, though he burned with the urge to demand of the emperor the reason for his summoning.

To his surprise, the emperor turned to Oneira, who smiled but did not take the proffered invitation. "I was hoping you would have those answers," the emperor said, setting aside his fork and resting his hands on the table in a clear signal of frank conversation. "With this war with Qui—"

"War?" Vidarian breathed, completely unaware of having interrupted the most powerful man on the continent.

"Yes," the emperor blinked, overlooking Vidarian's misstep, "and with my Sky Knights in such a shamble—"

Vidarian must have looked even more baffled, for Oneira, of all people, offered rescue, of a sort. "He has been on the farthest fringes since the Opening," she demurred, ostensibly speaking to Calphille, who already knew full well, rather than give the impression of correcting the emperor. "In the wild, where little hint of the consequences of his actions have permeated."

Heat crept up Vidarian's neck as he thought of their work to subdue the seridi as "little hint," but it would be worse than useless to contradict her. And was it true? *War?* With Qui? The rich meal rolled in his stomach at the thought. The great land nation to the south had always disputed the border provinces...

"Bloody savages," the emperor said, a cultured agony and affront twisting his lip, and Vidarian struggled not to boggle at his rough words. "Lurking,

67

always, at our southern border, and when they realized the time was right, seized Isrinvale, and are halfway through Lehria, according to the latest relays."

Now Vidarian's head swam. Even Ruby's stone radiated a deep, chilled shock. "And the Sky Knights . . . ?" Caladan's affront took on new color, and Vidarian regretted his obtuseness. He should have convinced the gryphons to land so he could gather news outside the capital. Surely the Knights were attempting to stem the tide of the Qui invasion—

"A shambles," the emperor repeated, and his dark eyes lifted to rest heavily on Vidarian. The burden in them seared through to the depths of his soul, but there was resolution there, too, and strength. He found himself pulled up by that gaze, and would never again wonder how such a young man could wield so much power. "And that is where I require your assistance. With my Sky Knights all but disabled, I rely much more on my skyships, and not only do I lack for captains that can show the necessary sharp thinking of captaining an entirely new *class* of ship, I require your unique knowledge of elemental magic to figure out what in the sacred names of all four goddesses is going on. We're dealing with towns turned upside down, waking relics, shapechangers . . ."

"The Company has provided the emperor with materials," Oneira began modestly. She went on about rare books the Company had obtained, but at the word "shapeshifter," Calphille had gasped, and Vidarian looked up at her, giving the slightest shake of his head. Now was certainly not the time to introduce that particular aspect of Calphille's family to the emperor.

* *Will there ever be a good time?* * Ruby giggled, and Vidarian thought sharp thoughts at her, warning her of Oneira's strange "hearing." For a blessing, she seemed not at all aware of Vidarian's thoughts, and he aimed to keep it that way. Ruby settled down, but still radiated damnable amusement at the whole thing, and now Vidarian understood why: it would be up to him to explain to the emperor that he was enamored of a shapeshifter, which the royal court—and perhaps even the emperor himself—would never accept as fully human.

All three at the table were now looking at him, and so he said the only thing he could say: "It's my honor to serve the empire," he managed not to sigh, "in any way I can, your majesty."

~~~

Relief and exhaustion washed over Vidarian as he sighted the door to his rooms. He knew that the numbness in his skull signified shock; if he consciously brought the thought of war against Qui or shapeshifting sky steeds to the fore, raw terror would lance down his spine, debilitating. But left alone, the panic submerged beneath that blessed buzz of nothingness, at least for now.

He opened the door, intent on falling immediately into the lavish bed. But someone had other plans.

A woman's legs, crossed elegantly at the knee, emerged from the shadow of the sitting room. His first thought was that he'd come into the wrong room by mistake, or she had—but perched on those slim knees was the pup, tongue lolling, sparks firing lazily from its crest, absurdly happy.

Beyond them, taking up all of the space between the sitting room and the bed, was the largest gryphon Vidarian had ever seen.

The creature was black from head to tailtip, speckled with points of light—not *white*, but *light*, as in stars. As he watched, convinced his eyes were playing a trick on him, he saw a comet streak across the gryphon's left wing. Its eyes glowed the faint gold of distant suns.

Hard as it was to tear his eyes away from this, the woman favored by the pup was also unnaturally large, not just in height but in every dimension. And *her* eyes were darker than the deepest shadow, with neither white nor pupil. Her clothing was like none he'd ever seen, her mannish trews made of what appeared to be liquid metal, and her blouse a dizzyingly patterned affair of black, yellow, and green silk, marbled like an exotic insect.

He still might not have recognized her until she giggled. "Poor, poor Vidarian," she said, and her voice set his head spinning for the third time that evening, heard as it was outside his head, rather than in. "We've been so hard on you." She stroked the pup, who leaned into her touch. Vidarian scowled at him, and his ears wilted soulfully.

Don't blame him, she said in his mind, smiling, revealing unnaturally white teeth. *Haven't you missed me?*

"I've been—busy." Vidarian felt behind him for the other armchair and sank into it.

"Oh, so have I!" The Starhunter stood and spun around with the pup in her arms, causing him to bark. She set him down on the carpet and proceeded to caper, dancing around the pup and laughing as he leaped and swatted at her with his paws. Then she spun toward the gryphon. "See?"

Vidarian looked at the gryphon again, trying not to be distracted by the twinkling of the stars on its feathers.

Then it spoke.

"They trapped me in ice," the gryphon rumbled, its voice three times deeper than any human's, with a quality that vibrated Vidarian's breastbone and threatened to turn his knees to jelly. "*Ice.*" Then it laughed, an even stranger sound, a kind of clucking wheeze. "Kind of ironic, really."

Being locked in ice for two thousand years has made him rather cranky.

"I can imagine," Vidarian said, after two false starts around a dry throat. "You know—the rest of your kind—" he wondered if they really qualified as "his kind," but barreled onward—"they don't speak . . . physically . . . anymore."

The gryphon blinked, eyelids casting patches of darkness over the golden sun-glow of its irises. "Fled entirely into telepathy, then? How odd."

A knock at the door set the pup barking madly again, spiking panic through Vidarian's veins. He stood and scooped the pup up in his arms, where it shocked him by accident, and then filled his mind with abject apologies. When he finally managed to convince it to stop barking—it shocked him twice more, but the jolts were decidedly losing force now, thank fortune—he turned back to the Starhunter and her gryphon.

But they were gone.

Get rid of him, the Starhunter said, and a shadow on the far wall moved, a slender hand making a very impolite gesture at the door.

Moving sideways, Vidarian shoved the pup under one arm—another shock, but a weak one—and opened the door just a hand's-breadth with the other.

A young man with nut-brown hair and eyes looked back at him, first hesitantly, then with mustering courage. "Are you Vidarian Rulorat?"

"I am," Vidarian said.

The boy stepped into the room without invitation, and Vidarian was so surprised—and so intent on making sure he didn't stumble into the pup's spines—that he took a step backward and let him in before he quite realized it.

Now you've done it, the Starhunter tsked.

"My name is Farian Reyali," the boy said, and a little chill sparked in Vidarian's heart. His oldest brother, lost to blood plague before Vidarian was born, had been named Farian. "Reyali" was almost familiar—a merchant family?

"What can I do for you?" Vidarian said, trying to maneuver the boy back around to the door.

"My father and grandfather belonged to the Court of Directors." That explained the pain in his eyes, the barely controlled anger.

"I'm very sorry," Vidarian said. And he was.

His father was three hundred and twenty-nine years old. Don't be.

"I'm their only heir," Farian said. "They've put me in the new Court. I suppose I should thank you." This last he said bitterly, and looked away as he said it.

The pup started to growl softly, and Vidarian turned again, placing himself between boy and animal. He summoned what little energy he had, and met Farian's gaze honestly, hoping to convince him of his regret, his own anguish. "If I could do anything to ease your pain, or make right the injury to your family, I would," he said.

For a moment, he thought he'd gotten through, that he'd be able to put the boy off to another time. But just as hope appeared, it fled, and Farian's face clouded over again with sorrow and rage.

"When you opened that gate, you had no idea what you were unleashing on us," he said, voice lifting with every word. "My family has lived and worked in the Imperial City for twelve generations. With my grandfathers gone, our guild secrets are gone with them! Some of those secrets kept people fed and clothed!"

He's becoming tedious now.

"Whether you think of it or not, people have died since the Opening, and more will die before long."

Honestly. Very bored.

A cold sweat broke out across Vidarian's brow, which the boy interpreted as guilt and an invitation to sail into another diatribe.

Sensing the Starhunter's impatience, but unable to cut through the boy's anger with reason, Vidarian tried entreaty instead. "Please—you should go—"

"I will *not* go! I will not let you hide away under your cushions from the consequences of your actions—"

Vidarian couldn't help himself. He launched forward and grabbed the boy by his shirtfront and hauled him close. "You genuinely," he said, through clenched teeth and fist, "have *no idea* about the consequences of my actions."

Ding! Egg's done!

Wait— Vidarian thought, then *no!* as he felt the Starhunter rush forward. He threw his own energy against her, holding her back.

For half an instant it worked. His mind and body strained against the weight of her will, and his elemental self, a twisting column of angry, confused sea and fire energy, flared bright, stretching to its limits.

Yes, that's amusing. Also pointless.

Vidarian felt himself casually pushed to one side, an alien chill in the "hand" that moved him.

Before Vidarian's eyes, the young man's face twisted from rage to surprise, then fear. He opened his mouth to scream, but it was too late. The Starhunter had opened up a void in the boy's chest, and first it seared him with starfire, burning him from the inside out. His body became ash, which collapsed toward the floor—and vanished before it could mar the rich blue carpet.

Vidarian staggered backward, covering his mouth out of reflex, sickened by what he'd just seen.

Aaaah, the Starhunter sighed happily.

He carefully drew one breath after another. By the tenth, he was reasonably sure he wouldn't be ill.

By the twentieth, he started to think about the implications of Farian's death.

"They're going to blame me for this," he said quietly. "The boy has a prominent family." He couldn't yet say *had*. Even now he shoved the memory of the boy's body melting to ash behind the wall of numbness that was all, at the moment, that was keeping him sane.

So not my problem, the Starhunter replied. *But I see you're going to be mopey about this. Toodles!*

The shadows on the wall vanished, lightening the room. Not quite believing they were gone, Vidarian set the pup down and staggered to the wall, placing a hand on its cool, papered surface. He lost track in moments of how long he remained there.

* *Is she gone?* * Ruby, who had been silent the entire time, now gave the impression that she was creeping out from a cave. Vidarian had never heard her so disturbed.

"Yes," he said, sinking down the wall and cradling his head in his hands. The pup whined and nosed his leg, and he dropped a hand down, carefully, to stroke its forehead.

* *That's what you had in your head, all that time?* * Now she was tentative, apologetic—also new.

"All that time." He lacked the strength to do more than repeat her words. And before she could answer, he slipped, unknowing, into sleep, there on the plush carpet, the pup curled up at his feet.

Chapter Eight

The Arboretum

Pain woke him.

A pounding headache dragged Vidarian from restless sleep. Opening his eyes made things much worse, so he closed them again, and clenched his teeth against the sear of agony that shot through his arms and legs.

Once the surge of red faded from behind his eyes, he cracked them open cautiously again, while pushing himself to a seated position.

Gingerly, and without quite knowing why, he reached out with his elemental senses—then immediately drew back as pain lashed him again. His subconscious fears were confirmed; he'd overreached, trying to resist the Starhunter's attack last night, and now those parts of his mind that controlled the magic were paying the price. He throttled them down, let go of the unconscious hold he kept on his abilities, and some of the pain dulled enough for him to think, if not clearly.

Gradually the room came into focus. First, the pup was staring at him, his white-tipped ears pointed up and forward. Vidarian leaned out to pet him, and as pain roared in his head with the movement, the little wolf howled in sympathy.

Wearily he thought reassuring thoughts at the pup, which seemed to calm him down, then took a quick breath and levered himself to his feet all at once.

This time he was ready for the wave of black dizziness and did not stagger, and the pup whined rather than howling. His sight came back in patches, and with it, rational thought, beneath the layer of still-throbbing complaint from his entire body. Given the soft morning light filtering through the expensive curtains, enough time had passed that the pup should have rendered the rooms a disaster area, from hunger or any assortment of physical needs.

There was no such disaster. In fact, a sniff of the air revealed a faint aroma of mint and lemons. The polished stone floor of the water chamber across from the bedroom gleamed even at this distance, his clothes had been neatly folded and shelved in the wardrobe, and a small folding table had been set up with a steaming silver meal service discreetly placed at the foot of the bed. Vidarian's stomach growled at the sight of that last, and his feet took him there before he'd quite consciously decided to go.

He lifted the engraved silver cloche to find a robust morning meal of thick toast, oatmeal porridge, dried fruits, and piping hot *kava*. Accompanying the breakfast was a plate of finely minced raw meat and a small porcelain jar of pungent hangover remedy. Vidarian realized with a flush of embarrassment that a servant must have come to clean his room, seen him sprawled in the antechamber, and naturally assumed the cause.

Nevertheless, the remedy jar, packed with willow bark and arrowmenthe, was as good for headaches as for hangovers, and he swallowed its contents down gamely, quickly chasing the blindingly bitter flavor with a gulp of *kava*.

* One imagines they keep quite a few of those little jars on hand around here, * Ruby observed dryly. It seemed her newfound humility in the face of the chaos goddess would be short-lived.

Instead of answering her, Vidarian set the plate of meat on the floor for the pup, who had been noisily salivating from the moment the breakfast tray was unveiled. Before the plate touched down, he was already greedily gulping down mouthfuls of meat, and in moments had devoured all and licked the plate clean. He then looked back up at Vidarian, wide blue eyes expectant, tongue lolling.

Vidarian reached for his spoon and the pup whined, very softly, beseeching. With a sigh, Vidarian instead picked up one of the thick, butter-slathered pieces of toast, and was rewarded by a frantically thumping tail. He handed it to the pup, who took it delicately between his incisors, and trotted off to chew with great contemplation beneath the shelter of the sitting room's small writing desk.

"You need a name," Vidarian told the pup. White-tufted ears swiveled toward him, but the rest of the pup's concentration remained on his toast.

* *Pest,* * Ruby offered. * *Mistake. Death-wish. Dirt.* *

"That's just mean," Vidarian said. He took up the bowl of oatmeal, dropped a handful of dried fruit into it, and sat on the edge of the bed to eat. Between the arrowmenthe, the food, and the *kava,* he was shortly feeling more human again, though his muscles still complained from the unceremonious night on the floor.

* *He's colored like old firewood, or ash,* * Ruby offered grudgingly.

"Ash," Vidarian said to himself, trying out the word, and suddenly the events of last night came pouring back into his mind. After swirling there for several moments they dropped like iron weights into his stomach, and he set aside what remained of the oatmeal.

The pup looked up at his distress and whined again, softly. He'd finished his toast, and after licking his paws and the carpet clean of crumbs came to settle at Vidarian's feet. Swimming out of his mental paralysis, Vidarian noted that the pup was quite a bit larger than he had been when he'd first found him, perhaps even twice as large.

When he'd found him. When he and Altair had killed the pup's pack. For an instant he fell into bleak self-pity: could he get nothing right? Was it his destiny to bring about destruction?

The pup whined again, deep in his throat. He lifted his head and rested his chin on Vidarian's knee, looking up with soulful cerulean eyes.

"Rai," Vidarian said softly, and the pup—Rai—thumped his tail.

* *'Blue'?* * Ruby asked. * *Is that Old Alorean?* *

"Yes," Vidarian agreed, reaching down to scratch the pup between his ears. "And 'lightning' in Qui, if I'm not mistaken."

* *It means 'trust' in Rikani.* *

Vidarian blinked. "I didn't know you spoke any Rikani."

* *I didn't know I did either.* *

Before he could press to discover whether she was joking or serious, a knock on the door startled him to his feet. He nearly knocked over the breakfast tray in the process, and the pup barked and rushed toward the door.

Deeply conscious of his rumpled appearance, Vidarian took a last swallow of *kava* and crossed the room. He pushed Rai to one side, glaring a warning against further barks, and opened the door.

A black-liveried messenger bearing the crest of the Alorean Import Company waited outside, his neatly oiled hair gleaming and accentuating the look of deep disapproval he gave Vidarian's rumpled attire. He made a token effort to mask his sigh, and said, "Captain Rulorat, my master requests the gift of your presence at luncheon today, to discuss certain matters of mutual concern."

Despite the man's attitude and clear assumption of compliance, the ice that shot down Vidarian's spine prevented him from even attempting defiance. Surely this "master" wished to discuss Farian's disappearance. "Have I a few moments—to prepare?"

The messenger eyed Vidarian up and down, then raised an eyebrow. "Take your time. The master takes luncheon in the Arboretum. Two marks." Then, without waiting for dismissal, he turned—almost lazily!—on his heel and left.

～～～

Two marks was long enough for Vidarian to scrub himself clean, severely trim his unruly beard, and throw himself into a set of clothes. What he'd found in the wardrobe was a mix of formal and working-wear, and the neckerchief he'd selected seemed uncomfortably tight no matter how he adjusted it.

When he asked passing servants for directions to the Arboretum, the looks they gave him, as though he knew something he shouldn't, further added to his discomfort. By the time he turned down the last hallway, with scant moments to spare, he was sweating, and not from exertion.

The doors to the Arboretum were of heavy cast iron, cold to the touch. Despite their size, they opened easily on well-oiled mechanical hinges—and brilliant sunlight poured through them, blinding.

Gradually his eyes adjusted, and he shifted his hand, which he'd brought up to shade them without thinking. As details began to resolve, he caught the silhouettes of tall, slender trees flanking sand-floored pathways, cast-iron benches, a bubbling fountain. Tiny birds too fast to identify flickered from tree to tree, their calls echoing.

As his eyes traveled upward, adjusting even more to the light, a chill rippled through his veins—for although there was sunlight, they were not outside. The glass panels that formed an octagonal ceiling far above also reflected diamond-white light that shone from a sphere hanging at their center.

"Astonishing, isn't it?" The voice behind him was muffled but close, and when he spun to confront it, heart hammering, he drew back without thinking. Painted eyebrows and a serenely smiling mouth looked back at him from a white porcelain mask, its eye sockets set with blue glass that hid even the wearer's eye color. The masked face tilted upward at the sun-sphere, then returned. "It ignited when you opened the gate, and as you can see . . ." he gestured eloquently with a black-gloved hand, ". . . the gardens have quite overgrown."

In his awe at the sun-sphere, Vidarian in fact hadn't noticed, but the masked man was right; vegetation spilled out of alabaster pots and carved stone beds, spread across sanded paths, and climbed the walls overhead.

"All will be attended to in time," the muffled voice added, and in its diction Vidarian almost recognized it, a memory that darted away as soon as he grasped after it . . . "But such details can wait. I did invite you to dine, after all." He could hear the genuine smile beneath the painted one, which unsettled him all over again.

Vidarian followed as his host led the way down one of the many branching paths, and they wove through sprawling vegetation until he utterly lost his tenuous sense of palace direction. It didn't seem possible that the room could contain so many twists and turns; the lush greenery must have made it seem smaller than it actually was.

They came upon a table draped with white linen, striking in the shaded vegetation. Glowing blue lights accompanied elegant silverware and glass dishes, providing light here where the tree canopy all but blocked out the artificial sunlight.

Without ceremony, his host—still masked—sat down and began lifting lids and serving out portions of food onto two plates. Aromatic mashed hornroot with peppery rockthistle seeds was joined by a savory lamb curry and chopped watercress and almond salad; the man apparently had a taste for Ishmanti delicacies. A dainty silver tray of imported sweetmeats confirmed this, as did the deep red tea served with the meal.

All this was carried out nearly before Vidarian could take his seat, and so shortly his host was lifting his spoon—then: "Ah," again the real smile beneath the painted one—and he cupped the mask with his left hand and pulled it free.

At first Vidarian stared at the man's face without recognition. His white hair and lined face, pale blue eyes that were almost gray—but then, a hint of agelessness, especially when he gave that superior smile, as he did now—

"Justinian," Vidarian said, so quiet he barely heard himself.

His host smiled again, droll this time, almost bored, agreeing. He gestured with a gloved hand, encouraging Vidarian to continue.

The man's smug satisfaction lit ire in Vidarian's heart, but his astonishment, and accompanying curiosity, still won out. "Oneira—the emperor!—they said you were dead. And you're . . ."

"Old?" Justinian offered, and now his irritating smile was reptilian. He jovially spooned up a mouthful of hornroot and gravy, ate it, and pointed the spoon at Vidarian. "But not dead. And that's the trick, isn't it?"

"You must have been—"

He waved the spoon again. "Six hundred and twenty-nine. Yes. Still am, actually." He dug into the curry this time, mocking Vidarian's lack of appetite with his elaborate flairs of the spoon. "You're wondering how I survived. It's fairly simple. Your little adventure did not eliminate healing magic, merely—severely—dampened it. I simply ensured I had sufficient concert-trained healers in my employ to offset the damage."

Vidarian took up his porcelain teacup and drank, taking courage from the hot liquid and trying to rally his senses. Justinian was showing a remarkable lack of desire to kill him. "And the rest of the Court?"

"Certifiably deceased, I assure you. A regrettable price, but so many prices have been paid, it hardly seems fair for the Court of Directors to be spared, don't you think?" Even for a Company man, this last was too glib, and it raised Vidarian's hackles.

"And your fellow directors—did they know about this 'price'?"

"The directors were unified behind the cause of moving our world into its next great stage," Justinian said. By now he had cleaned his plate; Vidarian's remained untouched.

"You didn't answer my question."

Justinian's pale eyes suddenly became flat and serious. "Let's not be naive, sirrah. Truth be told you did me a great favor, upending the Court like that. And I know my compatriots," his lip curled, ever so slightly, but the harshness in his voice was almost a kind of regret. "I held knowledge they did not, and I won our little gamble of world-changing events. They lost, and I am due the spoils. Things are as they should be."

"And now?" Vidarian gestured with his teacup at the porcelain mask.

The look that came over Justinian then was part cleverness, part victory, and part ecstasy: a wild kind that he had last seen in those who claimed to follow the chaos goddess. Destruction inevitably resulted. "Now—I have ascended." He wiped his fingers on a linen napkin and took up the mask again, tracing its painted eyebrows. "Our world is in shift, and these shifts have always seen the Company at its best. Now, though—" he cradled the mask between his two hands, running his thumbs along its cheeks as if to smooth it. "Now we wield the power to shape an entire age." He looked up. "An age in which you play an important role, Vidarian."

Even as he knew the familiarity of his given name was meant to agitate him, Vidarian had to work to contain the swell of outrage that lit in his chest. He stared at Justinian, and said nothing.

"Do you know why elemental magic faded from the world, until you opened the gate, Vidarian?" Justinian's voice was quiet, and still he looked at the mask, not across the table.

"The absence of the Starhunter—" Vidarian began, but knew his uncertainty to be obvious. None of the priestesses, or the gryphons, had ever answered that question.

Justinian shook his head ever so slightly, but enough to interrupt. "Population," he said, and now he looked up, lifting the mask to point at the overgrown greenery. "Human populations. Gryphon populations. Sentient populations—growing, thriving—blocking out the light." He looked back at Vidarian, and his eyes, old, but too young for the thoughts behind them, were piercing. "The Starhunter opens up the elements, channels energy between them, refreshes them—but only for a while. She is not a solution."

Vidarian pushed himself to his feet, suddenly aware of where Company logic would lead this line of thought. He wanted no part of it.

But Justinian rose also, smoothly, as if he'd intended to all along. "Imagine a world without suffering," he said, reaching across the table to pick up one of the glowing blue lights. He set it behind the porcelain mask, causing eerie blue light to pour from its glass eyes. "Imagine this garden, properly pruned, where sunlight touches every leaf, and every plant flowers and fruits."

A dull rumble sounded from the ground below their feet, and Vidarian jerked, looking for its source. When he returned his attention to Justinian, the man was smiling again—and holding out his hand to an adjacent alcove.

"Right on time," Justinian said, and started in that direction. "Follow me."

CHAPTER NINE
IRIDAN

Vidarian followed Justinian, not because he wanted to, but because it would be dangerous to do otherwise, in more ways than one. He needed to know what Justinian's survival meant—and why Oneira and the emperor had no knowledge of it.

In the next alcove, the primly dressed young man who had summoned Vidarian to the Arboretum waited beside an iron-handled trapdoor set into the floor. At Justinian's gesture he hauled it open, and the older—Vidarian tried not to dwell on how *much* older—man immediately trotted into the opening.

A set of steep and tightly winding stone stairs followed, and they would have been in darkness almost immediately if not for the small glass cube that Justinian produced from a pocket, which glowed blue as soon as he breathed on it. "The last Alorean grand enchanter favored blue, and so nearly all our remaining artifacts glow thus," he said in an aside, "I'll give you that tidbit for free."

The stairs ended at a blank wall. Justinian set the glowing cube on a nearly invisible ledge at the wall's center, and streaks of light immediately spidered out from it. When the light reached the four edges of the wall, the stone contracted, melting away from its center until there was nothing left but a kind of thick, glowing threshold.

Despite gryphons, despite his own elemental magic, Vidarian's heart quickened at the sight of such magic. Justinian wielded no magic of his own—Vidarian was sure he would have sensed it—and yet these devices, and his knowledge of them, allowed him tremendous power. In his wonder and astonishment at the skyship, he had never considered the existence of other enchanted devices. How many now were at work in the world? And how many more were waiting to be found?

All this swirled in his head as Justinian crossed the threshold, leading the way into a chamber lit at four corners and ceiling with more elemental lights, each of these in a different color. The diamond-white light above them seemed to be a smaller replica of the Arboretum's sun-sphere, and it cast a clear, gentle light down on a man encased in intricately engraved copper armor lying atop a massive stone slab.

A shiver of superstitious anxiety trickled up Vidarian's spine—clearly this was a tomb. He cursed himself for not knowing more imperial history; he hadn't known of the existence of the Arboretum, much less who might be buried beneath it.

Then the armored man sat up.

Vidarian reached for a sword he wasn't wearing, and then lifted his hand, all unthinking, a shield of water energy flaring out around his fingers. His bruised senses shrieked a complaint at such sudden use, but pure instinct had driven him, and couldn't now be taken back.

Justinian looked from Vidarian to one of the glowing lights, a turquoise-green one, which now flared brighter than the other three. He lifted an eyebrow, but turned toward the stone slab without comment.

The sitting man was turning his head to look around, and several things about him became apparent, chiefly: he was covered with glowing lavender gems, he radiated complex elemental energy, and he was not human. It took Vidarian several moments to reconcile this last, but upon close inspection it was obvious: the hinge-points at his arms, knees, and neck were far too thin to be covering flesh and bone. He wasn't wearing armor—he *was* the armor.

"You're Iridan, if my readings are correct," Justinian said.

"*I am,*" the metal figure said, head swiveling toward Justinian to fix him with glowing lavender eyes. His voice was inside and outside of Vidarian's head at the same time, the meaning of his words so immediate that Vidarian could not have said what language they were in. It was disconcerting, to say the least. "*I apologize for my ignorance—I don't believe we are acquainted?*"

Vidarian's heart beat faster at the—creature's?—eloquence, but Justinian took it in stride. "It is not ignorance, my dear friend," he said, and Vidarian would have bet money on the sincerity in his voice, "you have been asleep for just over a thousand years."

Iridan drew back, the joints along his arms and shoulders rattling. *"Yet that would mean . . . I recall . . . Parvidian bringing me here, I was so very tired . . . tell me, is he . . . ?"* The lavender lights flickered as he stared at Justinian.

"The Grand Artificer, I am sorry to say, left us about two decades after your sleep." At this the metal man's shoulders shuddered again, but he did not speak, his head turning stiffly to regard his hands. Grief rolled out of him, radiating from that strange hybrid of telepathy and speech. "I am deeply sorry to wake you to such terrible news," Justinian said, stepping closer to Iridan, and now his voice and body language were all caution and care. "And I must ask you, Iridan, if you know the whereabouts of your brother and sisters?"

The copper head turned back toward Justinian, lavender eyes flaring and dimming. *"My brother and sister—were away from the imperial city when last I woke. Do you know if they have yet awakened?"*

Justinian watched Iridan, giving no sign he had heard the metal man claim only one sister. "We do not yet know," he said, and again his voice was heavy with sympathy, "but had counted on your assistance in finding them. Before this, though," he turned and gestured to his assistant, who lurked in the doorway, "let us see to your comfort, and repair, if need be. Your joints must be feeling the effects of your long sleep."

Iridan lifted one of his hands, and in the glow of the elemental lights Vidarian could make out the intricate gears and curls of wire that formed it. The hand opened and closed, glittering.

* *Miraculous,* * Ruby murmured, stirring so suddenly from her long silence that he jumped. * *Only four were made . . .* *

What? Vidarian thought. But no answer came. He reached out with his mind, flailing, trying to reach Thalnarra or Isri. He had virtually no ability to speak of, but beyond that, this room was strange; where previously he had been aware of Isri's general location, thanks mostly to *her* skill, now it was as though this room was sealed off to the outside, as surely as if they'd been separated by a thousand feet of stone.

"*I would be quite grateful,*" Iridan said, and Justinian moved forward to place his hand on the copper shoulder. Did a creature of metal sense touch, Vidarian wondered—but the emotion that echoed with strange clarity from Iridan was appreciation for the gesture, nonetheless.

Then Justinian turned toward the doorway, motioning Vidarian after. The assistant passed them, moving for Iridan, carrying a steaming porcelain bowl, rags, and a flask of oil. Vidarian followed Justinian back up the stone staircase.

They emerged into the shaded alcove, pale white light filtering down through the trees. Justinian went back to the table, picked up his mask, and fitted it gently to his face. He turned back toward Vidarian, solemn beneath the painted smile. "You have begun this," he said.

An imperial summons reached Vidarian before he could retreat back to his rooms. The emperor planned to ride in the acres of parkland north of the palace, and wished for Vidarian's company. He wasn't dressed for riding, but was told a coat and boots would be waiting for him at the imperial stables.

The coat—imperial black and gold—fit with the same uncanny accuracy as the rest of the clothing, betraying Renard's hand. The boots less so, but serviceable, and waiting with them was a stablehand and a saddled black gelding. Being only the second horse Vidarian had ever ridden in his adult life, this one, called Aluhaar, reminded him of Feluhim, also night-black, also Irivedian, an Ishmanti breed long in favor with the imperial court.

His muscles cried out in complaint when the stablehand helped him into the saddle, and he landed awkwardly, earning flattened ears and a dissatisfied snort from the fine horse. The stablehand looked him over dubiously from beneath a mousy forelock, her hands moving automatically to calm the gelding, but led him out to the trailhead nonetheless. Eager to prove he wasn't a total tyro, he picked up the reins and rode ahead, thanking her with a wave.

The emperor was waiting, looking out over the low brush, just beyond the first bend in the trail. Vidarian wasn't sure whether to interrupt his contemplations, but Aluhaar decided for him, whickering as he caught scent of the emperor's horse and breaking into a trot—sensing with the strange wisdom of horses that Vidarian's inexperience meant he could take charge.

When they drew close, a familiar but shocking bark revealed what the emperor had been watching so closely: Rai, the wolf pup, launched out of the brush, and this time Aluhaar squealed and pranced, threatening to both unseat Vidarian and stomp the little predator.

Before either could happen, the emperor kneed his own mount close and reached across to grab Aluhaar's reins just below the chin. With his head restrained, and the other horse so near, the gelding rolled his eyes at the wolf, ears flat, but settled down. Rai, on the other hand, danced excitedly, barking— and then dashed back into the brush before Vidarian could correct him.

"My apologies," the emperor said, gradually releasing Aluhaar as the horse settled, "for both the surprise ride, and bringing your little—companion. I thought he might enjoy the park, and it would give my stewards a bit of a respite."

Embarrassment and panic rippled through Vidarian in turns. Of course the palace servants would not have restrained their complaints, particularly with how often Rai had been left unattended . . .

"Please, Captain, I truly mean no critique," the emperor said, his pale eyes gentle with concern. "I drag you into the heart of Val Imris unprepared, and you come to find the world has changed even more than you thought. Am I correct?"

"You are, your majesty," Vidarian agreed, striving to keep the dismay out of his voice, "though the responsibility for all this is mine."

"You give yourself too much credit, my friend," he said, but again the gentleness in his words removed all sting. The emperor kneed his mount closer again, looking Vidarian closely in the eye—searching, he thought. "I do not believe that any of us can escape our destinies. Nor should we linger unto paralysis on the strange times we find ourselves in. It is certain that the world will demand the best of us."

Vidarian met the emperor's gaze, marveling again at how so young a man, confronted with, as he said, such strange times, could maintain such an even keel.

He speaks truth, or thinks he does, Ruby offered, breaking the silence she'd inhabited since witnessing Iridan.

How do you know? Vidarian thought.

Years of trade alliances with far better liars than either of you.

It was a relief to hear something of the "old" Ruby again, and Vidarian smiled. The emperor smiled back, and indicated the trail. "Shall we ride?"

"Lead on, your majesty, and I will follow."

A surprised pleasure caught the emperor's face then, a mask pulled down, and for a moment they were only two men, gratitude rendering them equals.

They turned the horses down the path, and once the emperor took the lead, Aluhaar gamely followed. For a moment Vidarian worried that Rai was gone, but the pup tracked their progress, racing across the trail every hundred steps or so only to disappear back into the brush again. Both horses, after touching noses with the pup on one of his visits, decided that he was no threat and proceeded to ignore him entirely. Presently they rode into a copse of trees, their thin leaves golden, white branches carefully trained to arc over the trail to form a living tunnel.

"It's a heavy task I ask of you, Captain, but we need not weigh down our excursion with business," the emperor said, leaving a note hanging of what he would rather discuss.

Vidarian could guess at it, and Ruby clucked sardonically in his head. "My friend, the lady Calphille, seemed quite taken with your majesty," he ventured, and knew he'd struck true when again the mask of office slipped free of the emperor's face for just a moment.

"You know more of her than I do. Is it true she knows nothing of cities?"

"Her people . . . come from a small holding far to the south, beyond the Windsmouth," Vidarian said, hoping his voice did not betray him.

"An old country," the emperor said, surprised but—impressed? "Lost to civilization for centuries."

"They are a simple folk," Vidarian said, treading carefully, betting that the plausible slight to Calphille's people would reassure the emperor more than the truth.

"Simple," the emperor mused. "Yet perhaps that is why she is so intriguing. My court could do with a good deal more simplicity." The frank ruefulness in his voice shocked Vidarian, though he dared not show it.

"In the west I am educated, but here I fear I bring you too much simplicity, your majesty."

To his surprise, the emperor laughed and looked at him with wry wonder. "If only that were true."

He would have argued the point, but in just that moment, they emerged from the trees' golden canopy and into a meadow—where Altair and Thalnarra lay sunning, wings outspread.

Rai barked with recognition as he caught the gryphons' scent, and raced to meet them. In his exuberance, he loosed an arc of blue electricity, and though it missed Thalnarra's beak by inches, it set fire to the nearby grass.

Before Altair could voice his disapproval, Vidarian reached out with his own fire sense and drew the flames away, pulling their energy into himself. The water within him grumbled at this shift in energy balance, and it took him a few tense moments to quiet it.

"You were saying, Vidarian?" The emperor watched him with a strange expression, a mixture of amusement and fascination.

// *Compared to humans, gryphons are simple creatures,* // Thalnarra offered, languidly tucking her wings against her side and standing.

"Your majesty, may I introduce Thalnarra, adept of fire; and Altair, adept of air." The gryphons dipped their beaks at each of their names. "My friends— Emperor Lirien Aslaire, Lord of the Western Reaches." Then, after a quick glance, "For all our sakes, I hope he won't mind if I spare the rest of his titles."

To his relief, the emperor laughed, and urged his mount forward. Vidarian's own horse danced with agitation, and he worked awkwardly to control him, envious of the emperor's easy reassurance of his own mare.

Then the emperor swung down from his saddle, landing easily and walking up to Thalnarra, now well below her natural eye level. She lowered her head to his lifted hand, touching her beak to his palm. Throughout, she radiated an impressed curiosity, her thoughts like warm spiced apples where they brushed Vidarian's.

And the emperor's face, for his part, shone with awe and adventurousness. "I have read of your people," he said, returning his hand to his side, and turning to quiet his horse as she snorted at a frolicking Rai. The pup ran boldly up to the emperor, sniffed his knee, and then dashed back into the grass. Lirien chuckled and looked back to Thalnarra and Altair. "As a boy, I lost myself in tales from Alanndir, the sand kingdom on the far side of the world."

// *The most recent alliance between humans and gryphons,* // Thalnarra said, appreciation like melting butter in her thoughts. // *The last to dissolve, if our records are correct. Only eight generations ago.* //

// *I'd no idea they persisted so long,* // Altair said, an edge to his thoughts like smoked mint leaves. Vidarian was relieved that, for once, he was not alone in lacking knowledge Thalnarra possessed.

// *They were a fire pride,* // she explained. // *Distantly related to my own. Sun-chasers.* //

"Their legends hardly scratched the surface of your strength and beauty," the emperor said, and his words might have been all training, but the warmth in them was genuine.

Thalnarra turned one red eye on him, peering closely. Then her neck twisted and she bent her large head between her wings. Her beak, delicate for a weapon so large, closed around the shaft of a feather there, and with a precise jerk she pulled it free. It twirled as she shifted her lower jaw and brought it down to the emperor.

The feather was dark grey, edged with faded gold feather-paint. Against the emperor's hand it looked even larger than it had on Thalnarra, wider than his spread hand, and a third again longer. He accepted it with reverence, and lifted it between the two gryphons in a gesture of gratitude. "I will treasure this as it deserves, I promise you," he said, and again a boyish wonder humbled his voice beyond anything Vidarian had heard at the palace. "Tell me, are all of your needs being met? What gift might I bring you?"

// *We leave in the morning, with Vidarian,* // Thalnarra said, her feathers fluffed with appreciation for the emperor's words. // *We would ask only that you treasure his trust as our own.* //

Gratitude washed through Vidarian, spilling through him like sunlight. He reached out to Thalnarra with his thoughts, and she brushed them again, a faint sensation of wings arching around him.

The emperor turned, looking at Vidarian with thoughtful eyes. "I shall," he said.

CHAPTER TEN
SKY WAR

The next morning, a predawn knock on the door and Rai's answering riot of barking woke Vidarian from a deep sleep. As she had been the last several nights, Ariadel was in his dreams, and when reality cracked through, he woke to a wave of chest-crushing loss all over again.

He calmed Rai with a thought as he climbed out of bed, steering clear of his fully roused ruff of spines. In addition to gaining size, the spines on the back of the pup's neck were starting to show faint stripes of color, like his packmates'. This was another sad thought, and Vidarian brushed it away as he moved toward the door.

An apologetic messenger waited beyond. "I'm sorry, Captain," the boy said, "they told us you'd been informed. Fleet Admiral Allingworth will be preparing the launch at dawn."

"The Fleet Admiral?" Surprise, and the wafting aroma of *kava* from a breakfast tray carried by an approaching maid, chased the last of the sleepiness from his thoughts.

"Aye, sir," the messenger said, clearly relieved Vidarian wasn't angry. "He's asked to attend the delivery of the skyships. There'll be combat, scuttlebutt says." The boy was young enough to be excited by violence and old enough to know what it meant; a dangerous combination.

"Like enough," Vidarian agreed, letting his downward tone warn the boy off. He stepped to one side to allow the maid passage. She slipped adroitly by, set the tray on a side table, and, to Vidarian's surprise, passed Rai a bit of dried meat on her way back out the door. The pup wolfed it down, and the maid winked at Vidarian as she left.

"Do you think the Rikani stand a chance against the Qui, sir?" the boy asked, emboldened by Vidarian's distraction.

It was a good question, which was doubtless why the boy felt compelled to ask it of anyone, even a common stranger.

* *Or a less-than-common one. A strange stranger.* * Ruby corrected. Vidarian wondered absently if she ever slept.

"Wiser minds than mine believe they can, with our assistance," he said.

* *Such a politician.* *

The boy, too, seemed vaguely disappointed, but nodded. He was sneaking looks at Rai, who was insistently poking his nose into the back of Vidarian's knee, demanding breakfast. Vidarian excused himself and shut the door firmly.

Rai began beating the leg of the side table with his tail as soon as Vidarian turned around, and whined with anticipation as the lifted cloche revealed his meat plate. Vidarian tossed his toast on top of the meat without being asked, lowered the plate to the pup, and proceeded to wolf down his own breakfast—oatmeal, this time with pinenuts and dried plums—without tasting it.

He spared the time to wash thoroughly, as there wouldn't be another opportunity for some time (Tesseract he might be, but getting water and fire to cooperate enough to produce wash-water that was neither tepid nor superheated was embarrassingly difficult). Then he donned the only set of clothes left in the room—the others had been packed off for the voyage—and made briskly for the door.

In the hallway, he stopped just short of closing the door behind him. Rai had finished his breakfast and stood there, snout still damp, giving a tentative wave of his tail.

A voyage of the kind Vidarian was expecting was no place for a young animal. But neither was the palace, even with the stewards' forbearance.

In the end he succumbed to Rai's large, hopeful eyes, seeing the Precious Outside and Vidarian's hesitation. He waved his hand once and the pup gave a little yip of excitement and raced into the hallway, clawed feet skittering on the marble floor. As Vidarian headed for the north end of the palace, Rai raced up and down the hallways, crashing into walls twice without slowing down.

At length they came to the north palace walls, and then beyond to the parkland where Vidarian had ridden with the emperor. When he caught scent of the grass, Rai leapt ahead again with renewed speed, dashing across the open field. Initially he sped off to the west, down the trail they'd ridden, and Vidarian had to whistle loud and sharp to get him to return.

To the northeast, the grass had been stamped down where it had not been cut. Tents were laid out along the western tree line, and workers swarmed through one of the stranger sights of the new gate-opened world:

Skyships. Not one or even ten, but over twenty, and no two exactly alike. Most had watermarks, betraying a conversion to sea-going vessels, but some were utterly unmarked. Of these, some had been decommissioned entirely and were now receiving new rigging, while others looked spectacularly, impossibly new, preserved by some kind of magic Vidarian couldn't fathom.

The smallest skyships were in front, little messenger skiffs or fast courier boats. The *Destiny* was among them, also being tended by carpenters and ropemakers. And beside her was Corbin Allingworth, Imperial Admiral of the Fleet.

Vidarian had seen the admiral's likeness on imperial shipping documents, and there was no question to his identity. His coal-black hair, curled like wool, was grayer in the front than the last portrait he'd seen, but the stern, craggy face and broad build were unmistakable.

Rai, still showing no sign of fatigue, dashed up to the admiral, barking a greeting. The man did not draw back, but he did eye the pup's spines skeptically—which now and then flickered with electricity in his excitement.

Vidarian rushed to stare the pup down, nudging him away from the admiral with a foot. "My apologies, Admiral. He's been cooped up some time."

"This is your animal, then?" Allingworth said, his voice, too, gruff like old wool.

"I—had a commitment to his previous owner, no longer with us," Vidarian said. It hardly seemed helpful to share more details of his origin.

"I see." He looked up from the pup, the weight of his stare like an anvil, or a goddess. "And you're Captain Rulorat, I take it?"

"I am, sir," Vidarian said, extending his hand, meeting the man's gaze with what was not quite defiance. "Reporting at the emperor's request."

"I hope you're well in a scrap, then," Allingworth all but grunted. "Nistra knows we'll need all the wit we can get, sailing these against the Qui. At least you'll have a berth bigger than this one, eh." He poked the *Destiny* with the toe of his boot.

Vidarian felt heat creeping into his cheeks. "A small vessel, certainly, but she carried me well and safely across the Windsmouth Mountains all the way to this city."

Allingworth scrutinized him, clearly weighing whether he dared trust him with a weapon, much less a ship. Then, like storm clouds breaking, a grin split his saturnine face. "Temerity. Good. And you stand by your craft. We'll need that, by and by." Then he turned, waving Vidarian to follow.

They threaded their way through the lines of ships, workers flowing around them like steady streams of water. Most of the ships were supported by blocks, but a few hung suspended in the air, their elemental crystals aflame with blue light. As they passed toward the back of the field, the ships increased in size, until finally they came to a slender schooner so like the *Empress Quest* that Vidarian's heart convulsed.

A black melancholy settled on him as he looked on the ship. He realized now the root of his misgiving at this entire errand. The sight of the ships had only hinted at the shadow: now, seeing this vessel before him—the *Luminous*, according to her hull—the root of his misgiving crashed home. Vidarian, who had lived most of his entire life on the deck of a ship, could find very little he wanted to do with a vessel of this size now, since the destruction of his family's *Empress Quest*.

When he turned to gather his thoughts, Admiral Allingworth was there, the gruffness in his gaze replaced by compassion and sadness. He reached out to grip Vidarian's shoulder with a massive hand.

"Your pardon, my boy," he said, and some little part of Vidarian tried to remember who had last called him that, "I thought to reassure you with a familiar craft. The *Luminous* dates around the same time as your family's ship, if I'm not mistaken. And she's Targuli, too."

The familiar red teak was a giveaway, of course. And Vidarian would have recognized those lines anywhere. The *Luminous* was dwarfed by the flagship beside it, a monstrous twenty-eight-gun frigate half again bigger than Ruby's *Viere d'Inar*—but with familiar shape and build, Vidarian's eyes could only be drawn to the smaller ship.

"I thought, perhaps, a friendly voice—" Allingworth began.

"Captain!" But the voice was not familiar at all. Still, the man clearly recognized Vidarian, and came running down the steeply tilted gangplank to greet him.

Dawn hadn't yet made her appearance, and so the light was dim, even when aided by numerous witch-lights on long iron poles up and down the path. So it wasn't until the man was practically on top of them that Vidarian had the slightest recognition.

"Malloray?" Astonishment shook him out of his sadness. For here, sure as day, was Malloray, who had served aboard the *Empress Quest* for twenty years—but Vidarian had never seen him like this, buoyant, confident—and he had never *heard* him in his life. "But—you—" He didn't know remotely how to phrase it.

Rai, caught up in the excitement, started barking again, and Malloray laughed easily, crouching to pet the pup. Vidarian started to warn him, then swallowed his objection—for Malloray was looking into the pup's eyes, and Rai, unbelievably, calmed down, the spines along his neck relaxing and ceasing their electric vibration.

After a moment, Malloray looked up again, still aglow with secret satisfaction. "I know, sir. I ain't never spoken in the twenty years you knew me. Nor been on land a day all that time. But now I have some help, you see." He looked up, and Vidarian followed his gesture.

High above, from the rail of the *Luminous*, Isri, still wearing her black cloak, lifted her hand in greeting. To Vidarian's relief, she seemed at ease and happy.

// *He is a powerful mindspeaker,* // Isri said, and Malloray blushed. // *Extraordinarily so, to have been so affected he could neither speak nor tolerate populous places even before the gate opened. And now . . .* //

Allingworth, pleased at Malloray's appearance but oblivious to Isri's words, was still looking at Vidarian with concern. "The choice is yours, Captain Rulorat. I had thought to offer you the *Luminous*, and Nistra knows we have need of your leadership. But if it's too painful . . ." He lifted his eyebrows.

Vidarian looked from Allingworth to Malloray. "I could hardly refuse the vessel of so loyal and long a friend," he said, and meant it. "I'd be honored with the *Luminous*'s commission, Admiral."

Malloray clapped his hands, and Rai barked again. "You'll not regret it, sir." He thumped the polished side of the ship for emphasis. "*Luminous* is a relay ship!"

<center>~~~</center>

Vidarian had heard of signal ships being used in the Sea Wars, four generations past—but *Luminous* was a vessel of entirely different caliber. From the outside she had borne striking resemblance to the *Empress Quest*, but within— to Vidarian's relief—she was an entirely different creature.

Her crew was almost entirely officer class, and they moved about efficiently, many carrying stacks of paper tied with leather. Vidarian had never seen so many books aboard a ship before. And within, *Luminous* was a maze of cabins, all converging on a single large stateroom equipped with the same apparatus as the emperor's Relay Room: a single massive glowing sphere riddled with holes, and eight pairs of blue-lensed glasses that communicated with it. Thus, as Malloray had said, the "relay ship."

All this Vidarian knew from a fast tour of the decks, as he scrambled to get his bearings for command. Malloray was not just a signal officer—he was the *Luminous*'s first mate, made official when Vidarian accepted her captainship.

There was no time to become as versed as he would have liked in the launching and operation of the ship, with all able ships of the fleet taking off for Isrinvale and the front line of the Qui-Alorean conflict. And so after the ship took off—lifting easily into the air with a thrumming power the *Destiny* could not have hinted at—Vidarian, rather than standing at the wheel, was closeted in the captain's stateroom with Malloray.

Relay ships had an odd officer configuration, being as they served primarily to assist in reconnaissance and maintain communication between land command and a force abroad. Malloray was first mate, and second in command to Vidarian, but for all practical purposes, the actual function of the ship was given to the quartermistress, in this case a gruff dark-haired woman named Yerune. She was all business, and supervised the launch and movement of the ship, keeping it closely coordinated with the huge *Sunreign*, the admiral's flagship, whose cargo bays were large enough to host Thalnarra and Altair.

Yerune was Targulin, like the *Luminous* herself, but otherwise she reminded Vidarian of Marielle.

"Have you heard word from Ms. Solandt?" Vidarian asked Malloray, once the basics of the relay ship were clear in his mind. The last time Vidarian had seen the *Empress Quest*'s first mate, he realized with a pang, she had been fleeing the burning wreckage of his family's ship.

The crease of worry that passed over Malloray's features quickened Vidarian's pulse. "Not in weeks," he said, after a long pause. "They gave her the *Ardent*, as you hoped—" at this Vidarian's heart leapt, "—but they sailed west from Val Harlon, and passed beyond our communication three weeks ago."

Three weeks was not a long time for a ship to be out of range, but something in Malloray's tone said otherwise. "Out of range?" Vidarian pressed. "Even—for a relay ship?" He wasn't quite sure, but from what Malloray had described of the ship's capabilities, any vessels in the West Sea should have been well within the range of a Val Harlon relay ship.

Malloray was nodding reluctantly, troubled still. "Aye, sir. The *Ardent* hasn't made her checkpoints the last three running. I confess it concerns me."

To hear such sharply articulate words from a man who had never spoken in Vidarian's lifetime still startled him, but far more disturbing was the thought of Marielle lost at sea.

"I have a commitment in the West Sea, and would be there if it weren't for the emperor's summons," Vidarian said.

* *And here I thought you'd forgotten entirely.* * Ruby had been distracted by the presence of the relay sphere and many other elemental artifacts aboard the ship, but not absorbed. The barb in her tone stung true.

"I don't forget a commitment," he said. At Ruby's words, Malloray had looked thoughtful, a bit puzzled, as though he half heard her. "And I'll find Marielle, if I can."

~~~

The skyships were fast—at top speed, half again faster than a gryphon's long-distance pace—but still the southern border was two days' flight away. These days flew by faster than the ground below as Vidarian immersed himself in ancient tomes on aerial warfare. In the process he learned, to no comfort, that the ship, her artifacts—including the books, rare and prized beyond price—had been provided by the Alorean Import Company. Yet the Company, despite its name, had long also operated in Qui. Why would it supply a war that cut off trade between two of its partner empires?

Also contained in the ship's library were artifact indexes detailing the usage, description, and history of several elemental artifacts. The similarity between the water amplifier he'd used against the Vkortha and the relay sphere was no coincidence—the technologies were related. And the book also contained a chapter on an entire class of objects that most closely resembled glowing gemstones . . .

A pulse of thought energy pulled Vidarian, bleary-eyed, from the latest passage. It was Isri, who still sat, eyes closed and legs folded in a meditation pose, on the carpeted deck of the stateroom.

She opened her eyes, naturally gold but now brilliant blue with the light of the relay sphere she embraced with her mind.

"That presence . . ." Isri trailed off, the feathers on her forehead standing stiff in agitation, her eyes somewhere far away. "Strange, even impossible . . ."

Vidarian flipped the book closed and moved toward her, crouching to bring his face into her line of sight. Beyond the walls of the ship, a dull boom of cannonfire sounded from far below.

The blue eyes faded to green and then gold, pupils narrowing with vision at last. "The Qui. And the Rikani. We are here."

CHAPTER ELEVEN
COMPLETIONIST

When they ran up the ladders to the deck, they found the *Luminous* surging with the controlled chaos of battle preparation. Sails had already been furled and cannon prepared, but still the spar deck swarmed with activity.

Yerune, the quartermistress, shouted commands from the aftcastle rail, her eyes obscured by glowing blue relay glasses. Malloray was nowhere to be seen; for the last day he'd been shuttered in with a handful of other powerful mindspeakers in the ship's relay room, coordinating communications from the imperial city to Admiral Allingworth and the dozen skyships in his armada.

Far below, shreds of white cloud obscured parts of the sky, and even farther below them, a land and sea battle raged: the Rikani, true to their word, had sailed into the great crescent arm that was Parelle Bay, and harried the Qui invasion force occupying the green lands of Isrinvale.

"Fire forward cannons!" Yerune's cry carried clearly, and below the gundeck answered, shuddering the entire craft. As gunsmoke painted the air, Vidarian realized what damage they could do from this vantage, where their guns could reach the Qui, but none on the ground could reach them.

// *Ahoy there!* // Altair's voice, surreal and cheerful amidst the smoke and military precision, "tapped" Vidarian on the shoulder. He looked up in its direction and saw both gryphons floating, wings angled to glide with the ship's movement, off the starboard bow.

An impact from the ground far below pulled all of their attention, and Vidarian and Isri ran to the rail.

Thousands of feet beneath them, the cannon-strike was marked by giant burning circles. Impact craters blackened with soot showed the starburst center of each, and beyond for a hundred yards tiny figures silenced by distance writhed in flames, or did not move at all.

// *Fireshot,* // Thalnarra said, and the wreath of cedar smoke around her voice was blended respect and dread. // *Wherever did they find some still intact?* //

"You've heard of this weapon?" Vidarian said, half his breath taken away in attempted comprehension.

// *Heard only. It hasn't been seen in a thousand years. They can't have much of it.* // He tried not to think that this last was hope and not fact.

Rattling steps on the ladders, followed by a flurry of cursing, pulled them away from the carnage below.

A fire priestess—though dressed in leather, and like no other Vidarian had ever seen—ushered two initiates ahead of her up the ladders. All three of them carried odd lanterns, and the priestess wore blue relay glasses held in place with thick, riveted leather straps.

"Priestess Goldwind, can we assist you?" Vidarian shouted, as the cannon thundered again, and he tried not to imagine the result of their landing. He recognized the priestess from the ship's roll only, a Velinese woman aged fifty-three. The quartermistress had written "feisty" next to her name.

"No, you can't, Sharli burn it!" the priestess shouted, setting down the lanterns with a care contrasting her ire, and shaking her hands at the initiates to do likewise. Only when all six lanterns were settled did she look up over the rim of her strangely fixed glasses to squint at Vidarian. She offered no apology, but added grudgingly, "Well, perhaps *you* can," and waved him impatiently over.

Her two assistants were carefully arranging the lanterns, tilting them toward the sun. As they did so, the flames within picked up strength, and Priestess Goldwind seemed to relax just a little.

"The blessed lamps aren't stably made," she grumbled, an engineer's affront in her diagnosis. "They're pair-lights, clever enough—the little skiffs don't have mindspeakers aboard, but they do each have an opposite to these lights." She cocked an eye at Vidarian, then rolled it when he didn't immediately "ah" with comprehension. "Each pair of lights has the same life-flame. Adjust one and the other adjusts with—now *don't* be touching that, Amara!"

The initiate in question flinched away from the priestess's scolding, then gestured helplessly at the lamp in her charge. "I just—"

"I don't want your excuses! Sending me up here to a fool's war with naught but babes in swaddling . . ." She actually purpled, but only for a moment, and turned her searing attention back to Vidarian. "But they weren't properly made. Not enough energy. I thought the sun would help them, and it has, a . . ." Her eyes suddenly lost focus, and for a split second Vidarian thought she would faint, but then he saw that she was deliberately focusing on the lenses of the relay glasses.

The pair-lights all started to flicker, six different messages coming in at once. It was not any signal code Vidarian knew.

Priestess Goldwind's attention moved from lamp to lamp. And her face slackened with alarm. "They're saying—but it's impossible —"

The sky bloomed with orange light off the bow, some hundred yards ahead. Isri leapt into the air with a cry of recognition and dismay. She arrowed forward; Vidarian had not known she could move so fast.

He leapt from the deck and ran for the bow, lifting his head just in time to see a sear of orange and white light streak through the sky. The gryphons shrieked as the light appeared, and Vidarian felt their wave of astonishment and denial also. He cried out as the light burned his eyes, but kept lurching forward, and reached the bow just as his eyes cleared.

The gryphons each peeled off, Altair diving to starboard while Thalnarra curved to port, instinctively evading the attacks from below.

The little skiffs, as Priestess Goldwind had called them, weren't so lucky, or half so agile. A second blast of light tore through the port- and mainsails of the leading craft, which tipped crazily to one side. A topman pitched off his mast and into the open sky, falling—

Altair shrieked, drawing Vidarian's eye. The gryphon was poised in midair, talon raised in a gesture wreathed with pale energy. The falling sailor was blown upward, back within range of the skiff. The blast was coarse, but it would save his life.

Or it would, if the whole skiff itself wasn't tipping to starboard, its side-sails failing entirely.

"Altair!" Vidarian cried, "The ship!"

Altair dove, arrowing downward faster than a falling stone, then snapped his wings open and sailed beneath the beleaguered vessel. A *crack!* split the air, and seconds later the pulse of wind reached Vidarian—well after it filled the sails of the falling ship and carried it upward again. The men and women aboard saw certain death snatched away from their futures, and cried out in relief and gratitude.

But Altair, despite his enhanced strength, was struggling under the weight of the skiff and all it carried. He slowed its fall rather than supporting it. // *Thalnarra! The sails!* //

Thalnarra dove, a palpable anxiety, focus, and determination burning from her mind. She was not as fast as the white kite-gryphon, but she was upon the faltering skiff in moments, her broad, dark wings fanning out to brake her descent.

Now Thalnarra's talons reached out toward the sails, her mind radiating caution and delicacy across the distance between the ships. The torn sails lashed in the wind, erratic—but when their edges touched together, little by little, they began to re-knit, under the slow and painstakingly gentle fire energy of Thalnarra's claws.

"Breathtaking," Priestess Goldwind murmured, all trace of her acidity gone for half a moment. Then she recovered herself, turning on her initiates with redoubled ire. "You there! You'll not witness such precision in all your lives again! A single breath's more intensity and she'd have shorn those sails clear through, a single less and they'd not mend!" The initiates summoned suitably awestruck expressions, and Goldwind leaned toward Vidarian. "Even among gryphons, I'd lay my eyeballs on her touch being exceptional. I've not seen anything like it."

Below, the skiff was stabilizing, to more cries of relief from its crew. Altair, too, sounded less strained as he called back another command: // *Tell them to adjust the stabilizers! Transfer energy to the right half of the craft!* // Altair showed a "picture" of what to do, and Vidarian repeated the instructions as best he could, while Priestess Goldwind and her assistants relayed them to the damaged skiff.

Shortly, both gryphons were angling away from the repaired vessel, minute movements of their wingtips carrying them carefully away to the renewed cheers of the skiff's crew.

Their celebration was short-lived, as two more bursts of searing strange fire, one after the other, rocketed up from the ground. These were followed by three more, two of which found the bow of the *Destiny.*

The gryphons' shrieks of anger and fear echoed the silent pitch of Vidarian's heart. He reached out helplessly as the tiny craft pitched forward, its propulsion failing, and plummeted toward the ground.

Thalnarra and Altair cupped their wings to dive, but broke off with cries of fury as they realized the *Destiny* was falling too fast, and their magics could not repair its shattered frame. They might all have stared, transfixed with horror, at the falling ship, if two more sizzling lances of fire hadn't split the air between them.

Altair had spun, using the wind to angle back up toward the *Luminous.*

"We can't fight them from here!" Vidarian shouted. The gryphon replied with a wave of smoky, frustrated ascent. Not quite believing what he was about to suggest, but without another option, Vidarian added, "Can you get me down there?"

Altair was close enough now for Vidarian to read the pinning of his pupils as he cocked his head, looking from the *Luminous* to the ground and calculating.

// *I can,* // Altair agreed, just when Vidarian was sure he would refuse. He tried not to think about the distance between the ship and the ground. Or the homicidal magic-wielder that awaited them.

Altair tipped his left wing and slipped closer to the ship, positioning himself as close as he dared. He gestured with his beak, and Vidarian climbed up onto the rail. Isri let out a little squeak of protest, but subsided, nodding unhappily when Vidarian looked back at her.

It was one thing to talk about leaping off a skyship, and another to contemplate doing it. The pale, smoking dots far below made Vidarian's stomach turn over.

"It didn't turn out so well the last time we did this!" Vidarian called down.

// *Neither of us* died, // Altair snapped, with a whiff of affront like lightning in dry air. // *And last time it relied on the Breath of Siane,* // he added gruffly. Vidarian still carried the crystal whistle, though it no longer functioned, its energy spent. Altair had lifted a sailor from hundreds of feet away; his confidence in carrying Vidarian to the ground was not unfounded.

Vidarian closed his eyes and dove out into the air.

Sound engulfed him: the whistling of the wind past his face, the low susurrus of Altair's wingbeats, the thunder of the Alorean armada's cannon.

When he opened his eyes, he was falling—he and Altair angled sharply toward the ground. He'd instinctively spread out his arms like wings, ridiculous as that was—and beneath him, Altair's expansive wingspan guided them arrow-sharp toward their goal. Beyond the gryphon's feathers, vivid to the tiniest detail at this distance, the painted earth spread out far below. The waves of Parelle Bay still crashed against the shore, indifferent to the battle, and the fighting and dying of men.

Vidarian was trying to take in all that went on below them when another blast from the enemy magician blazed up below, causing Altair to shriek and pivot his wings. The gryphon's bubble of air energy carried Vidarian with it and out of range of the fiery blast, but Vidarian's stomach did three more flips as they spiraled away.

After an eternity the gryphon leveled out again, a "hand" of air energy brushing over Vidarian and steadying him. Two more blasts of pale fire shot past them, and it became obvious that they, and not the ships above, were the new target. A savage flush of victory pulsed through Vidarian, followed immediately by panic; they'd succeeded in protecting the *Luminous*, at least for now, but would they even make it to the ground?

Said ground, however, had been rushing upward during their maneuvers, and was now quite close. A sudden memory of crashing through trees sent panic shooting through Vidarian's veins, but already Altair was slowing, spreading his wingtips and bringing them down in a graceful arc.

The ground rushed up beneath them, and Altair's wings stretched farther, bringing them into a swift glide just above the top of the marsh grasses. As they slowed, his wings tilted deeper and his hind legs shot downward, tearing at the ground.

A brush of air and Vidarian slid to the right, then dropped down onto his feet.

He only had a breath to appreciate the landing, and then the grass to his right burst into angry flame.

The next burst was preceded by a whisper of energy, barely enough warning for both of them to throw themselves to the ground. Even then, Altair's wing coverts were smoking as he stood and shrieked a terrible full-throated battle challenge, his pupils flaring with fury.

Vidarian had to shove him to get his attention, and even then Altair nearly lashed out with a talon from pure pitched reflex. "Go! You're no good on the ground!"

Altair looked as if he might argue, but another blast of energy seared between them, forcing them to leap away from each other or be torched on the spot.

Vidarian hit the ground and rolled, gripping the hilt of his sword as he used momentum to get back to his feet. He turned, and through a shimmer of heat haze saw their attacker. Behind him, the thud of wings signaled Altair taking back to the sky—and the enemy magician's arms were lifting to bring him back down.

He drew his sword, slicing an arc in the air, and with the blow sent a pulse of fire energy arcing out toward her. Her arms immediately dropped, palms flat to deflect the attack—but now Altair was safely rising, and soon would be out of her immediate range.

She wore the multicolored robes of a Qui noble, tightly wrapped under-clothes covered by a short-sleeved garment that hung at her elbows and knees. Her hair, black and silken, lifted in wild cloud about her head, electrified by the bolts of energy she sent slicing up into the sky.

Vidarian spent half a precious moment looking for another attacker, but there was none—only this woman, originator of the strange blasts of not-quite-fire, was the source of the devastating assault.

She lifted a hand, fingers grasping like claws, and another punishing lash of energy swept out from her, this one finer and more controlled. Vidarian's fire wanted to leap out toward it, but he held it back, instead straining to shield himself with a wall of water.

The elements fought him, as they always did. They sniped at each other, wearing him down in the process—but at last the water soared upward, and the Qui magician's energy melted into it.

Most of the energy was absorbed, but a remaining arm of it sailed through the water, reaching. Vidarian only just raised his hand in time, letting fire leap from him out of desperation rather than finesse—and the energy, airlike, was eaten by the fire.

As he dropped the water shield so that he could see his opponent, he stared, unbelieving. There was only one explanation for such partially deflected energy, and suddenly the "strangeness" of the energy bolts made sense—

The Qui was wielding two elements simultaneously, braiding together the energies so tightly that they could only be pulled apart by a shield of an opposing element.

It should have been impossible. The Book of Sharli explicitly called it so.

While he struggled to comprehend, Altair was making his second attack, diving and shaping the weather around him into an ice storm in miniature that sliced down toward their enemy.

The Qui magician was undaunted by Altair's stoop, and retaliated with a broad arc of her fused air-and-fire energy. It melted through Altair's ice and threatened to singe his feathers again, forcing him to bank off and abandon the dive.

Vidarian ran at her, lifting his sword and calling water and fire around its blade, bending the elements to his will through sheer force.

His gambit worked; the Qui woman hadn't expected his physical assault, and now spun to retreat.

Vidarian pressed his advantage, striking out with a knifelike bolt of fire energy. The woman spun even as she ran, kicking into an acrobatic backflip that brought her hands up to easily repel his attack.

Then she spun again, this time in an arcing kick from her hip, one foot planted firmly on the ground—and with the momentum of her kick came a meteoric burst of searing, white-hot energy.

He realized too late that she hadn't been retreating—she'd been running *toward* an artifact on the ground, an amplifier—

His hastily raised shields of water and then fire were useless against the blast at this range. It rushed at him and time seemed to slow; in that bare instant he saw *into* the energy, saw how the air wove itself with fire so tightly that they seemed one. Then his feet left the ground as the leading edge of the blast lifted him—

Then, blackness.

Silence, for three moments.

Then, noise—slowly hearing returned, the muffled boom of cannon from far overhead; then sight, blurry at first, the blasting blue of the sky—

The Qui woman, leaning over him, one fist lifted and haloed with white-gold energy, a snarl on her face.

For one crazed moment he thought she was Ariadel. The dark, almond-shaped eyes, the silken hair—

"Who are you?" he choked. "Priestess—"

Her eyes widened with affront and she snarled again, the energy around her fist brightening like a small sun. "I am no priestess," she said, words heavily accented but distinct.

A horn sounded off to the north, and the woman's face went slack with disbelief. She looked back over her shoulder, then at Vidarian, rage incandescing her expression anew—

Then she turned and ran.

Vidarian tried to get up, and a wave of darkness turned his muscles to water. He lay there on the ground, listening to the call of the armada's guns, breathing in the incongruently fresh, bracing scent of the marsh grasses, and the tang of swamp water beneath them.

Seconds, or perhaps minutes later, Altair landed beside him, hitting the ground hard. The gryphon's face passed over his body, checking worriedly for serious injury, and his wings stretched out protectively.

// *They've retreated,* // Altair said, when he seemed satisfied that Vidarian's damage was not fatal. // *The battle is won. You did well.* // This last seemed to be for Vidarian's pride, which felt about as battered as he did.

The knowledge that they'd successfully distracted the enemy magess from destroying more of the ships was cold comfort. She had brought down the *Destiny*, and what crew had been aboard—all yet unavenged. And that energy—wounded, half-coherent, Vidarian could not put it from his mind.

His body, however, had other ideas. He managed to lift his hand to brush Altair's beak as the gryphon fussed over him again, then fell back into darkness.

PART TWO
TIGERS GATHER

CHAPTER TWELVE

THE LANCE

For the second time, Vidarian woke in his opulent palace room wracked by pain. A pounding ache through his entire body brought him out of a dreamless sleep, and when he opened his eyes, he wished he hadn't; white light shot to the back of his skull like a hammer blow. He cried out involuntarily, and Rai started barking from somewhere painfully close to his head.

Feet shuffled on the marble, then a muffled voice, young and high: "I could take him to the knights' training field, ma'am? They're all cleared out on patrol."

// Very good, Brannon. Can you manage him? //

Then a rustling of thick paper, a drifting scent of spice-dried beef, and Rai's barking paused, then resumed, twice again as loud. Every bark lit another starburst across the inside of Vidarian's eyelids.

When the barking finally receded into the distance, Vidarian's senses cooperated enough for sight to return, first in patches: the rumpled sheets, the glass balcony door open to the air—and Thalnarra, sitting on a mat, its pleated fibers protecting the marble from the knife-sharp tips of her talons.

// You're awake, then, // Thalnarra said, her mind's voice pitched low and carrying notes of sage and burning hickory.

"So it . . . seems," he managed, halting around a throat dry as paper.

// It was a near thing, // the gryphoness replied. // The armada's healers wanted to dunk you in ice water for your fever. //

A crawling sensation, as though thousands of spiders skittered under his skin, drove Vidarian to shiver and lever himself up in the bed. His stomach flipped beneath another wave of ache, but when it subsided, so did the "spiders." He blinked against the light, trying to get a better look at Thalnarra—and as he forced his eyes to focus, caught the way her left wing hung lower than it should, a huge patch of feathers burned away at the elbow joint. "You're hurt—" he began, startled at the wave of distress this thought brought.

Thalnarra clicked her beak. // *A triviality. You should be grateful for it. Without it I might not have known what had hit you.* //

* *You should thank her,* * Ruby murmured, and even her soft voice set Vidarian's head ringing again. * *The healers' treatment might have killed you if she hadn't intervened. And she bears more pain than she admits.* *

"Thank you, Thalnarra."

// *You're welcome. Now put it out of your mind,* // she admonished, shifting her wing to hide the bare skin. // *In another few days it'll hardly be noticeable.* //

"Another?" He rubbed his itching scalp, then started at the grimy state of his hair. "How long have I . . . ?"

// *Four and a half days,* // she said, a crispness in her tone brooking no surprise. // *You've quite missed the celebration. Though I daresay there may be another now you've rejoined us.* //

"Celebration?" Still repulsed by his hair, he ran a hand along his arm, then choked with startlement when a layer of skin came off in his hand.

// *Take care. It's good for that dead skin to come off, but gently. And yes,* // she added, her voice going from hearth-gentle to sharp, bitter smoke. // *The Aloreans celebrate their victory. None alive today recall the weight of an imperial war, or else they'd mourn.* //

"What did she do to me?" Vidarian said, resisting the urge to peel the rest of the dried skin away. It was like a sunburn, but the dead skin was oddly colored, gray like ash.

// *We were hoping you could answer that.* //

Vidarian's stomach sank with a chill that momentarily blotted out his pain. A numbness in his heart showed him just now much he'd come to rely on Thalnarra's knowledge. And now—how could he explain what his attacker had done? "She . . . hit me. With this strange energy—it was air and fire, together."

// *'She'? There must have been two.* //

Vidarian stared at Thalnarra, trying to read her expression. Had she been human, knowing her personality, it still might have been impossible. "No," he said slowly. "There was only one. She wielded the two elements together."

// *The way that you do?* // Her voice was dubious, metallic in his mind, and the tip of her tail flicked thoughtfully. // *It's unlikely, but perhaps the opening of the gate created multi-element rogues . . .* //

"No, not like I do. She wielded them *together*, like they were the same element."

// *That is not possible.* //

"I should have demanded more education from the beginning in 'things that aren't possible,'" Vidarian growled. Thalnarra only blinked at him, unreadable.

// *You are tired,* // she said finally. // *And the battle was intense. If they had some clever way of masking the presence of another—* //

"There was no other." And as he said it, some of the astonishment he had felt just before the battle returned to him. The implications set his head spinning. *I am no priestess,* the woman had said. If she could meld air and fire, could she also meld water and fire? Did the Qui bear the secrets to mastering his warring magics? Secrets even the gryphons knew nothing of? "They must have a technique—"

// *Technique has nothing to do with it. You are suggesting a refutation of the fundamental laws of the elements.* // Annoyance licked outward from Thalnarra's mind like flickering flamelets, and would have provoked a surge of heat from Vidarian in return, but he sternly reminded himself he owed her his life.

"I apologize," he began, and her neck-feathers sank back down. "I've had—"

The door banged open, and Brannon tumbled in, speaking before Vidarian or Thalnarra could chastise him. "Sir Vidarian? We need your help, sir."

// *What is it, child?* // Thalnarra said, and the concern that wafted from her voice like bread on the edge of burning told Vidarian that the boy had done much to earn her respect. She'd taken the heads off of younger gryphons for less than Brannon's intrusion.

The boy turned worriedly between Thalnarra and Vidarian. "It's Rai. It's just—you'd better come see, ma'am, sir. And hurry!"

Vidarian had fallen out of bed, not out of clumsiness, but by virtue of the nervelessness of his legs when he pushed himself out from under the heavy blankets. Blood surged through his limbs, tingling his nerves, and then he'd forced himself to his feet out of sheer will. Getting clothed was even harder—anything coarser than silk pulled at his burned skin enough to peel it to blood, and finally he threw a thick, soft woolen cloak around his shoulders and had done. Even the cool marble floor bit at his feet, and shoes were out of the question. Doubtless his appearance would scandalize any courtiers who saw him, but he couldn't bring himself to sufficiently sympathize.

He made his way as quickly as possible toward the Sky Knights' training field, even though "as quickly as possible" turned out to include several stops where his legs gave out again or his vision blackened. What *had* that woman done to him? Had he really almost died?

Thalnarra kept an agitated eye on him, surreptitiously positioning herself to his right, where her uninjured left side could quickly lean in to support him when he started to fall. By the time they closed on the corridors that led to the Sky Knights' keep, then beyond it to their training fields, Vidarian was drenched in sweat and fighting to breathe without gasping.

Sounds of a commotion reached his ears when they stopped thundering with blood: Rai's urgent warning barks, the raised shouts of knights, and the squeals of their angry steeds.

"They came back early because the eggs were hatching, sir," Brannon explained quickly. "If I'd known—" The boy's eyes were large with agony.

"Not your fault, lad," Vidarian said between breaths, trying to put as much feeling into the words as he could, and floundering.

// *Eggs?* // Thalnarra asked. Her voice was all thistle and hot pine sap, flickering sharp.

"Three of 'em, milady. They think one's a royal, I heard. And . . ." The boy trailed off, dropping his eyes.

// What is it, child? I have told you, a gryphon-ward speaks his mind. //

At this Brannon stiffened, marshaling himself and lifting his head. "Yes, ma'am. It's just—it's rumor, part of it." When Thalnarra's neck-feathers lifted with the beginning of irritation, he rushed on, "The last steeds hatched haven't survived the bonding, you see. They're—willful. And they die without getting riders."

// You're not telling us everything, boy. What do you think is causing this? //

"I think . . ." He flushed again, then pressed his lips together and threw caution to the wind. "I think they're becoming more like you, ma'am."

// What? //

"Well—they're smarter, you see. And one of the squires says her steed started talking to her. No one believes her. They think she's gone off in the head. It started when the changes happened."

Bridge for change-bringing . . . The gryphon Arikaree's words echoed back to Vidarian, chilling him. And there was no doubt that Rai spoke in his mind. He hadn't lost all of his sanity yet . . .

* *They used to,* * Ruby mused, and Vidarian bridled, thinking she was commenting on his lost wits. * *Sky steeds. Shapechangers . . .* *

The opening of the gate had amplified elemental magic all over the world, and more than that, it seemed—it had awakened shapeshifters, trapped these thousands of years in single shapes, their abilities forgotten by humankind. He thought with a pang of Ariadel's little ash-grey kitten, which had abruptly— in his presence, while he "carried" a connection to the Starhunter—manifested the ability to change into a tiny golden spider. How could the presence of the chaos goddess in the world change so much?

* *'Chaos' is an odd way of putting it.* *

He started to argue, but there were more pressing issues than a philosophical discussion with one of Ruby's strange new fragmented memories. "So what you're saying is, three of the last sky steed eggs are hatching, the knights have come to bond new riders to the hatchlings, they'll probably kill them, and Rai is in the middle of it. Wonderful."

As if speaking his name caught his attention, Rai's barks increased in urgency, and they hurried through the arches to the training field.

The scene that they found paralyzed Vidarian where he stood. Four full knights and their steeds stared across the field, stamping for battle. Opposite them, Rai bristled, his head low and spines lifted along his entire body, barking and snarling warnings. Behind him were three cracked eggs and three hatchlings. One had bonded to a child that crouched protectively with it, while a second, indeed a royal, struggled from its eggshell and squalled, lifting its proud black-green head. And the third was dead.

For now, the knights were holding back their steeds, hauling on lead-lines and keeping them from attacking Rai—surely for fear of their own safety, or the hatchlings', rather than any charity for the wolf pup. The steeds all fought their knights, their eyes rolling with near madness.

The knights had a boy in front of them that they were pushing toward Rai—a squire who, though he looked on the little royal with avarice, wanted nothing to do with the snarling creature between them.

"Rai!" Vidarian shouted, or meant to shout, if his throat would have cooperated. He struggled on, mustering all the authority he could. "Leave them! Come over here!"

Rai whined, his spines drooping for a moment, and his tail also, but when one of the knights took a step toward him he bristled again, lip curling up to expose what had become a set of fearsome white fangs.

// Those creatures are exhausted, and distressed, // Thalnarra said, her red eyes pinning as she sized up the hatchlings. *// And—the large one is fighting. She doesn't want this boy they're giving her. //*

She dies, brother, Rai said, shocking Vidarian three times: once for his intelligence and clarity, again for the emotion that laced his words—they burned in Vidarian's mind with pain and sadness—and finally, that he called Vidarian "brother." Then he released another surprise, filling Vidarian's mind with a chaotic series of memories heavy with sensation—the knights pushing the squires toward the hatchlings, trying to force a bond, as even their own steeds resisted them. After the smallest had died, Rai rushed in, warning them all off.

"Enough of this rot," one of the knights sneered and loosed his steed, slapping it on the hip. "Kill that mongrel."

The steed reared, and now Vidarian could see from its flattened ears and wide eyes that it was upset, not enraged—but so on edge that it obeyed this command from its rider, and leapt at Rai.

Vidarian cried out hoarsely, first in objection, then in surprise. As the steed leapt, it changed shape—hooved feet curled under, shortening into clawed paws, its tail stretched out and collapsed into a coiling thing, and its head pulled inward, growing larger eyes, broader ears, and teeth. As it landed, snarling, it was a striped cat, a huge one, with wings more sleek and compact than it had in its native horse shape. It lashed out at Rai with a clawed paw.

Rai, far from abandoning his charges, leapt back at the steed—and changed. Massive wings spread from his shoulders, feathered and striped green like his spines; he grew and his paws thickened, his tail lengthened, until he, too, was a winged cat, pacing in an arc around his foe.

The knights all shouted again, in mingled astonishment and fury, while Vidarian tried to make sense of what he'd just seen. The two cats were growling at each other and circling, here and there lashing out with a claw, but neither striking true.

When he regained control of his senses, Vidarian staggered out into the field, stumbling between the two great, hissing creatures. He reached out with his water sense, but immediately recoiled, falling to his knees. All his elemental sensitivity, too, was "burned," and far worse than his body. It seemed an eternity before the wave of misery passed, and he pushed himself back to his feet again, lifting his hands between Rai and the steed.

She dies! Rai cried again, and roared as he did so, a terrifying sound that cut straight to the ancestral prey creature in all of them. Thalnarra, not quite so affected, rushed over to the hatchlings and spread her wings over them.

"Who can save her?" Vidarian asked Rai, facing him down, trying to block him from seeing the still-snarling steed behind him.

He felt the pulse of Rai's surprise, and then, immediately, a picture: the older steward's girl. Brannon's sister.

"Bran!" Vidarian shouted, "Fetch your sister! Quickly!" He had no idea how she might heal the royal hatchling, but at the very least it would calm Rai down. Brannon yelled something and dashed off toward the palace.

"You've no right to do this!" One of the knights cried, and the others called agreement.

"Hardly," Vidarian agreed, fatigue beginning to catch up with him in earnest and attempt to force him to the ground. He grit his teeth. "But seeing as you lot were making such a mess of it . . ."

They started shouting again, enraged, but an arcing line of fire rose up from the ground in front of them, flames licking hungrily toward the necks of the steeds. Vidarian turned, and Thalnarra dipped her beak in acknowledgment. She was still crouched over the little royal, and radiated a steady fury.

Running footsteps sounded, and the girl who had first greeted them in the city arrived two steps ahead of her brother, looking surprised and a little afraid. She skidded to a stop when she saw the battling steeds, the line of fire, the gryphon—and Brannon pushed her, murmuring something urgent. The girl colored, and she turned to leave, but Brannon grabbed her hand and hauled her bodily toward Thalnarra and the little royal.

Vidarian had just long enough to worry that the girl wouldn't know what to do—how could she?—but then, as soon as she caught sight of the hatchling, she broke away from Brannon and rushed toward it, crouching, reaching out to comfort it, heedless of Thalnarra's presence. And for its part the little royal stumbled toward her, lowing.

The royal's eyes flashed blue, bright enough for Vidarian to see even at this distance—and he was reminded suddenly of the way the setting sun had caught the kitten's eyes when Ariadel had first picked it up, so long ago at the dockside in Val Harlon. Or rather, he *thought* it had been the sun . . .

Now that it was done, Thalnarra slowly lowered the fire-line, and the cat-steed returned to its original shape and paced back over to its rider, its head low. The rider glowered at Vidarian, ignoring his steed. "You've started a war, *Captain*. Not in a hundred years—"

// *Only that long?* // Thalnarra interrupted, laying down on the packed dirt of the field, her body still curled protectively around the royal hatchling and her new rider. A pulse of heat emanated from her, almost lazy, and stirred the smoke that still crept upward from where she'd scorched the ground.

The man purpled, muttered several things under his breath, and stomped off, leaving the other knights to calm their steeds and follow him. The steeds themselves had besieged expressions, if such could be said for horses; their ears lay flat and they held their heads low, wings drooping. All of them stared at the hatchlings, clearly drawn to them, but turned back toward their riders and left one by one.

Rai, still cat-shaped, pushed his head under Vidarian's hand, looking up in apology. Vidarian shook his head, as he fought against another wave of exhaustion that threatened to steal consciousness again. "You saved that creature's life." With what little remained of his thinking mind, beneath the terrible tiredness, he turned over what Rai's new growth and intelligence meant. Had the other thornwolves been so? He thought back to their attack, and doubted it.

Brannon was crouching beside the hatched royal with his sister, whose face was tear-streaked, but not with sadness. They had lost the one hatchling, but this one survived—and the girl, whose name Vidarian still did not know, would not be returning to the steward's quarters.

"What now?" he asked Thalnarra dully.

// *I will watch over these,* // she said, extending her wing over Brannon, his sister, and the hatchling. // *Now, you go back to bed.* //

CHAPTER THIRTEEN
MUSIC

Huge golden eyes met Vidarian's when he woke again in his palace chamber. He flinched, and they changed: shrinking and darkening, pupils widening. They became Rai's eyes, and the wide, striped cat face became the thornwolf—and barked.

The sound rattled Vidarian's skull, and as he sat up, the burning complaint of his arms and legs told him he'd again been asleep for more than a day.

Rai barked again, then yipped with surprise as he slid backwards, his claws ripping at the carpet. Brannon's head popped up when Rai was safely away from the bed; the boy had dragged the wolf away by his tail.

"Sorry, milord . . . Captain," Brannon corrected his address before Vidarian could start to object. Rai lunged forward again, but the boy gamely threw his own weight against him.

"How long have I slept this time?" Vidarian asked, rubbing eyes that stung with the stiffness of disuse. The room seemed not to have changed, but Thalnarra was not there, and for a moment her absence stung like a mother's disregard.

"Three days, m . . . sir." The boy grunted as Rai changed back into the winged tiger, but not with surprise. At this size Rai easily lifted the boy up and made his way back toward the bed, but Brannon swung his legs down and dug into the carpet with his heels. When this proved ineffective, he dug into his pocket, and Rai froze at the sound of crinkling waxed paper that emerged. He stopped, and Brannon gave him a bit of dried fish from the bag. Rai tore it up delicately and with full attention.

Good, the wolf-turned-tiger offered, "sharing" with Vidarian the taste of the pungent fish. He tried not to gag.

"Would you know where Thalnarra is, by any chance?"

"In the fields out back," Brannon said, pushing Rai's wide nose away from his pocket now. "She'll be wanting to know you're awake, sir. An' see you, even, if you're up to it."

As if his three days of sleep had just released all of their pent-up energy into him at once, Vidarian pushed himself out of bed, anxious to discover what he had missed. His legs gave way as soon as his weight was upon them, and he swayed, thumping into the bedpost. Rai whined, and Brannon visibly swallowed a startled yelp.

Instead the boy pointed to the bed. "You should at least eat first, sir? They've sent a tray."

After everything, it still hurt his pride to be grateful for the excuse to sit back down. Feeling was crawling back into his limbs, and not quietly; it was all he could do to remain still as his skin prickled over nerves that had turned to stinging nettles. Rai, wolf-shaped now, rested his chin on Vidarian's knee and sighed.

Brannon brought the promised tray from its place by the door and set about fussing with the linen and silver. Vidarian waved him off, then tossed him the currant-studded bread roll, ignoring Rai's accusatory stare. The boy bit into the roll and pulled more fish from his pocket to soothe the wolf's hurt feelings.

The porridge today was a lumpen one, heavy with fruit and some kind of congealed grain that tasted faintly unpleasant but must have been medicinal for the way that it rushed strength into his wasted muscles. By the end of it he was beginning to feel real alertness wake in his mind. With alertness came awareness of a certain week-long-bed-rest stench, and so he spared the time to wash thoroughly in the marble water chamber.

The hot water seemed to take off at least two layers of his skin, and so when Brannon and Rai led the way to the north parkland, the air stung his face.

It was strange to think that only ten days ago these fields beyond the north palace wall had been filled with skyships. Now only a handful remained, most actively undergoing repair. All that was left to mark the absence of the rest— which Allingworth had moved to defensive positions or currently led against the Qui—was an expanse of trampled grass and the occasional dropped tool or gangplank.

The yawning field was an uncomfortable reminder that the Imperial City itself had few defenses when it came to skyships; they were being deployed as soon as they could be discovered and their crews trained.

Rai dashed ahead as soon as their feet had touched the grass, and now bounded through the underbrush that separated one field from another.

"He seems to have even more energy than he did before." Vidarian shaded his eyes to look ruefully after the young wolf.

* The first change invigorates them, * Ruby said, and Vidarian started at the sound of her voice, which was dreamlike and distant. * He's likely relieved—like a bird molting, or a snake shedding its skin. *

"How do you know that?"

* It's in here. *

"In where?"

But Ruby didn't answer. Brannon lifted his fingertips to his teeth and whistled long and loud. Rai dashed back toward them, running as fast and low to the ground as his long legs would take him.

They crossed the brush to the second field, and Altair and Thalnarra both reclined in the grasses, their wings half-spread under the midmorning sun. With them were three Sky Knight apprentices and their young steeds: the boy who had bonded to the small colt three days ago, Brannon's sister, and a gangly young girl Vidarian didn't recognize.

As they drew closer, Altair's voice reached them:

// And if your opponent was an archer? //

"Sky Knights are archers, too," the boy said.

// So you would fire on them? // The gryphon's blue eyes pinned as he tilted his head at the boy.

"Cross-dive," Brannon's sister—Linnea, Rai pushed the name on him—said, almost too quietly to hear.

Altair's tufted ear twitched in her direction. He dipped his beak, gesturing for her to continue.

"The combat training manual recommends a cross-dive against a mounted archer," she said. Her hands were clenched around the mane of the royal foal— who had filled out nicely, and now glittered violet and green at her socks and sloping head.

// *Correct,* // Altair said. Then his aquiline head tilted toward Vidarian. // *Welcome, brother. We are assisting these young ones with their training.* //

When she caught sight of him, Linnea flushed anew, but to his surprise, she gently patted her steed on the head and then stood to advance on Vidarian.

He froze, unsure what to make of her approach. At first, she wouldn't meet his eyes, but finally she lifted her head and fixed him with a determined stare. He still wasn't sure what to expect, and never would have guessed that she would next pull a hanging pendant from her waist pocket and hand it to him.

Vidarian accepted the pendant gingerly, letting it lay across his palm. It was a simple stone oval framed in darkened steel. When he turned it, the stone gleamed with purple-black iridescence. He realized what it was, and inhaled. "Is this . . . ?"

"It's from Trakari's eggshell," Linnea agreed, dropping her eyes with embarrassment only for a moment. "It's a gift. If it weren't for you, she would have died."

"You should thank Rai, really," Vidarian said, surprised at his own diffidence. "Without him, we'd never have known that the eggs were even hatching."

Linnea turned to face Rai, who noticed her attention and immediately bounded over to leap into her arms. She staggered under his weight and laughed with delight. Along with his shapechanging ability, Rai was learning how to more tightly control and maneuver the shocking spines, an endless relief.

// *Vidarian can teach you much about wind patterns and navigation,* // Thalnarra said.

"I'd be pleased to," he said, addressing both of them. "But your wing-leader wouldn't want you here, I'd wager." The girl flushed, confirming his suspicion, but her jaw firmed.

"There's nothing we can learn from the other knights," Linnea said, and beneath the steel of her defiance was a wounded heart that cut at Vidarian's own. "They won't say I'm a real rider, and anyway they spend their days drunk into stupidity."

"What happened to them?" Vidarian asked. The knights were clearly in a shambles, but no one had yet explained why.

"Their steeds are rebelling," the other boy said, pushing himself to his feet. "Half of 'em can't even get in the saddle. They're trying to hide it, though."

"The old ways aren't working, not since the steeds started shapechanging," Linnea agreed.

"And getting smarter." The boy reached down to scratch between the ears of his foal.

"Well," Vidarian said, extending his hand for Linnea's royal to sniff, "we can certainly do something about that. I seem to have surrounded myself with excessively intelligent creatures."

Altair snorted, a strange sound from his hooked beak, and called them all back to his combat puzzles.

// You are performing courier duty, flying at three bars' height . . . //

They practiced and played and lay in the sun until afternoon faded into evening and the sun was beginning to fall behind the trees. The oldest apprentice had a fully-grown sky steed; Rai and the steed wrestled in their winged cat forms, winning whoops and whistles of delight even from the two gryphons.

Just as Vidarian was going to present the apprentices with a navigation puzzle his father had begun his own lessons with as a boy, a portly imperial messenger came trotting into the field, panting with fatigue.

"Captain Rulorat," the man said between breaths, relieved and just a touch annoyed. For a moment Vidarian worried that word had gotten back to the Sky Knights that he and the gryphons were instructing their apprentices, but then the man pulled a cream envelope from his sleeve. "The emperor was pleased to hear of your recovery, and invites you to dine this evening—and witness a musical performance by the miraculous metal creature called Iridan."

"Iridan?" Vidarian said, forgetting for a moment his anxiety. "Music?"

His disbelief cracked the messenger's marble veneer. "Damndest thing, is't not, milord? I'm told the music is the most amazing you'll ever hear. Makes grown men cry, and babes sleep as though enchanted."

// We should send these younglings back to their stable. Doubtless they'll be doing chores into the night as it is. //

The messenger jumped when Thalnarra spoke, but made an admirably quick recovery, turning to give her and Altair a little bow. "I'm given to understand you both were of critical assistance at the Lehrian border engagement. We're all deeply grateful."

// You speak like a soldier, sirrah. //

He drew himself up. "I was, milady. And may be so again, with what's been brewing."

"With Qui? I should think the imperial forces . . ." Vidarian trailed off at the man's solemn expression.

"Not just Qui, Captain." His voice lowered. "There's rumors of rebellion in the western provinces. Attacks—sabotage."

"I'd heard none of this," Vidarian said, turning to Thalnarra and Altair, who also twitched their beaks in agreement.

"It's rumor," the messenger allowed, "but the kind as usually turns out truer than not, ye ken?"

Vidarian nodded, and caught the worried looks of the three apprentices. "The emperor surely is acting on them even as we speak."

They murmured loyal agreement, and the cloud over their expressions lifted slightly. More, at the moment, would be difficult to ask.

ᔕᔕᔕ

As with his last imperial supper, they had left him just enough time to rush back to his chambers, scrub the field dirt and animal musk from himself, and fall into clothing that he hoped would pass muster for an imperial event.

When he'd returned from the skyship battle, there had been a hand-tailored imperial captain's uniform waiting in his wardrobe, which he only now discovered. Unsure if it had been Renard's doing, Allingworth's, or both, he donned it, and tucked Linnea's pendant behind its white silk dress scarf.

The performance and dinner were to be held in the Arboretum, which both unsettled Vidarian and piqued his curiosity. The heavy doors were held open this time by ornate brass pillars, and hanging blue lights led guests along the garden paths.

It may as well have been a completely different place for how they had transformed it. Far from being overgrown, every hedge and tree and hanging vine had been meticulously trimmed. Flowers bloomed and filled the room with their rich and wild fragrances. The sun-sphere high above had been dimmed to a pale blue light, casting the twisting paths and hanging branches in false moonlight. It was deeply beautiful, but Vidarian could not help the dropping sensation in his stomach.

There were perhaps a dozen guests, all fantastically garbed. The ladies in particular bore jewelry that changed color with their movements. Vidarian had never heard of or seen such gems before; they must have awakened with the gate. The emperor was surrounded by such ladies, and after a moment's hesitation Vidarian abandoned any hope of speaking with him.

He turned, and met intricately worked brass and lavender gemstone eyes. Beside the metal figure stood Justinian, resplendent in heavily embroidered robes, recognizable by his porcelain mask.

"*It's a pleasure to meet you, Captain Rulorat,*" Iridan said, quite as if they had never met before. A chill crept down Vidarian's spine as he tried to ascertain politic from sincerity. But Iridan's metal face revealed nothing.

Justinian—at least, Vidarian was certain that it *must* be Justinian— gestured, a rolling movement with his hands. And he kept gesturing until Iridan spoke again.

"*Please pardon my friend. A terrible accident rendered him unable to speak. He wishes me to tell you that it is his pleasure to meet you as well, and that he has heard much about you from the emperor.*"

Vidarian stared, poleaxed. Clearly this was politicking—Justinian must have remembered their meeting. Or didn't he? No—surely this was some elaborate ploy. "I'm—pleased to meet you both as well."

"*I do hope that you'll enjoy the performance.*"

"I'm sure that I will."

A small gong sounded, and the guests drifted toward the chairs that had been assembled in a particularly brightly lit clearing. Iridan bowed, and turned that way himself, his body rotating silently on perfectly worked hinges.

Vidarian made his way to an empty seat in the second row, and their brass-bodied performer took his place beside a fountain of flowers set in front of the chairs.

"*I was created to assist in diplomacy,*" Iridan began, his torso swiveling at his waist as he turned to address the guests. Despite his distance from the seated guests, his voice carried with preternatural ease, as though he were right in front of Vidarian. "*As you have experienced, my voice is simultaneously telepathic and aural. It is beyond language, and indeed beyond words' intent. No creature may successfully practice deceit in my presence without my knowledge. Yet my creator's path in generating this effect passed through music, the universal language of beauty and truth. Music, perhaps, was always intended to be my greater purpose, for a time without deceit.*"

And with this, he began.

At first there was no sound, and then—the barest thread of vibration. The audience leaned forward, grasping for it; Vidarian found himself moving with them before realizing what he was doing. A rhythm emerged: it was a subtle clicking, the brush of a leaf against a window, and yet it pulsed, slowly but steadily increasing in tempo.

Then, the most extraordinary sound. Iridan's jaw opened only slightly, and what issued forth was something like a violin, something like a horn, but exactly like neither. It seemed to cut straight to the soul, and then it began to dance, capering through melodies and rhythms that called to mind spring winds, chirping birds, spreading hills.

The glowing gems at Iridan's arms and shoulders pulsed more brightly then, and more sounds emerged: the soft, buttery pluck of a harp, the low solemn burr of a stone flute.

Music transported them, pulled them away from the Arboretum with its soft sun-sphere and marble fonts, sang of the stars on a summer evening, of distant worlds. There was truth here, the truth Vidarian had felt to his bones when the Starhunter showed him the world beyond the gate. He was there again, caught up in its majesty, its splendor, its terror. A melancholy crept through—lines of melody rose and fell as if looking for a companion, leaving space for a song that never materialized—but the sense was fleeting, replaced by surety, a plucking overture.

And Iridan brought them back again. Gradually the other instrument sounds faded, made their gracious exits, and the horn-violin remained, accompanied only by low and steady notes from the stone flute. They returned to the Arboretum, heard the little night birds chirp softly from their nests, saw the blue lights against the leaves once more.

* Four were made, * Ruby said, and a dozen faces turned toward Vidarian as sharply as if he'd thrown water at them.

Ruby? he thought wildly. What are you doing? But she did not hear him.

* Four were made, * she said again, a strange and distant cadence in her words, as if someone else spoke with her voice. The sun ruby in Vidarian's pocket grew hot, glowed red. * Iridan, the youngest, brass-voiced, singer of truth. Modrian, brother, silver-voiced, chanter of law. Arian, sister, golden-voiced, keeper of verse. And the fourth— *

Justinian turned, his hands at his face—and the mask slipped away, falling. Gasps from the audience covered the sound of the mask striking the sand path and breaking in two.

Iridan shook his head, a strange and human movement from his gem and metal body. He seemed to awaken from a trance. As he looked out over the audience, he took a step backward, startled to see them all watching him.

The emperor stood, lifting his hand to Iridan in concern, but to no acknowledgment.

Iridan turned, the stiffness in his movements betraying a return of memory, of betrayal. "Justinian, my friend? You know of the existence of my brother and sister?" The fourth he did not mention, as if he hadn't heard it.

Justinian stared, his jaw slack. He looked out at the audience, wild with shock—and suddenly froze, his eyes widening even further.

In the front row, Oneira's face, perfectly painted and framed by her precisely sculptured hair, lost all of its poise. She stared at Justinian, the shock and betrayal written for an instant in her eyes, telling Vidarian that Justinian had never revealed himself to her. Shock melted into grief, then lit into rage, only for a fraction of a moment. Then she lifted her skirts in white-knuckled hands and strode from the clearing without a word.

The guests all stood in a flurry, and the Arboretum erupted into shocked conversation. The emperor's face was already an unreadable mask, which said as clearly as Oneira's that he, too, had not known that Justinian lived. Vidarian stood and carefully made his way to the exit by means of a winding path that looped far from the main clearing.

"What happened?" he said softly, once he was sure he was out of hearing range of the guests.

* The music . . . called something out of . . . this shell. I need to get out of here, Darian, * Ruby said softly. * This . . . thing, * she shoved an image of the sun ruby at him, and the feelings that clung to it were revulsion, horror, fear that gripped his stomach. * It makes me think things that I don't know . . . and now . . . that wasn't me, saying those things. It wasn't me. *

"It's my fault, not yours," he said, and the truth of the words cut at his throat. "We'll get you back to your ship. I promise."

CHAPTER FOURTEEN

TEN THOUSAND FATHOMS

"I wish that I could give you a ship, Vidarian. Truly I do."

They were not in the throne room, for which Vidarian was quite grateful. Lirien—Vidarian worked, still without total success, to think of the man and not "the emperor"—looked haggard, here where his subjects and courtiers could not see him, bare of the mineral treatments and tricks of the light that Renard used to keep him appearing at all times vigorous, fresh, indomitable.

Calphille sat to his left, poised like a butterfly on her chair. Renard's hand was there with her, also; the gown she wore, black and sunshine yellow, would have been unthinkable on any other maiden Vidarian had seen at court. She wore it effortlessly, and as she looked with naked worry on Lirien, she was surely unaware of the classical stylishness of her golden hairclips, the enviable cut of her gown. Vidarian would hardly have known any of these things, but he'd heard the whispers from the other noblewomen, which Calphille herself could not be immune to.

Oneira, immaculate as always, would have been aware of Calphille's aesthetic perfection, had she not been drawn deep into herself, listless as Vidarian had never seen her. She sat to the right of the emperor, but the distance of her gaze belied faraway thoughts.

Vidarian felt his shoulders sinking as he took in Lirien's sincere regret, and consciously firmed his jaw. "I came here in a skyship," he said carefully, watching the emperor for any sign of outrage. "The *Destiny*. It was lost in the errand for which I was summoned."

Lirien sighed: tired and remorseful, to Vidarian's relief. "You are right. But every single one of my skyships is committed to the war effort, and cannot be diverted." He stood and strode away from his chair, pacing.

Vidarian watched him, straining for any sign of judgment or doubt. He had not told the emperor the nature of his errand, only that urgent business called him away from the city, a matter of personal honor.

Lirien stopped in his tracks and turned. "Oneira—the Company has provided you a skyship, has it not?"

Oneira stirred, blinking as if waking from a dream. "Pardon, your majesty?"

"The *Wind Maiden*. She is at your disposal, yes?"

Now Oneira's dark eyes sharpened. She let a moment pass, visibly calculating how she might resist the emperor's will without losing his esteem, then said, "Apologies, majesty, but the *Wind Maiden* is currently commissioned for my research expedition to Rikan."

The look that Lirien gave Oneira then bordered on impatience, and Vidarian wondered if he was about to see the imperial will made manifest, but Oneira scented the direction of the wind.

"There is a way I could continue my studies," she said. "No other single artifact is a complete subject, but the automaton Iridan would be more than so."

Now it was the emperor's turn to be taken aback. "You're suggesting that he journey with you?" Lirien asked, voicing Vidarian's thoughts. The notion of traveling with—as Oneira called him, an automaton—had not entered his mind.

"Yes, your majesty. I have requested to study him before, but the proper opportunity has not arisen." Unspoken was the notion that she had not been permitted, and this was her price.

Lirien remained unsure. "Iridan is tremendously valuable. To transport him over an ocean—"

"With respect, majesty," Vidarian said as gently as he could manage, "I am a water elementalist. Iridan would be under no threat of loss to the sea."

Oneira's head turned toward him, a mixture of speculation and gratitude on her face that quickly turned to ice, then thawed again as she turned back toward the emperor.

"An acceptable arrangement," Lirien said at last. "Vidarian, I will hold you responsible for Iridan's welfare."

"Of course, your majesty." He was nowhere near as certain as he sounded, but to an imperial command there was only one answer.

"If you will excuse me, I have an audience with the Rikani ambassador."

Vidarian and Oneira rose, bowing first to the emperor, and then exchanging nods with Calphille. The dryad's eyes were full of worry again, and Vidarian was surprised to find it directed at him. He smiled, hoping to reassure her, wishing that there had been more time to see to *her* welfare. The currents of the palace pulled as determinedly as any he had encountered at sea.

They left the small audience chamber, passing into the hall. There was only one way back to the main arteries of the palace, and so Vidarian and Oneira were forced to walk together, or risk obvious impropriety.

"What is this errand of yours, anyway?" Oneira muttered.

Vidarian told her.

Oneira stopped, and Vidarian stopped with her, certain she was about to refuse the use of her ship. But she only stared at him, calculating, then nodded once, and set off down the hall again.

∿∿∿

The *Wind Maiden* had a crew of able-bodied men and women all precision-trained by the Alorean Import Company, but for the journey they would need supplies, and preparing the ship took the better part of two days. A skyship was not limited by the tide, but every item brought aboard must be justified, for it directly impacted the ship's maneuverability.

There was also the matter of charting a course. Ruby was clear on the location of her body—* There is only one place my crew would have taken me. * But safe airspace must be found between the imperial city and that West Sea location, and a means of recovering her body once they arrived.

This latter Vidarian tried not to think on overmuch. He would be the one to pull her corpse from the waves—a thought that had shadowed his dreams since first she had reawakened.

Thalnarra and Altair joined them as a matter of course, much to the complaint of their erstwhile Sky Knight apprentices. The gryphons would be a welcome guardian force—but the surprise, as they charted course and negotiated delicately over the supply of the ship, was Isri.

The seridi appeared one morning in the planning room—a side chamber graciously donated by Oneira—with a young olive-skinned girl with bright green eyes. Save for her eye color, she reminded Vidarian painfully of Lifan, his ship's windreader. He told himself Lifan and the rest of his crew would be safe with Marielle, but in spite of everything he couldn't help but be weighed down by a sense of having failed them all.

The girl, Isri said, was a Finder. She was possessed of a unique telepathic sense specifically tied to objects. If she touched an object belonging to a person, she could find that person, living or dead.

Her name was Alora, and she had nearly driven herself mad before Isri had found her and brought her to the mindcrafters in the Imperial City for training.

"You will know the general location of Ruby's body," Isri said, the sleekness of her feathers conveying a calmness Vidarian envied, "but you'll need someone with Alora's talents to find its exact location, and convey it to you mind-to-mind that you might bring it to the surface."

"I'm grateful, as always, for your advice and assistance," Vidarian said, and meant it, "but will her parents allow her on such a potentially dangerous expedition?"

"She is an orphan," Isri said, placing a feathered hand on the girl's shoulder. "And I have agreed to mentor her, if we might accompany you." Now the tiny feathers around her beak lifted in a seridi smile. "In truth, it will be good for her to get away from the city and its multitude of sensations. It's little wonder so many go mad here."

Vidarian thought painfully of Malloray, and how he must have suffered without knowing why, working all of those years for Rulorats. But the sea had helped him, too. Vidarian knelt and held his hand out to Alora. "I'm pleased and honored to have your service, then," he said.

The girl smiled shyly and shook his hand, then looked to Isri for approval.

The seridi nodded, and Alora giggled—a high, delighted sound. Then she blushed and ran from the room.

"She's shy yet," Isri said, looking after her. "But incredibly talented."

"I have misgivings on bringing so young a child on so dark an expedition," Vidarian said.

Isri's golden eyes turned toward him, staring, as they often seemed to, straight to his heart. "Times are dark," she said only. "We must all learn, and grow, faster than we might like."

The ship was a fine one, a build and trim unfamiliar to Vidarian but impressive. Her measurements made no sense to him, and he suspected she might be Malinari, which raised more questions than it answered. But she was solidly built, and outfitted with more navigational and luxury mechanisms than even the *Luminous* had borne.

The greatest of its technologies remained hidden, however. For the first three days of sailing Iridan spent all of his time below decks, shuttered in his room. At first he would admit no one, to Oneira's outrage, but on the second day he permitted her entry, and they remained closeted for most of the day and night.

Oneira's crew was circumspect—assiduously so. None would engage beyond the most basic conversation, and so the trip was a strange one to Vidarian, taken on a foreign ship among sailors who rarely spoke. The gryphons flew alongside the ship, preferring to exercise their wings rather than ride, and Isri spent most of her time with her young apprentice.

Even Ruby was subdued, though Vidarian could hardly blame her. She provided a heading to the steersman, an uncharted expanse of ocean off the coast of Ignirole, and then she withdrew within—wherever she was.

On the third day, when Vidarian was beginning to give names to the cloud formations that passed below them, Ruby started speaking without prompting.

* *'Dead' is still the wrong word. When I awoke, I didn't know where I was. It took me days to realize I no longer had a human body, and I started to discover things about the place I was in. About here. It was as though doors opened, and beyond them was space, knowledge.* *

Silence stretched between them, punctuated by the whistle of wind against the rigging, and Vidarian was afraid to answer, lest he break the spell that had caused her to so suddenly describe what she'd been going through all this time.

* *There are things in here . . . things. I find them and I know things that I couldn't have known before. Sometimes they jump right out of me, skip 'Ruby' and go straight out into the world. And they're getting bolder. I'm not sure what I'm becoming.* *

"Regardless of where it came from, that knowledge has been a great help," he ventured.

She didn't seem to hear him. * *I'm not dead, Vidarian.* *

"I—" he started, unsure where he would finish, but she was gone again, back behind one of the many doors in the "prism key," as she referred to the sun ruby.

And as if Ruby's sudden speech had broken free the ice that stiffened the air of the *Wind Maiden*, Oneira emerged from the hold, blinking her eyes against the white light of the cloudscape, and joined him at the bow.

"He's a remarkable artifact," she said after perhaps two leagues' worth of travel.

To ask if she meant Iridan would be to invite scorn, and so Vidarian said, "Your interest in him seemed rather abrupt."

She cast him a look that was perhaps five degrees warmer than total dismissal. "Justinian came all the way to Val Imris, risked exposure to awaken and study the automaton. He desires to be near it, and so I will take it far from him."

It would have been a relief if there had been simple coldness in her voice. Instead there was something much sharper, much subtler, an emptiness that stilled Vidarian's heart for a breath. He tucked away her words and reached for diplomacy. "I've been remiss. I never thanked you for the use of your ship."

"You needn't," she said. "Your hand is reasonably well played, and I have been curious about your trapped friend for some time." She indicated the stone in his pocket with a glance. He must not have masked his shock adequately, for she smiled, hollow as bird bones. "Don't toy with me, Captain. The Company was keeping secrets before your grandfather was born. Remember that."

∽∽∽

On the fifth morning, as Vidarian was drinking a steaming cup of *kava* at the bow, Altair landed on the deck behind him.

Vidarian started to offer him a sip from the cup, in jest—gryphons were violently allergic to both *kava* and alcohol—but stopped when he caught sight of the gryphon's roused neck-feathers.

// *There's a disruption here,* // he said, and the peppermint brightness in his mind-voice was curious, worried. // *There is a signature on the water—it came from a gryphon, a powerful air wielder to impose a geis this long-lasting.* //

* *His name was Urri,* * Ruby said softly. * *He left a mark on the water where my mother was slain. I thought it was respect, but years later realized it was a warning-mark.* *

Ruby's words called up a cloudy memory of the largest tattoo on her body—a white gryphon, and one of the only stories she had never told Vidarian. They must have been related.

* *This is the only place my crew would have buried—my body.* *

"Then we should begin this now, and be done with it." The voice was Isri's, and from behind them. She stood with her hand on Alora's shoulder, her wings partly spread.

Vidarian whistled, then signaled the boatswain to direct the *Wind Maiden* down to the surface of the water. They would approach as closely as they could, and then he would lift Ruby's body from the water.

He had managed to put off specifically envisioning the task Ruby had demanded until this moment. Now, as they descended through the clouds, passing interminably toward the water, he could imagine little else.

Vidarian had seen rotting bodies before, but none pulled up from the seafloor. She would be wrapped in linen, tight. The thought of Ruby's body, as he had last seen it, now emerging from the waters, desiccated, eaten by sea creatures, made the gorge rise in his throat. Grimly he fought it back down, worked his thoughts through what they must do.

The ship leveled out, and below them stretched the glass surface of the sea. A shadow flickered overhead; Thalnarra, keeping a watch from high above. She gave a short, piercing cry, then angled into her circling patrol pattern.

Isri's touch on Vidarian's forearm made him jump. He turned toward her, and had to look away from her golden gaze, too full of sympathy. She realized his discomfort and dimmed her presence, withdrawing. He hadn't known she could do that. "You have the object that she carried?"

"I only have—her," he said, drawing the ruby from its pouch at his side. He passed it wordlessly to Isri.

The seridi raised the ruby to the light, staring through it. The sense of her presence increased, and he knew she was focusing herself through the gem, testing its safety. "It will be a challenge," she said, turning to Alora and offering the stone. "But she is up to it."

Alora, seeming even smaller than Vidarian remembered her, reached out to take the stone.

As soon as the ruby touched her pale skin, Alora fell to the deck, writhing. Vidarian dropped to his knees beside her, diving to break her fall.

"No!" Isri said. The sharpest word he'd ever heard her utter, it stopped him mid-movement. He pushed himself away, losing his balance and falling to the deck. "Don't touch her! If another object touches her, she may not be able to contain the reaction." Isri spread her wings, arcing them around the girl, who still convulsed, her throat opening and closing in ragged gasps.

Vidarian stood and turned away, stung at his own helplessness. He nearly ran into Oneira, who, to her credit, looked as sick as he felt. Without being asked, she turned to the nearest crewman and gave orders for blankets, hot drinks.

"Shh, it's all right," Isri murmured, insinuating herself around the girl without touching her, dodging her thrashing arms and somehow making sure she was turned in just the right direction to keep from injuring herself.

"Can't you help her?" Vidarian asked, when the fit showed no sign of stopping.

Isri's eyes came up, and for a moment there was outrage in them, an otherworldly focus that made him take a step backward. "It must pass on its own. She will grow stronger in overcoming it with time. Any interference only jeopardizes her sanity."

At length, the convulsions diminished, replaced by a wordless murmuring of syllables that seemed to have no beginnings and no ends.

"She is ready," Isri said, and without warning, touched Alora's nerveless hand to Vidarian's arm.

Ruby's life, and several hundreds of other memories, facts, places, objects, hurtled into Vidarian's mind. It was a faraway self that fell again to the deck, knees banging against wood, back slamming into the rail. Everything Ruby had ever been, every object she had touched, invisible threads spun out from his mind to where they had been. A hundred thousand memories, more—

Push them away, Isri's voice was in his head, an island of cool identity. *Imagine her body. The flesh as it was. Imagine what you seek.*

It was there, ten thousand fathoms below, resting against the silt and rocks, dark beyond darkness. It was there, her body, like an extension of his arm, pressed in by miles of water but as real as his own hand.

Vidarian reached toward it, shaped the water around it with his will, separated it from the silt until it was weightless, encased only in water.

"I've got her," he whispered. He centered his focus deep beneath the waves, and began to pull.

CHAPTER FIFTEEN

ANOTHER WAY

The surface of the sea bubbled and frothed, spraying the deck and everyone on it. Vidarian kept his mind locked on the task of drawing the body from the water; the mechanics of it were not difficult, but he had to fight to keep his grip on today's reality when Alora's object-sense still bombarded him with the chaos of the past, a million million moments experienced all simultaneously.

Over his shoulder, Oneira was shouting for the deck to be cleared. A very small part of him was aware enough to be grateful; the thought of strangers witnessing what they were about to do clawed at his gut.

He continued to pull, aware now that the heaviness was receding; the closer he brought it to the surface, the less the sea seemed determined to haul it back to the depths.

Then—a presence.

It loomed up out of the water, a mind Vidarian had felt before; Ruby had lived then, and steered her ship around the deadly storm-tossed arc of Maladar's Horn. He very nearly lost his grip on Ruby's body: pain lanced through his eyes as he forced himself to concentrate.

A face formed in the water, and human voices around him gasped. Altair and Thalnarra each said something in a language he didn't recognize.

* *Nistra!* * Ruby exulted. She had always been absolute in her loyalty to the goddess of the sea, but now she was a nomad dying of thirst.

What you attempt cannot be done, the words swirled in Vidarian's mind like drops of oil in water. *You should not take from me what is mine.* Weight suddenly settled on Ruby's body, preventing him from lifting it further. But neither did it draw her back into the depths.

* *What is she saying? I can hear her voice but not her words!* *

"Beloved Nistra," Vidarian said, and starbursts of white light bloomed against his eyelids as he fought to keep his concentration. What little mind's energy he could spare from keeping the body from dropping again into the black now spun with furious calculation. He chose his words as an archer chooses fletching. "Will you deny us the attempt to return your daughter to her rightful vessel? A captain who has served and honored you always?"

I will not, the words bubbled now, and the presence withdrew. Ruby's body began to rise once more. *But you are warned, blood of my waters. The knife-reefs line your path.*

Then she was gone, the shadowy face surrendering itself to the chop and roll of the waves.

* *What did she say?* * Ruby asked again.

And then her body broke the surface with a crash and rush of water. The shrouded shape tilted, bobbed, and then floated. Now that he could see it, Vidarian stepped away from Alora—parting from her touch was like emerging into clear air, and his thoughts became his own again—and pushed the waves up underneath the body, lifting it gently up and over the rail, then down onto the deck.

Part of him was still in denial about what he was seeing. He had seen bodies prepared for sea burial before, and this was one such, wrapped tightly in binding linens. The left foot was missing; the linen would have been treated to repel the appetites of sea creatures, but this was no guarantee.

The linen was stretched, loose where it had been pushed outward by bloating and then fallen in with decay. As the wind shifted, gaps in the fabric carried a mordant air of death to their faces. Vidarian choked, and brought his forearm up to cover his nose and mouth.

When the wave of nausea passed, he said, "Ruby . . . I don't think . . ."

* *NO!* * Ruby barked, a hysteria creeping into her voice. * *We have come this far! You swore an oath!* *

Numbly, Vidarian held out his hand to Alora, who stared wide-eyed at Ruby's body. He cursed himself for allowing her on the journey, even if Isri approved. The seridi squeezed the girl's shoulder, and she started, then handed Vidarian the sun ruby.

Keeping his forearm across his mouth, Vidarian approached the wrapped body, and knelt. He turned to look at Isri, who was concentrating very hard on the shape in front of him. She gave a slight shake of her head, as of uncertainty, and so he turned back, and placed the ruby on the forehead of the corpse.

The ruby flared just as it touched the linen, growing hot, and for one terrible moment Vidarian was sure they would see the corpse lift itself and stand.

Then—nothing.

He choked in one breath after another, staring at the linen shape that part of him still would not accept had been one of his dearest friends. There was a rustle of feathers, and Isri was there, kneeling beside him. She spread her hands over the body, concentrating.

They waited for long minutes, and at last, Ruby spoke.

* *This isn't possible. Why can't I go back?* *

A fury burned in her, something beyond human emotion, something that resonated through all the "chambers" of her prison. It was as if the alien thing that lived within the prism key with her now manifested itself alongside her will—and it was preternaturally angry.

The force of that inhuman consciousness jarred Vidarian from his shock. He realized, almost for the first time, what he was looking at, what he was doing, and suddenly it all seemed quite, quite mad. He turned his head away from the body, seeking anything else to look at.

Tears streaked Isri's face. Vidarian had not known seridi could cry. "It seems . . ." Her voice rasped, and she coughed. "It seems that Ruby's body is too far gone to house her. The . . . place . . . that her mind would go is unreachable to me, as if it were not flesh at all." Though her words stung, the truth of it again seemed obvious; there was hardly anything left of her body that could be imagined to live.

At Isri's words, Ruby let out a cry of despair and frustration that clawed straight through his soul. None of them could bear to answer her, and so they sat again in silence.

"We should," Vidarian began at last, choking over his words, realizing that tears were running down his cheeks and throat. He coughed. "We should return the body to the sea."

* No! * Ruby snapped again, rage pouring out of her, lighting the prism key from within. * This is Nistra's doing! She would not let me hear her, and now would deny me my own body! She shall not have it again! *

Vidarian reeled anew, struck to some deep part of him that had been raised to revere the sea goddess. Her words echoed back, stirring dread. He started to object, but Ruby cut him off again.

* Burn it, Vidarian. Do me this service, at least. *

Dread crystallized into ice. Fire was a landsman's burial, not a sea captain, much less a Queen of the West Sea.

* It isn't me, my friend. And it has already been taken from Nistra. *

Ruby's sudden composure, the air of command and confidence once more in her voice, did not dispel the dread, but it loosed its hold.

They could not burn the body on the deck. Which meant in all likelihood, the crew could not burn it at all. Vidarian called a wave up from the ocean's surface with a murmur, and directed it under the body again. He lifted it out, and back to the surface, holding it there. Then he turned away, and willed fire into it.

The fire did not go willingly. It fought him, both at being summoned while he still held the body aloft with his water sense, and in objection to the water energy that saturated the body. Vidarian closed his eyes and redoubled his efforts, clenching his teeth, pressing the water from the body and commanding the fire to enter it.

He heard the fire, and felt it, but would not look back. This might be Ruby's will, and a fulfillment of his oath, but he retreated within himself as he carried it out, searching within for a meditative mind that an exercise from the Book of Nistra had taught him. And he mouthed silent prayers to the goddess of the sea, asking forgiveness for Ruby, and for himself. Nistra was not a goddess to contemplate forgiveness, nor the owing of debts or action, but he asked it anyway, offering himself up to the sea.

An oily smoke and char stained the air, choking them again, until Altair silently summoned a wind to chase it back across the water. The tall gryphon stole up next to him, spreading a wing around him, and Vidarian leaned into his feathered shoulder, reaching for a peace that would not come.

∿∿

Clouds spread below them, rolling white here at the heights, their every detail revealed by the bright and golden afternoon sun. Far below, a storm rumbled close to the ocean's surface, charcoal clouds lit by intermittent punctuations of lightning.

He had asked Oneira to return them to the Imperial City, his task fulfilled. The dread that ate at his stomach had not diminished. If the ship had been a quiet one before, now it was silent as a tomb. For the first day of sailing Vidarian stood at the stern, looking down and back over the clouds, and spoke to no one.

Ruby, too, had been silent, her thoughts only her own. When she spoke at last on the second day, it was to stir Vidarian out of a solemn and wordless meditation.

* You have to destroy me, Vidarian. *

The breath stopped in his chest.

* I can't live like this. It's not living at all! I am not dead, and I am not alive. And I am losing myself to . . . whatever this is. *

"Ruby, I . . ." His head spun.

* I'm dangerous. I'm a danger to you and to anyone around me. You know this. *

He must have radiated his agony and shock, for Isri was suddenly there in his mind, whispering up around him as she had never done before, wordlessly radiating reassurance. Far to starboard, Thalnarra gave an upward-lilting call, inquiring.

"I have fulfilled my obligation to you, Ruby," he began, knowing in his heart that it felt untrue, but resisting her would be truer than admitting he could now bear to destroy her, which he knew he could not.

* You don't believe that, * she snorted, an ire raising to stiffen behind the moroseness of her first demand.

Footsteps sounded on the deck, and he turned, stunned to see Oneira approaching the stern rail. He shook his head, but to his further astonishment, she only lifted her eyebrows, and continued forward.

"I know that I cannot destroy you," he said, reaching for the words that would deter her from the chase. But she only bore down harder.

How can you lack the strength to do what you must do? Are you no captain at all? Perhaps you were never? He clenched his jaw, but she plowed on relentlessly. *Or has 'destiny' weakened you? First that mongrel wolf, and now you flinch again.* He flushed, aware of Oneira's presence, as Ruby must have known he would be, and that the woman could hear her.

This was a Ruby he knew, a woman ferocious in negotiation, a master of sea politics. She was pushing him, hoping to seal him in his own anger so that he might do what she asked. Perversely, it made him all the more inclined to resist her. "I won't do this, Ruby. I can't."

Then you betray me for the second time.

He wanted to argue with her, but felt all composure slipping away. He closed his eyes, and a kind of madness yawned under him, a panic; Isri's presence wrapped around him again, soft as a down blanket—a specific down blanket, one that smelled of lavender and cedar, pulled from his memories of his mother—but it could not reach the knife of breaking within him, the fissure, opened by the Great Gate, that now threatened to swallow him into unbeing.

"There is another way." The voice was soft, gentle. Unrecognizable. It was Oneira's.

Vidarian opened his burning eyes and looked at her. The world seemed tilted, and he worked to straighten his head, assaulted on all sides by sensation. The sun seemed far too bright, the scent of the varnished rail suddenly stifling, the sky too huge and bearing down on them.

Oneira took his silence for permission. "The vessel that you now inhabit, the prism key. It is one of many, some larger than others. Some are so large that they can contain the fullness of a human mind. They can even give it a human shape."

Ruby's attention palpably turned away from Vidarian, felt as a cooling of his skin. He struggled to breathe. *You speak of automaton bodies. Like Iridan's.*

Oneira nodded, folding her lace-gloved hands in front of her. "The creation of automata is assumed to be a lost art—but not for the Company."

You can craft me such a body?

"Not I," Oneira said. "But I know someone who can."

CHAPTER SIXTEEN
A PROMISING YOUNG MIND

Try as he might, Vidarian could not bring himself to eat the lavish meal Oneira had laid before them in the forecastle's stateroom. He had never been seasick a day in his life, but even looking at the poached rock crab before him turned his stomach.

Oneira had no such difficulty, daintily downing chilled oysters and wilted pepper greens with sweet plum vinegar.

It didn't help that Isri also went without eating, though she was offered plate after plate. The seridi ate no meat, by choice and not biology, and it had taken subtle pressure on Vidarian's part to have her included at the table at all. Now he wasn't sure that he'd truly done her a service by insisting.

Iridan did not eat, but he did have a plate in front of him, an etched silver platter set with a translucent sphere that glowed a soft blue. It was an attunement sphere, Oneira had said, and it had some sort of meditative effect on automata.

Now that Oneira was openly acknowledging Ruby, she, too, had a place at the table, set in an ornate golden jewelry box. She and Iridan could communicate silently, which meant that the meal, awkward already, was made more so by punctuations of long silence.

"*I would be very grateful,*" Iridan said after one such, "*for any information about my siblings. Any of them.*"

He addressed this to the table, and Vidarian wasn't sure whether it was with honest openness or to pressure Ruby—or Oneira—by voicing his question publicly. It was unfair to hold his origins against him, but the mere fact that he was created for diplomacy—or created at all—made it difficult for Vidarian to feel comfortable with his motives. If an automaton could be said to be motivated for anything other than its purpose.

* *I wish I could tell you more than I already have,* * Ruby said. * *What I . . . said . . . in the Arboretum—it came from a part of this prism key that I can't open on my own. It's as though a door is shut, and I can't control what opens it. I'm genuinely sorry.* *

"My *plight* is certainly not worse than yours. Perhaps we can help each other."

Ruby and Iridan warming to each other was hardly surprising under their circumstances, but Vidarian couldn't help but be disquieted by the thought that Ruby was testing the waters of Iridan's intelligence, imagining herself in such a body. Oneira's offer presented more questions than it answered, but while they were still leagues from the Imperial City, there was no prospect of answering them.

Iridan's lavender eyes were on Oneira. She set aside her silver fork and lifted her linen napkin to her lips, then set it aside, all thoughtfulness. "What I am about to tell you is a Company secret, and you should know already how covetously knowledge is guarded." She lifted the napkin again and carefully folded it. "I only tell you as I suspect you know already, and what I know isn't much. The existence of the four automata created by Grand Artificer Parvidian nearly a thousand years ago has been continuously known to the Company, which has also paid handsomely to preserve the knowledge of the Animators, whose guild in turn trained Parvidian."

"Four," Iridan repeated, his inflection flat, his mind somewhere far away.

Oneira nodded, watching him carefully. "Three known to each other and to the public—the fourth known only to the highest echelons of government, and, of course, the Company."

* *Do they exact some kind of loyalty oath from you, to keep you from disclosing your secrets?* * Ruby asked. Her tone said clearly that she did not trust the Company, even if she remained tempted by Oneira's offer of an automaton body.

"They don't need to," Oneira said, and rang the serving bell. A black-uniformed maid entered promptly with a steaming pitcher of *kava* and a tray of sugar, cream, and spices. "Knowledge is disclosed only with advancement into genuine wealth—and the Company controls access to that wealth. No one would jeopardize what they had earned."

"Unless someone else offered more wealth?" Vidarian ventured.

The bemused look Oneira gave him was chilling in its implication: no one in the world had more wealth than the Company. She gestured, and the serving maid set the tray on the table, then poured a silver cup of *kava* and spiced it. Vidarian had known the Company was powerful, but only the opening of the gate had revealed the glacier of strength that lay below the surface. "And Justinian?"

Oneira accepted her cup and gestured the maid to pour Vidarian's. She took a long and deliberate sip. "I should have known that he of all the directors would have had a contingency plan."

Her tone was neutral, a subtle rebuke on her analytic abilities, but the wound was clear: whatever Justinian's contingency plan had been, it did not include her. Vidarian decided not to suggest to her that it had appeared to include him. It felt oddly oily to withhold information with her when she had shared a piece of her own, but he reminded himself as he accepted the silver cup that he did not trust her at all.

The next morning Altair arced down to hover just off the starboard rail where Vidarian stood.

// *Thalnarra has heard something from below,* // he said, curiosity giving his voice a metallic tang. // *A contact. She is coming in to land.* // Generally, Altair flew at higher altitudes than Thalnarra, but lately they had been reversed.

"Can't you hear them yourself?"

// *Her telepathy is quite a bit stronger than mine.* // He didn't seem embarrassed, though Vidarian was; certainly, as telepathic strength varied in humans and seridi, so must it also in gryphons, but the thought had never occurred to him.

Altair cupped his wings and allowed the wind current produced by the ship's wake to carry him up and over the rail with a slight tilting of his right wing. He touched down gently on the deck, just before Thalnarra, as promised, angled in from above and dropped down next to the port rail. Her landing was not so delicate and tilted the ship, but it soon righted itself.

Her dark-backed primaries brushed the deck as she extended her wings for balance. // *Arikaree is here. An'du is with him.* //

"An'du? Here?" Vidarian went to the rail and peered down, but could see only clouds.

// *I asked about that. Now that she can change shape at will, she's no longer confined to the An'durin. She's rejoined her people in the West Sea.* //

"Her people?" An'du had said there were "many" of her kind, but it had been hard to believe. He'd never heard of another whale like her.

The round, red eye that Thalnarra turned on him suggested that the Company wasn't the only group to hoard knowledge. // *There are quite a few of them. She has one with her, some kind of ambassador from one of the other clans. She wants you to meet him.* //

Vidarian found Oneira in the navigation room consulting with her boatswain. He hadn't quite figured out the *Wind Maiden*'s arrangement; the crew clearly answered to Oneira alone as the Company representative, but she did not fulfill a captain's duties, and indeed they seemed not to have one. He apologized for interrupting, then explained about their new guests.

"The sea-folk?" The flatness of her eyes said that she was neither surprised nor inclined to elaborate. More secrets. Vidarian fought not to grind his teeth. "I'd love to meet one of them," Oneira said, and instructed the boatswain to anchor the ship on the water again.

Above, Thalnarra and Altair had returned to the sky, and circled the *Wind Maiden* as she descended toward the water. They called out greetings to unseen—to Vidarian, anyway—targets below. The ship hove along a starboard arc and the ocean loomed up beneath them, all chopping whitecap under a brisk northeasterly wind.

// *Be greeting, good-friend,* // the pelican-gryphon said joyfully, voice fresh like a north sea breeze. // *Nistra's blessing to be seeing you once more.* //

The gryphon might be able to see Vidarian, but not the reverse; it was some long moments before he made out the bobbing shape far below on the water. Arikaree spread his wings in greeting, and flipped an arc of seawater up into the air with his beak.

Beside him, a scaled equine face broke the water's surface, followed by a long, muscled neck. Vidarian only had a second to attempt to make sense of a horse—a green one—in the water, and then An'du's grey-green head surfaced as well, perched atop the creature's back.

The horse reared, another impossible-seeming feat, until the churning foam cleared to show the massive scaled fish torso that continued downward from its waist. Its forelegs, split and webbed where a horse's hooves would be, pawed at the waves, and it squealed, a sound more dolphin than horse.

An'du laughed and cursed the beast in a language Vidarian had never heard, then released the reins. As soon as it had its head, the horse dove back beneath the water's surface to glower at her. How he could tell it was glowering Vidarian had no idea, but it rolled off the creature like water.

"A pleasure to see you again, Vidarian—especially on the open sea." An'du smiled, and Vidarian knew her words to be genuine; she glowed with health, a fact that must have been attributable to the ocean return. "May we board your handsome vessel?"

The *Wind Maiden* still hovered above the water's surface, and Vidarian turned, looking for the nearest davit, or some way of bringing them aboard. Oneira was already there, supervising the lowering of something better—a rope ladder.

There was a kind of chirp from the water, and a splash. A sea otter had hopped from its camouflaged perch between Arikaree's wings to swim over to An'du's shoulders. She wrapped him around her neck like a fine lady with a foxtail stole, then swam to the ladder. One muscular arm wrapped between two rungs, and she waved with her free hand. Three strong sailors set to pulling the ladder back in, while Arikaree swam with surprising speed and flapped his broad, rectangular wings, laboriously—but impressively—taking off from the water.

When An'du stepped up to the deck, Vidarian realized he'd forgotten how large she was—or perhaps she had always looked smaller in the water.

He'd become accustomed to the size of the gryphons, but An'du at least *appeared* human, though her dark eyes without iris or pupil, not to mention her mottled green skin, loudly proclaimed that she was not. Still, as she towered above all of the humans, easily half again as tall as Oneira—no small woman herself—Vidarian appreciated her strangeness anew, trying to imagine the great green whale of the An'durin somehow being the same creature, and not quite succeeding.

An'du knelt and the sea otter leapt from her shoulders, shook water from his pelt in a sinuous head-to-tail twist, then grew, becoming a slim, dark-olive-skinned young man.

He was slender and strong, so wiry that he seemed taller than he was. But where An'du was much larger than a human, her guest was slightly smaller, fine-boned and sharp of feature. And the quiet burn of his eyes as he took in Vidarian, Oneira, the sailors, and the gryphons said that he was not terribly impressed with his new company.

"My friends, I introduce to you Tepeki Underbranch, prince of the Velshi," An'du said, coming to stand behind the boy and put a hand on his shoulder that easily could have cupped his entire head. She squeezed gently, almost unnoticeably, and he gave the slightest possible nod of his chin.

"I'm pleased to meet you," the boy said, a soft voice that tried to be low but couldn't.

* *Another shapechanger,* * Ruby said. * *Fantastic.* *

Oneira invited An'du and her young guest into the state room for tea and refreshments while Thalnarra and Altair saw to Arikaree's comfort and doubt-less set about exchanging gossip. Though it was morning still, the fare spread out by one of the black-coated attendants was seafood, which, to their collective relief, seemed not to offend An'du or the boy. Quite to the contrary, Tepeki tucked into the steamed clam soup with verve, possibly to avoid being drawn into conversation. Isri had joined them as well, and Vidarian cast a grateful look at Oneira for providing her a more appropriate tray of sliced fruit and shelled nuts.

Upon seeing An'du, Isri, to their surprise, had gone straight to the massive woman and embraced her. They exchanged several words in a language that, this time, Vidarian could almost recognize—an antique dialect of High Alorean? Or if not, certainly related.

The seridi's cheek-feathers were puffed out with happiness as she took a seat next to An'du. "It's such a relief to know that the Traenumar survived the Long Dream," she said. At this the boy looked up from his soup. Isri caught his eyes, and her feathers flattened again. She even gave a small gasp. "And— is our young friend . . . Velshi?"

"He is," An'du said, a motherly pride evident in the quiet way she beamed at Isri's recognition. "One of the few remaining. A prince of his people."

Isri raised a feathered hand toward him, as if not quite believing he was there, and then gave a soft chirp to herself. "Please excuse my curiosity, young friend. I have never in my life met one of your people, though my own people, the seridi, much desired to, before the Dream."

"The Velshi have always been notoriously private," An'du explained. "Historically they have treated only with the Traenumar, and that rarely— and on their terms, not ours."

"How are your people, An'du?" Isri asked. Vidarian had never seen her so animated.

"Many have yet to awaken," An'du replied, with a sigh that rang in her chest like the low note of a stone flute. "Which is why I've brought Tepeki to you." She took a sip of her soup, then lifted her spoon to Oneira in a small salute at its flavor, and turned to Vidarian. "It's our strange good fortune to have found you," she said. "I had thought we would have to travel overland to the Imperial City, and then we sensed a strong water wielder not far from here, next to the wind bell."

"The wind bell?" Vidarian asked, pausing over his tea.

"It is an energy signature that my cousins say has marked the water near here for twenty years or so. Surely you felt it?"

"There was a pattern," he agreed. "I had no idea it was a bell."

"Well, it rang for leagues," An'du chuckled. "And we are lucky it did." She hesitated, then folded her hands on the table. "I had hoped you would consider bringing Tepeki with you," she said, delicacy in her posture and tone. "As an ambassador to your Alorean emperor."

"You and master Tepeki are welcome aboard the *Wind Maiden* for as long as we may host you, gracious mother, and I would be honored to see the young master to the hand of the emperor personally," Oneira said, speaking for the first time since the meal started, and Vidarian worked to avoid choking on his tea. He did not quite dare glare at Oneira, but he did allow himself a frown, which An'du thankfully—or perhaps deliberately—missed.

"I would be in your debt," An'du said, tipping her steepled fingertips toward Oneira in a gesture of thanks. "As I said, many of my own Traenumar have not yet awakened, and I am needed in our five seas to search them out and bring them to consciousness." Now she smiled at Vidarian. "There is much Tepeki could learn from you, Vidarian, of the Alorean culture and how his people, and mine, might work together peacefully with your empire."

"And if I do not wish to learn?" the boy said quietly, setting his spoon aside. "With respect, gracious mother? If I believe that my place is with our people?"

An'du's face did not change, but as she turned toward her young charge, the air in the stateroom seemed to cool a degree. "Then it is all the more important that you have the opportunity to do so—for the future of your people. We will not speak on this further."

The boy bobbed his head, though his black eyes still glinted with roguish defiance. What was An'du getting them into?

"I would be pleased to assist him at the palace as well, dear An'du," Isri added. The boy looked at her and seemed to thaw just a degree, and Vidarian realized that his objection was to interacting with humans. A seridi, not being human, ranked lower in his mind than a Velshi or Traenumar—but higher than a Tesseract.

"We are both grateful for that, friend Isri. Some of my Traenumar have found seridi over the ocean, and we extend to them the same guidance, and assistance if they require. That is to say . . . when it can be received." This last she said delicately, and sadness touched her large, pupilless eyes.

"More we cannot ask," Isri said, and Vidarian did not need telepathy to know her thoughts. She saw in her mind, as he did, the last insane seridi they had captured, and thought of how many more still ranged over the seas and mountains.

"We will all recover in time, Nistra willing," An'du said, and Isri reached over to clasp her hand warmly. Within it, Isri's feathered one looked like a child's.

"Nistra willing," Isri agreed, and even Tepeki, for a moment, seemed to forget his insolence. Vidarian watched him while Oneira proceeded to make genteel small talk about the Traenumar and the Velshi. The flash of the boy's eyes when they accidentally met his across the table made him think that, whatever he learned, it would not be what An'du was hoping for.

CHAPTER SEVENTEEN
A SILENCE OF
BRANCH AND LEAF

O nce Tepeki found out about Iridan, there was little speaking with
him about anything else.

It was not surprising that a young man should be fascinated with a
mechanical being—but Tepeki's focus was unwavering and single-minded.
For his first day on the ship he peppered anyone who would listen with questions about his function and creation, an obsession that couldn't help but
recall an otter cracking open a clam.

The thought itself widened a fissure that had been growing in Vidarian's
heart. First An'du, then Calphille, Iridan, and now Tepeki—they looked,
sounded, and behaved human, except when they most manifestly did not.
An'du and Calphille he had trusted from the first moment he'd met them, a
"gut trust" as his father would have said. Iridan he could make neither heads
nor tails of, and now the young Tepeki seemed hells-bent on showing him just
how strange and unknowable a shapechanger race could be.

Vidarian had seen enough bigotry between the elemental families and the
many cultures that dwelled even in Alorea to know the signs of it in his own
heart. It was Iridan that confused him; surely his intelligence and humanlike
capacity for grief and pain warranted fairer treatment than he'd received, yet
Vidarian could not put his machine nature—purpose-built with intentions
now lost to the centuries—out of his mind. And it had made Vidarian avoid
him, even when part of him knew the shape of his body was the genuine solution to Ruby's predicament.

The puzzle of Iridan would not be easily solved. But he could attempt to
remedy Tepeki's animosity.

He found Oneira in the ship's solarium, a lavish compartment abaft the forecastle with glass walls all around. The glass brought in the sun's heat but kept off the wind, and consequently the air inside was tropic warm and thick with the herbal scent of the tiny white flowers that sprawled from stone pots just inside the walls.

For once, Iridan was not with her, and so neither was Tepeki. She reclined on a plush divan, reading an antique book embossed with a flame and gear-wheel insignia Vidarian didn't recognize. When Vidarian took a seat opposite her, she closed the book and delicately removed her reading spectacles, setting them on a jade-topped side table at her right hand. "Good afternoon, Captain."

"A lovely one," Vidarian agreed. "And a remarkable solarium your *Wind Maiden* has."

"You find it ostentatious."

"I would never so accuse a vessel of the Alorean Import Company."

"See that you do not, while her decks are below your feet, anyway." Oneira looked him up and down. "Well, what can I help you with, Captain? You certainly didn't come out here to insult my livelihood, I should hope."

"It's about Tepeki," Vidarian said, leaning back into the plush upholstery. "You graciously offered to introduce him to the emperor."

"Yes?"

"I greatly appreciate the gesture," he said carefully, "And most certainly Tepeki does as well. But the promise for his welfare was mine." Vidarian leaned forward, folding his hands. "I've not properly counseled the boy. I'd like to begin to make amends by conducting his introduction myself."

A silence stretched between them. High above, a feathery cloud drifted across the sun, painting a line of shadow across the glass.

"The solution is simple," Oneira said, folding her hands. "We shall introduce him together."

He looked at her a long moment, calculating, and finally nodded, standing. "Thank you."

"Of course." She picked up the spectacles from the jade side table again.

Vidarian bowed, then walked to the door. His hand was on the brass latch when he turned back. "Can you truly provide Ruby a body like Iridan's? What artificer could create one today, if the Grand Artificer who made only four such in his lifetime died almost a thousand years ago?"

Oneira gave him a long look over the wire rims of her spectacles, lifted an eyebrow, and pointedly opened her book again.

$\sim\!\sim\!\sim$

They moored back at the palace four days after the failed attempt to retrieve Ruby's body; a prevailing wind had made the homeward journey faster.

When they were gliding downward to land in the north field, tiny, moving specks far below showed that they would be met by a small welcome committee. There were three small, humanish figures and three distinctly non-human ones—and Vidarian guessed that the one racing through the grass in wide, wild arcs was Rai. When the ship drew closer, the racing shape barked, and twice released a small shower of sparks in its excitement. One of the sparks started the grass to smoking, and the three humans ran to stamp it out, while Rai took up a post nearby and barked even louder. Vidarian laughed, once it was clear the small fire was out.

"What is that?" Tepeki said, leaning over the rail.

"His name is Rai," Vidarian began.

"That's Rikani for 'trust.'"

"You are full of surprises," Vidarian said.

"And you are full of assumptions."

"I would not have assumed," he kept his voice as even as he could, "that any young man your age would speak Rikani."

"They are an ocean-faring people, not so different from mine." He vaulted up onto the rail, and it was all Vidarian could do to stop himself from lunging after. Any warning would only amuse the boy, or worse, goad him to even greater risks.

Tepeki reached out to the great, braided cables of the mainstay, leaning even farther, and Vidarian's thoughts raced, planning even now how they would rescue him if he should fall. By his size, Altair should be able to fly with him, he hoped . . . and there was some chance the wide starboard wing mast just below them would slow the fall . . . The boy became the otter, and lightly ran up the mainstay, then leaped off—this time with the *Wind Maiden's* deck thankfully beneath him—to clamber over the foremast shrouds.

Vidarian shook his head, and when he returned to watch the landing from the rail, they were almost on the ground. A slow grinding motion signaled the furling of the lower fin-mast as the ship prepared to land.

Rai ran up the gangplank before its base had even touched the ground, to the annoyance of the otherwise precise crewmen who lowered it. They were also less than impressed by the dashing arrival of the thornwolf, his spines throwing off sparks, and so Vidarian pushed his way down the gangplank alone, the better to distract Rai from leaping onto the ship itself.

Tepeki followed him down, and though Rai ran several circles around Vidarian, desperately pleased at his return, he was rapidly distracted by the young sea boy. The wolf capered, and Tepeki laughed, dancing with surprising agility for a boy who must have spent most of his life in another shape, and swimming. The two seemed to understand each other, and find a special joy in that understanding.

My creatures know things, the Starhunter had said.

Though it gave him a pang—it felt strange how much he'd missed the wolf pup, who was noticeably larger than he had been a fortnight ago—he left them to play and turned toward Brannon, his sister, and the other Sky Knight apprentice who was so often with them.

"Welcome home, sir. We were sent to watch for you," Brannon said. "The emperor has asked for you—and he wants to meet a 'Prince Tepeki' also."

Oneira must have had one of the relay spheres aboard the ship for news to travel so fast. He couldn't help but wonder what else about the empire had already changed as a result of the things.

"Of course," Vidarian said. Behind him, Oneira was descending the gangplank, meticulously coiffed and smelling of expensive jasmine. She must have spent the entire descent, as perhaps Vidarian should have, preparing.

As it was his usual function, Brannon fell into the role of page boy again, leading them across the field and through the corridors of the palace. Rai had expunged his excitement, and now paced beside Vidarian, strolling and panting.

The emperor was waiting for them, and as soon as they arrived, sent the two stewards and secretaries that had been attending him out of the room. This was a central audience chamber, albeit a simple one—intended to impress, but also intended to comfort familiar friends. Calphille was with him, and they both stood as Vidarian, Oneira, Tepeki, and Rai entered the chamber.

"Ah, Vidarian, Oneira—welcome home," Lirien said, and the warmth in his voice was genuine. Vidarian marveled at how this man—one of the most powerful in the world—had seemed so terrifying scant weeks ago, and yet now evoked only warmth and friendship. "I trust you had a successful journey?"

"I found what I was looking for," Vidarian agreed, still careful. "Thank you, your majesty, for your tolerance of the expedition when you have much need of us. I promise you that it was a necessary one."

Tepeki was smiling at Calphille, a silly, ogling smile that Vidarian had to restrain himself from correcting with force. Calphille was a striking woman—today resplendent as a rainforest blossom in a gown of crimson and forest green—and perhaps the boy had no experience with ladies at all, though he had not reacted the same way to Oneira, who by all accounts deserved similar.

Vidarian contained his response to gripping Tepeki's elbow firmly. "I'm pleased to introduce to your majesty Tepeki Underbranch, a prince of the Velshi people."

"And I am pleased to meet him," Lirien said, stepping forward to offer the boy his hand. Tepeki seemed not to know what to do with it, and Vidarian guided their hands together with his own. "Oneira tells me your people are an ocean-faring one, like our allies, the Rikani."

"*Modo dalashi kure*," Tepeki replied, and though Vidarian was hardly much judge, his Rikani accent seemed flawless. The emperor, too, was impressed. "We are kin, of a sorts," Tepeki repeated. "My people have sent me to learn what may be learned from yours." There was a challenge in his eyes, but not one of the emperor's authority. But then the boy's gaze strayed again to Calphille.

"You admire my consort, the Lady Calphille," Lirien said, the slightest edge to his voice.

Vidarian only had a moment to be surprised at the title.

"She's a shapechanger," Tepeki said. He shrank, gliding into his sea otter form, then back to human again. "Like me."

Silence dropped, thrumming in the air as if someone had shattered glass in front of them.

Lirien was staring at Tepeki, clearly taking in with shock what he'd just seen. He'd drawn back, ever so slightly. Vidarian's thoughts raced for the second time that day. Did he know about Calphille already? Surely she must have told him, and yet if she had, the gossip at court would have taken on a radically different tone. Perhaps she had told the emperor, and he had been keeping her secret? Or perhaps, wildest of miracles, the court had accepted what she was already.

"You may all withdraw," the emperor said at last. Calphille stretched a hand toward him, and the coolness of his reply was knife-sharp. "All of you."

Calphille's hand stopped, curled. She knelt, gathering her skirts with deliberate care. Oneira led Tepeki out by the elbow, and for a moment Calphille stood, chin down, eyes iron flat. Vidarian was sure she would say something, and then she strode from the room, all pretense at courtliness abandoned. She was, though wrapped in silk, the warrior again. Vidarian turned quickly to follow her.

His hand was on the door when the emperor's voice stopped him.

"Vidarian."

He stared down the hall. In a moment she would turn the corner, and he would lose her. Slowly, he turned back around.

There was a cold anger in the emperor's eyes, and something worse. "I thought that we understood each other." He turned away, walking back to his chair. He did not sit, but placed a hand on the carved golden eagle on its arm. "I was wrong."

∿∿∿

A slender dark-barked spruce stood in the center of the north field.

Vidarian went to the tree, his thoughts and his feet heavy. "Calphille?" he said, when he reached it. She didn't answer, and so he sat on the ground, leaning against the trunk.

For a few moments he watched the palace bustle, what little of it he could see from the field. His eyes wanted to go up and into the sky, and eventually he closed them.

At length the tree shivered, and he jerked out of his half-sleep, then pushed himself to his feet and brushed dust from his trouser legs.

Once she was human again, Calphille looked at him, waiting for him to speak.

"How could he not know?"

She turned away, but not angrily. "It just—never came up." When he didn't answer, she turned back to him. "You know how the court is. Once we'd discussed it there'd be no escaping it. I thought that once he admitted that he cared for me . . ."

"He called you his consort," Vidarian said.

Calphille blushed, dark skin turning darker for a moment. "He'd never done that before. I—don't know if it was to warn off Tepeki, or . . ." She shook her head. "I should go. I should return to my people." She turned her face southward, eyes hard and shining. "I should never have left them."

"He's right about one thing. It's my fault for bringing you here."

"You didn't *bring* me. I came with you." She knelt and traced her fingertips through the dirt and dry grass. "I wanted to know this place."

"You're supposed to be here," he said.

"Maybe I'm supposed to be there, seeing to the awakening of my brothers and sisters." Her voice cracked as she said it, guilt welling out like maple sap, or blood.

"And how would you do that?" He tried to say it gently, treated each word as if it were made of porcelain, and breathed a little easier when no explosion came. Slowly, gingerly, he took her hand, pressing it between his own. She looked at him, and there was her wildness again, her uncertainty. "Destiny and I have not always been on speaking terms," he said, and waited for her to smile before he did so himself. "But yours is obvious. It's with him. He knows it. We all knew it as soon as you saw each other." It was sentimental, and he knew it, but it was also the truth, and one he thought she needed.

"I didn't come to your human palace in search of a mate," she said.

"Why did you come, then?"

She flushed again. "To learn what had happened. To bring alliances back to my people."

"And that is what you will have done," he said. "And more. You are an ambassador to everyone that you've met here. And to Lirien. What you are to him is important. It's changed him . . ."

Her jaw firmed. "*What* I am."

"Calphille, I didn't mean—"

"Please go," she said. And before Vidarian could say another word, she changed. Slender arms lifted toward the sky, then stretched, sprouted branches, bloomed with hairlike evergreen needles. Her toes spread outward, growing into roots as thick as his wrist and pushing down into the turned earth. The tree was there in her place once more.

The Sky Knight arena was just beyond the south field, between Vidarian and his rooms. Now that they'd returned to the palace, a thousand tasks weighed on his conscience: he needed to find out more about the metal body Oneira had offered Ruby, he needed to find out more about and from Iridan, and his gut ached to know the status of the war with Qui. Admiral Allingworth and the emperor had both made it quite clear that they preferred Vidarian in the palace, but that hardly meant he had to remain uninformed.

Inside the arena, Rai barked, which meant that Brannon and his sister were likely there as well. Vidarian owed him thanks, and some kind of payment, for watching the pup while the *Wind Maiden* had journeyed. Part of him wished Rai had been there with him, but a more practical part was glad he had missed the journey.

A booming familiar voice, giving laughing commands, told Vidarian that the young apprentices were not alone. Caladan had returned from his dispatch. His voice was a relief—now the children would have the benefit of real Sky Knight training, instead of the gryphons' best analogies.

"Greetings, Sir Caladan. Excellent to see you again." When they'd met, there had been some friction over Isri, which surely lingered; relief swept through him when the knight smiled heartily and extended his gloved hand. Vidarian clasped it, wondering what had provoked the change in humor. The man's eyes were on the young apprentices, who played with their steeds in a chasing game that Vidarian guessed was intended to train agility.

"Beautiful creatures," Vidarian said. "Particularly the royals."

"And she has you to thank, I understand," Caladan said. So thus came the repair.

"We both have Rai to thank," Vidarian said, gesturing to the capering wolf with his chin. Hearing his name, Rai dashed over, circled around both of them, then galloped back to his game.

"The Knighthood is in your debt," Caladan said. The chase game had turned on Brannon, who now had to dash in an attempt to catch either of the two girls or their steeds.

"I had a rather different reception at the time," Vidarian murmured, not wanting to cause difficulty, but feeling for where Caladan stood.

"It's not so bad as you might imagine," he said, then lowered his voice. "Confidentially, Captain, there may as well be two Knighthoods now. Those of us who adapted—with joy—to the changes in our steeds . . . and those of us who did not."

"And how many are the former?"

Caladan sighed. "Not enough."

"Enough to protect the emperor?"

The knight's eyes turned sharply on him. "From whom?"

Vidarian looked to the apprentices, noting the speed of their steeds' growth, speculating things he did not wish to speculate. What kind of world was it, to think of bringing children into a war?

"Whomever we need to," he said, finally. Caladan followed his gaze, his chin firm with an argument at first, before it dropped, and he nodded.

CHAPTER EIGHTEEN
THE ANIMATOR

Vidarian hadn't the slightest idea how to go about finding someone who could build a mechanical body—but he knew someone who seemed to know more about the palace than many of the people who lived in it.

Since they'd returned to the palace, Ruby had been staying with Oneira and Iridan. Her reasoning was obvious, but stung nonetheless; it was difficult not to wonder how much of her remained whole inside the prism key. Such thoughts didn't help her, but despite the lashing of guilt that accompanied them he couldn't seem to keep them away.

Oneira had been locked in Company meetings from the moment the *Wind Maiden* touched down, and so Vidarian went to the Arboretum to find Iridan. Ruby had a "radius," and as soon as Vidarian pushed open the Arboretum's massive stone door, he knew she was there.

"Good afternoon, Iridan." The automaton was bent over a manuscript, but looked up when Vidarian greeted him.

"*Welcome, Captain. I trust you've recovered from our long journey?*"

"I have," he said only. His instinct was to protest that he was hardly as taxed as he might have been, but that thought, too, was unproductive. "And yourself? I never got a chance to thank you personally for agreeing to come with us. Without you, we certainly would not have been permitted the ship."

"*Most of my interests are portable,*" Iridan said, brushing the edges of the manuscript with copper fingertips. "*I was not duly inconvenienced, and the travel itself was refreshing.*"

"You're searching for your siblings? Modrian and Arian?"

The lights on Iridan's face brightened. "*That is well remembered, Captain. Yes, I search for them still.*"

"I wish I could be of more assistance to you," he said, and meant it. "Your world is a foreign landscape to me."

"*Mm*," Iridan agreed, managing to lace more meaning into a single syllable than Vidarian had known diplomats to weave into an hour. "*How may I help you today, then, Captain?*"

"I—came to speak with Ruby, actually. Is she here?"

"*She is here—but I'm afraid she's asleep.*"

Vidarian drew back. "Asleep?"

Iridan made a musical sound, a brief rolling flute trill. "*We do sleep. Prism intelligences, that is. But special tools are required. I'm afraid Ruby was quite sleep deprived.*"

"She'll be better when she awakens, then?" He tried not to sound too relieved.

"*Improved, yes.*" There was a cloud of ambiguity around the words, something almost like worry. "*I'll have a note sent when she wakes. In the meantime, perhaps I can help you?*"

Vidarian worked not to frown as he considered how much to confide in Iridan. It was entirely likely that any words he provided would go straight to Oneira. "I'm looking for the history of crafting elemental devices—from comparatively simple ones, such as the relay spheres, even to such intricate and magnificent works as yourself."

This time the musical sound was a kind of multinote pipe. "*You needn't waste a silver tongue on me, Captain.*" There was amusement, and also a hint of challenge. "*But what you seek is the Animator's Guild. There should be a history of heirs in the Great Library. You could request the volume from their office in the palace. I admit I would be quite curious as to what you find.*"

Vidarian blinked. "Do you mean to say you haven't spoken with them yourself?"

"*The emperor, and my sponsors here, think it would not be wise for me to go abroad in the city.*"

That was not difficult to believe, but somehow the thought was offensive. "You are captive here, then?"

Iridan's lights dimmed momentarily, then brightened again. *"This is my home, Captain. I do not consider it captivity."*

He bowed slightly. "Of course. I apologize for the rash suggestion."

"Think not on it. But I would like to hear what you discover."

"I'll return tomorrow and tell you everything I can."

"Thank you, Captain."

⌇⌇⌇

Once he knew what he was looking for, the palace office of the Great Library was simple to find. The attendant, a bored noble's son, had a clear and manifest disinterest in whatever he would request, and so in short order he had a ticket providing claim to the most recent rolls of the Animator's Guild. The book took about an hour to retrieve from the library itself, and during the wait Vidarian thought of attempting to see Calphille, but worried that if he missed the delivery he would not be able to keep his promise to return to Iridan tomorrow. And he doubted that Calphille would have forgiven him, or the emperor, by now as it was.

The Animator's Guild roll proved surprisingly well organized. Assisting in its organization was the sad fact that only a handful of guildfolk remained committed to their craft. With over five centuries between the current practice and the last functioning elemental artifact, it was astonishing that any persisted at all. A striking concentration of them persisted in Rikan, and another tightly knit contingent in Qui—but there was one registered as alive and living in the Imperial City. And the roll provided an address.

Vidarian copied down the address onto two pieces of scrip and returned the book, then went to find Brannon, who would doubtless be with Thalnarra, and Rai. They were in the Sky Knights' training arena, and he left one of the address copies with them. Rai complained bitterly at not being brought along, but Vidarian had a difficult time imagining what he could bring to a delicately raised scholar that might disturb them *more* than a shapechanging wolf covered with electric thorns.

The Animator's name was Khalesh vel'Itai, and he lived in a modest but respectable district on the northeast side of the city. A light cab took him there—lit, as more than half the cabs in the city now were, by elemental lanterns. The effect as they bounced over the cobbles beneath a red sunset was striking and unsettling, a sea of bobbing pale blue lights that called to mind painterly visions of the spirit world.

Above the door at the address listed was a sign that said "Locksmith," and Vidarian was quite sure the roll must have been out of date. He sighed heavily, and turned to call the cab back—but it was already gone.

The cab's quickness, however, turned out to be fortune; just as he turned back to the sign, looking to the east and west to see if perhaps the numbers had been changed, he caught sight of a small mark on the bottom corner.

It was a flame and gear-wheel insignia, the same as the one on Oneira's book.

He knocked on the door, and was rewarded almost immediately: first by a shout to go away, and second by an opening of the wrought-iron peephole cover.

"Who are you?"

"Khalesh vel'Itai?" Vidarian asked.

"No, that's who *I* am. Who are *you*?"

Vidarian gave a little half bow. "Captain Vidarian Rulorat, good sir, and I come seeking your copious wisdom regarding—"

"Not interested."

He drew back. "But I—"

The iron peephole cover clanked shut, louder than should have been possible. "*Not interested.*"

"I'm willing to pay you," Vidarian began, but only earned laughter. "I also come on request," he said loudly, unable to keep an edge from creeping into his voice, "and on behalf of the automaton Iridan, created over a thousand years ago by the Grand Artificer Parvidian."

The laughing stopped. There was a silence.

The door opened.

Khalesh vel'Itai stood there, his black-bearded head nearly brushing the doorjamb. He wore a battered leather apron covered with burns, thick wool arm-coverings even in the heat of the afternoon, and gloves that looked to be reinforced with metal and a pattern of tiny glowing gems. "You've met the automaton?" he said.

"I have," Vidarian said. "He was quite interested to learn the fate of the Animator's Guild."

Khalesh stuck his head out and looked up and down the street. Then he turned and beckoned with a glowing, gloved hand. "Come in."

༄༄༄

The Animator's house was a rabbit warren of narrow corridors, not by any architectural intent but by virtue of the number of objects he had crammed into the small space. Cabinets and drawers and armoires were everywhere, and coated with mechanical devices of all shapes and sizes.

Khalesh led Vidarian through the maze. They passed several small rooms, one of which had a large, multicolored bird on an iron stand that squawked a welcome with bone-scraping volume. Another was lined with tables laden with glass flasks of at least twenty types of meticulously labeled fluid in a rainbow of colors.

At last they came to a crowded drawing room. It was lined with bookcases on every wall except a narrow vertical band of stone that held a strange and wonderful fireplace. It was elemental fire, and it burned pure and clean—the finest Vidarian had ever seen other than the Living Flames of Sharli at the temple of the fire priestesses.

"Where in the world did you find that?" Vidarian couldn't help but ask.

Khalesh grunted, gesturing Vidarian to a tapestry-upholstered couch as he lifted an iron kettle onto a hook above the flames. "It's been here for generations. Turned itself on some weeks ago out of the blue. Rather startling, you see, as we'd been using that chamber to store books for the last half century or so. Lost a few to the flames, Lady bless."

Yet another little thing for Vidarian to feel guilty about. The surge in elemental magic that had accompanied the gate had awakened the blue lanterns now carried by the cabs, and must have lit this fireplace as well. He decided not to mention it. "How long have you been here?"

The big man removed his gloves and set them on a lacquered side table—the gems dimmed as soon as he removed them—and spooned tea into an earthenware pot, touching his fingertips together to count as he did so. "Well, it's thirty-six generations, I think. Before that we were just a low merchant family in Khodu. My clan mothers instructed the family to become Animators—paid for my many-times great-grandmother's instruction—and we have been ever since."

"Your ancestor was an Animator during the last time Iridan was awake, then," Vidarian said. "The declining years of the Ascendancy." He'd only heard it called that recently: more books, courtesy Oneira and the Company.

Khalesh nodded. The kettle rattled with its boil, and he slipped on a glove, picked it up, and poured steaming water into the teapot. Vidarian watched, struck by the speed and heat of the pure blue flame. "She met Iridan, once, family legend says." He looked up, wordlessly challenging Vidarian's knowledge.

"I've just returned from a skyship journey with him."

Eyes bright, Khalesh laughed. "A skyship as well. You must be quite the important fellow."

"I was summoned by the emperor," Vidarian said, to avoid being more direct, "and it's in his service—as well as on a private errand—that I sought you out. How did your family manage . . ." He realized what he was about to say was impolitic, and trailed off.

Khalesh laughed again, and poured black-green tea into a pair of silver-rimmed glass cups. "How did we manage to survive, practicing a trade that's been dead a thousand years?" He handed Vidarian a cup and gestured to the silver sugar dish. Vidarian took a piece of caramelized sugar, and Khalesh took one also, putting it directly into his mouth before picking up his glass and taking a sip. "The Guild has always known that Animation is a luxury art. Our creed as guildsmen and women is to protect the old knowledge at all costs, during times of waking and sleep for our charges, and in the meantime earn our bread through simpler mechanical devices." He pointed around the room, which, though less cluttered than the others, still contained everything from laundry pulleys to padlocks to devices for which Vidarian had no names. "But you mustn't tease me, Captain. You enter my house with a promise of news of the automaton."

Vidarian put the piece of sugar into his mouth as Khalesh had done. It was candy-sweet but pleasantly smoky, and the hot tea added just the right bitterness. "I will tell you all that I can, and find out for you whatever I can," he said carefully. "But the Alorean Import Company keeps him quite closely guarded."

Khalesh gave a violent wave of his hand, and his expression darkened so deeply and swiftly that for a moment Vidarian thought he would spit. "The Company. A scourge on the free traffic of information, and on the Animator's Guild, from the moment they began." He took a long draught of his tea, and visibly mastered himself. "They were the ones who awakened Iridan, you say? It explains why we've been able to find out so little."

Vidarian nodded. "A senior partner named Justinian Veritas, one of the only Company elders to survive the gate opening." He blinked, remembering something. "And—as it occurs to me—the last time I saw him with Iridan, he seemed to be controlling him."

Khalesh had been about to take another sip of tea, but halted mid-sip. "How do you mean?"

"He was giving a kind of musical performance. I was there when he first woke—" Khalesh's eyes widened with speculation at this, but Vidarian plowed ahead— "and he was asking about his brother and sister. He didn't ask again for some time, until that day. It was strange—he heard a word, and seemed to wake up from a dream."

"What you're describing sounds like an inhibition geis," Khalesh said, caterpillar-thick eyebrows drawn down with worry. "By the northern guild, they're forbidden altogether, and by the southern, strictly avoided except in the direst circumstances—such as an automaton going mad."

"That can happen?" Vidarian gripped his glass, then deliberately relaxed his hands. He had not thought of the possibility of Iridan losing sanity, and now that he did, he imagined the terrible strength of that metal body bent against a human. A terrifying thought.

"Very rarely, thus the application of inhibition geasa was tightly controlled in my forefathers' day. I can only think of a handful of recorded uses."

"I have to confess," Vidarian said, "I came here for information of a rather different sort. I wanted to know if you, or anyone you know, would be capable of crafting a body like Iridan's."

He expected thoughtfulness, but Khalesh homed immediately in on the oddness of his request. "A body."

"I have a—a soul for it already." Vidarian reached into his coat pocket and brought out a supple leather pouch. He untied the strips of leather holding it shut, and emptied its contents into his palm—a sun ruby, the empty companion to the one that now contained Ruby. Gently he passed it across the table to Khalesh, who accepted it and peered closely.

"This is a prism key." He held it out to the light of the fire, and it brightened. "Finely made. A very complicated kind of opening device."

"You recognize it? My friend's mind has been trapped inside one of these—"

"You bound a prism key to a human mind?" Khalesh had been turning the stone between his fingertips, but now he stopped, powerful jaw slack as he looked at Vidarian.

Vidarian couldn't bring himself to answer, and Khalesh carefully set down his glass and stood. He went to one of the tall bookcases and extracted a heavy, leather-bound volume. Still balancing the sun ruby in his left hand, he thumbed through it, then returned it and pulled another. He repeated this for four more volumes, then finally seemed to find what he was looking for—a particularly old book, its metal cover spotted with mineral residue—and returned to his chair.

Pushing aside the tea service with a massive forearm, Khalesh set the book down and began flipping through pages, calluses on his hands brushing through them so quickly that he seemed to move them with his thoughts alone. "It shouldn't be possible . . ." He murmured unhappily to himself as he pored, sometimes stopping to read individual pages, but more often flipping through entire sections. "Here . . . yes." He traced a passage with his fingertip. "An elementalist who wields multiple polar elements could do this in theory. The binding occurs *between* the elements . . ." His eyes came up, his words slowed. "And then the subject must die."

"That—is a fair description of what happened." Vidarian closed his eyes, then rubbed them with his thumb and forefinger. The binding—foolishly, he'd agreed to bind the gem to Ruby the way that Endera had bound the sun emerald to him. Her words came back to him across what seemed an eternity: *In order to bind that stone to your life, I had to bind some of your life—just a little part—to the stone.*

And so he had bound Ruby's life to the prism key. A chill crept through him—did this also mean that, should he die, part of him would persist in the sun emerald? Was it also a prism key, or something else entirely? He'd given the stone to An'du . . .

"I'm sorry to say that what you've done is not advisable at all," Khalesh was saying, clearly torn between sympathy and professional outrage. A slow dread had been congealing in Vidarian's stomach as Khalesh spoke, and now it was bubbling over.

"Could a body like Iridan's be made for her?" he asked softly.

"It could, but it would be—well, it could be disastrous." Khalesh flipped the book shut, boring urgently into Vidarian's eyes with his own. "You have no idea how much of her made it into the stone. By its size, it's not possible that it was all of her. And you don't know what was already in the stone when she was put in there."

At this Vidarian looked up, and Khalesh's jaw firmed.

"You've seen evidence already. Knowledge she shouldn't have, things she says outside of her own control and consciousness." Miserably Vidarian nodded, and Khalesh leaned forward, his voice low with sympathy. "Whatever is in that stone, my friend, and however much it seems to be this woman you know—it isn't. Not all of it. It's a mirage, an echo—and possibly a dangerous one."

"She's my friend," was all that Vidarian could say, knowing that the words were a child's.

"If she was," Khalesh said firmly, "what you owe her is to protect her—and those you care about—from what she has become."

CHAPTER NINETEEN

SHADOWS

Vidarian left Khalesh's home that evening in a haze of shock. He'd promised to bring the Animator more information as soon as he could obtain it. If he could, he'd bring Khalesh to the palace himself—if there would be a way of getting him there without Oneira's knowledge.

He'd promised Iridan a report, and so when he arrived back at the palace—long after dark, the place was a moonglow fantasia of multicolored elemental lights—he went straight to the Arboretum.

Whenever it was that Iridan slept, it didn't seem to be by night. The automaton sat at a small wrought-iron table in the main atrium, poring through one of his many books.

Sitting across from him, revealed too late to allow a hasty retreat, was Justinian. He stood as Vidarian drew near. "Ah, Vidarian!" He smiled for all the world as if they were old and dear friends. "I had hoped to see you. Iridan said you would be paying a visit."

"I thought that I might," Vidarian said, carefully choosing his words. He intended not to let on that he even knew of the existence of the Animator's Guild.

Justinian turned toward Iridan. "My friend, would you mind terribly leaving us for a bit?"

"*I'm quite interested in what the good Captain has to say,*" Iridan said. It was too genteel to be an argument, which the automaton surely intended.

"Well, he can deliver it to me, and I can deliver it to you. You look a bit peaked—perhaps you should rest for the night?" With that, Justinian placed a gloved hand on Iridan's shoulder.

Iridan's eyes dimmed, and his arms lost their tension. Vidarian managed not to gasp, but inhaled sharply. Justinian only smiled, and Vidarian relaxed;

let him think that Vidarian was merely impressed by his exertion of control. He wanted to fight him, to destroy whatever it was that Justinian was using to control Iridan, but showing his hand now would only jeopardize them both.

"He'll sleep for some hours. Perhaps we should leave him?" Without waiting for an answer, Justinian turned then, walking down the corridor and disappearing through an archway obscured by thin, willowy vines that hung from floor to ceiling. Vidarian followed, brushing through the plants, and found himself in another hallway, a dark one, that sloped gently downward to another vine-covered arch and one of the Arboretum's many subterranean chambers. He emerged shortly into a brightly lit room with polished stone walls, and it took several moments for his eyes to adjust to the light.

Justinian stood over a sand table—the most expensive and detailed Vidarian had ever seen. Terrain was picked out in different colors of sand, and landmarks, even forests, had been re-created in miniature. As he watched, Justinian passed his hand over the table, and some of the sand shifted, rearranging itself. A narrow "river" of it carried cavalry markers toward an opposing force.

Vidarian could not sense the power that Justinian used directly, but it hummed in his bones. Earth magic.

When he looked back up, Justinian was leering at him, an unpleasant expression that may not have been intentional. A long, jagged cut marred the left side of the man's otherwise lined but perfect face, distorting his smile into something that could not appear anything other than sinister. "So shocked, are you, Vidarian?" he said. A genuine sneer curled the corner of his lip. "Your friends in the priestesshood are no longer the only keepers of elemental power. A little earth magic has always run in my family." He turned back toward the sand table and beckoned Vidarian closer. "And like so many things," he said softly, "it can be manipulated."

At this distance Vidarian could see that he wore gloves not unlike the ones Khalesh had worn, though these were no workman's garment. The gems set into them were tiny and subtle, and tuned to Justinian's life energy; they glowed and dimmed with his thoughts.

Try as he might otherwise, Vidarian's eyes kept trailing back to the cut on Justinian's face, and he noticed. "Women," he said, and the sneer was back redoubled, though he tried to cover it with a conspiratorial grin. "Would you know broken ceramic has quite a keen cutting edge? I think the Qui have been using it for weaponry for some time . . ." Not much could have brought Vidarian to pity Oneira, but Justinian's derision came close.

"At least you've come out of hiding, then," Vidarian said.

"I hadn't much choice, had I?" Justinian chuckled. "The emperor is quite put out."

"You lied to all of them," Vidarian said. "They were genuinely grieving."

"You must stop pretending to be so naive, my boy." There was just a hair too much flatness in Justinian's voice. "You'll have me wondering whether you can do what must be done."

"I'll not be tasked by anyone," Vidarian said. "Much less your Company."

"Of course, of course." Justinian picked up one of the figures from the sand table, a carved Sky Knight. "And yet you are here at the bequest of the emperor."

"As are you," Vidarian said, probably too sharply.

But again Justinian only smiled. "That's where you're wrong." He put the knight back in its place on the sand. "This is the beauty of commerce. Commerce recognizes all lines of force, and bows only to the greatest among them. Commerce is not bound by tradition or mindless loyalty."

"If you're suggesting that my loyalty to the emperor is mindless—"

Justinian raised a placating hand. "The furthest from it. I am suggesting that balances of power change. Kingdoms and empires come and go." He looked closely at Vidarian. "Power changes hands."

Unsure what Justinian was implying, and uncomfortable with many possible variations, Vidarian turned his attention to the sand table. The battle it displayed appeared to be north of Isrinvale, a coastal front. "And yet the Company itself expends resources even on nations not our own, and for no foreseeable profit." An array of little skyship and infantry markers had been painted red, as had the supply ships coming from the southern island nation of Rikan.

Justinian shrugged. "The Rikani are quite excellent at killing Qui. Much practice, you see."

"So it's about efficiency?" Vidarian asked. "Dispatching the enemies of the Alorean empire?"

Now the look that Justinian turned on him was measured. He was silent for several long moments. "My colleagues—the young Partners—would think this foolishness, but I believe that the future health of the Company depends upon cultivating relationships with the new brokers of power in this changed world of ours. People," he paused, reaching out to knock over a handful of the cavalry figures, leaving a blue-marked one standing. "Like you. And I believe that the way to earn your trust is to give you information, which so many of your other allies have denied you."

The mark hit home, and Vidarian tried not to show it. The tension of the conversation was pulling him apart, and he felt a sudden bone-deep exhaustion at all of it—the palace, the Company. The world.

"I know you to be a man of integrity," Justinian said slowly. "And therefore trustworthy with such information, which the Company has gone to great lengths to obtain." He walked away from the sand table then and toward a low bench upon which was sitting a silver tray with a wine bottle and two tall glass flutes. He poured a delicate blue ice wine into each, and presented one flute to Vidarian before sipping delicately at his own. Then he took a seat on the bench, quaffed the rest of the glass in a single gulp, and poured himself a second. "Some years ago," he began, "in its ongoing study of the patterns of inheritance in elemental magic, the Company came across a rather startling finding." He drank again, a long draw. "Over the centuries there have been many changes to the dynamics of inherited magic, but one consistency: as sentient populations—humans, gryphons, humanoid shapechangers—increase, inherited magic decreases. As I've told you, the Company has always been interested in—a pruned world. Nicely trimmed. More to go around." Justinian's eyes came up, and this time they seemed almost tired. He rolled the ice wine around in the flute. "And therefore . . . ?"

"The Company benefits from any war," Vidarian said, not believing it could be possible even as the words left his mouth. "It benefits from any large-scale loss of life that does not directly impact the Partners." It was impossible. "But—you're not suggesting that the Company was involved in *starting* the war."

"Come now, Vidarian," Justinian said softly. "You don't think the Qui just up and decided to cross that border all on their own? We've had advisors at Emperor Ziao's court for decades."

The room seemed to spin, and he closed his eyes, which made the effect worse. He opened them again and looked at the ceiling. When he recovered himself, he could barely look at Justinian. A basic instinct said to kill him, to stop anyone who could seek such an insane path before they could do more damage. But to do so would be to cut off his only reliable source of the Company's true motives. "And all this, for . . . what?"

"For future generations," Justinian said softly. "A smaller population—a larger, more thriving world. A world organized by strength of elemental magic."

"Why would you trust me with this? What if I go to the emperor?" Vidarian said, his mouth dry as dust.

To his shock and annoyance, Justinian laughed. "And tell him what? That this war he's now embroiled in is sheer folly? That he has sent his own people to die for no proper cause? Do you think even the great Lirien Aslaire can hear that message? And then what?"

"I trust him with his own empire," Vidarian said. "With my empire, my home. For centuries his family has been entrusted with this."

"Ah, but Vidarian," Justinian said, raising his glass. "You are power. You are our future."

Justinian seemed unsurprised when Vidarian left the Arboretum without another word. He hadn't touched the ice wine, but nonetheless felt drunk on his feet. He staggered back to his rooms, nearly tripping over Rai, who had stretched himself just inside the door, stripped off his clothes in a half-aware haze, and fell into the bed.

But in spite of the exhaustion that sent his head into a kind of perpetual whirling dervish, sleep would not take him. Rai, cat-shaped, came to lay his massive head on the corner of the bed, and Vidarian reached over to scratch between his ears. Rai's head started to rattle, and he jerked his hand back with surprise; it stopped, and he realized: he was purring. The effect on an animal with thorn-spines the length of one's forearm was rather striking. When his heart calmed back down he resumed scratching again, and the purring returned. He shifted and rested his head in the crook of his free arm.

When he opened his eyes again, the angle of the moonlight coming cool through the window had changed. And there was a presence, a sense in the air like the moment before lightning. Rai's purring had turned to a low, menacing growl.

A pair of slender legs, folded neatly at the knee, faded into view feetfirst. On the feet were pointed shoes of silvery metal, and the rest of the legs, disembodied, flowed upward from them.

"Poor, poor Vidarian," a voice echoed. "Does he need someone eviscerated?"

"Go away," he mumbled.

"No," she twinkled. "But thank you for asking." Now all of the Starhunter was there, wearing a feathered hat and a strapless dress made out of some silver satiny material that stretched with her movements. To Vidarian's annoyance, Rai had stopped growling, and came over to rest his head in the Starhunter's lap. She cooed at him and his tail flicked happily.

"The Company wants to kill millions of people. Don't you give a damn about that?"

She blinked pupilless starscape eyes. "You weren't here before the millions got here. It wasn't so bad. I can see where they're coming from."

Ice seeped through his veins, and he started to choke on an answer.

"On the other hand," she tapped her lips with a fingertip. "Mass death is such a downer. Total buzzkill, like imagining your grandma naked." Her face turned into his grandmother's face, and her dress started to disappear.

Vidarian realized she was toying with him, first with strange words and then the clothes. He turned over and pressed his face into the pillow.

"Oh, don't be boring," she sighed, and bounced restlessly off the bed. Vidarian turned and opened one eye. Rai had followed her, tail swishing, and she pounced, turning into a cat that was a purple copy of him. At first Rai was startled, but then fell into the game.

"Rai," Vidarian barked, and the cat sat, tail curling contritely around his feet.

"It's getting a little tedious around here," the Starhunter said. "I think you should leave."

And then she was gone.

⌇⌇⌇

A soft *clink!* against the window glass woke Vidarian from dark dreams.

Rai was growling again, and this time the spines along his back lifted. Vidarian threw back the covers and slid out of bed.

Someone had broken the latch and was climbing through the window.

There was no time to get to his sword. Vidarian summoned up fire, riding out its unruly objections and sharpening it into a spear of energy.

The figure wore a long black cape, and she pulled back its hood as soon as she landed on the carpeted floor.

It was Ariadel.

For a moment he was sure it was the Starhunter come back to torture him, but even the Starhunter could not have devised this particular incarnation. As she straightened, fixing him with a look that was hard and pained at once, the shadows wrapped around the unmistakable swell of her stomach.

"You're—" he breathed.

"I tried to tell you," she said.

Vidarian learned a new definition of miserable as he remembered the last time they'd spoken. "*We should talk*," she'd said—and then he'd flown off to the Imperial City. With Calphille.

The world shifted under his feet. This changed everything. Didn't it? Why was she standing so far from him, unmoving?

There was something different in her. Something harder, sharper. But even that thought brought with it the realization that they knew so little of each other. A year ago he had not known her name or that she existed. And now—

Circumstance had brought them together. A romantic might say "destiny." But it was romance in the cruelest sort, of elemental forces and lines of power that had pushed them to seek solace in each other. In a peaceful world, would they even have found each other?

But a child—the word itself sent his thoughts reeling—it changed everything. The future shifted in front of him. And everything about this—the Imperial City, the Company, Ariadel sneaking through the night to climb through his window—seemed so much more real, and completely mad, all at the same time.

"You don't have to worry about me," Ariadel said at last, breaking open his thoughts. There was a distant hurt in her words, almost an accusation, but it lurked beneath miles of ice. "But I need your help. That's why I'm here."

A thousand things vied for his voice, filling his mind. Where had she been? Would she forgive him? And—she was here for his help? Had she even missed him? Surely if they were to raise a child—

A skittering on her shoulder made him flinch backward instinctively, interrupting his thoughts. It was the little golden spider. It crawled out from beneath Ariadel's hair, then leaped off her collarbone, spinning a thread of web as it fell to slow its descent.

Halfway to the floor, it changed shape.

No longer ash-grey, the kitten had grown into an elegant young cat with flame-colored fur. Its body was striped with cream, and its face was maned almost like a lion. It snaked around Vidarian's feet, then strode fearlessly up to press its nose against Rai's.

"Raven missed you," Ariadel said softly.

Vidarian pressed her hands between his. "How did you get here?"

"It's complicated," she said, and turned. The chill dismissal stopped him from pressing further. "Who is this?"

"His name is Rai. He's a shapechanger from the forest near the gate." He knew he was rambling, relieved at having something clear to say in the face of all it seemed he couldn't. Rai had lain on the floor to keep his head more politely near the smaller cat's. "What's happened? Is everyone all right?"

She looked at him, searching, then sighed. "They've managed to keep it a secret from the cities."

"Keep what a secret?"

In answer, she pulled a gemstone from a pocket of the dark cape and tapped its surface. To his astonishment, a cloud of mist emerged from it, and within were images. There was no sound, but there needn't be—a long line of raggedly clad people, black-haired and dark of eye, were being shepherded into a crudely constructed fort of some kind. Old men and young, women and children, all of Qui descent.

"What is this?" he said, distracted momentarily from what she so clearly did not want to discuss. "Where is it?"

"In the south," she said. "Near Astralaar. The desert."

"Here?" Vidarian said, so sharply that both cats looked up at him. "In Alorea?"

"My father sent word that my mother had contacted him using a far-speaking device. They'd come for her and were taking her to the desert along with all of the other Qui in the village where she was staying. They said it was for her protection, but she knew it wasn't." Her eyes glittered and her voice hardened. "We've been able to stop them rounding up more—disrupting the caravans, helping them escape. But my mother is still missing."

"The saboteurs . . ." His blood went cold again. All of Val Imris had its eyes on the war. The "Qui dissidents" within Alorea weren't dissidents at all . . .

Ariadel laughed coldly and without humor. "That's what they're calling us? The old and the young are dying. There aren't enough resources to supply the front, much less these afterthoughts. And they keep bringing in more. Trying, anyway."

The image that came into his mind, of Ariadel's people loaded onto carts and wheeled to one of these makeshift cities, woke realization with a pang. "They're consolidating people. Moving entire groups into the same place. Sorting them." He looked at her. "This is the Company's doing."

"Come with me," she said. "Help me undo this."

It was as if his legs were frozen beneath him. He wanted to go; to throw himself after her and fight the problem in the most honest way possible, by assaulting it, bringing it down by force. To win her back with his passion. But something pulled him in another direction. The complex lacework of the palace politics told him that a smaller movement from a place of greater leverage could have much more effect.

"The emperor must not know about this," he said. "If I can talk to him—"

Darkness fell over Ariadel's expression like a tide of shadow. Her voice was harsh and quiet. "*If* he doesn't know about this, which I very much doubt, then he will not have the power to correct it, not from within this web."

"You don't know him—"

Her eyes filled with tears. "They told me I was wrong to come here. I don't know you," she whispered. She murmured something else to the gem at her wrist, and a hole in the world opened beside her. Vidarian cried out, assaulted by memories of the Great Gate—but beyond it wasn't a spread of universes, a nothingness speckled with galaxies—instead, there was land, somewhere where the sun was high in the sky. Five gryphons, three of them species he did not recognize, held the portal open. Ariadel picked up Raven, stepped through it, and was gone.

The portal vanished after her, leaving emptiness in its wake.

CHAPTER TWENTY

ONE TOLERABLE PRICE

idarian woke just as dawn was beginning to filter in through his window. For a moment he wondered if it had all been a nightmare—but the window was still open, its latch hanging broken, and Rai was toying with a long purple plume that must have fallen from the Starhunter's ridiculous hat.

His entire body burned with complaint, but he forced himself out of bed. The emperor was an early riser, and he hoped to catch him before the day's business began. Although he hadn't yet used the summoning bell, one of the maids had shown it to him on his first day in the palace, and he rang it now. A soft chime rang in his room, and if it was functioning properly, a louder one would ring in the page room.

A boy came knocking on the door within moments; the bell relay must have been closer than he thought. It was not Brannon, but a smaller mouse-haired boy, and for a moment Vidarian missed seeing Bran's familiar face. He asked for breakfast and *kava* after realizing he was staring with exhaustion.

The boy left, and Vidarian stumbled to the water chamber to draw a bath. He pulled the chains for hot and cold water, then sank down next to the tub, tilting his head back against the cool marble surface and listening to the soft roar of water against the stone. The palace's sophisticated water-channeling system was still novel—he well remembered arduous water-carrying for his mother's baths as a child—but his thoughts remained on the coming conversation with Lirien.

Part of him still had trouble believing Ariadel had been in his room only hours ago. Gryphons had opened the portal that brought her here, which must have been related to the Great Gate, but somehow it was moveable, and trained not just between worlds but within them. The amount of energy it had taken felt enormous, which was somewhat reassuring; likely only the gryphons retained the technique of creating them. And, given that she had had to climb through the window, their targeting must not be very accurate.

And Ariadel—was she pregnant?

The sudden returning memory of her stomach silhouetted against the window made his heart pound and adrenaline climb through his blood. He was grateful to be on the floor already, even as he knew that he would have to keep the thought of a child far from his conscious thoughts to do what he must. It was easier thought than done, and he allowed himself a few moments of reaction—astonishment, terror, wonder, an odd thing that he thought was gratitude or joy, followed immediately by spine-crushing anxiety. For the first time in a very long time, he missed his mother with fresh sharpness, as he thought of how overjoyed she would have been, and how she would have told him, no matter how dark the world seemed, that new life was to be celebrated and treasured.

The only thing that was certain was his galvanizing drive to protect her and the child, and to earn her forgiveness if he could. Part of him screamed to be demanding the portal technology from Thalnarra and Altair and finding Ariadel however he must, but the steadiness he had earned painfully from years at sea knew that, if these prison cities were what she claimed they were, the greatest hope of rescuing her mother—and therefore his responsibility— lay with the emperor.

The adrenaline had the side effect of temporarily beating back the exhaustion, and so he stood, stripped off sweat-soaked underclothing, and stepped into the bath. The hot water was a welcome shock, and he plunged down under the surface. He held himself there until his chest ached, then rose again, gasping. The air, though thick and humid in the heat of the water chamber, felt new and invigorating.

By the time he left the tub, rubbed himself dry, and dressed, a breakfast tray was waiting with his requested large pot of *kava*. Though he usually limited himself to a single cup in the morning, today he had three, and ate the piping hot breakfast quickly. Rai was more meticulous with his plate of meat (and Vidarian still gave over his toast), and was still eating when Vidarian strode out into the quiet hallway.

His time in the palace had at least earned him a modicum of trust: when he asked a passing steward where the emperor was, she replied promptly and without suspicion. He was in the Relay Room receiving the day's news. Vidarian made his way there quickly, glad that he wouldn't be interrupting a public audience.

Luck, in this, was further with him. Just as he entered the Relay Room, the chief relay officer was finishing his report. Accompanying him, to Vidarian's surprise, was Malloray, who smiled a quick greeting before returning to a professional stoicism.

"A good morning to you, Vidarian," the emperor said, once the officer had bowed himself out. Vidarian gestured quickly for Malloray to stay. The man looked confused, but nodded, murmured a few words to his commander, and hovered near the door. The emperor was looking at Vidarian with curiosity, surprised to see him so early.

"Good morning, your majesty. I apologize for interrupting—" Lirien waved off his apology. "But I have . . . rather urgent . . . news."

For a moment no one answered, and Vidarian could feel the ears of all the relay officers—though they remained studiously bent over their message spheres—straining to listen. For his part, the emperor looked at Vidarian for a long moment, then nodded. "Come with me," he said, and left the room.

Two imperial guards moved before the emperor like water, holding doors and remaining ever near. Malloray had fallen in with them, earning Vidarian's smile of gratitude. The emperor did not seem to visibly direct the guards, but somehow they stayed with him, noiselessly following his every move.

Vidarian expected an audience chamber, but instead they wove even deeper into the palace than he had ever been before, coming at last upon a suite of rooms attended by less ornate stewards than appeared elsewhere in the palace. There was an air of business, aided largely by the adjacent small chambers filled with men and women bent over calculation beads.

Lirien led them to a large room near the rear, and, after the guards opened the large carved double doors before them, turned, and said, "Leave us."

The guards paused for a moment, all that betrayed their unfamiliarity with the situation, but quickly bowed and took up posts outside the room. Then the emperor led Vidarian and Malloray inside and shut the door. Malloray, for his part, was white as a sheet, Vidarian noted guiltily; for all he knew, Malloray had never even seen the emperor before, and now was closeted in a private strategy chamber with him.

The room was plush with creature comforts—ornate silk rugs, dark-varnished wood, overstuffed tapestry-upholstered chairs—and resplendent in red, black, and gold. For all its opulence, though, it was a room with a purpose, as evidenced by the tall stacks of parchment atop the heavy, claw-footed desk, and the wear marks on the floor and chairs.

"Thank you for seeing me so quickly," Vidarian said, and suddenly felt overwhelmed. He had half expected not to be able to find the emperor at all, and now struggled for words.

"I can see you're quite upset," Lirien said, concern lowering his eyebrows. "And you look half-dead with exhaustion."

"I've—had quite the couple of days," Vidarian admitted.

"Well, have a seat," the emperor said, gesturing them to a circle of four armchairs arranged around a small, lacquered table. And then, to Vidarian's surprise and Malloray's open gawking, the emperor himself proceeded to turn over three cut crystal glasses from a stack atop a polished liquor cabinet and pour generous helpings of a translucent amber liquid into them. He handed one to Vidarian, who took it, and held one out to Malloray, who tried not to accept.

"You're not fooling anyone," Lirien smiled at him, pressing the glass firmly into his palm. "And it's quite all right." Malloray relented, and the emperor then picked up his own glass and settled into one of the chairs.

Vidarian and Malloray took their seats awkwardly, and the emperor raised his glass, a toast and a prompt. Casting an encouraging look at Malloray, Vidarian took a drink, and felt his own eyes widen involuntarily at the strength of the liquor. He cleared his throat, and raised his glass a second time to the emperor, blinking to clear his watering eyes. "I was visited last night in my room," Vidarian began, having decided to tell the story backwards. He described Ariadel's appearance, her condition, what she had said, and finally her exit, including the strange portal magic that had taken her. He knew that he should be drilling immediately to Justinian's assertions about the Company's strategy, but also knew he would not be able to put Ariadel's concerns from his mind until he heard an answer directly from Lirien.

As he spoke, the emperor's expression grew grave, and beyond grave, into something Vidarian feared might be dangerous. Gone was his politic ease, and now he looked sharply at Malloray. "You trust this man?"

"With my life," Vidarian answered immediately, and the emperor nodded, then sighed.

"Even still, I should not," Lirien said, and drained his glass. When he looked back at Vidarian, his eyes were tired. "What she told you may be true," he began, and Vidarian's blood went to ice. "But not in the way she describes. The Court of Directors, and the Alorean Import Company, as a branch of their actions to support the war effort, have taken on the task of building and maintaining prisoner of war camps for captured Qui."

"From her descriptions, and what I saw, these were not soldiers, your majesty," Vidarian said, working to keep his tone even. "They were Alorean citizens. Women and children."

Lirien looked up, a pained grimace twisting his face. "Could she have been mistaken?"

"I saw the images with my own eyes, your majesty. I know of no way such a thing could be fabricated to such quality."

"It is possible," Lirien said heavily, "that they may have become overzealous in their prisoner selection." He rubbed his eyebrows for a moment. "In truth I had feared as much with their latest report—but the war has required my full attention." At Vidarian's silence, he added, "It is no excuse."

"Now that you know about it, can you stop it?" Vidarian asked. His head began to swim when the emperor didn't immediately answer. "There's more," he said, and described, as close to the exact words as he could, everything Justinian had told him. That the Company actively desired the deaths of Qui and Alorean soldiers alike—and likely more, all across Andovar. That they had been collecting and separating knowledge for centuries, in preparation for a new kind of world-governing body that did not include the survival of the Alorean Empire, or Qui, as they currently existed.

As he spoke, Lirien stood and returned to the liquor cabinet with his glass. He paused there, then took the entire crystal decanter and brought it back to the table, pouring for himself and Vidarian. Malloray, despite instruction, had still not touched his drink, but as Vidarian continued his explanation he took a healthy swallow.

When he finished speaking, Vidarian waited. Lirien said nothing, and in fact stared into his glass, his eyes far away, but his countenance dark. At last he stood, setting down his glass without having taken a second drink. For a moment his hand lingered on the crystal, so tight Vidarian feared he would break it—but then he let go. He went to the desk, beginning to rifle through the stacks of parchment. His easy navigation of the stacks made Vidarian suddenly realize that this must be his personal office.

At length the emperor returned to the table, sitting and dropping a large, leather-bound book in front of Vidarian. A page was marked with a bit of red ribbon. At Lirien's gesture, Vidarian exchanged his glass for the book, and opened it to the marked page.

It was a ledger, a massive one. Tiny script marked out expenses laid down in columns that ran down all of the pages.

With rare exception, the tallies were in a middle column, with credit markers. To the right of the marker was the symbol of the Alorean Import Company. The symbols ran down the page—and the page before it, and the page before that—like a row of ants. At first Vidarian wasn't sure what he was seeing—and then he saw the key indicating scale of currency, and nearly dropped the book.

"These are the imperial finances," Lirien said. "You can see that it isn't a good situation."

"This is impossible," Vidarian breathed.

"I only wish it were," the emperor said heavily, and now he picked up his glass again, though only to sip. "You can see that the debt begins with Qui's invasion of our southern border. Prior to that, I had been making headway on repaying it."

"Repaying it?" Vidarian looked up, then back down to the ledger, flipping through tens of pages at a time.

"I regret to say that the debt itself long precedes my birth," Lirien said, rolling the crystal glass between his palms. "And my father's, and my grandfather's. Alorea has carried debt to the Alorean Import Company since the last Sea War."

"I had no idea," was all Vidarian could manage.

"Few do. That is the only copy of that ledger in the empire's possession, and the Company certainly does not share their own records. The empire operates, even prospers, but you see why correction of their behavior at this point is—complex at best."

"But you see what they're doing? The Company benefits from this war! Not only does it accomplish their strategic objectives, it gives them more and more power over the empire itself." Vidarian's voice shook, and he tightened his grip on the ledger in an attempt to master himself.

"Believe me, Vidarian, war was the last thing I wanted. But Qui invaded. They started this."

"We can end it. Call for peace."

The look the emperor gave him was somewhere in between incredulity and disappointment. "After the blood they've shed? There can be no easy peace."

A quiet had spread through Vidarian, a resolve that came purely from the center of a mad storm. "Your majesty, you know that my loyalty and my family's loyalty to the Alorean Empire is absolute. We have served you for generations." He took a breath. "But what's here," he tapped the book. "Is not our empire. If the Company can wage war, and stop you from policing even within your own borders, this is no longer the Alorean Empire."

"Careful, Vidarian," Lirien said, and the hard emotion in his eyes said he was straining to remain Vidarian's friend. "You tread close to treason."

"It is not, your majesty," Vidarian said, voice taut with diffidence. He turned to Malloray. "My friend, will you check to ensure our privacy?" Malloray blinked, and started to rise, but Vidarian lifted a hand. He stopped, Vidarian nodded slowly, and then he understood, taking his seat again. His eyes drifted shut for several moments, and Vidarian waited.

"None listen," Malloray said, opening his eyes again. "And I have set some—precautions—that will warn us if they should try."

Vidarian thanked him solemnly, then turned back to the emperor. He hesitated, weighing the look on Lirien's face, the soul-deep tiredness, the man on the edge of wielding an authority he did not want to wield. "Your majesty, I think you need to leave the Imperial City."

Lirien stiffened, not quite jumping, but jerking his head upward in surprise. He squinted, lips pursed, obviously waiting for Vidarian to say he was joking and present him with the real plan. When he realized no such explanation was coming, he reddened, slightly. Elegantly. "No emperor in a thousand years—"

That wasn't entirely true, but now was not the moment to correct him. "You wouldn't be retreating," Vidarian insisted. "The Company is singularly business-minded. They do not benefit from an outright abdication of your throne." At the word *abdication* Lirien's face flushed again and Vidarian hurried on. "But they must be reminded of your value if you are to reassert your bargaining position—and regain control over your empire and people." At this last he allowed a bit of hardness to creep into his voice. If his father had known that his own emperor had indebted himself to the Alorean Import Company . . .

"The goddesses know I have lost my leverage here," the emperor said, at once on the edge of despair and with a father's regret.

"Come with us, then, your majesty, and negotiate from outside the city. Couch it as a morale tour for your people."

Lirien snorted, looked into his glass, and took another drink. "With you, is it?" His sad smile, pained and friendly, took any sting from the words.

"We'll have the gryphon clans, the fire ones at least, and the loyal remnants of the Sky Knights."

"What you propose is very likely suicide," Lirien said. Then he sighed, and drained his glass again. "But it is an honorable death. And you are correct." The defeat in his voice was excruciating. "The empire has not been truly an empire in my lifetime. Perhaps this is its chance to be so again, if only for a moment." He set his glass on the table, and Vidarian could feel him gathering strength. "A royal voyage. We will take the *Empress Cimeria*."

"I'm afraid we can't take that ship, your majesty," Vidarian said. "Who knows what the Company will have equipped it with. But we should send it away. Perhaps to Rikan?"

"A ruse," Lirien said.

"Malloray, can you send a message to the chief steward, and tell him to prepare the *Empress Cimeria* for an imperial flight to Rikan? And—the *Luminous*, for a reconnaissance flight, destination not to be disclosed."

Malloray blinked. "It's done," he said.

"Thank you, my friend."

"And we will bring that bloody automaton," Lirien said, and the growl that crept into his voice now, evoking the lion for which he was named, made the hair on the back of Vidarian's neck rise. "If Justinian wants him, he shall not have him." Now was also not the time to inform him that he so precisely echoed Oneira's hurt words. For a moment, Vidarian felt a pang of sadness for Iridan, even if he could not trust him: torn between one manipulating hand and the next, wanting only—so he said—to reunite with his brother and sister.

"I'll see to it myself," Vidarian said only.

"I hope you know what you're doing, Captain," the emperor murmured.

CHAPTER TWENTY-ONE
A FIRE SPREADS

When Vidarian left the emperor's office, a single steward—a short, dark man who moved with a purpose that, in spite of what appeared to be duller livery, said he outranked the "front" palace stewards—filed in to speak with Lirien. Before Vidarian had even left the hallway, the man was jogging out, calling to three more of his staff. And by the time Vidarian reached the main palace, the east wing was a hive of activity.

Vidarian made a circuitous route, anxious to avoid even idle curiosity. He found his legs taking him automatically toward the skyship field north of the palace, and decided this was a plausible enough place to go. As he walked, he organized his thoughts. The memory of Ariadel still burned like a brand in his mind, but he convinced himself that every step he would take to fight for the empire was to fight for her, and for their child. There were several people whose aid he wished to call upon, and most could be reached from the *Luminous*'s relay room—but one must be convinced to leave the city.

A simmering impatience to put his plans into action crept through his body as he forced himself to nonchalantly stroll across the skyship field. He exchanged waves and greetings with the sailors and carpenters who moved continuously among the ships, and feigned surprise when he heard that the *Empress Cimeria* was being prepared for an imperial visit to allies in Rikan. After three passes around the field, during which he surreptitiously checked the preparations for the *Luminous*, he permitted himself escape.

Vidarian left the skyship field and jogged to the stables, where he asked for and obtained three horses. Beyond the palace gates, Val Imris was alive with activity even at this early hour, and he only dared urge his mount to a dignified trot lest he attract the attention of the constables.

He didn't remember Khalesh's home being so far from the palace, and expected to see the wooden sign with its gear-and-flame symbol around every turn. By the time he arrived on the correct street, he nearly missed the sign again, so many times had his hopes been raised and dashed. Without dismounting, he kneed his horse up the three slate steps to Khalesh's door—quite to the gelding's flattened-ears disapproval—and knocked.

If the big man was surprised to see Vidarian, horsed, at his door, he didn't show it. He did take a look to right and left, as he had the first time Vidarian had visited, but then cheerfully asked, "How can I help you today, Captain?"

"There's someone I'd like you to meet," Vidarian said.

Khalesh eyed the horses trailing behind Vidarian. "And I take it this someone is not within a day's ride of the city. I do have my own horse, you know."

Vidarian hadn't, but it was obvious. The little apartment where Khalesh lived was on the second story, up a flight of stairs that immediately followed the front door. Below it, evident now by the grassy scent of straw and grain, was a small stable. "I should have thought of that," he admitted. "But I'm on a rather tight schedule. Bring your horse, and your things; the horse can remain at the imperial stables."

"Remain?" Khalesh asked, his thick eyebrows lowering.

"Where we're going," Vidarian looked pointedly at the sky, "You won't need him."

The Animator looked at him, brow furrowed, then his eyes suddenly widened. "How much time?"

"Minutes," Vidarian said. The gelding pawed impatiently at the slate in unintended emphasis.

Khalesh nodded, then disappeared back into his house and shut the door.

Various clanks and crashes sounded from within, and Vidarian looked nervously up and down the street. What was Khalesh worried about his neighbors seeing or hearing?

Promised minutes later, the Animator was pushing open the half-rotted stable doors with a woven lead-line clamped between his teeth. A shaggy grey mare followed him, loaded with saddlebags full of books, and Khalesh had two more such thrown over his shoulders and under one arm. The other arm wrapped around a wrought-iron cage that contained the huge squawking bird Vidarian had passed by on his first visit. Only now, at this vantage, it was quite apparent that underneath its colorful feathers the bird was made out of metal and wire. Its eyes glowed orange.

"Rrawk?" the bird squawked, once the sunlight hit it and it noticed Vidarian. "Hello!"

Vidarian flinched back, spooking his horse. He wrestled it back to composure, and Khalesh apologized. "It's remarkable," Vidarian cut him off.

"She," Khalesh grunted, setting down the cage and belting the saddlebags onto the rear horse. He lifted the cage on top of the saddle and lashed it down, then, with easy strength and surprising agility for a man his size, lifted himself into the saddle of the middle animal.

Vidarian spared a few moments for him to settle onto the new mount, then kneed the gelding back toward the palace. He didn't dare trot with the mechanical bird fixed rather tenuously to that saddle, but he pushed to a fast, smooth walk.

"Are we fleeing the city?" Khalesh murmured.

"Not *fleeing*," Vidarian said, and the Animator made a sound of agreement indicating quite clearly that he did not believe at all.

"But we're leaving," Khalesh said. "Quickly."

"Yes. Is that a problem?"

"Not at all. I just should have watered my plants."

"Perhaps we can send a messenger," Vidarian said, before he realized that the big man was laughing at him.

At the palace, Vidarian gave their horses to the stableboys, instructing them to take Khalesh's belongings and stow them aboard the *Luminous*. Khalesh started to object to his bird being trusted to children, and Vidarian told them to find Brannon and bring him to the stables. In minutes, the boy was there, and Vidarian asked him to take the bird directly to the gryphons aboard the ship, and to trust it to no other.

"You'll find no better protectors at the palace," Vidarian assured Khalesh, when he still looked nervously after Brannon, who carried the cage awkwardly but carefully across the field.

One of the other stableboys—a sharp-looking child with dirty blond hair and an air of trouble about him—Vidarian pressed into service also, asking him to lead them to the Arboretum along the least traversed routes. When he understood the task, the boy first looked suspicious, but gradually lit up as Vidarian and Khalesh proved genuinely interested in his "secret" routes. Khalesh, for his part, had clearly never been to the palace before, and visibly relaxed when the stableboy's guidance brought them quickly away from polished marble and hammered gold.

They passed into narrow servants' hallways, and though they were not forbidden, it was as if they entered a secret world. There was an etiquette to the narrow passages, and fortunately the stableboy—who shyly had provided Elan as his name—knew all of the side-nooks and detours that would keep them out of the path of the rapidly moving stewards, maids, and pages that were the legitimate travelers.

When at last Elan opened a narrow stone door, Vidarian had no idea where they were—until he saw the cathedral-like arches of the Arboretum tree canopy. Twinkling through it was the light of the sun-sphere, and the purpose for the door—which Vidarian had not ever seen or knew existed—was right beside it: a divided little trough of several colors of birdseed.

Vidarian searched through his pockets for some token to give the boy, but had found nothing of appropriate value when Khalesh pulled a tiny metal sphere from a pouch at his waist. It was made of a lacework of brass laid over another lacework, and another beneath that in intricate succession—and when Khalesh breathed onto it, the interior spheres spun and shone with a pale blue light. Elan was old enough to insist it was far too lavish a gift, but young enough to accept it once Khalesh applied light insistence. The boy cradled it between his hands, bowed, and dashed back out the door to show off his prize.

The only sounds in the Arboretum were natural ones: the twitter of birds as they sang or battled over seed, the soft bubble of fountains. Vidarian didn't realize he was straining for any sign of Justinian's voice until he saw Khalesh anxiously watching him. He smiled an apology, then started down the path toward the main building where he'd first met Iridan, silently rehearsing what he would say if he encountered either Justinian or Oneira.

Iridan wasn't—quite—alone. Vidarian could detect a soft buzz of conversation, almost as though he were hearing a conversation in the next room, and in another language. When Iridan heard their approach, he turned, and suddenly his voice became coherent and audible. *"Good afternoon, Captain."*

Khalesh's soft gasp as he saw and heard Iridan was suddenly worth all of his ribbing and superior attitude. Vidarian had not told him *whom* he wanted him to meet, and Khalesh, large and fierce-minded though he was, now openly shook with reaction as he pulled a pair of amber-lensed spectacles from his pocket and fitted them to his face.

Iridan tilted his head. *"And who is your friend?"*

"This is Khalesh vel'Itai. He is the last Animator in Val Imris," Vidarian said.

To Vidarian's surprise, Iridan startled—or rather, that was the only way Vidarian could describe his reaction. His gems all flared in unison, and the mechanisms that slowly rotated in his chest picked up speed. He stood, and strode toward them to clasp Khalesh's hands in his own. *"Thank you, friend Vidarian, for bringing me such a treasure,"* he said, radiating gratitude and hope.

"Extraordinary," Khalesh murmured, hoarse.

Guiltily Vidarian realized Iridan must have assumed he'd brought Khalesh to assist in his search. Knowing that it was useless to try to deceive him, Vidarian said, "I must confess, Iridan, I brought him for another task beyond assisting in finding your sibs, though I hope he will help you with that also." Iridan's bright face turned toward him. "We have been summoned to another journey, this one to assist the emperor." He tried to put as much feeling into his words as he could, hoping Iridan would read his desire for discretion.

"I am at the emperor's service," Iridan said, an evenness to his cadence that said he understood. *"Have I time to pack a few things?"*

Guilt sparked in Vidarian's chest again when he felt his eyebrows lifting with surprise. Of course it would be possible for the automaton to have belongings. "We can spare a few minutes," he managed.

"*Thank you,*" he said, then turned and disappeared down a passageway leading deeper into the underground hall.

On the table, Ruby sat, still cradled in the jewelry box Oneira had provided for her. To either side of the sun ruby that housed her were a pair of small sapphires. Though he didn't need to, Vidarian went to the table and knelt beside it, putting the jewelry box at eye level. "Ruby?" he said.

* Oh, hello, Vidarian, * Ruby said.

Beside him, Khalesh stiffened. He'd clearly heard her, and realized what she was. Vidarian lifted a hand to stop him from speaking. "We're about to depart on another skyship journey."

* Enjoy yourselves. *

Vidarian blinked, a chill curling in his stomach. "I—had thought to bring you with us."

* I should stay here. Oneira is sourcing the parts for my body. *

Unease rolled off of Khalesh, and Vidarian was thankful for Iridan's absence. "I've spoken with an Animator," Vidarian said, turning again to shake his head at Khalesh lest the man think of speaking to Ruby directly. He took a deep breath when he turned back to Ruby. The last thing he'd wanted was to deliver Khalesh's pronouncement under the pressure of an imminent departure. "He . . . strongly believed that your . . . condition . . . should not be connected to an automaton body. That we should find another solution."

Ruby was quiet for a moment, and the hope sparked that she would listen. Then—

* What have I got to lose? * she said. The quiet, tired defeat in her voice cut deep, eroding Vidarian's resolve.

"Your sanity," he said, after reaching for and discarding many wrong words. "He said—"

* I have precious little sanity left, Vidarian, * she cut him off. * I'm afraid you'll have to take this journey without me. I know where it leads. *

Vidarian's hands tensed on the table and his thoughts raced. He hadn't even considered that Ruby would refuse to go. Yet—deeply aware that the walls most certainly had ears here in the Arboretum, he said, "I'm not sure when we'll be returning."

* Then Oneira shall have all the time she needs. *

Frustration and anger lit in Vidarian, combusting suddenly from tinder of anxiety and guilt. He reached for the box.

An answering anger leapt outward from the stone, stopping his hand. * Don't you dare. *

"You don't know her," Vidarian said, straining not to betray their mission, or Khalesh's trust. "This is the Alorean Import Company, Ruby."

* She's the best deal I have right now, Vidarian. * The heat of her anger was still vivid against his mind, but her words softened. * Go on your journey. When you return, maybe I'll be whole. *

Iridan returned, wearing a hooded black cloak that covered all but his hands and carrying a large basket covered with blue cloth, like an odd kind of picnic kit. "I am ready, Captain," the automaton said.

Slowly, Vidarian turned back toward the stairs. "Good-bye, then, Ruby," he said.

* Good-bye. *

⌇⌇⌇

They went directly to the *Luminous*. Out in the north field, they passed Calphille, still a tree and planted in the same spot on the field. Large white flowers covered the tree's branches. Vidarian slowed his pace as they approached, hoping she would speak. In the end, they passed quietly beneath her spreading branches, and she did not stir. In her silence Vidarian could only read rebuke, and could not bear to force the issue and risk starting another argument with one of the few people he trusted. Part of him screamed to stay, to help her as he should have from the moment they arrived, and hated every moment of speed that had so many times now stopped him from paying proper attention to those he valued most. *If you can hear me*, he thought at her, *you'll be all right. Lirien will come to his senses. You'll see.*

The skyship field was aswarm with activity. Ordinarily it would have taken days to prepare the ships, but imperial initiative could move time itself, it seemed. As promised, Thalnarra and Altair had been summoned, and were supervising the building of large makeshift nests on the forecastle deck with Brannon, Isri, Tepeki, and Khalesh's mechanical bird. Vidarian approached them and made introductions; Khalesh fawned over both the gryphons and his bird, and thanked Brannon for his attentiveness.

In a black mood from the argument with Ruby—a simmering heat that masked his deep worry and sadness poorly—Vidarian excused himself, making some prevarication about checking the hold. As he turned, he met another black-hooded face—the third on the ship, after Isri and Iridan.

The eyes within were familiar, but it took several moments to make sense of the rest. "Lir—" he began, before he could stop himself.

The emperor smiled and raised a finger to his lips. "Renard is a wizard, is he not?"

At that moment, a swell of sound from below turned Vidarian's head toward the *Empress Cimeria*. A man in the emperor's gleaming black satin robes was ascending the gangplank, surrounded by attendants. "He is," Vidarian agreed.

"Shall we adjourn to the relay chamber for the launch?" the emperor said.

Vidarian started, then nodded. He would never become used to being aboard a ship and not being at its command—even as his life aboard the *Empress Quest* now seemed more than a lifetime away.

Lirien was correct, though, that their place was in the room equipped with relay spheres. Malloray was there awaiting his orders, as Vidarian had left word that as soon as the *Luminous* launched he was to begin contacting allies. The emperor took a seat at the table, and Vidarian followed suit, picking a chair between the three other bespectacled relay officers that stared intently into the relay sphere at the center of the room.

"I was able to make contact, sir," Malloray said, and the way he said "sir" was an obscure comfort, a decades-long familiarity. "You were right, she does seem to have a relay sphere of her own." Malloray handed him a pair of the now-familiar blue-lensed spectacles.

Vidarian fitted the spectacles to his face, and the world turned blue. It also changed in height and depth, in floor and furnishing.

To his surprise, the room that he saw was not in Kara'zul, but the fire tower in Val Harlon. Less surprising was the burgundy-robed figure that sat in the room, picking up blue-lensed spectacles while he watched. "Endera. It's been quite some time."

"It has indeed, Captain. You've made some new friends."

"I have need of old ones, also." Mere months ago Vidarian would have choked on his beer to hear that he would refer to Endera as an "old friend," and yet there was no denying now that he felt a flush of warm relief at seeing her. Dancing carefully around his words, he told her that they had a relay ship, that he was in Val Imris, and that he and the gryphons required safe harbor for some very precious cargo.

"Come to Val Harlon. The Fire Council—"

What she said next vanished in a buzz of sound, and the world went black. Across the table, Malloray cursed, and started barking orders to the other relay officers.

The blue world returned, but Malloray's orders only increased in volume and intensity.

And the room they looked in on was not Val Harlon. The ground shifted beneath Vidarian's feet, and part of him was aware that it was the *Luminous*, taking off and gaining altitude.

Justinian had had a new mask made. In basic shape it resembled his first mask, but its ornamentation, lavish with gold filigree and gems, suggested a much more open statement of station.

"I believe you have something that belongs to me, Captain," Justinian said.

"The automaton belongs to the empire," Lirien said, and Vidarian's pulse quickened at the steel in his voice.

To his astonishment, and Lirien's fury, Justinian did not answer him.

"This is a declaration of war, Vidarian."

"I'm sorry you feel that way," Vidarian began, channeling some of the patronizing arrogance that Justinian had spoken with from the day they first met. A day when Justinian's face had been whole, Ariadel had stood beside him, and Ruby still lived.

He opened his mouth to say more, but the glasses went dark completely, and after long moments of blindness he finally removed the spectacles and set them aside.

Malloray stood near the door, and had hauled one of the relay officers up by his elbow. Both were breathing heavily, as though they'd just come out of hand-to-hand combat, despite Vidarian having heard nothing of the sort. When Malloray turned toward him, his bearing reeked of misery. "A traitor," he said, between heavy breaths. "A Company man. I'm so sorry, Captain. I should have known. His defenses were nearly perfect."

Vidarian touched his palm to his forehead and closed his eyes for a moment, reeling with the implications. "Justinian, at least, will know that the emperor is aboard the *Luminous*."

"He has his own problems with the Court of Directors," Lirien said, clearly still shaken from the encounter. "There's no certainty they'll even believe him."

"Begging your pardon, sirs," Malloray said, face flushed red with embarrassment and anger. "But what shall I do with this slime?"

"Take him above," Vidarian said, and Malloray nodded, hauling the man out of the chamber. Vidarian followed, and they made their way laboriously up the ladders.

The wind whipped, and only sky was visible for miles around when they came atopships. Around the ship was arrayed a small contingent of Sky Knights; when he emerged, one of the riders to starboard lifted his lance—Caladan. Amidst the ever-advancing threat of their situation, Vidarian experienced a moment of deep gratitude for whomever had brought him—probably Thalnarra. At Vidarian's indication, Malloray hustled the relay officer toward the stern.

The gryphons were reclining in their freshly made nests. Before them, Tepeki and Brannon were sparring with wooden swords.

"I apologize for interrupting," Vidarian said, and the boys lowered their weapons. "But I may need some assistance. We've discovered one of Justinian's men among the relay officers."

// *I can return him to the ground,* // Altair said.

Vidarian turned to Altair, searching his tone for any sign of irony or suggestion. There was none, only the cool breeze of a problem solved. "Please do. Gently," he glanced at the man, whose eyes were widening as he realized how he was going to leave the ship, "but not too gently."

Altair chuffed, a dry, amused note in the back of his throat, then tipped his beak in a nod, climbing to his feet and giving a luxurious and illustrative head-to-toe stretch of his muscles and wings.

Malloray's grip loosened on the man's arm, and at first Vidarian assumed it was out of shock at Altair's formidable height.

"Captain!" Malloray shouted. "I've made contact with another ship! Another relay chamber received the distress call that went out with the interrupted contact with Val Harlon." The man turned, and the blue lenses slipped away from his eyes in his urgency. "It's Marielle, sir!"

PART THREE
EAGLES ASCEND

CHAPTER TWENTY-TWO
FIRE COUNCIL

"Good afternoon, Captain Rulorat." Through the blue lenses of his relay glasses, Marielle stood, well turned-out, in a stateroom Vidarian almost recognized. His former first mate looked superb; whatever she'd been up to in the months since the burning of the *Empress Quest* had suited her. The burr in her voice was confidence, a kind of lightning contentment, the kind that came from action and strength.

"It's been a long time, Captain Solandt," Vidarian replied. Beside Marielle, a massive and excessively armed man frowned and opened his mouth. Marielle stilled him with a lift of her fingers.

Back on the *Luminous*, the relay chamber onto which the blue glasses projected Marielle's images was growing crowded. Iridan and Khalesh had joined Malloray and his remaining two officers. Khalesh had some kind of elemental device in his hands, a narrow metal tube set with three differently colored glass spheres evenly spaced along it.

Squinting at the double vision provided by the glasses, Vidarian caught Malloray's attention and lifted his chin in Iridan's direction.

The voice in his head was quiet, pitched for him alone, and unmistakably Malloray's. *Iridan asked about the configuration of the ship's relay sphere. He seemed to think he could stop an outside presence from interfering again.*

Not completely convinced, but neither desiring an argument, Vidarian nodded. "We heard that the *Ardent* has been lost for months."

"Is something lost what doesn't want to be found?" Marielle smiled again, and this time her silent burly companion joined her.

Vidarian looked at Marielle as closely as the spectacles would allow. What she was suggesting—that she and the entire crew of the *Ardent* had abandoned their commissions—was close to treason on its face. He was glad suddenly that Lirien had not come to the relay chamber with them.

Marielle took pity on his clumsily calculating mind and said, "I'd like to explain in full, but not at such distance." Even her manner of speaking had changed; was she emulating him, he wondered? Or had her adventures been so transformative?

"We are on route to Val Harlon," Vidarian began. Marielle's face darkened ever so slightly.

"Fire priestesses?" Marielle asked. Val Harlon was not the mountain stronghold that was the fire temple at Kara'zul, but it was their nearest port, and certainly, among other things, would be what Marielle most associated the city with for some time.

"They are our allies," Vidarian said, choosing his words carefully. He wanted—badly—to know what had become of Marielle and the *Ardent*, which should be accountable as loyal defenders of the emperor against the Company, but could not afford to abandon his initial plan of seeking out elemental supporters. "We have need of robust friends."

"Well," Marielle smiled, all business. "When you have need of stronger ones, come to this location." She began to rattle off a set of coordinates and further instructions on the safest routes toward them. Malloray swatted at one of the relay officers, who scrambled after parchment and pencil.

"We look forward to seeing you there, and hearing more of your journey, old friend," Vidarian said. He spoke slowly, without quite meaning to, though well aware of how much he missed Marielle's steady wisdom. It was enough of a lift in his spirits merely to know she lived.

"Who are you calling 'old'?" Marielle asked, folding her arms. She winked, and then vanished.

Around the table the relay officers all gasped, then fell into a cacophony of discussion, remarkable considering that there were only three of them, including Malloray.

"She's gone again, sir," Malloray said at last, and rather unnecessarily, owing to his state of fluster. "I can't make contact with the ship. It's as if she's vanished entirely."

"*They have a masking device,*" Iridan said. Vidarian started, then turned toward the automaton, having forgotten he was there. *"It's an effect I can duplicate, if you'd like."*

"You can make us invisible to other relay spheres? And telepaths?" Vidarian asked.

Iridan nodded, an eerie expression from a metal head. *"Such a device is built into my body. A diplomatic tool."*

"Of course," Vidarian sighed. "It seems quite wise, if it's not an undue tax on your resources."

"It is not," Iridan said. He was silent a moment, then his gears rotated for a few more. *"It is done."*

One of the relay officers, the youngest of them, put his hands around his temples. "It's like a blanket," he said. "A big, fluffy quilt—or a blanket of snow."

"It's excellently done," Malloray said, and seemed to have recovered somewhat from his mortification at having missed the spy in their midst. "Thank you kindly for it. We'll sleep easier a-night."

"I am of course pleased to be of any assistance."

∿∿∿

Since the awakening of the skyships, Val Harlon's tallest towers, long abandoned, now saw new life. Strange bridges that seemed to lead nowhere proved to be skyway piers; most had not survived, but Endera had taken over a tower near one of the few that did, flying from it the three-flames banner of Sharli. Slender balconies that wrapped the towers in long spirals punctuated by broad open courtyards also disclosed their original purpose: landing platforms and open-air roads where gryphons could spare delicate interior carpets and marbles their sharp talons. A passing rumor in the city held that some enterprising soul had developed woolen knit "gryphon mittens" that allowed safer indoor walking, but rather mysteriously they weren't catching on.

They docked at the pier, which had been marked with small golden elemental lanterns, and Vidarian disembarked with Thalnarra.

As they descended the spiral walkway toward the large, arched door, Thalnarra walked proudly beside Vidarian. It was a somewhat subtle attitude to catch in a gryphon, since they always looked somewhere between angry and proud by dint of sharp-beaked predator faces, but in Thalnarra it was recognizable in the shift of her wings, the length of her stride.

"You've painted your feathers," Vidarian noticed obediently. It wasn't hard to feign admiration—the golden patterns weren't as tightly executed as they'd been when he first met her, but they were beautiful nonetheless, gilding the tips of the blue-black feathers on the tops of her wings.

Thalnarra's cheek-feathers puffed, pleased. // *Brannon's work. He's coming along.* //

"Are you sure it was wise to bring him away from his family?"

She turned a narrowed red eye on him without tilting her head. // *He's chosen to become a gryphon-ward. It is his life, not theirs.* // Vidarian wanted to ask what it meant to be "a gryphon-ward," exactly, but the pinning of Thalnarra's pupil said that asking would only get him a riddle, and he couldn't muster the will.

An acolyte greeted them at the door, summoned by the sound of claws on the walkway. Slim and spectacled, she bowed deeply to Thalnarra, who dipped her beak in return. // *We are here to see Priestess Endera,* // Thalnarra said.

"The High Priestess takes luncheon in the solar," the acolyte said cautiously. "Whom may I say is calling?"

Vidarian looked at Thalnarra, surprised at Endera's new title, but her eyes were fixed intently on the acolyte. Thalnarra's tufted ears lowered just a fraction. The girl had enough experience with gryphons to be intimidated. // *Tell her that Thalnarra is here, and the Tesseract, Captain Vidarian Rulorat.* //

By now Vidarian was used to priestesses and their ilk ignoring him if there was either a woman or a gryphon around, but the way that they scrambled when they learned who he was still had a bit of sparkle. The girl began apologizing, and Thalnarra gestured with her beak, sending her vanishing back inside the tower with a squeak.

In moments, a different acolyte, this one with gold stripes on the grey sleeves of her robes, came out and immediately ushered them into the tower.

In the hall, they were plied with luxuries: a steaming hot towel for Vidarian's face and hands, an oil-rubbed cloth for Thalnarra's feathers, glasses of chilled melon water and a peppery dried venison that gryphons favored. More still they offered: bathing chambers, clothing, meals—but Thalnarra gently insisted that they be taken straight to Endera.

They wound down through the tower to the fifth floor, and then out onto a round rooftop garden enclosed in glass. Endera was there dressed in rich golden robes, sitting at a small, wrought-iron table set with tea, pears, and delicate cress sandwiches. Her carnelian circlet had been replaced by one of silver set with garnets and rubies. She smiled sardonically at Vidarian's theatrically raised eyebrows and waved him to a seat. As they approached, another acolyte entered the solarium bearing a tea service for Vidarian with more cress sandwiches and a plate of seared fish for Thalnarra.

"We're honored to merit the audience of a High Priestess," Vidarian said, by way of complimenting her promotion with just the right dash of impudence.

Endera stirred fragrant coconut sugar into her tea. "I have you to thank for that." She lifted her cup to him.

Vidarian took one of the chairs and Thalnarra sat to his left, delicately lifting one of the fish by its tail and swallowing it whole. Endera lifted her own teapot and poured him a cup of tea. "Me?" he asked.

She picked up her own cup again, sipped, and nodded. "The Fire Council believes now that it was Sharli's intention that we should be part of your journey, that our . . . friction . . . was part of that path, and that I acted in accordance with the will of the goddess in shaping it. They are here in Val Harlon for my ascension ceremony."

"Congratulations," he managed. He looked at Thalnarra, searching for the protocol for a newly promoted priestess, but she was no help at all. She continued eating the fish and actually seemed to be pretending that Endera wasn't there. It seemed she hadn't quite forgiven her for the betrayal that had caused Thalnarra to win a separation from the priestesshood with her pride—by ritual combat.

She waved a hand. "Temple politics. Had I been a High Priestess when we first met, who knows what might have happened?" Delicately she picked up a sandwich—a tiny thing with pressed cream-colored bread and bright greens—and pushed the plate at Vidarian. He took one out of politeness and ate it. The cress was pleasantly peppery. "But come. You said you were in need of friends." At this, Thalnarra snapped through the body of one of the fish, crunching bones.

As he explained all that had happened—the sky skirmishes with the Qui, the collapse of the Sky Knights, the arrival of Ariadel, the revelation of the imperial finances—a quiet fire visibly ignited in Endera's eyes. She watched Vidarian like a cat stalking prey. He gave as much detail as he dared without disclosing exact statements, or the fact that the emperor had left the city with them. When at last he trailed off, she folded her hands and stared at the table for several long moments. He half expected the plate of sandwiches to burst into flames.

At last Endera gave the slightest shake of her head, waking from a tense meditation. "We've known pieces of this," she admitted. "Ariadel—sought my help . . ."

"Where is she?" The words escaped him before conscious thought.

Endera blinked, and her eyes slid over to Thalnarra for only a moment. "She's with Thalnarra's flight—"

Vidarian started to stand, but Endera's hand on his arm, startlingly hot, kept him in his seat.

"You can't go there now," she said, her circlet sliding lower on her forehead as she frowned. "If half of what you say is true, your ship could only draw attention to their location."

His free hand came down on the table, rattling the dishes. He looked up in an apology he couldn't bring himself to voice, then rubbed his eyes. "What exactly am I to do, then?"

"We can give you the assistance the imperial court could not afford," Endera said. In her eyes now was something he never thought he would see: an age, a tiredness, even—regret? Even as he watched, it hardened. "I will personally guarantee it." When his head jerked with surprise, she smiled sadly. "The priestesshood, despite some miscalculations, has not been so foolish as to chain itself to a mercantile master. And we owe you."

"Owe me?"

"Well, I owe you for this," she said, touching her circlet. "And, of course . . ." She trailed off deliberately, tilting her head.

Vidarian shook his head, not understanding.

Endera waited, then laughed, a surprised golden bell of sound. "Did you ever *read* the Breakwater Agreement?"

Endera summoned an acolyte—the same one who had first met them, who blushed red when she saw them again—and sent her immediately to convene an emergency session of the Fire Council. If what she'd said was true, it must have been her first time doing so since being added to the council as a High Priestess. As Thalnarra tersely explained, the priestesshood had no more than seven High Priestesses at any given time—one for each of the districts claimed by the Sharlin Temple—and three additional Robed council officers who filled different facilitation roles. In theory these officers, indicated by three different robe colors, were impartial, but—and at this Thalnarra trailed off onto a rapid track of thinking that Vidarian could make out little of other than its anti-human tone.

It took some time to assemble the council, and so they were moved to another hall, this one indoors, wherein the luxuries descended again: scented oils, aromatic steam, imported delicacies. It was never so lavish as he recalled Endera pressing upon him before—attempts he now knew intended to impress and even intimidate—and at any rate anxiety over Ariadel made him stare at the double doors of the council chamber with a wolfish persistence. There was no use pressing Thalnarra on whether she'd known where Ariadel had gone; she had shown no sign when Endera had said so, which meant that she was unsurprised, and also uninterested in commenting.

At last, the council convened, and there was more waiting. Vidarian thought of returning to the ship, but dared not leave the vicinity lest some answer came, or worse, some question to which they *needed* an answer.

When shadows stretched long across the alabaster tiles, Endera emerged from the tall double doors. She radiated exhaustion, but also a cold determination. "Come with me," she said, and disappeared back behind the door. Vidarian exchanged a look with Thalnarra, and they followed Endera into the chamber.

The hallway beyond the door was dark, but it quickly opened up into an octagonal chamber lit by beacons that used a system of mirrors to channel sunlight from outside the tower. Each was spaced around the white-walled chamber with geometric precision, and the pale light that slanted through the room as a result created slowly shifting patterns doubtless intended to suggest the movements of fire energy itself. Now that Vidarian had wielded his own fire magic, albeit still crudely, he saw the temple artifacts with new, and humbling, eyes.

Nine fire priestesses—High Priestesses, he corrected himself—sat around the table in the center of the chamber. Six wore golden robes like Endera's, and the remaining three were dressed in burgundy, black, and white. One chair was empty.

The white-robed priestess, a tall, sharp-featured woman with white-blonde hair, held a large, black stone shaped into an octagonal prism, which she now rapped on the polished stone table to call the meeting back to order. She did not bother with a greeting, and Vidarian was at first unsure whether to take it as a slight. "We have brought you into this council meeting to clarify certain matters . . . Captain." A slight it was, then.

"Arbiter, you claimed that you had information from Val Imris that would make our decision clear." Endera's voice was tired, and the leash on her tone tight.

"The Company has released a banner," the white-robed priestess—the Arbiter, apparently—said. "They say he's kidnapped the emperor."

"*What?*" Vidarian managed not to shout only because shock stole the breath from his lungs.

The Arbiter's cold, silver eyes turned toward him. "You deny this, then?"

"Of course I do! Why would I come here if I'd kidnapped him?"

"But you admit that he is on your ship, and not aboard the *Empress Cimeria*."

"The *Luminous* is an imperial vessel—"

"Which, by rights, we should detain until further clarification can come from the Imperial City."

"By which you mean the Alorean Import Company."

Thalnarra's cedar-smoke voice was pitched for him alone. // *Her family has close ties with the Company. A cousin is one of the western directors, I believe.* //

Vidarian focused his thoughts. He still did not quite understand what allowed some gryphons, or seridi, or humans, to speak mind-to-mind and others not, but tried to think as loudly as he could. *How many of them have such ties?*

// *You don't really want the answer to that.* //

"I remind the council only for our record," Endera began, "for surely my fellow councilwomen recall that the Rulorat family entered into an agreement on behalf of the Priestess Aelana Wintermark some seventy-five years ago—"

"We are of course aware of the Breakwater Agreement," one of the golden-robed priestesses said, "but it cannot outweigh our fealty to the empire, Endera."

"The priestesshood is beholden only to Sharli," Endera said.

"In spirit, High Priestess," the white-robed priestess's cadence implied she was speaking to a child. "Our souls answer to Sharli, but our bodies must be fed, our daughters sheltered."

"Fed and sheltered by mercantile masters," Endera finished, venom curling her lip.

"You overstep, High Priestess," the Arbiter said.

"This is quite disappointing," Endera said. Her voice was low, dangerous.

The white-robed priestess seemed not to notice. "The needs of the greater priestesshood must outweigh individual concerns."

"You are of course correct," Endera said softly. Her palms were flat on the polished table, her eyes fixed somewhere between them. "I am left with only one course of action." Vidarian watched the Arbiter, and so saw the exact moment when her satisfaction turned to outrage. "The west branch of the priesthood divides from the mother temple. My priestesses will come with me, or be permitted to transfer to another district."

"This is madness, Endera!" one of the golden-robed priestesses hissed.

"You've no guarantee any will follow you at all," the burgundy-robed priestess said, and unlike the others, she seemed genuinely distressed, not angry.

"*Madness*," Endera said sharply, and silence cut across the table like a whip, "was allowing the Alorean Import Company to so thoroughly infiltrate and influence matters that should be the exclusive purview of the goddess of sun and fire." She looked directly at the Arbiter, and the woman nearly rose out of her seat with fury. "I happen to agree with Vidarian. And it is within my authority to split my district from the mother temple when I perceive corruption within her. I have once adhered to the temple's strictures when they did not agree with my own." Now she looked at Thalnarra, who returned her gaze for the first time since they'd arrived. "I will not do so again."

Three of the golden-robed priestesses listened to Endera with jaws slack with astonishment. The Arbiter pounded on the table with the stone octagon until Vidarian was sure it would shatter. All of the remaining priestesses except Endera began talking at once, their voices echoing off of the high walls and ceiling.

The black-robed priestess, who had been entirely silent, cleared her throat, which cut through the cacophony instantly. She was old, older than any of the other priestesses, her hands thin-boned like bird claws or fine ginseng. "High Priestess Endera is correct. This divide is within her authority." She said no more, and after three moments more of silence, the din of voices erupted again.

Endera stood, and the rest of the council stood with her. But they didn't follow as she circled the room toward Vidarian and placed a hand on his shoulder, turning him toward the door. "We should go." Vidarian looked between her and Thalnarra, dumbfounded. She snapped her fingers. "*Now*, Vidarian!"

They rushed from the chamber, and Endera brushed the acolytes aside as they converged on her with a flurry of questions. "It won't take them long to relay messages back to Val Imris. How much room have you got in that ship?" Vidarian told her, and she nodded, calculating. Then she barked a quick order, and one of the acolytes produced parchment and stylus. She wrote a message, then ordered it to be copied and distributed. When she was done, she said, "I hope you have somewhere to go, by the way. I'm afraid Sher'azar is rather out of the question."

"Thalnarra," Vidarian whispered. "Would you be so kind as to contact the *Luminous*? Tell them to prepare Marielle's coordinates. Quickly."

CHAPTER TWENTY-THREE

QUEEN MARIELLE

I t was not the first time that Vidarian had led a band of refugees fleeing Val Harlon, but he vehemently hoped it would be the last.

"Last time we did this—" Vidarian began.

"You left by land," Endera said, leaning over the rail of the *Luminous* to look down through cloud-threaded sky at the city spires dwindling beneath them. "I must say this is rather an improvement."

"It soon won't be, if the Company reserved any skyships," Vidarian said, peering down at the clouds through a borrowed spyglass.

"They didn't," Endera said, satisfaction heavy as honey on her words. "At least not in Val Harlon. There aren't *so* many of these ships left, you know. Has it occurred to you that you take them for granted?" She was watching him speculatively, as if gauging the potential of a child, or an exotic animal. While he was considering her question, she asked, "Isn't that rather redundant?" indicating the spyglass.

"I've just learned recently that not only can telepathic communications be disrupted even via relay, entire ships can be hidden from telepathic contact if they have the right sort of device on board."

Endera frowned. "Such devices are exceedingly rare. In their heyday they were contraband."

"That may explain why Marielle has one," he muttered, almost to himself. Ever since he'd seen the burly officer reporting to Marielle, the seed of a theory had planted itself in his mind, fed further by the instructions she'd given about her location. But it hardly seemed possible. . .

"High Priestess," a voice said from behind them, pulling him out of his thoughts.

They turned, and waiting three steps away was a burgundy-robed fire priestess, a costume that could only ever remind Vidarian of Ariadel. But this priestess otherwise was as far from her as could be, with silver hair cropped short around her face, and large, hazel eyes. She had a look of mischief about her that made her look younger than she probably was, though with priestesses it was usually hard to tell.

"What is it, Ilara?" Endera said. The girl's face was a mask of formality, but Vidarian felt her flinch; he wondered if Endera knew the terror she so casually induced.

Visibly Ilara hardened, summoning boldness. "I have asked my Sisters to begin combat practice," she said, and quickened when Endera's eyes widened ever so slightly. "I know you wished us to omit such training at Val Harlon, but circumstances have clearly changed."

Endera watched the other priestess for a long moment, measuring. "You'll need the permission of the quartermistress," she said, finally.

"I've asked," Ilara said, and now the quickness of her words was relief. "She directed me to the training space to the rear of the ship."

"Aft," Endera corrected. "The training deck." She sighed, very softly. "Carry on, then."

Ilara bowed. "Thank you, High Priestess. We won't disappoint you." She bowed then to Vidarian, and turned to beat a hasty retreat.

"Ilara," Endera said, and the girl turned back. "Ask the gryphons. Their knowledge of combat techniques far exceeds our own. And don't offend them!" The last she added sternly when the younger priestess lit up at the word *gryphon*. At Endera's rebuke, she studiously dimmed her expression, bowing and excusing herself to hurry across the deck.

Endera turned back to the rail, her eyes tight with worry. "I've tried to keep them away from combat," she said. "This ludicrous war business . . ."

"Qui invaded our southern border," Vidarian objected.

Endera turned one of those scathing looks on him that said he might amount to something if only he hadn't the wit of a flea. "And surely this isn't the first time Qui has dared aggress, yet for the last hundred years we have found diplomatic solutions. Until now."

He felt foolish for refusing to believe that the Company alone could be so pivotal in something as titanic as an imperial war—also realizing how much he hadn't wanted to believe that Alorea was capable of such corruption. There was no good answer, and so he returned to searching the clouds, sure any moment he'd find the white sails of imperial pursuit.

The instructions Marielle had sent carried them far west from Val Harlon, out over the open West Sea. Miles and miles they went with only the azure glass curve of the ocean below, correcting course by the stars. They passed beyond even known pirate territory and into the Deep Outwater, past the boundaries of the maps captured from West Sea Kingdom vessels. After three days above the Deep they came upon a ring of knife-reefs that jutted far out of the water—a mark Marielle had described—and one day north from there passed into a wall of mist. The crew of the *Luminous* steered her skyward, but thin air and straining sails gave way before the weather did.

Thalnarra, Altair, and Isri stood with Vidarian—Rai curled protectively around his feet, cat-claws gripping the deck—at the bow. Altair had tried to repel the mist, but even his formidable ability could not grasp it. At first the gryphons had considered scouting above and below, but it was quickly deemed too hazardous, as there was no guarantee they'd be able to find their way back to the ship.

// *Something is creating this,* // Altair said, closing his eyes for long stretches as he reached out, trying to find the mist's edge. // *Something strong.* //

"We're at the location," Vidarian said, looking at the logbook where one of Malloray's assistants had quickly taken down Marielle's instructions. "We'll have to try to make contact using the relay sphere."

Isri's eyebrows were drawn down, the closest her beaked face could come to a frown. "Whatever's masking them is equally strong. I should be able to break through, but I can't, not without potentially injuring whomever is hiding them."

"Or *what*ever," Vidarian said, but added, "Better not to risk it."

The gryphons returned to watching the mist for any sign of opening, and Isri went with Vidarian to the relay chamber. Rai followed close on his heels, shrinking to wolf-shape to more easily fit down the ladder. Ever since Vidarian had returned from his last voyage, Rai had refused to let him out of sight without intense complaint.

They found Iridan and Malloray already in the relay room, and in contact with Marielle.

"*She's asked to speak with you and the emperor,*" Iridan said, a note of thinly veiled worry in his words.

Moments later, Lirien, looking haggard—the attendants said he'd hardly slept since boarding the *Luminous*—entered the room, and donned relay lenses. Vidarian did the same.

"You've made good time, sirs," Marielle said, once again in the hauntingly familiar stateroom.

"Skyships do that," Vidarian said, cutting around formality. "We're rather taken aback by the weather, though."

"The mistwall," Marielle agreed. "A formality, but a necessary one, I'm afraid. Before we lower it, I'll need your word, Vidarian, that whatever you see here will not under any circumstance be reported back to Val Imris." She turned and gave a slight bow to the emperor. "And your word as well, Emperor Lirien."

Lirien stiffened slightly, affronted at her audacity. He looked at Vidarian, pressing his unhappiness into a glance.

A chill tickled up Vidarian's spine, combated by his trust in Marielle, whatever mysterious role she now held. The thought that they—whomever she was with—controlled the "mistwall" was both unsurprising and unsettling. "We're well within their territory already, your majesty," he said slowly. "If you had an envoy from a foreign nation at the palace, you would ask the same."

"This presumes the West Sea Kingdom to be a sovereign nation," the emperor said, his mild tone saying that he wasn't objecting, merely making it clear to Vidarian that his agreement to Marielle's request represented a concession that the Alorean Empire had not made toward the Sea Kingdoms in over a century.

"They are our friends," Vidarian said. "Or can be."

The emperor inclined his head, closing his eyes for a long moment. When he raised them, it was with a mask of a dynasty's pride and authority, and also its weariness. "You have my word."

Vidarian let out a breath he didn't realize he was holding. "And mine."

Marielle smiled, gently, a friend's relief. "Then I bid you welcome, and advise you to return atopships. You'll want to watch the landing."

Malloray sent messages to the crew to prepare for the descent, and Vidarian turned to Isri, whose neck-feathers puffed in a shrug. Her eyes lost their focus. "I can see them," she said, then blinked with surprise. "All of them!"

They hurried back to the top deck to watch the landing as instructed. Even as they ascended the main ladder, the mist was parting around them, giving way to blindingly blue sky.

As the ship descended, the gryphons fanned out their wings, letting the updraft carry them light as dandelion seeds into the air. They arced out around the ship, circling—and each uttered an aquiline whistle of surprise when their sharp eyes picked out what lay far below them.

"What do you see?" Vidarian shouted.

// It's—a city! // Altair replied, struggling for words.

They were descending fast, and before Vidarian could press for a better answer, he saw for himself.

There were ships down on the water's surface, large ones—but spread out between them and stretching beyond for leagues was a network of floating piers, stationary rafts, and walkways. The rafts came in all shapes and sizes, some of which, incredibly, carried pyramids of soil studded with crops, or multistory chicken coops. Sailors walked the piers on errands, or caroused, or worked; merchants plied wares on a particular set of rafts; children raced and leapt from pier to raft to walkway with the alacrity and fearlessness of youth.

Altair was right. It was a city. A floating city.

The largest ship among them floated some distance from the rest, accessed via a wide pier decorated with banners. The flag of the West Sea Kingdom flew from its highest mast—it was the *Viere d'Inar*. Ruby's ship.

As they descended, a pair of sailors with small hand-flags waved them to a pier not far from the *Viere*. The ship turned serenely toward it, and in minutes, they were lowering the gangplank.

Vidarian descended to the pier first, even as Thalnarra and Altair landed on wider open spots on the pier. Isri followed him, and Iridan, Lirien, and Malloray.

A small group of three met them at the end of the pier. Two were officers—one of them being the big man weighted down with weaponry that they'd seen on relay—and the third was Marielle.

It was all Vidarian could do to not to rush straight to her. When he thought of all that had happened, and the tortuous echo of the destruction of the *Quest* from when he'd last seen her, chained and escorted by Endera's fire priestesses—the sight of her here, hale, free, stung his eyes. But he blinked measuredly, reached for professionalism. As they drew closer, the big man at her right stepped forward.

"I present Queen Marielle, Captain of the *Viere d'Inar*, Admiral of the Free Armada, sovereign of the West Sea."

Marielle's—*Queen* Marielle's—familiar smile twitched at the corner of her lips, tired and amused by the world all at once. "Welcome to Rivenwake, Captain Rulorat."

∿∿∿

Their three hosts escorted them to the *Viere d'Inar*. As they ascended the gangplank, Marielle gave commands for meat and whatever else they should request to be given to the gryphons, and food and water offered to the crew of the *Luminous*. An odd crawling feeling spread across Vidarian's stomach as they crossed the familiar deck of the *Viere*, peopled as it was with unfamiliar crew. It felt like an insult to Ruby, and he wondered if it would have felt worse had she remained dead.

Marielle led them to the captain's stateroom, and even before Vidarian saw the relay sphere that now sat at the center of its main table, he recognized it. Someone had changed the decor—gone were Ruby's Targuli carpets, and thin geometric Rikani ones replaced them, likewise the linens. Even as he was cataloging the changes, Marielle turned to her two officers.

"Anglar, Yuril, there are matters I wish to discuss with our guests privately."

"Your majesty—" Anglar, the bigger one, made it two words into his objection.

"Need I ask you again, sir?" The evenness of her tone was a greater threat than steel.

"No, ma'am." He bowed stiffly and left the stateroom, stealing a glare like a jealous tomcat at Vidarian as he did so.

When the door was shut behind him, Marielle gestured them to the velvet-upholstered chairs, pouring tea into four cups with her own hand. "If you have need, we have elemental channeling stones you are welcome to," she said to Iridan, addressing him as she would any other guest. His eyes glowed appreciatively.

"How did this happen?" Vidarian asked, as soon as they'd settled into their chairs.

"It's as unlikely a thing as can be imagined, I grant you," Marielle said, taking a long draw on her tea. "I was captain of the *Ardent*, you knew."

Vidarian nodded.

"We hit a squall off the coast of Ignirole—not surprising for that time of year, but its strength was. A wild thing, unnatural. It was all we could do to keep the rig upright. We came out of it, but the *Viere* —" she knocked on the deck with the heel of her boot—"was waiting, looking for easy prey among the jetsam." Thoughtfully, she rolled her silver teacup between her hands, then took another long pull on it. "We gave it an honorable fight, but 'twere never a hope. They boarded us."

Vidarian winced. He well imagined the misery she must have felt, newly a captain and her first commission lost to pirates.

"I had a choice. I could fight, and if I won we would all become pirates—citizens of the West Sea Kingdom—or I could refuse to fight, and they'd slaughter us all."

"They offered you combat?" Vidarian said, surprised.

"Aye. Foolishness. The captain was a young pup named Warrick. Thought himself invincible, thought he'd make an example out of a woman-captain from the landers."

"What did you do?"

"I killed him," she said, and in the hesitancy, even regret, in her voice, Vidarian recognized the Marielle he had known. "I hardly meant to, but he was an oaf of a boy had no business on either end of a sword. Ran right into me."

"Did you . . . ?" The beginning of the question escaped Vidarian before he could think better of it.

In answer, Marielle turned over her wrist and pulled back the sleeve from her forearm. There, just below her palm, was the mark, a pattern inked from reed needles into her skin, a blue dragon, albeit a small one. "Stupid boy," she said softly, her thoughts far away in a memory.

"You could have gone home," Vidarian said.

Marielle shook her head. "Not then. If we'd fled, they'd've filled our hull with lead. They don't permit anyone to just pick off a monarch—even a temporary upstart of one, as he was, having successfully seized the *Viere*—and sail away."

"But you've always hated pirates," Vidarian said, aware that he sounded plaintive.

Marielle looked up over her cup, a tired glance that Endera would have been proud of. She turned to Lirien and gave him a little deferential nod. "Yer pardon, majesty, but I hope you've enough a head on your shoulders to know what a mess the admiralty has become." Lirien sighed, but didn't answer, and Marielle took it for agreement and turned back to Vidarian. "To save my crew, I told them I'd take the crown I'd won—and once I saw this place," she gestured roundly with her cup, "and met their people, I saw what the Sea Kingdoms had become, and how badly they needed leadership. Also how badly the world needs them."

"On that, we can agree," Vidarian said, seeing his opening. He told her of their flight from the Imperial City, of the Company's machinations—without mentioning, in Lirien's presence, the imperial debt—and what Ariadel had told him, of the prison camps full of Qui.

Marielle's face grew progressively graver, and then darker, the more Vidarian spoke. When he mentioned the prison camps, she cursed roundly. "It explains other news we've received. Lifan, the *Quest*'s little windreader—she's disappeared."

Vidarian's stomach sank. "How do you—?"

Marielle glanced at the relay sphere. "One thing the Kingdoms learned to do very well from the beginning was to maintain lines of communication. I had gotten wind of Lifan's disappearance some months ago. Thought it odd, especially with Ellara watching over her. They'll have taken her, I'm sure of it."

A cold anger rolled through Vidarian's veins. He thought about how he would dismantle the Alorean Import Company, if it took his last breath and beyond. "Surely, the West Sea Kingdom has power to bring to this cause. I need to destroy those camps."

Marielle's expression was grave. "There's little choice, then. I don't have the authority to provide what you're asking for."

Surprise pulled him out of his reverie of vengeance. "I thought you were the West Sea Queen."

Marielle shook her head. "Not that simple, 'm afraid. The Kingdoms make it look like their monarchies are absolute, but there are protocols—strict ones, for things like this. It requires a Sea Council." Vidarian blinked, and she continued. "You think this place is big now, wait until you see it with every pier filled. The last one convened to confirm my rise to Queen." The word sounded even stranger coming from Marielle. She set down her cup, stood, and went to the door. None of them were surprised when her burly officer, whom she called Anglar, was hovering just beyond.

"Mr. Anglar," Marielle said, and the big fellow straightened. "I've called a Sea Council. See to it."

"At once, your majesty."

When he'd left, Vidarian said, "How do you get used to that?"

Marielle chuckled, her green eyes tired. "I try not to think about it."

CHAPTER TWENTY-FOUR
SEA COUNCIL

The next morning Vidarian ventured out into the floating city, crossing from pier to pier. He carried a mug of *kava* from the ship; its hot bite was sharpened by the heavy, cold air that had come in over the water with the dawn hours.

Far from the sleepy village the place had seemed by late afternoon, by morning it was a bustle of activity. There was some logic to the way that they made use of the narrow raft bridges, but he couldn't make sense of it, and eventually stopped at an unused spar and stood aside.

Across the network of bridges, far from where the *Luminous* and *Viere d'Inar* moored, a pair of familiarly-shaped figures bobbed in the water to starboard of the great Rivenwake structure. They were pelican-gryphons, and as he had only ever seen one before, Vidarian assumed one must be Arikaree—yet, as he squinted at them, it was clear neither was he. The water-gryphon had returned to his people with the opening of the Great Gate, and Vidarian had not seen him since he'd reappeared with An'du. These two, at the very least, must be members of his flight; Thalnarra had never spoken of more than one small group of the pelican-gryphons. Even as he watched, another ship glided between them, hiding the creatures from sight.

When he returned to watching the stream of merchants, tiny delivery carts, and sailors, a passing fruit vendor noticed his confusion and pressed half of a ripe mango into his palm, all while waving away any attempt at payment. In moments the vendor had reentered the trail of passersby and quite vanished.

Vidarian bit into the mango, more out of a desire to free his hand than hunger, but blinked with surprise as the rich, bright, spectacular flavor hit his tongue. The fruit was perfectly ripe, its flavor like pure liquid sunlight, a taste he'd only experienced once before when, in his childhood, his father had sailed to the far southwestern islands where mango trees grew. But those were miles away—these mangoes must be grown here in Rivenwake, miraculously on one of the garden-rafts.

Emboldened by the fruit's tap-dance across his senses, he ventured back out onto the raft-bridges, and this time managed to move with the stream of travelers long enough to come into some kind of trading district.

It was strange to call the collections of rafts "districts," but they could be nothing else. Rivenwake was a city, with a city's specialization of tasks—the massive flat garden-rafts tended to cluster together, as did the different rafts for cloth-selling, grocery, herbery, and more.

The merchant's-way onto which he'd stumbled seemed to be a hybrid of several raft types, repurposed for small shops like those in the central Val Harlon tradegoods market. And like Val Harlon's, the noise here was deafening, as shop-keepers shouted over the passing travelers and over each other in an attempt to ply their wares. Vidarian moved along with the eddy of the raft-bridges, but at length stepped off onto the quietest of the merchant rafts he could find.

It was an elemental lights shop, or perhaps a curio shop that happened to have a terrible lot of lights. They hung from the steel canopy of the place, bunched up in clusters or spread out in lines, dozens of lights in more colors than he had seen even in Val Imris.

As he passed through one of the two narrow aisles, still taking in the scenery more than genuinely perusing the wares, another kind of sparkle caught his eye, deep red:

A prism key.

The shape, size, and color of it were all unmistakable; what he would have called a "sun ruby" mere months ago. And as then, it should have been nearly priceless.

This fact did not deter him from making an embarrassingly modest offer to the wizened shopkeep tucked into a tiny cubby in the rear of the raft. He expected denial, even derision, but what he got instead in response to the entire contents of his leather coinpurse still came as a surprise.

"Eh? I bain't a-been'n land fer forty year, m'boy! What use've I fer yer shiny bits? Gold fer'ma teeth maybe?" The old man took his silence for confusion—which it was, but at his accent, not the meaning of the words—and made a shooing notion with his hands. "Gitchee tootha moneychanger, lad, they's a'visitin' by sailers what might've use fer Alorean silver."

Vidarian was taken aback, and tried to hide exactly how much. He'd never met a sailor who would turn down silver, yet the old merchant's point was clear and reasonable. Still, for the sake of appearances he tried to argue him into taking the coin and changing it himself, but the old man would have none of it. Finally, he left the shop, glum about departing without the prism key, but educated in the ways of this strange place that Marielle had roosted.

～～～

Time slipped away quickly in the labyrinthine market quarter, and shortly the sun had advanced high in its march, signaling the convening of the council in a few short hours.

Vidarian found Lirien on the *Luminous*'s pier, sitting next to Tepeki, who held a book in his hands. As Vidarian approached, the boy set the book carefully aside, gestured to Lirien, and leapt off the pier. Midway through the air, he changed, his body rearranging itself to become the otter. He struck the water smoothly, cutting below its surface with hardly a splash, then bounced up again to whirl and cavort through the water.

"He's remarkably well read," Lirien said. "His people long ago made translations of many of the Alorean classics, and it seems they've bartered for books for ages." While they watched, Tepeki spun again in the water, and changed shape as he did so, this time into a strange hybrid form. Vidarian had seen An'du like this—from the waist down, a whale, she'd remained human across the rest of her body, though larger than she was in her full human shape. Similarly, here Tepeki was smaller, half boy and half otter, and kept several otter details, including the tiny black claws that tipped his tiny, clever fingers. A long and powerful tail let him leap high out of the water, performing, before he swam back to the pier.

Lirien was watching the boy, his thoughts transparent: was Tepeki a different race, or a different species? When he appeared to be a boy, did he think like a boy? When he was an otter, were his thoughts human? Were Calphille's, as she slept with branches outstretched in the palace's north field?

Standing up in the water again, Tepeki gave another strong thrash of his tail and leapt, sailing up onto the pier. He landed on human arms and otter legs, and Vidarian was sure he was flaunting the strangeness of his hybrid body to the emperor.

"You're a superb swimmer," Lirien said, declining the challenge. Tepeki turned boy again, his otter pelt blurring into fur-clothed human legs, and he took his seat again on the edge of the planks, sluicing water from his hair.

And regardless of what they'd spoken of before Vidarian's arrival, it was clear Tepeki intended to steer the conversation straight to what was in his heart. "She's not one of you," Tepeki said at last. "She is of my people."

"But yours are sea-folk," Vidarian said. "An'du told me of your five clans."

"It is not right that you should be with her," Tepeki insisted, ignoring Vidarian.

"Perhaps you are correct, my young friend," Lirien said. Tepeki cast a satisfied look at Vidarian, and so missed the sadness in Lirien's voice. It was not a sadness that faded easily or was forgotten; it gave the lie to his words. All this was lost on the Velshi boy, who grinned with triumph and leapt back into the water, shivering into his otter form and capering through the waves.

"I hope you are keeping your own counsel when it comes to Calphille," Vidarian said, sitting next to Lirien on the pier.

Lirien turned a glance on him that was purely imperial. "On all things."

It was not a good place to make his next appeal, but time was slipping away. "On the subject of the Sea Council, my friend . . ." The emperor's eyebrows lifted, even as he frowned ever so slightly. "All who care for you would prefer that you remain safely in the *Luminous*. I can conduct whatever business there may be."

"Certainly not," Lirien said, as mildly as he would have asked for milk in his tea.

"Your majesty," Vidarian pressed, twisting the irony in the title with deliberate care. "These pirates are dangerous. My family has treated with them for nearly a century, and there's no telling—"

Lirien shook his head, reaching out to clasp Vidarian's shoulder to take the sting out of his disagreement. "I can't let you do everything for me, my friend. And it is idleness that's created all this. You can't expect me to sit by like a closeted princess."

"You were hardly idle," Vidarian said, taken aback and again stunned by the strangeness of the entire affair.

"I am also responsible," Lirien replied. He ran a hand across his sleeve, and the embroidered emblem there. "Perils of the station."

"And I hope I am not responsible for introducing you into yet more such."

"Shall we bicker over this? Perhaps ritual combat?"

"I'll bring the gryphons, at least," Vidarian said at last.

Lirien smiled. "I hoped you might."

～～～

Thalnarra and Altair were not the only two gryphons at the council meeting, as it turned out.

The council meeting was held in the largest stateroom of the *Viere d'Inar*, a chamber so heavy with gilt-chased mahogany cabinets and a monstrosity of an oval dining table—all hailing, if Vidarian's history was correct, from the opulent age of Alorea's third emperor—that it likely served as the ship's primary ballast all on its own. As children, Vidarian and Ruby had never been allowed in this room, and so entering it now was nearly as intimidating as its occupancy of nearly a dozen hardened pirate captains.

Fortunately the stateroom was in the aftcastle, sparing the gryphons the indignity of stairs. The wide stone stairways of the elemental temples were one thing, but Vidarian shuddered to think of what their talons would make of the narrow ladders leading down into even the *Viere's* broad holds.

Vidarian had told Marielle of his intention to bring Thalnarra and Altair, as well as Iridan and the emperor—a tense conversation that had been half request and half negotiation. At first Marielle had resisted the idea of bringing the emperor to the council at all, sharing many of Vidarian's concerns, but at length she had been convinced by its simple expediency. And while she was clearly not much enamored of the idea of two more large gryphons in her grand stateroom, she saw the sense of their inclusion as well. Iridan's presence she accepted with only cordiality, and again Vidarian was surprised by the ease with which she seemed inclined to include him.

The third gryphon was halfway familiar: one of the pelican-gryphons he'd seen out on the pier, here in the flesh, larger than he'd remembered Arikaree being by a good head-height. The knack he'd developed for deciphering gender on the goshawk, kite, and hawk-gryphons was useless here, though he suspected that the creature's sheer size hinted at a "she."

Lirien had dressed carefully for the occasion, in a partially formal variation on his black silk robes. As he had in the palace, he wore a simple circlet of gold embossed with the imperial insignia. He stood with Vidarian, Iridan, Thalnarra, and Altair far aft of the doorway, around the narrower end of the oval table, as the rest of the captains filed in. Those who did not look with wonder at Iridan stared openly at the emperor with a mix of expressions varying from curiosity to open hostility, but took to their seats without issue.

Marielle sat at the head of the table, a black geode in front of her acting as a ceremonial gavel, a wiry bespectacled girl with a large leather-bound book and a quill sitting just behind her. She began the council meeting as soon as all the captains had taken their seats, leaving no room for chatter. "Thank you, Captains, for your swift attendance of this three-hundredth and thirty-second meeting of the West Sea Council," she began, and struck the table heavily with the geode. "I would also like to welcome our new council members, Shaman Te'lu of the Traenumar, and Kiowa of the Kado'a fisher-gryphons."

The one she called Shaman Te'lu could have been An'du's brother, though he was white of hair and had a bluer tone to his pale green skin. Like An'du, he was a giant of a man in human form, requiring an oversized chair brought down from one of the sitting rooms. He nodded and smiled to Marielle's greeting, an unassuming openness to his features that Vidarian liked immediately.

All told the council itself numbered nine, including Marielle; in addition to Kiowa and Te'lu, there was a sun-hardened thin man of dark features, a short broad-shouldered man also of unclear nationality, a small and precise-featured Rikani, a slim Ishmanti with her long hair in hundreds of tiny braids, a tall blonde Alorean whose even stare reminded Vidarian painfully of Ruby, and a pair of surprisingly young men who both wore captain's-rank badges for the same ship.

"We convene for one reason," Marielle continued, looking around the table. "As your seconds will have told you, we are approached by the Alorean Emperor, Lirien Aslaire, with an offering of partnership in repelling the Alorean Import Company from the continent and the West Sea. Attending Lirien—" Vidarian watched the emperor out of the corner of his eye for any sign of reaction to the familiarity of Marielle's address, and relaxed when he saw none—"is the automaton Iridan, created by the Grand Artificer Parvidian, and Captain Vidarian Rulorat, called gryphon-friend, who bridges many cultures, including our own."

"He's a lander," one of the captains sneered, a whip-thin fellow with a greasy black mustache, Maresh under all his grime, Vidarian thought. Though from the sound of it, calling him from Maresh might result in bared steel. An island it might be, but an island was still land. "Soft and dry as barn-cat bones."

"He is no lander," Marielle said, and however long she'd been here, the pirates knew well enough to take her casual tone for the threat it was. "And you'll button your insults, Kalil, or we'll settle it here between us."

Kalil bared his teeth, a shocking and animalistic gesture, but said no more.

"I welcome Emperor Lirien and Captain Rulorat to this council," Marielle said, steel under the wool-frankness of her tone. "And open our discussion with a question for the empire. If the West Sea Kingdom agrees to provide martial support for your resistance and expulsion of the Alorean Import Company, will you extend in return a binding peace agreement recognizing the sovereignty of the West Sea Kingdom over all our disputed territories, lasting at least three generations?"

Vidarian drew in his breath, and a soft rustle behind him sounded as the gryphons lifted their neck-feathers. None of them had expected Marielle to move so quickly into a negotiation—but even as his mind reeled with what she was suggesting, Vidarian saw the brilliance of it: by forcing the emperor to extend his agreement first, she would make it nearly impossible for the council to refuse. To do so, if Lirien would support her offer, would be to reject what their forebears had striven for with blood and gold for the better part of a century. Though he strained, Vidarian did not dare even look at the emperor, for fear of his reaction.

Silence stretched across the table.

// *I know little of your human empires,* // Altair said, his voice pitched for Thalnarra and Vidarian alone. // *But this is a great concession, yes?* //

Very great, Vidarian thought back, and as he did so Iridan's head turned slightly toward him. He reminded himself again to beg some kind of thought-training from Isri. *The Alorean Empire and the Sea Kingdoms have warred for nearly a hundred years.*

"I will," Lirien said, and around them Vidarian could feel the energy in the room quicken. Like it or not, they accepted the emperor's authority, perhaps even revered it, and to reverse the imperial position toward the Sea Kingdoms was to change the course of Alorean history itself.

"But we won't," Kalil growled. Marielle made an exasperated noise, but he ignored her. "What guarantee do we have that he'll keep his word? Why would he not throw us overboard the moment he dared? We've received nothing but the boot from the Alorean Empire, and I say faugh to his peace offering." He looked ready to spit, and only narrowly contained himself, but his eyes widened with fervor. "Perhaps we should move on imperial territory while we know them to be distracted!"

A chorus of objections rose around the table, and Kalil shouted back to them: "They'd do the same to us!"

The table devolved into three separate arguments carried on simultaneously. The pair of young captains—their closeness and familiarity reminded Vidarian of the co-captainship his grandfather and grandmother were said to have—derided and mocked Kalil, who puffed up with fury, while the other captains fell into separate arguments about territory and trade routes respectively. Marielle pounded the table with the black geode until Vidarian feared it would crack.

"They seek to pull us into a war of their own making!" Kalil shouted, pushing himself to his feet and glaring across the table. "This war with Qui is as ridiculous as the imperial squabbling that began the Sea Wars our forefathers and foremothers abandoned to create this kingdom! And we are called here to discuss a peace agreement with the same madmen?"

"A century ago, our forebears warred over this very issue," Vidarian said, thumping the table with his fist. "The separation of the empires and the common people caught between them. And you—" he pointed at the Maresh captain, who glowered—"would have us sail into another war with each other even as you decry the foolishness of the conflict with Qui." Kalil puffed up again, but Marielle banged the table, and Vidarian's interjection served to distract him long enough for the other captains to continue a real discussion.

"Qui control over the Eastern Sea has been a choke hold on the Sea Kingdoms for decades," the blonde captain said, looking around the table for confirmation. "If we could open relations there . . ."

"It would mean a world of expansion and trade," the Rikani captain said. "You know that I of all of us have least love for the Qui, but neither do I believe that war with their ports is in our interest. By opposing the Alorean Empire in this resistance, do we not in fact support the Qui Empire?"

"But he's talking about war on the empire itself," the broad-barreled captain said. He had been quiet during the bickering, but when he spoke now, the others paused and listened. "War from within."

"On the Company," Lirien corrected gently, leaning forward. "I will establish the imperial position. They will do their best to cloud it to the populace, but we have evidence on our side."

"*And communication,*" Iridan added. Thirteen heads turned toward him. "*Proper use of the relay spheres should allow us to cut through the lies they will attempt to spread, at least in the larger cities that have working relay rooms.*"

"It sounds like we've moved on to tactics," Marielle said into the silence that followed Iridan's words. Undoubtedly they were all considering what the presence of the automaton meant. How much more ancient technology did the Company still hold in reserve? "I'll therefore call a vote. Those in favor of supporting the Alorean Empire in its repulsion of the Alorean Import Company, in exchange for a peace treaty recognizing the West Sea Kingdom as sovereign over the territories now held and known as the Outwater, indicate your agreement."

Around the table, hands lifted, heads nodded, "aye"s were pronounced. The scribe at Marielle's right hand scribbled furiously.

"Those opposed?"

Kalil muttered a general obscenity at all of them, folding his arms across his chest and glaring nowhere in particular.

"We must meet them on the open ocean," Marielle said. "They must not be permitted to learn the location of Rivenwake."

A chorus of agreement answered her, and she rapped the table with the geode again, ending the council. One by one the captains stood, moving toward either Lirien or Marielle, proffering greetings or battle strategies. Others approached the gryphons, and Iridan—between them, Vidarian moved to catch Marielle's eye, only long enough for a smile of thanks. She returned it, guardedly, and he did not need to be a mindspeaker to read the caution there, the resolve; once again, the true work now would begin.

CHAPTER TWENTY-FIVE

OPEN OCEAN

A piercing whistle, softened by the walls of the ship but still shrill, woke Vidarian from troubled sleep before dawn the next morning.

He dressed quickly, and when he emerged into the pale blue of predawn with Rai following on his heels, Rivenwake was alive with activity, this time with a seriousness of purpose. Gone were the jubilant calls from the market; now the merchants tied down their wares, sealed barrels, and prepared goods of a different kind. Casks of powder and crates of lead rolled down the floating walkways; sailors drilled and smiths fed their forges as the free people of the West Sea Kingdom prepared for war.

On the *Luminous*, he went first to the relay chamber, the natural gathering point for information across the entire armada. Iridan, Isri, and Khalesh gathered there, Iridan with his gemstones dim and the other two with heavy eyelids that spoke of late nights and heavy burdens. An array of devices lay before them on the table, and a steady stream of messengers flowed through the chamber, removing some and adding others. Rai padded up to the table and sniffed it, then sniffed at Iridan.

?, came his thought, a wordless note of curiosity surrounding Iridan's sharp smell. *Metal*, Vidarian thought back. *Clockwork man.* The wolf was getting bigger again; with only a slight lift of his head he could now see over the edge of the table.

"I heard a pipe whistle," Vidarian began.

"They've sighted imperial scout-ships," Iridan said. *"Not here, thankfully,"* he added, when Vidarian's eyes widened. *"In the Outwater. Searching."*

"Skyships?" Vidarian asked.

"Afraid so." A new voice, this time, but equally tired—Malloray, entering the chamber with a tray piled with *kava* and meatrolls. There was even a plate of raw chicken for Rai; Isri must have told him that Vidarian and the wolf had arrived. In spite of the intervening months he still wasn't quite used to living with telepaths. "They must think you're quite important. One of our scouts says the flagship is flying the banner of Admiral Allingworth." Malloray set his tray down, then put the plate of chicken on the floor for Rai.

"They've been sounding all morning," Khalesh added. "Did you just hear that one?"

Just then, the relay sphere at the center of the table brightened. Iridan opened two latched panels on either side of his palm, baring a blue lens embedded within, and placed his hand over the sphere. Light poured through it, and, miraculously, a moving picture began to take shape in the air above it.

"Lovely trick," Malloray murmured, squinting at the picture. Iridan adjusted his hand until the image sharpened into recognizability.

It was a scout, his hair whipped by a stiff wind over the Outwater. His mouth moved, and Iridan spoke, but not with his own voice. It was higher, and accented—the voice of the scout: *"Reporting from the third waypoint, sir! We've spotted the ships! Reports that it was Admiral Allingworth're right true, sir! They 'a'ven't spotted us, but we're circlin' some distance away—hope to keep ourselves from discovery for as long as we can!"*

"Well done, Rioque. Stay out of sight, stay safe, and we'll look to your midday report," Malloray answered.

The sphere's light faded, and Iridan took back his hand.

"I've got to go out there," Vidarian said. "I've got to speak with Allingworth. He'll listen to reason about all this. They must have sent him for diplomatic purposes." Khalesh and Malloray looked doubtful, and Vidarian pressed again. "He's the most important man in their war right now. They wouldn't pull him from the line if the object were simple destruction."

"You'll need a skiff," Malloray said. "One of ours will do. And Sea Kingdom ships will have to follow beneath you."

"They haven't much chance against skyships, have they?" Vidarian asked quietly, not wanting to, but unable to avoid it.

To his surprise, Khalesh smiled, a vicious expression. "That's our job." He waved a hand over the table.

"All these bits? What are you doing?" Vidarian picked up one of the elemental tools. It flared as he touched it and he nearly dropped it again.

"They've been working on converting the *Viere* into a skyship for some time, apparently," Malloray said. "Khalesh and Iridan have been conscripted into speeding up the process."

Khalesh shook his head. "Not a lot of good we are thus far. We need power sources."

"I saw a merchant among the tradegoods rafts," Vidarian said. "He had a strange lot of elemental artifacts—including a prism key."

The eye Khalesh turned on him was a mixture of interest and reproach at the reminder of their last interaction with a prism key, namely the one containing Ruby. But his curiosity won out, and he grunted a question. "Whereabouts?"

"Past the grocers and the growers, the luxury rafts farthest down the main walkway from the *Viere*," Vidarian said.

"We'll go presently," Malloray said, picking up a pair of relay lenses. He stepped back out the door and shouted for a messenger before he put them on. Then he was looking deeply into the relay sphere, his eyes somewhere far away. When the messenger appeared, he blinked, and said, "Summon the emperor, if you would. I have his Qui ambassador here, as requested."

Iridan and Khalesh were intent on their devices, and so Vidarian withdrew, wanting to seek out his skiff and get under way as fast as possible. Isri followed him, walking quietly out into the hall and shutting the door after Rai trotted out behind them.

The sight of her reminded Vidarian of how far they had come since the opening of the gate. As strange, quiet sadness accompanied those thoughts, for so many reasons.

"I had not thought to bring you into a war," he murmured.

A soft thrumming sounded from Isri's chest and throat—laughter, he realized, or a kind of it. "You assume that, before we entered the Great Gate, my people were accustomed to peace," she said, and when the laughter faded her voice turned downward into sadness. "Which we were not. And even if we had been . . ." Now the laugh was half sigh, and sliding quickly somewhere darker. "You know her. *Adrasti*. They—you—call her Starhunter. I have seen things, Vidarian, that our world ought never see."

"The seridi," Vidarian said, an echo of their living nightmares coming back to him, making him shiver. "They say things—"

"They are still seeing those visions of which I speak," she said sadly. "They are trapped in them."

"They're real, then? The visions?" Somehow the question, though distant and seeming inconsequential, felt critically important.

"To them, yes," Isri answered simply, crest-feathers just lifted in mild surprise. "They exist in those visions. They're quite real to them. But where they come from we don't know. Certainly other worlds, many of the other worlds that *Adrasti* can see and travel to, worlds beyond our ken. Even times, we think. Ages past and possibly even future." She started down the hall, then turned back, and Vidarian nearly ran into her. "Have you been sleeping?"

Vidarian didn't know how to answer. He also couldn't remember the last time he'd had a truly solid night's sleep, one not plagued by nightmares that would wake him panting and disoriented, spectres of dreams fading like threads of old spiderweb.

"It's good if you can sleep," Isri said, her cheek-feathers lifted in a tentative smile.

"I—have nightmares," Vidarian confessed.

He would have continued, but just then Lirien came striding down the hallway, a small entourage in tow. One of the attendants was the scribe who had annotated the council meeting. Vidarian stepped out of the way, and Lirien smiled as he passed.

"Qui?" Vidarian asked.

Lirien nodded. "I've made contact with our ambassador. He's been trapped in the embassy in Shen Ti, but Iridan was able to make contact with a dormant relay sphere there. It will take some doing, and time, but I intend to reach

Emperor Ziao." A hardness, and a fire, had stolen into Lirien's bearing. For the first time since they'd left the palace, Vidarian began to see the rebirth of the empire, and a new kind of future.

∿∿∿

Before he could leave, another authority would need to be convinced. Vidarian strode up the gangplank to board the *Viere d'Inar*, rehearsing repeatedly the explanation he would provide to Marielle for his journeying alone to treat with the admiral.

What he saw at the edge of the main deck stopped him in his tracks, and drove all thought of persuasion from his mind.

Altair crouched in the center of the deck, legs folded as neatly as a statue's, his wings half-spread with wingtips brushing the deck. His eyes were narrow slits, and eddies of invisible wind lifted the feathers all over his body. Around him sat a circle, evenly spaced, of glowing, fist-sized blue gems, and before him sat an elaborate device, roughly square, made of metal wheels all interlocking and studded with more blue elemental tubes.

Altair's eyes opened wide, and beneath them, the *Viere d'Inar* stirred, rose.

Vidarian flailed with his arms, catching at the rail. Beside him, Rai hissed, spreading his wings partway and cutting into the gangplank with his claws.

The ship only lifted a scant inch or two out of the water, but its rise was faltering, far from steady. After much shifting and rocking, it stabilized—then sank back into the water with a soft crash as hull met wave once more.

Now Altair was shuddering, coming back to himself. He blinked, and the white haze that had misted across his eyes faded, returning sense to them. His wings drooped with exhaustion. Nonetheless, when he came back to himself, his beak lifted in a smile of greeting.

"We'll have this old sea queen converted in no time," a cheerful voice said behind them. It was Marielle, ascending from the main ladders with a double-armful of iron and leather equipment. She set it down next to Altair—not getting too close, for the volatile wind energy crackled between the elemental stones at random intervals—and came up to meet Vidarian. When she drew near, she held out her hand for Rai to sniff, which he did, cautiously, his wide striped tail flicking back and forth as he did so. "Altair has been a tremendous help. Without his touch to fill and calibrate these salvaged controls, we wouldn't have a prayer of getting into the sky."

"Speaking of which," Vidarian began, by now having totally abandoned his carefully rehearsed argument.

"The sighting whistles," Marielle said, her voice darkening like clouds over afternoon sun. "You want to go and meet that imperial admiral. By yourself, I'll wager."

"Well, I—"

"You'd better leave quickly if you want to run advance of the rest of us," she said only. "And I'll send two ships with you, of course. Not a terrible lot they'll be able to do from the water—but Ulaine and his partner captain the best gunnery ship we've got. They'll suit you."

Taken aback by Marielle's forthright agreement to his dangerous mission, Vidarian could only nod, and finally salute, to which Marielle raised an acerbic eyebrow, and only smiled. "I take it you'll have notified them already," he added, once he began to get an inkling of how much further she'd thought the plan through.

"They'll be waiting for you at the northside docks. Don't make them wait too long."

He bowed then, though it was odd for so many reasons, and turned to go.

"Vidarian."

Slowly he turned back around.

"Keep them safe for me."

He smiled, making the pledge to himself as well as her. "I will—your majesty."

The *Luminous*'s small scouting skiff was not the *Destiny*, but it was a fine little craft, trim and merry. Or it would be, if not for the weight of their task. Vidarian had insisted on going alone, insofar as he could. Far below on the water were the *Kadari Knife* and the *Sunray*, two ships that had, if he recalled, been particularly good at opposing imperial craft in the past. The two young men helmed the *Knife* while the *Sunray* belonged to the blonde captain; they'd been perfunctory but perfectly pleasant, and fortunately unsurprised, when Vidarian went to meet them on the north side of Rivenwake.

Other than the water escort, he'd gone alone, taking only Rai, and that because the wolf absolutely insisted on going. Now that he could fly, there was little keeping him in a place he didn't desire. Thalnarra had been a harder sell, but he had at length prevailed upon her with the urgency to protect and assist Altair's recovery.

The handling of the skiff took all of his attention, and became a kind of meditation, a rhythm of rope and beam. As he guided the little craft into the air he was able to lose himself for a few moments in the sounds of wind hitting sail, the scents of sun on canvas and wood varnish.

Vidarian's spirits rose even as the ship did, and the blue arc of the sky, limitless, washed away the heaviness in his heart one worry at a time. Thoughts fell like raindrops into a well: the stiff breeze was cold and getting colder; was a storm coming in? He missed Ariadel; her absence was a simple ache that never seemed to abate.

In the silence of their rising altitude, there was little to pull him from these gentle ruminations, and his eyes began to absently follow cloud patterns. They traced shapes automatically: a topsail, an eagle, a cedar tree.

Then a face, curling up in the cloud, a familiar sharp chin and all-white eyes.

Rai started barking, his tail wagging furiously.

"How are you doing that?" Vidarian called to the formation.

Not so loud! the Starhunter said. *You never know who's listening.*

It would take longer, and frustrate more, to argue with her than comply, and so Vidarian thought: *How are you doing that? Doesn't the air goddess resent you intruding in her territory?*

Dowdy old things, she clucked. *I haven't even seen Siane since you let me out. She might be ignoring me. Always was a bit of a drama queen.*

A *what?* Vidarian thought, confused and annoyed.

Never mind. Look, you've got to help me out here. The cloud-face bit its lip, then swirled, losing cohesion. *Stupid . . . cloud!* She was pulling the surrounding cirrus blanket toward her "face," and the clouds darkened as they drew inward, condensing.

Vidarian leaned out over the rail, concerned for the ships far below. What kind of storm was she capable of summoning?

The face in the clouds gritted its teeth, and webs of frost crackled out over the mist. *I can't work like this! I'll be back.*

And then she was gone.

Three sharp notes sounded from below, a bosun's pipe from one of the ships. Rai whined, and the pipe sounded again, high and clear. Vidarian searched the sky, wondering what they were warning him of—

An imperial frigate cut through the mist, practically on top of them.

Rai started barking again, and Vidarian dove for the wheel, spinning it wildly to starboard to swing them away from the swift-approaching hull. Once they were out of the collision course, he leapt forward again and hauled on the spinnaker pole, spilling air from the skiff's little mainsheet and slowing their advance.

When he pulled the skiff around, sailors were shouting from the main deck of the frigate—marked *Starscape*—and two men in imperial regalia hailed him from the rail. Behind the ship were two smaller ones, also emerging from the mist: slender, battle-ready skyships with the marks of cannonfire and scorching fresh on their hulls.

The port wingmast brushed the hull of the *Starscape,* and Vidarian cursed, turning and stabilizing the skiff again. Then he sat back, hauled Rai—still barking—back from the skiff's rail by his neck-ruff, and shouted a greeting up to the frigate.

"Good morrow, Captain," the older of the two called down, first obscured by sunlight, then revealed. It was Admiral Allingworth. "I had hoped you might meet us here."

"And I am grateful for your presence, Admiral," Vidarian said, guiding the skiff up to eye level with the admiral. "Truly. Though disturbed that you were called away from the front."

"We're sent to escort you back to Val Imris, Lord Tesseract," the young man at the admiral's left hand said.

"I'm afraid that's not within my plans, sir . . . ?" He offered the 'sir' only for peacemaking, but was shocked when the man replied:

"Lieutenant August Kaine. I—"

"*Lieutenant*?" Vidarian repeated the title incredulously before he could stop himself. The younger man's face clouded.

The admiral had more sense, and a bit more diplomacy. "He's assisting on behalf of the Alorean Import Company," he cut in. Kaine looked displeased as his origin was revealed, but quickly schooled his expression. "They sent me with these ships to—see if this misunderstanding could be sorted out," Allingworth said, glancing at "Lieutenant" Kaine. "I told them," the admiral continued loudly, "that there must be some misunderstanding. There are some preposterous rumors, my boy—rumors that you've kidnapped the emperor!" He tried to laugh, but it was so forced that it died in his throat.

"We understand your strategy, Lord Tesseract," Kaine called. "The Court is impressed, and—" he smiled, thinly, visible even at this distance, "once recovered from their shock, glad to witness your strength. There will be much need for leadership in the future, leadership to guide our people through dark times."

"My loyalty is to the Alorean Emperor, and the imperial family!"

Kaine drew back, a slight motion, but his voice changed. "So you will not be returning with us?"

"I will not, Lieutenant." At his answer, Rai bristled, and began to growl softly.

"Then perhaps what you require is a demonstration of *our* strength." He turned. "Admiral Allingworth, open fire upon this vessel."

"I certainly will not," Allingworth said, his voice climbing in volume again. "And I advise you to remember your place, sir!"

Kaine's hand moved, drawing something from his waist sash, and light flared. Shock rippled through Vidarian along with the light—it was some kind of weapon!

And then Allingworth was tumbling from the *Starscape*, hurtling through the clouds, his side torn open and burned, mouth open and eyes already unseeing.

The admiral's body disappeared into the mist below them.

A terrible rage coursed through Vidarian—a thunder beneath his skin, a rattling in his chest, his claws sank into the wood of the skiff's deck—

He was leaping, wings outspread, two strong beats, and then he was tearing out the throat of the screaming human who had killed the admiral. Blood filled his mouth, hot and thick, and he bared his teeth, hissing.

Vidarian came back to himself with a gasp, falling backward in the skiff.

Rai was mantling over the body of Lieutenant Kaine, his back and tail stiff, claws extended. Sailors were shouting behind him, and advancing with drawn swords.

"Rai!" Vidarian roared, trying to catch the cat's attention. He reached out with his thoughts, clumsily—but Rai's mind was a cloud of rage, impenetrable. He only hissed again, crouching over his fallen prey.

The sailors closed in, an arc of blades, angry shouts spurring Rai to more growling and hissing.

Vidarian flung his elemental awareness outward, fire surging upward and spilling out of him, wild and uncontrolled. By sheer will he pulled the lash away from Rai, slicing it across the sailors. The water energy, strong and heavy where the fire was light, incandescent, rippled across the mist of the clouds around them, pulling water from the sky. It came drenching powerfully over the sailors, a torrent that disarmed several of them, clattering their swords to the deck—and soaked Rai, startling him out of his fury.

When he called Rai back this time, he flattened his ears but obeyed, leaping back to the skiff. The sailors might have lost some of their swords, but more of them now swarmed the deck, and command shouts called for cannon and muskets.

Vidarian dove for the wheel again, sweeping his hands across the elemental crystal that powered the craft and turning it until the light flickered out completely.

The skiff plummeted, and Vidarian threw one arm around Rai and the other around the mainmast, pressing himself to the floor. Cannonfire sounded overhead, and then from below, as the *Kadari Knife* and the *Sunray* answered the *Starscape*'s volley. When they'd fallen as far as he dared, Vidarian touched the crystal again, restoring power, and threw his weight against the rail downhauls, flying open the wingsails. Another spin of the wheel tilted the craft further, but they evened out into an arc, drifting fast down toward the waiting ships below.

As soon as the skiff stabilized, Vidarian hauled himself to his feet against the mast, waving frantically to the *Knife* and the *Sunray*. "Hail the *Luminous*! Prepare to fight!"

Chapter Twenty-Six
Promise

The *Starscape* was massive and slow to turn, even as a skyship, being a stocky imperial titan and not one of the agile, fast frigates favored by pirates, like the *Viere d'Inar*. She was a long time coming around, long enough that the *Knife* and the *Sunray* loosed multiple volleys, tearing the wide wingsails and snapping the leading edge off of the great keel-mast that kept the ship balanced. The frigate might have them on crew and armament, but she was headless, likely in disarray.

Vidarian thought it was going quite well, and then the firepipes opened.

Shuttered doors like square gunports opened near the base of the hull, below where a sea-going ship's waterline would be, giving way to long metal tubes, also like cannon but narrower. From these slim pipes poured fountains of fire, raining down on the ships below.

The *Sunray* was too close, and fire cut across her nose. Bright as it was, it incandesced even more brightly to Vidarian's vision, burning against his elemental sight. It did not explode on contact, for which he thanked every goddess there was, but it seared and consumed, melting through the *Sunray*'s deck like hot water through snow.

When imperial ships had fought the Qui off Isrinvale, they'd had cannonballs treated or forged with elemental fire energy inside them, weapons Thalnarra had called "fireshot." This was a completely different kind of weapon, somehow a flowing liquid that contained condensed fire energy, energy that was angry and charged—fire that hungered.

Plumes of steam poured up from the seared hull of the *Sunray* as the liquid fire met the surface of the ocean. With a sickening lurch Vidarian realized that this meant it had eaten through the entire face of the ship. With that realization came confirmation, as the *Sunray* took on water and began to dip downward from the fore.

Men and women swarmed across the decks of both Sea Kingdom ships. The *Kadari Knife* was coming around, heeling hard to port in an attempt to bring its rail close enough to rescue leaping sailors abandoning the *Sunray*. The two young captains shouted encouragement to their crew, brandishing their swords at the looming *Starscape* high above them in a spectacular dearth of any self-preservation.

The streams of fire had stopped, but the *Starscape* was turning in an arc, readying itself for another deadly pass.

Vidarian turned to the controls of the little skiff, searching through the cryptic markers that were ancient indicators of the strength of the elemental power source. From the slow speed with which it had ascended, he extrapolated how many sailors it might hold—how many he might rescue from either ship. By his quick calculations, the answer was not nearly enough.

The *Starscape* had nearly made her turn, and the other two skyships were tipping into position to unleash their cannon on the Sea Kingdom ships. If either of them had fireshot, the *Knife* would be lucky to last minutes.

Vidarian looked up again, desperately gauging the distance between the sea ships and the belly of the *Starscape*. Then, before he could remind himself that it was completely insane, he thrust his entire awareness down into the ocean.

Cold shocked him first, followed by a rush of water energy, the electric tang of salt and the cataclysmic depth that only the open ocean could provide. Voices filled his mind, distant, indecipherable—thousands of voices echoing throughout the sea. A tiny part of him that remained Vidarian wondered who they were, and why he had never heard them before. He tried to call out to them, but his voice only echoed, swallowed up by wave and sea life.

Other parts of him darted away, and he began to lose his grip on himself and his consciousness. The bits that were Vidarian spilled away like grains of sand, dancing through the sea. He strained so hard after them that, far away, hanging in the sky, his body gasped, his chest compressing. And this pulled him back, helped him draw a line around the bits that were him and push away the seeming-infinite bits that were not.

When he had circled himself, he reached out to grip the ocean itself, and pulled.

Vidarian opened eyes he hadn't realized he'd closed and nearly fell to the deck in a rush of doubled vision and nausea. He closed his eyes again, gritted his teeth, and pulled harder, lifting the sea itself. He reached deep into the heart of the water, down as far as he could go, and then farther.

And the sea rose. It climbed into the sky like the top of a bell, curving upward and taking the sea ships with it.

The weight was enormous, stretching Vidarian to his limits. And at the heart of his being, his fire magic curled like a venomous snake, a parasitic worm, eating away at his spirit with flame and tooth now that he was consumed by water.

He continued to lift, blinking as sweat poured down his forehead and into his eyes. He hoped that the *Knife* and even the *Sunray* had enough sense to train their cannon on the imperial ships as Vidarian pulled them into range.

They did. Cannonfire sounded, plumes of black smoke climbed into the air; high above, wood shattered and sailors cried out as holes opened up on the *Starscape* and the other two ships.

The echo of the cannonfire pushed the Sea Kingdom ships against the upward-curving sea—and Vidarian lost his grip.

All at once the ocean slipped away from him, sliding through his "hands" like wet silk rope. The sea began to churn and roar as he accidentally set it free, and he flailed after it, but it was too late. Already resenting being held even for a moment, the water churned, and high above, storm clouds closed in over the battle.

They all sank back to the natural surface of the water, Vidarian exhausted beyond thought and falling to the deck of the skiff. The shadow of the *Starscape* passed over them, and Vidarian prepared to meet death.

As the sea ships tipped up and down in the water, the *Sunray* more than half sunk below the green waves, a bugle call sounded, high and far, from the sky to the south.

Gathering mist parted, and the white sails of the *Luminous*, spread like bird's wings, its keel-mast an elegant tail, swept toward them, one of the most welcome sights of Vidarian's life. Around the ship were Caladan and his handful of Sky Knights, an honor guard for Lirien. And behind them—

Behind the *Luminous*, its new wing-masts bright in the morning sunlight, supple steel and translucent airsilk, was, impossibly, the *Viere d'Inar*.

As the fast frigate of Vidarian's childhood drew closer—he could not see her without feeling a blow to his heart, for Ruby and for her mother before her, who would never see this strange and wonderful sight—the method of her flight revealed itself. Altair stood, legs braced and wings spread, atop the fore-castle, winds of his own making spinning around him and lifting his feathers. In the center of the main deck, the tube and clockwork device Vidarian had seen earlier glowed like a great blue beacon, and all of the gryphon's attention was centered on it, keeping them aloft.

Even as it advanced, the *Viere* started to turn, bringing its wide body around to present its gunport-studded side to the *Starscape*. It opened fire, and the sound shattered the air, knocking Vidarian off his feet.

More holes opened up in the now-overmatched *Starscape*, and this time sailors spilled from them, plummeting toward the water. Though Altair was bound to the *Viere*, another gryphon leapt from the rail—Thalnarra—arrowing out over the water and then angling around an updraft, carrying herself high and fast. She proceeded to harry the *Starscape*'s surviving crew, lashing out with lances of fire energy even as she swooped and dove, pulling men from the rigging and dropping them into the sea.

Relieved, Vidarian pointed the skiff toward the *Luminous* and laid on its power, sending them scudding through the air toward the relay ship.

Cannons tore the air as he sped for the *Luminous*, the *Viere* opening with all guns on the three ships. A great shadow slanted across the sea as the *Starscape* tilted to port in the sky, its wingmast snapped in half on that side. The two other ships returned fire, but chaotically, thrown into disarray by the looming collapse of their flagship.

Vidarian had just pulled upon the *Luminous*, rising along her starboard hull, when the ripples hit him.

He dove to the deck, pulling Rai down with him. The hammer of water energy preceded by the rippling warning tore through the skiff's single mast, snapping it and slamming them into the hull of the *Luminous*. Rai screeched, leaping upward, throwing out his wings, and Vidarian was lifted off his feet, carried upward.

The skiff fell beneath them, cracking its keel as it bounced off of the larger ship, and Rai's wings were pumping, lifting them into the air. Panic had given him strength, but after two wingbeats he began to falter, not strong enough to carry Vidarian's weight. Despite the long fall that awaited, Vidarian prepared to push himself away from Rai, to save him from being pulled down with him.

Rai snarled, not with anger, but determination, hissing *Stay!* into Vidarian's mind, mimicking a command Vidarian had often given him, and renewed his desperate wingbeats, throwing himself—and Vidarian with him—at the *Luminous*. Even as his wings worked, he reached out with his forepaws, swiping at the wooden hull with claws extended. They sank into the wood, but Rai kept moving, clawing his way upward with Vidarian clinging to his neck.

Light poured into their eyes as they reached the top of the rail. Rai curled his paws around the beam, kicking furiously with his hind legs to push them the rest of the way. In a tumble they rolled onto the deck, and Vidarian pressed the sanded wood with his hands, breathing deep to calm his pounding heart. Rai stood over him, claws sunk into the deck as if he expected it to fall out from beneath them, his tail lashing. When Vidarian looked up, Rai lowered his head and licked Vidarian's cheek with a large sandpaper tongue. Vidarian reached up to bury his hand in the thick fur of the underside of the cat's neck.

A crash followed by shouts split the air, and Rai hissed again, crouching. Vidarian pushed himself to his feet and went to the rail, searching.

Another fist of wild water energy—seawater pulled up from the still-rolling ocean—had thundered into the *Viere d'Inar*, tearing a wide hole in its starboard wing-mast. The ship pitched to the side, and sailors yelled, sliding across the deck. Two of them rolled off the side, crying out in horror before their lifelines snapped taut, suspending them in the air.

Vidarian traced the residual water energy up into the air, expecting to see one of the imperial skyships. Instead, a seridi, only a silhouette against the gathering thunderheads, hovered there, her eyes unseeing as she turned and unleashed strike after strike of water energy.

Thalnarra landed beside them, breathing heavily with exertion. Patches of feathers were ragged, and blood flowed sluggishly from a shallow sword cut on her left flank. // *She must have been drawn by your trick with the waves,* // she said, gesturing with her beak to the seridi, then moving to the rail and looking down.

Below them, the *Viere* was angling unsteadily toward the water. She struck the sea with a boom that rippled the water's surface as far as the eye could see. Her lack of keel-mast now was an advantage as she took to the water and quickly reoriented.

Behind, from the aftcastle of the *Luminous*, Isri burst into flight, shedding her black cloak behind her as she took to the air. She flew directly toward the attacking seridi, reaching out with her hands as she flew.

The seridi turned toward her, crest raising with alarm. As the mad ones did, she seemed to see and not see her at the same time. It was clear that she saw *something*, but it was not Isri. Whatever she saw caused her to lift both hands and draw water from the sea so forcefully that it compressed Vidarian's chest even at this distance.

Isri continued hurtling toward her, even as another arm of water lifted itself from the sea. Sweat broke out over Vidarian's forehead as he watched, waiting. She was too far away, and her hold on the water too strong, for him to simply overpower her at this distance—he would have to wait until she released the water, and hope that he could deflect it in time.

When Isri saw the water, she turned in midair, and for a moment Vidarian hoped the strike would miss her entirely. But the other seridi tracked her with mad eyes, curving the water even as she released it.

Vidarian strained, reaching out to touch the flying water, hundreds of lengths away though it was. He almost touched it, and then his own fire sense roared up within him, even angrier than it had been before. It had become a living thing, almost its own consciousness, and snapped at him, eroding his grip.

A rolling growl sounded beside him, and he had no time to decipher whether it was anger or annoyance. But Thalnarra's own fire sense reached into him and crushed his, creating a sudden sinking feeling in his stomach, but freeing his water sense to knock the blast of seawater explosively to one side just before it reached Isri.

The two seridi collided in midair, the mad one—Treune, he could almost hear Isri saying—snarling like an animal and fighting Isri with fingers crooked into claws. But as soon as Isri touched her forehead, the other seridi fell limp.

Altair, watching the engagement from below, and now no longer needed in keeping the *Viere* aloft, leapt into the air, his wide wings a flash of white against the dark wood and sea. He flew arrow-swift toward the two seridi, reaching out with air magic to stop the unconscious one from falling. Isri fluttered, her wings strained, but the three of them soon glided toward the *Luminous*.

Though the arrival of the mad Treune seridi had distracted the imperial ships—she had struck blindly, and so had damaged one of the smaller ships in addition to striking the *Viere* and the *Luminous*—it had done little to pause their onslaught. Cannonfire still shook the air, and the *Viere*, once it settled on the sea, rejoined the fight, adding its thundering guns to the exchange.

Altair and Isri landed on the deck, gently setting the unconscious seridi down between them. Her feathers were an iridescent dark blue, streaked with black. A pair of medics ran across the deck from the forecastle, but Isri waved them away.

"Altair, my friend!" Vidarian lifted his hand, and Altair tiredly pressed his charcoal beak into it. "You have already done more than these ships could have imagined, but I must ask you—can you get me up there?" He pointed to the more intact of the three skyships, the smallest vessel that hovered to the rear.

Altair shook out his feathers, but nodded. // I can. // Then, without preamble, he lifted Vidarian into the air, just before leaping off the deck himself.

Coming too, Rai said, and leapt after them. It was strange to see him flying side by side with Altair. Vidarian knew he was big, but here he nearly matched the gryphon for length, if not for height or girth.

Now that he'd done this before, Vidarian liked to think he was a little better at balancing his body atop Altair's. It was not *riding* a gryphon, per se —he quailed to think of how Altair would respond to such an idea—but by flattening himself close to the gryphon's back and using his arms to balance, he could make the flying easier on his tired friend.

// *Where shall I drop you?* // Altair asked. A cannonball flew by them and he twitched his wing, swinging effortlessly out of the way, though sending Vidarian's heart convulsing.

"Near the prow," Vidarian shouted over the wind. "Get us to the front, if you would. Then tell Malloray and Yerune to get the *Luminous* up next to us!"

They were coming fast upon the smallest of the three ships, though it was still larger than the *Luminous* herself. Altair brought them swiftly in, banking in a wide arc, and the ship loomed large before them. Tall letters on its side marked it the *Argentium*. Vidarian drew his arms and legs inward, preparing for a rolling landing, and his stomach gave a lurch as Altair's air touch released him. He hit the deck feetfirst and rolled, drawing his sword as he regained his legs. Beside him, Rai landed as well, snarling.

Sailors ran toward him, shouting, but both their shouts and their attacks were exhausted, demoralized. Vidarian shouted back at them: "Drop your weapons and surrender! I am Captain Vidarian Rulorat, and I act under the authority of your emperor, Lirien Aslaire!"

One of the men fired a musket at him, and he reached out with an arc of fire energy, which leapt snakelike at the flying ball, relishing being released at last. He brought the fire down in an arc, disrupting the curve of the shot and sending it flying aside into the deck. Rai snarled, advancing on the men, but one of the other sailors was already pulling the musket from his comrade's hands.

A blast of wind carried smoke into all of their faces, and they turned toward the port rail. Beyond it, and far below them, the *Starscape* had caught fire in earnest, and her sailors were losing their battle against the flames. It pitched even further toward the water, nose first, and sailors spilled out of it by the dozen.

The defending party of the *Argentium* threw down its swords, and Vidarian lowered the tip of his blade with relief. One of the sailors, a slender Ishmanti, pointed behind Vidarian and shouted.

Vidarian turned, dreading yet another unexpected enemy. But it was the *Luminous*, drawing upon the final ship remaining in the air and fighting. Caladan's Sky Knights flew out in front of them, surrounding the imperial ship.

The three ships were close, and at the prow of the *Luminous* Vidarian could easily recognize Lirien. The sailors of the *Argentium* recognized him too, and a murmur of shock and dismay rippled through them. A scuffle broke out toward the rear, as three of the sailors wrestled a sword out of the hands of a Company commander.

Lirien called out to the final ship, beseeching its sailors. "Men and women of the empire! Do not spend your lives so needlessly! Put down your weapons, and renew your loyalty to Alorea and its emperor!" Aboard the other ship, sailors turned, the tips of their swords dropping, incredulous as to what they were hearing, responding to the voice of their sovereign.

As Lirien drew breath to shout again, Tepeki came to stand beside him, waving to the other ship.

Vidarian only saw the flash of a blade, and then the knife's bone handle, protruding from Lirien's side.

Tepeki, the snarl on his face far older than his years, yanked the knife free—blood arced across the deck of the *Luminous*—then struck again, slicing across the emperor's stomach, then a third time, sinking the blade into his chest.

Rai leapt from the deck of the *Argentium*, roaring, wings spreading—and Vidarian, caught up in the strength of Rai's emotion again but not consumed by it, dropped his sword to the deck and leapt with him.

The sea opened up beneath them, hundreds of lengths below. Vidarian's heart flew into his throat, and he scrambled in midair toward Rai, even as he knew the big cat could not support both their weight. He drew breath to shout for Altair, but then, as his hands came down to grip the base of Rai's feathered wings, Rai began to change shape again.

The feathers beneath his hands flattened, hardened, spread. Before him Rai's neck stretched long, his striped spines growing even longer, protruding knifelike from a long, swanlike neck. His head was stretching too, along length and width, and a crown of horns erupted from his forehead. The cat's face narrowed, eyes stretching, and his skin everywhere had become rough, pebbled with scales.

Even as Vidarian clung to the now-broad back, leathery wings stretching three times as long as Thalnarra's to either side of him, Rai roared again, a bone-rattling reptilian sound, and dove at the *Luminous*.

The dragon's roar became a hiss, and the hiss became an explosion, a flash and a crackle as Rai discharged a bolt of lightning, this time very directed and deliberate, that struck the ship moments before his massive body crashed against it.

Tepeki blanched pale as soon as he saw Rai transform, dropping his knife to the deck. He flung himself over the rail, diving for the sea.

Rai pushed away from the *Luminous*, cracking wood with his claws, and dove after Tepeki, hurtling headfirst toward the water. As he fell, Tepeki changed, becoming the otter, dwindling in the air and darkening, far smaller than Rai's head alone.

The otter slipped into the water with hardly a splash, only moments before Rai struck down with a titanic one, his neck flailing and wings buffeting the surface as he scrambled after his small quarry. Vidarian fought to keep his seat, sliding on the scaled back, but able to wrap his legs around one of the huge spines that rose from Rai's back.

Furiously Rai thrust his head beneath the water, searching, but Tepeki was gone. The dragon roared, and electricity crackled from his body, arcing out across the water. Sailors that had fallen from the ships but survived in the sea now writhed, their bodies wracked by electricity.

"He's gone, Rai!" Vidarian shouted, now beyond shock, a numbness creeping through his entire body. He thumped at the dragon's shoulder, not knowing if, in this new shape, and in his state of rage, Rai would even recognize him.

The dragon's head whipped around, spines roused, hissing—

But when he saw Vidarian, he drew back, huge eyes clouding with confusion. He hesitated, then growled, a preternatural reptilian sound.

"Can you get us back to the *Viere*?" Vidarian asked. "Back to Marielle?"

Rai's head tipped down in a nod, and he flapped his wings, striking the water with each movement, but lifting them into the air. As had happened when he had first turned into the winged cat, he seemed to have trouble speaking, perhaps even trouble forming his own thoughts. This close to him, Vidarian felt the waves of grief, confusion, and fury that rolled off of him, and in moments his own cheeks were cold, chilled as the wind blew against the tears he did not know he was shedding.

Only the *Viere* was large enough to bear Rai's weight now, and even still the ship listed as he landed at the bow. The two gryphons were there, uncertainly taking in Rai's new shape, and so was Marielle. Malloray stood beside her, his face red with emotion; the *Luminous* had no doubt already relayed what had just happened.

"We've seized the remaining ship," Marielle said. Her face, through the soot of the cannon battle, was tear-streaked. "Her crew put up a token resistance only." As well they might, seeing their emperor, unexpected in the first place, cut down before them. "We don't dare return to Rivenwake," she said. "With all this commotion, we'll be lucky if they don't find it as it is. We need to travel far, distract them."

// *We can lead you,* // Altair said. The gryphon's exhausted mind-voice, pale as sawdust, turned all their heads toward him.

"To where?"

// *To friends,* // Thalnarra said, and Altair tipped his beak in a weary nod.

Chapter Twenty-Seven

Gryphonslair

Lirien's body was wrapped in velvet and hides, bunches of dried herbs raided from the herbery of the *Luminous* lain around him to stave off decay. Yerune, who, in defiance of her private demeanor, seemed the most openly devastated of all of the crew, insisted that he be transported in the largest stateroom of the *Luminous*. That he would be returned to the Imperial City was never questioned; even the most ardent of the Sea Kingdom sailors would have found the notion of his sea burial unsettling.

Vidarian stood in the stateroom, alone except for Rai, who had positioned himself just inside the doorway when the emperor was brought there and would not be moved. He had spent so much of his time in his cat form while they had been sailing—a practical enough choice for sky travel—but now that he lay on the floor, head on his paws, Vidarian could see again how much he had grown. The spines that had seemed small and awkward when he was a pup had now grown into a fierce mane, now more closely resembling his forest kin. It was an odd way to measure time, Vidarian thought, the length of a thornwolf's spines.

Lirien's stillness could only feel like a reproach. It was still impossible to believe he was dead, and yet all too real at the same time. Vidarian had been haunted for so long by the dead: his brothers, his father, Ruby, and now Lirien. When he began to count them up, more crowded in: the priestesses the Starhunter had killed, the Sky Knights sent by the Alorean Import Company, the sailors who earned death by following orders from a corrupt authority. There was so much death in the world, and it was hard not to think it was needless, especially as he looked upon the body of a friend, something he had done too often these last months.

He tried to mourn, and part of him had already caved in with sorrow, but the larger part of his awareness burned with wordless rage. Tepeki had been young, impetuous, full of contempt for the empire, but to kill Lirien? How had he had it in him, and more painfully, why had Vidarian not seen it?

There was one person aboard who might be able to provide answers, though it weighed on Vidarian to ask it of her.

The *Luminous* turned and the deck creaked beneath his feet, pulling him from his reverie. He shook himself, then left the stateroom, pausing only to reach down and scratch Rai's ears. The wolf's tail swished across the floor, but he did not lift his head.

Abovedecks, a small group conferred at the bow. Clouds traced by beneath them, and far aft was the *Viere d'Inar*; Endera and her fire priestesses had been able to restore the flagship's wing-mast with impressive quickness, melting the steel back together, and she had once again taken to the air, shepherded by Altair but under her own power.

Before the bowsprit, Marielle stood supervising Isri, Alora, and Malloray, who gathered around the bone-handled knife that Tepeki had left behind. When Vidarian arrived, they all turned toward him, sympathy and grief a palpable miasma that he tried to push away from his thoughts.

Vidarian knelt in front of Alora, putting his eyes even with hers. Despite the long history of child windreaders aboard sailing vessels, Alora still seemed too young by far to be witnessing such things. Ship children were tough, wise beyond their years; Alora with her large, soulful eyes and thin body seemed sensitive, youth embodied. "You don't have to do this, my dear," Vidarian said.

But the girl stiffened, her eyes going wide and then strong. "I want to help, sir. I know it will be—dark. But this is the price of my ability." The words were full of competence, comprehension, incongruous in her high voice—but still she looked to Isri for approval. The seridi nodded, and Alora flushed with pride.

Vidarian looked at Isri, knowing she would feel his discomfort. She only nodded again, the smallest motion, and a wave of reassurance wrapped around him, a warmth that said she understood, and regretted, also.

Alora turned back around and picked up the knife. She had quietly held her breath as she did so, and only when she held the bone pommel between both hands did she breathe in again.

The girl shuddered, her eyes rolling back in her head before she recovered herself. Isri placed an encouraging hand on her shoulder. "He had—some kind of arrangement with the Alorean Import Company . . ." Her eyes went distant, then widened with horror, still unseeing. "They were going to kill Tepeki's people. All of them. Somehow—hunt down his entire race . . ." Her forehead wrinkled and she squeezed her eyes shut, searching. "He didn't know how. But he knew that they could do it, that they would hunt every Velshi in the five seas. *Makkta chichinot'ta Aielu*—" She shook her head, focusing. "Unless he killed the emperor."

Vidarian's throat closed, a wave of exhaustion and dizziness rushing to his head with the dread, but he fought them back. "Did An'du know about this?" He did not want to hear the answer, but knew that he must.

"No," Alora said, her eyes still closed. Relief flowed through Vidarian like water. "An'du wanted him to befriend the empire. She will be very angry. He is afraid. The one-skin man is nothing to him, but it is anathema to kill *ta'alewa*. He fears it bringing a curse upon him, but must bear it for his people. He fills his heart with apologies to Akawe Sea-mother." All this Tepeki had experienced as he dealt the killing blow, unknowingly infusing his heart into the blade for Alora to read. "A man from the Company directed him to this. He wears a smiling mask like the death-god of the Velshi shadow shamasal."

"Justinian," Vidarian growled. But fast beneath the fury that crackled through his heart came another realization. "And this happened when Tepeki was in the Imperial City. In my trust."

"Belay't," Marielle said, harsh but not unkind. "An'du wanted you to take him to the city. And now we know our enemies' hand." She looked hard at Vidarian, a steel in her now that he had not known even in the decades that she had sailed knife-reefs and worse under his command and his father's. "You were right to bring us into this."

The *Luminous* and the *Viere* flew east under the gryphons' direction, long days of sun and silence that slowly baked the sky battles into more distant memories. After two days, the Alorean coast appeared, and then the snowy ridges of the Windsmouth Mountains. The Sea Kingdom ships dispersed, tasked with harrying the ships of the Alorean Import Company still conducting trade in the West Sea, and the four skyships—the *Viere*, the *Luminous*, the *Argentium*, and the captured *Skyfalcon*—continued on alone, heavily loaded with as many Sea Kingdom sailors as would volunteer to meet the Company again in battle. It was a satisfying population.

But where they had numbers, they lacked in training. Fortunately, when it came to skyships, the Company should be at an equal disadvantage, still bridging the gap between what could and could not be adapted from sea-based warfare. And Vidarian's ever-growing force had two advantages: the gryphons, who had been skilled in aerial warfare for thousands of years, and, surprisingly, Iridan, who had both seen and studied live skyship battles in their heyday.

Once they reached the coastline, the days moved fast, heavy with drills and strategy. A new life took over the ships, an energy of anticipation and focus unlike Vidarian had ever experienced, though his father and grandfather had described it. There was fear, hanging unsaid in conversations about the size of the Company's mercenary forces, but there was also readiness and determination.

On the eighth day, they passed over a desert and began to turn northward, following a curve of the Windsmouth that changed here from granite megaliths to craggy shale cliffs, and finally to high, dry buttes of white-banded red rock. They passed beyond the snow flurries that spiraled ever off of the Windsmouth and into vaulting dry skies scudded with only the occasional thin, white cloud.

On the ninth morning they were well into high desert, and Thalnarra joined Vidarian at the bow as he surveyed the land below, trying to determine where they were.

// *We've been granted permission to land.* // Her voice had an electricity to it.

Vidarian turned, about to ask her why they would even consider landing in such an inhospitable place, but even as Thalnarra spoke, the encampment unveiled itself below, animal-hide tents and log-built training courses, herdbeast fields and storage buildings. They coalesced into view one at a time, then three at a time, six—multiplying as they grew closer.

Then, visible in the air below and even above them: squadrons of gryphons. Wings, Thalnarra would have called them. Groups of five to ten gryphons that flew together in formation, their every twitch of a feather perfectly synchronized, in lines and arrowheads and rows, flying patrols around their territory or practicing drills.

As they began to descend, other flyers became clear. Vidarian didn't quite believe it until they had landed, and the sight was indisputable:

Seridi practiced in groups or alone, spread out among the gryphons. And these were no mad wildlings, nor mindspeakers like Isri, nor magic-users at all, it seemed—they were warriors. Those that did not already have naturally grey or black feathers had their plumage dyed in mottled greys, blues, and blacks—the better to disappear against the sky. Their movements had a deadly grace not unlike what he'd seen in Maresh honor guards . . . who, now that he thought of it, had always claimed to inherit their long hand-fighting tradition from ancient extinct allies.

But the seridi were not the most surprising denizens of the camp. Off to the side, tucked into their own smaller encampment but no less active for it— almost beyond explanation—were Sky Knights.

As soon as they lowered the gangplank, Caladan urged his mount to the ground, then cantered toward his brethren. The apprentices, whose steeds were still colts and not ridable, stayed aboard the *Luminous*.

"He sent word around the whole empire," Linnea said, her hand on the sprightly mane of her royal. "Some kind of code that hasn't been used in generations. He said the ones we wanted would answer the call."

And "the ones we wanted" numbered, at a glance, nearly two hundred.

Vidarian had known that there were nearly two thousand Sky Knights spread across the empire—they were trying, and failing, to increase the fertility rates of the steeds and especially the royals—but he never would have guessed that this many would be willing to openly rebel against the men and women who held their purse strings.

Caladan came cantering back up, his tricolored steed tossing its head and snorting with happiness to be among its brothers and sisters. The knight was smiling, the first time he'd done so since Lirien's death. It was not a joyous smile, but a satisfied one; small and hard. "Nearly two hundred have come," he said, confirming Vidarian's estimate. "And more are coming in every day. The smaller provinces especially, and those far from Qui. They too have felt the heat of the Company for months." He trotted back to the other knights, then, after a hasty bow; Vidarian felt a flush of gratitude to see him truly among his own people again.

Vidarian worked his way toward what appeared to be a command tent, Rai so close to his side that his spines brushed against Vidarian's leg. Small girls and boys ran back and forth endlessly across the camp, packs of them forming fluidly whenever one or more of them was on an errand to the same location. They were wild and swift, tough-soled and utterly unsocialized; // *Gryphon-wards,* // Altair offered, when he too had descended from the *Luminous* and followed Vidarian. // *Honorary members of the pride.* //

"That's what Brannon wants to be?" Vidarian only barely kept himself from raising his voice. "'Gryphon-wards'—they're real? I thought Thalnarra was just trying to . . . inspire him to good behavior."

A low sound that was almost a growl, but pitched upward into laughter. // *They are very real, and very needed, particularly for the prides with especially large gryphons who can't even manage a buckle with their own talons. The little ones are our hands and sometimes even our eyes.* //

"And what are you teaching them?" Vidarian asked.

Altair's head drew back, his tufted ears low as he thought over the question. // *They learn wildness. Survival. And a bond with their pride as strong as the bond between gryphon pridemembers.* //

"Wait—you said 'especially large gryphons.' What do you mean? Thalnarra seems quite able to manage herself—"

Altair was looking at him, wry amusement radiating from him with a scent like fresh-cut basil. // *Well—I imagine you'll see in a moment.* //

They were almost upon the tent when Thalnarra herself landed next to them. She panted softly with exertion; she'd been busy greeting all who needed greeting, and well she might; Vidarian had never seen so many gryphons—or so many different *kinds* of gryphons—in his life, nor his imagination.

There were two tents that looked command caliber, and Vidarian entered the one on the left at a quick nod from Thalnarra's beak. Inside, his eyes took a moment to adjust—and then, sitting there, waiting for them, were the two largest gryphons he had ever seen, short of the Starhunter's giant companion, which he half suspected he may have imagined.

// *Pridemother, I bring you Vidarian Rulorat, and Altair, our wind brother.* //

Vidarian realized that the standard against which he had measured gryphons—Thalnarra—was an excellent one, but not nearly large enough. The pridemother was massive, an athlete among gryphons, her shoulders half again as broad and her wings long and gleaming. On seeing her, Rai actually barked a warning, and Vidarian hurried to shush him.

But large as she was, the pridemother herself was dwarfed by a gryphon beside her, whose long head—bearing the single largest beak Vidarian had ever seen, an eagle's hooked weapon twice the length of his spread hand—was several handspans above the pridemother's at rest. His rectangular wings were also the largest Vidarian had seen, with powerful golden primaries. And next to the large-beaked gryphon's, Thalnarra's talons looked slim and dainty; not only were her claws smaller overall, they were significantly smaller by proportion.

Looking at the monstrous creature—and boggling all over again when he realized that he was a drake gryphon, a male, meaning that a female of his type would be even larger—Vidarian's entire view of gryphons shifted. Thalnarra was a striking creature, without doubt, but he had been so used to thinking of her as the largest of her kind, as she was broader and larger than Altair or the other gryphons he had met. Now he realized that he had only encountered scouts and supporters—excellent creatures, well-suited to border tasks, but hardly the fighting core of gryphonkind. And Kaltak and Ishrak, whom he had always thought of as average in size, now seemed awkward and adolescent, as no doubt they were when compared to the elders of their pride and flight.

// *Welcome, Captain Rulorat, to our camp. I am Meleaar.* // The huge gryphon's voice was warm and rich, almost like hot butter and a sharp spring morning.

"Thank you, Sir Meleaar," Vidarian answered, at a loss for what to call him. "And Pridemother. I—had no idea you were out here, that there were gryphons on the northern continent."

All four gryphons clicked their beaks gently, chuckling. // *We would hardly call our own home 'Gryphonslair,'* // Meleaar said. // *Our allies refer to it thus. We are a temporary encampment, owing to the eastern campaign.* //

"Eastern campaign?" Vidarian blinked. Thalnarra had said nothing about this.

Meleaar and the pridemother exchanged startled glances. // *Well, of course. We assume that your forces are here for that reason—and quite welcome they are.* // When Vidarian did not immediately answer, Meleaar continued. // *We won't keep you long. We are sure there is someone you should be seeing at once.* //

⌇⌇⌇

After the pridemother, Thalnarra shepherded Vidarian to the tent adjacent, pushing him and Rai through its flap with her beak . . . and then leaving. Vidarian started to call after her, but knew by the determination in her step that she would never hear him.

Rai whined, and Vidarian turned around—almost directly into Ariadel.

She had stood from her desk, piled high with parchment and message tubes, and walked halfway to the tent flap, her arms folded across her chest. Her stomach very visibly swelled now, and her cheeks were red—and not, he thought, out of joy at seeing him. Heat and pressure filled his chest at the sight of her, and it was all he could do to keep his hands at his sides.

"What are you doing here?" she asked. "I never authorized a landing."

Vidarian started to answer, then blinked. "You—command this place?"

"Of course I do," she said, turning back to the desk. "This is the heart of the resistance. They didn't tell you that?" And then, without waiting for him to answer, "Someone had to do something."

Parchment crinkled on the desk—Raven, the cat, even larger than Vidarian remembered, still flame orange and striped.

Rai started barking and charged, the puppy-wolf taking over his brain. Vidarian shouted wordlessly and dove after him, tackling. He earned an accidental shock for his efforts, but Rai immediately left off, whining apologies.

"I've done what I could," he said, more sharply than he meant to, standing, his arm smarting from the electricity. "I've brought you two dozen Sky Knights, nearly two hundred Sea Kingdom sailors, and four skyships."

"You brought them?" Ariadel said, moving to the opening to draw back the tent-flap and peer out. "Skyships?" Her eyes had gone dark and thoughtful, calculating.

Vidarian stood, and before he could blink, Ariadel rushed into his arms, pulling him tightly against her. His own arms fell around her, carefully, hardly daring to touch her, and especially careful of the fragile curve of her stomach. The feel of her pressed against him, and the thought of her condition, the child she carried, made his head spin. Something started to break loose in him, but then her head was coming up, and she kissed him, fierce and with abandon at once. Her hands lifted to bring his face even closer, and then there were no thoughts at all, only fire and ocean, depth and height, as it had always been with her from the moment they met.

"I'm sorry," she said, when she drew her head back, then pressed her forehead into his collarbone. "I thought—I didn't—"

"It's all right," he said, kissing her hair. "Of course it's all right. I never should have . . ." He couldn't finish the sentence.

She laughed softly into his chest, saying without words that he didn't need to. They stood that way for a long time, and yet if it had been years it wouldn't have been long enough.

"I didn't think you'd ever forgive me," he said. The words fell out, as they had so many months ago, but this time not nearly so disastrous.

"I wasn't going to," she said, looking up at him, then looking away. "But—spending this much time around gryphons has a way of sinking in."

"I didn't know gryphons were the forgiving type."

"They're not," she replied, and his eyebrows lifted. "But they mate for life." She pulled away, but only to look at him.

Vidarian rested his hands on her shoulders, searching her eyes carefully. "At risk of losing everything I care about right this moment—that doesn't seem an especially good reason."

Ariadel covered one of his hands with her own. "They have—a more distant perspective. Whatever this is, and much as we'd hate to admit it, something larger than either of us has brought us together. And it didn't think about taking its time or making it easy. But that doesn't mean it was wrong."

Vidarian straightened, startled at hearing his own thoughts echoed back in Ariadel's voice.

"Just promise me a future when we can learn more of each other," she said.

"I would move worlds to make that happen," he said.

"All right. We're even."

Turning back to the desk, she drew away, and again he fought not to move immediately with her. It was enough to have the terrible pull in his chest alleviated, if only for a moment. It was enough to have true purpose again.

Raven, the oddly named cat, perched on the edge of the desk, her head down and nose almost touching Rai's as he looked up at her in fascination. A tiny spark of electricity jumped from his nose to hers, and she hissed, slashing at him with a paw. She missed, but he yelped, more than half an apology, and ran back behind Vidarian, tail low.

Ariadel moved behind the desk, shifting stacks of parchment with one hand. "There have been rumors of a weapon, something large and terrible, capable of killing multitudes at once. It was also rumored they would test the weapon on the prison camp."

"Have you found your mother?"

She looked up, the answer already on her face when she shook her head. "We believe she is in the camp. But we don't know." Then, as she dropped her eyes to the desk, searching, her face hardened again. "But with your skyships, we'll have tipped the balance."

"The ships and all we bring are at your disposal."

Ariadel smiled, but only halfway, a world of sentiment in half a movement. "Rest today, but we must attack tomorrow, before they can send reinforcements."

Chapter Twenty-Eight

Mastery

When Vidarian emerged from the tent, Thalnarra was waiting for him. // *Come with me. There's someone I want you to meet.* //

She turned northwest and Vidarian followed with Rai pacing alongside him. Thinking of Meleaar, he wondered whom she meant for him to meet, and whether he would have to revise his notions of gryphons again. It seemed foolish in retrospect to think that they should be contained to the types of the handful he'd met, and now his mind roved in speculation.

But as they passed beyond the command tents, busy with gryphons and seridi moving among them with purpose, the next path she chose led them to a different "village" of tents, these positioned much more closely together. Gryphons moved here, too, trotting down the narrow roads, often with burdens hanging from their beaks or strapped to harnesses at their sides, but the farther they went, the more the population changed to human.

A mixture of faces turned to look as they passed, mostly dark of hair, but with the occasional blond or mop of red. Very few had any identifiable ethnicity that Vidarian could recognize, and none of them wore clothing he had ever seen before. They were dressed predominantly in leather or doeskin, more varieties than he could count, with decorations of feathers—small and large—and beads of precious stone. They paused in their work—blacksmithing, carpentry, cloth weaving—as Vidarian passed, staring at him almost as openly as they stared at Rai.

Thalnarra threaded her way through the tents, bringing them around to the far side of the encampment and a lean-to surrounded by racks of leather. There were straps of all sizes, and more varieties and treatments of animal hide than he'd seen on all the villagers so far. A man sat on a worn leather stool in the center of it all, working rivets into a piece of thick harness. Thalnarra scratched on a bit of thick hide stretched across a little rack for that purpose, and the man looked up, then stood and approached.

His thick, black hair falling in unruly waves to his shoulders would have been the envy of many an imperial countess. The leather he wore was extraordinarily fine, its origin animal unidentifiable, and a strap of darker hide across his chest was covered with cabochons of amber, each with a tiny feather trapped inside. He bowed first to Thalnarra, and when he turned to Vidarian, his silver eyes were intent but wild, untrusting.

// Kormir, this is Captain Vidarian Rulorat, and this is the shapechanger I told you about. // To Vidarian's surprise, Thalnarra turned as she spoke, dipping her head at Rai.

Kormir looked from Vidarian to Thalnarra, and then to Rai. "It is true, then?" He knelt and held his hand out to Rai, who crept forward with a hesitant wave of his tail, and sniffed.

// Kormir is the finest skin-worker in my pride, and in the entire flight, // Thalnarra said, and Kormir waved his hand negligently. There was something warmer in Thalnarra's tone than respect for a craftsman; a lilt of vanilla and *kava* steam.

"She shows partiality to her ward. It is unseemly." Kormir's eyes twinkled as he turned back on his heels to Thalnarra and swatted at her foreleg. Vidarian had never seen any human so forward with a gryphon before.

// You have been kinsman for a decade now. I am therefore unbiased. // She leaned her head down to Kormir, nudging his shoulder.

Kormir shook his head, pushing at Thalnarra's beak. "It is good to see you, *akrinha*."

Thalnarra preened a piece of Kormir's hair, then turned her head toward Rai. *// Go on, little one, //* she said, gesturing at Rai with her beak. *// Show him what you can do. //*

"Come around on him, have you?" Vidarian asked.

// Even a gryphon eventually accepts being out-stubborned. //

"Or learns to respect creatures that grow substantially bigger than them?"

Rai shuffled backward, then became the dragon, stretching behind into the scrub brush clearing to their west. He crouched in the dry weeds, long, spiked tail swishing like a cat's, rather to the detriment of the foliage. His huge head was now even with Kormir, who drew in his breath.

// *It should be impossible,* // Thalnarra said, with a fresh rosemary note of bemusement that said she had grown used to contemplating impossibilities. // *In five thousand years there has never been a dragon shapechanger. I verified this with Kree. It must have been the influence of the Gate.* //

"He is stunning," Kormir said, and then, to Vidarian's surprise, eeled up next to Rai and began feeling at his legs, his barrel, his wings. Rai's head jerked upward and curved on a swanlike neck to look at him, but did not intervene. "I would be honored to make you a harness and saddle, if you would allow it," he told Rai, patting him on the shoulder.

Rai's horned head lifted again with surprise, then looked to Vidarian before returning to nod at Kormir.

// *I hoped you might. You will have an assistant, if you'd like. My new ward.* //

Kormir gave a little hop and a whoop, startling Rai, then apologized, but turned immediately back to Thalnarra. "This is excellent news! They said you would never!"

// *Come, he will want to meet you, and then you can see to this harness.* // Thalnarra deftly ignored the young man's effusiveness, but her cheek-feathers puffed. Kormir stood, brushing his hands on his trousers, beaming, and Thalnarra turned back to Vidarian. // *We will take care of Rai. You should go to Malinai. He has asked for you.* //

Malinai was a dying gryphon.

When Vidarian asked for him, gryphons and humans alike pointed with solemnity at a red stone plateau to the south. None would discuss Malinai, but one of them gave him a waterskin and told him to ration it. It was a long, hot trek followed by a climb hundreds of feet in altitude, back and forth along the sage-bordered switchback trails that led up to the summit.

At the top a persistent wind whipped, cooling his skin but drying his tongue almost instantly. And there, across the stone, was Malinai.

The old gryphon was slow to move, and under the constant beat of the sun overhead it was hard not to emulate him. His feathers at one time may have been a rich russet red, with cream secondaries banded with black, but here the sun had bleached them to cream and white with delicate tan striping. With a shiver Vidarian realized he was the same type of gryphon as his friends Kaltak and Ishrak; was this the aged fate that awaited them?

"Malinai, sir?" Vidarian asked, when he approached the gryphon and his eyes remained closed.

// *I give myself to the sky and the sun. They are almost done devouring me. You interrupt my sacred journey.* // The voice was pale as powder, but complex, with notes of sage and burning rock, spearmint and citrus.

"They—said that you sent for me," Vidarian said, hoping desperately the old gryphon wasn't senile.

The narrow slits of the gryphon's eyes opened, revealing vivid orange-umber eyes beneath. // *Did I?* //

Then, without warning, he lashed out with an arm of fire energy, scorching the ground just to the left of Vidarian's feet. He tried to stop it, to lift his recalcitrant fire magic up to deflect the blow, but could not move in time.

// *Your fire is unruly! Whoever trained you should be ashamed.* //

"One of your people trained me," Vidiarian grunted, brushing at soot from his trouser leg.

// *Then I fear for our future,* // Malinai said, his eyes sliding shut again. // *I am almost gone to the goddess. She fills me with light.* // At the last of his words, his voice took on a strange harmonic tone, as if two twins sang the words with him. // *What would you ask of Ele'cherath, light of the world, goddess of the sun?* //

"I—" Vidarian began, but could not pull the words out of his dry throat. He coughed, then tried again. "I would ask her to release my potential," he pointed up at the *Luminous*, where Endera and her apprentices were drilling, little flashes of fire magic arcing into the air. "To give me control over the warring elements that she released within me."

// You do not need a goddess for that! // The gryphon growled, his voice returning to a single pitch. His eyes opened again, but squinting, and he tilted his rough-feathered head to one side, dissecting Vidarian. *// You know what you must do. You have seen it. //*

"Thalnarra told me that what I witnessed was not possible," he said, fighting to keep bitterness from his voice.

// The young are creatures of certainty, // Malinai said, and Vidarian had to repeat the words to himself before he realized the old gryphon was talking about Thalnarra. *// They are governed and reassured by rules and their heritage. It is to battle against the great fear in their hearts, the true unnamed certainty that their parents and their elders have left them, bequeathing the world into their claws. //*

"I'm not sure I understand how that relates to the physical effects of the elements."

Malinai's beak clacked dissatisfaction, a hollow sound like an old dry bone. *// Reality—physical effects—are mostly what we perceive them to be. And, it often follows, what we expect them to be. //*

"That's not my experience," Vidarian said carefully, swallowing annoyance. "If I drop a rock on the ground—" he picked up a triangular stone, then dropped it, "perceiving that it did not fall will not keep it in the air."

// It will not, // Malinai agreed. *// But you can perceive that the ground instead rises to meet the stone, or that the stone is drawn to the center of the world, which happens to be toward the ground, and these will cause your realities to be quite different. //*

"And that means . . . ?" He was beginning to grow impatient, and incredulous that a creature who had so little life remaining could be so indirect.

The great beak clacked again, and Malinai roused his feathers, shaking off a small cloud of dust and several loose secondaries that were caught and spun about by the wind. *// Your culture, Thalnarra's culture, expects the elements to behave a certain way. She needs them to behave. Your Qui opponent perceived reality differently. //*

"So you're saying I just need to think about my elements and they'll be happy?"

// No, // Malinai said, as if speaking to a particularly slow student. *// I'm saying it behooves you to speak with a Qui elementalist. //*

"That's become rather complicated, thanks to the war."

// *There are three Qui elementalists in this camp,* // Malinai said, and Vidarian's heart lifted, but then, // *but none of them have the pair of elements you require.* // Frustration flickered up again, but then— // *You'll have to make do with me.* //

"You?"

// *Yes, but I'll need your assistance. I have a flicker of water ability, but not nearly enough to demonstrate anything up here. You're going to have to channel some to me if you want a demonstration.* //

"Channel . . . ?"

// *They haven't even taught you basic conduitry? A kitten in straw knows how to conduit.* //

"There hasn't been time," Vidarian began.

// *Excuses!* // The gryphon shook his feathers again, and Vidarian was afraid he was going to lose all he had if he kept it up. // *Now, hand me your water energy. Just—draw some together, and push it toward me. Be ready to release it.* //

Vidarian gamely pulled the water out of the air, drying it even more than it had been before, and shaped it into a column of water. As it had before, his fire sense reared up in him, hissing, striking. He gritted his teeth, and passed the water toward Malinai, ready to let it go.

Suddenly the water lifted away from him, and despite being warned, he was pulled with it, and nearly stumbled. He let it go just in time, and the water moved away from him, though a thread remained with which he could feed more energy to it to keep it alive. Malinai turned it deftly in the air, clicking his tongue in approval, and then drew out his own fire: a bright, pure flame so strong and true it stirred memories of love in Vidarian's chest.

Then there was one energy, not two; a braided, fused thing that amplified both of the elements, so bright he had to force himself not to look away.

"That's it!" Vidarian exclaimed, so shocked that he dropped the water thread. Malinai's energy flashed bright, then vanished, leaving spots across Vidarian's eyes.

// *Again,* // Malinai barked.

Once more Vidarian drew the water, this time passing it more gracefully to Malinai. He watched intently, staring so fiercely at the two elements that a little needle of pain opened between his eyebrows.

Without moving, somehow the two energies tilted to one side—or perhaps it was the world that tilted—and then fell together, interlocking into a band of brilliant white. Malinai passed it back to Vidarian, who took it reverently in his elemental "hands," and turned it, inspected it. Inside was a world of possibility, of brightness, of visions yet to be coalesced. And for the first time since the fire goddess had awakened his water magic, his soul stilled, and was at peace.

// *Very good,* // Malinai said softly, and banished his fire magic with a whisper. Vidarian drew the water back into himself, released it back into the air as mist, and sighed. // *You'll be able to do that again, I'll wager.* //

Without realizing it, Vidarian had kept his eyes strained open, and now they stung with dryness. He blinked them several times.

// *Go now,* // Malinai said, fluffing out his wings and turning to tuck his beak between them. // *I must return to my meditations.* // His voice had thinned to vellum, translucent as spring frost.

"Thank you, sir," Vidarian bowed, holding his head low for a long moment before he straightened. The gryphon did not move, and after several moments he turned and went back to the trail.

// *Vidarian,* // Malinai said, and he looked back. // *Tell your mistress I am coming, and I am not afraid.* //

The wind stirred stronger, and the old gryphon stared at Vidarian, the sun shining through his thin feathers, already more than half a ghost. Despite his insubstantiality, now Malinai looked deeply at him, his orange eyes full of fire and will. "I will, sir," Vidarian said softly.

∿∿∿

"Why would you send me to Malinai?" Vidarian demanded of Thalnarra, when he'd returned to the village and found her in front of the command tent with Meleaar.

// *We thought he'd help you,* // Meleaar said. // *Or, he'd eat you. Either way, problem solved?* //

// *And I am sorry to pull you from one errand to the next,* // Thalnarra said, and Vidarian turned to her tiredly. // *But the* Luminous *has summoned you. They say they've made contact with Qui.* //

"The ambassador?" Vidarian asked, already turning, shading his eyes and looking for the relay ship.

Thalnarra's beak nudged his forearm and he looked down again—then started when he saw the *Luminous* ground-anchored not a hundred lengths away. He looked back at Thalnarra, gave a small bow of thanks to her and to Meleaar, and ran for the ship.

In the relay chamber, a handful of folk were already gathered: Iridan, his hand on the relay sphere, projecting the images of an opulently dressed Qui woman and the Alorean ambassador; Malloray, watching from the rear with his arms folded; Marielle, staring intently at the Qui woman; and Khalesh, for the first time in days focused on something other than the *Viere's* power stones.

Vidarian took his seat, after bowing to the two women, though he wasn't sure if they could see him. The ambassador's face was fresh with tears; they must have just told her of the emperor's death. The Qui woman looked grim. She spoke a string of liquid syllables, the musical language sounding sophisticated no matter what it contained.

The ambassador translated, after clearing her throat, "Madam Councilor wishes to know, what is the status of the Alorean government?"

"It is a government-in-exile," Marielle replied, and waited for the ambassador to translate between sentences. "The emperor was murdered by the Alorean Import Company. Prior to his murder, he had wished to open peace negotiations between Alorea and Qui, while the corruption of the Alorean Import Company is rooted out."

"How do we know you represent the Alorean Empire?"

Marielle looked at Vidarian, as well she might, her imperial status being tacitly revoked when she became a pirate queen. "You don't," Vidarian said. "Alorea has been invaded from within, and wars now with itself. What you know is that we will offer you an alliance, and the Alorean Import Company will not."

"And if the Alorean Import Company is stronger?"

"Then you still have reduced forces attacking your army," Vidarian replied, "as those loyal to the empire will draw down. They will wish for time to grieve, if not to abandon the conflict entirely."

"And those territories our armies have already won?" At this the ambassador darted looks between the councilor and Vidarian, betraying her own feelings on the matter.

Vidarian in turn looked at Marielle, who gave a slight shake of her head. "This is something to negotiate more formally," Vidarian hazarded. "We wish for an end to hostilities. If you would sign a treaty to allow free passage between Qui and Alorea, we would be willing to discuss some adjustment of border lines."

The two women conferred, words passing between them like fish in a stream. Vidarian could only listen, fascinated but uncomprehending.

"You may come to us at Shen Ti," the councilor said finally, in her own clear but accented High Alorean. "When you have established yourselves as rivals to the Alorean Import Company. We will send instructions. And, of course, guarantee your safety."

"I will come myself," Vidarian agreed, standing and resting his palms on the table. In any other circumstance he would offer his hand as proof of his intent.

The councilor seemed to understand, and said, "That will be most appreciated."

A shudder rippled through the *Luminous*, and Vidarian grabbed the arms of his chair out of reflex. He looked to Khalesh, whose eyes had widened with horror and puzzlement. He gave the slightest shake of his head.

Vidarian rose, offering a quick, "Your pardon," and left Khalesh and Iridan to explain his exit. He ran from the relay chamber, raced up the ladder, and searched the sky above the top deck, half expecting to see a punishing assault of skyships.

There were none, and he began to breathe a bit easier, and also to feel a bit silly for leaving the chamber so hastily. But then a flicker of movement caught the corner of his eye. He turned, lifting a hand to shade his sight, and searched for it.

When he saw it, Vidarian was sure his eyes had deceived him. It must be some artifact of the landscape, low brush that made the figure seem larger than it was, and farther away. But as he squinted and the shape drew nearer, its polished surface gleaming under the desert sun, dust swirling behind it as it tore through the ground on which it walked, his eyes insisted they did not deceive. And when the figure raised a glowing golden hand, and the ripples passed over him like a cold wind, preceding a thundering torrent of water energy that set the gryphons all around the encampment murmuring with almost a single voice, a cold and clenching dread in his stomach was terrible recognition:

It was Ruby.

Chapter Twenty-Nine
New War

Vidarian ran for the *Luminous*'s bell, hauling on its line to raise the alarm throughout the ship. He rang furiously for several seconds, then stilled it, following the alarm with a single ring to draw the crew to the bow.

Marielle had been fast on his heels up the ladder, and stood by while he repeated the alarm signal again, scanning the sky. She hardened when she saw the line of skyships just appearing on the horizon, a hand drifting to the sword pommel at her side, but when Vidarian released the bell, he pointed to the rising dust below them on the ground. Shading her eyes, she stared, uncomprehending, then gasped as she, too, realized what they were seeing, the giant golden automaton closing on the camp.

"You need to get into the air," Vidarian said, even as the figure on the horizon raised its arm again, fiery against the red sunset, and released a blast of water energy that drew a long line into the desert scrub, pointing south into the encampment.

"*I* do?"

But Vidarian's eyes were locked on Ruby's faraway figure. There was something more ominous still about the line she had blasted into the brush. "It's pointing right at us," he breathed.

"They're attacking," Marielle agreed slowly, her tone raising in a question.

"But how do they know where we are? The camp is masked by a camouflage sphere." He desperately willed it to be a coincidence. There were elderly and children in the gryphons' tent village . . . But the ships above—a round dozen of them, large and small—were turning in the direction Ruby had pointed.

Vidarian ran across the deck, shouting behind him, "Get airborne! Get all of your ships away from the camp! Send them in different directions!"

If the imperial forces were advancing on the camp now, it could only mean one thing: whatever had given them their heading was aboard one of the Sea Kingdom ships.

Even as he charged down the gangplank, Marielle was already shouting orders, and a pair of sailors hauled the plank up almost before Vidarian's feet touched the earth. He started toward Kormir's village, but skidded to a stop as he caught sight of a rider loping fast toward the *Luminous*.

Ariadel rode out on a black horse, sitting her saddle with the ease of a born equestrian. The animal she rode was half warhorse, with lean, athletic lines paired with massive feet and a thick, indomitable neck. "They've attacked before we could!" she cried. "They know that the longer they wait, the more they stand to lose!"

"It's worse than that," Vidarian said, hating to admit it, but needing to. "I think they're drawn to something on one of the ships—one of the ones we captured, most likely. We've drawn them to you."

She turned, spinning the horse with one rein and a heel, looking up at the ship. "They've got to get into the air—away from the camp!"

"They're already moving," Vidarian said, and so they were—sailors were calling out readiness checks, and even as they stood there the *Luminous* began to lift off the ground. "I need to get to Rai."

Ariadel turned back to him, then reached down, offering her hand. "Come on."

He blinked, frozen for a moment, then took her hand. She slipped her foot free of the stirrup and he stepped into it, levering himself up and over the horse's back behind her. It was awkward, and he had to take hold of her waist quickly as she spurred the horse into a gallop.

Vidarian clung to the saddle and the tents flew by. Overhead, another low boom echoed across the desert, this time as the imperial skyships fired sighting shots from their cannon. They weren't yet within range of the camp, but would not be kept off for long.

Once he was sure he wasn't going to tumble off the back of the fast-moving horse, "Did you really think I would have supported the empire against you?" Vidarian said over Ariadel's shoulder.

She drew up before Kormir's tent, and Vidarian slid from the saddle, levering himself to the ground. A hand on his shoulder steadied him, and then she leaned down, kissing him. Then, without answering, she turned her horse back to the command field and was galloping off again.

Kormir and Rai were where he'd left them, and now Rai was draped with harness. A modified bareback saddle sat between his shoulders, thick with padding and sewn with additional thick leather straps.

"Thank the goddesses that you are so quick," Vidarian said, walking up to the dragon and tracing the leather straps with his hands.

"It's not done," Kormir said, his eyebrows up with alarm. "I still have—"

Vidarian turned, pointing at the sky, which was now blooming with light around the advancing skyships as they continued their weapons checks. "We need to be up there in moments. I'll ride him with nothing at all if I have to."

Kormir followed his gesture, then cursed, turning back to his racks to thread three needles at once with thick sinew. He attacked the harness, reinforcing stitching, connecting straps, hauling on them to test their strength, all the while muttering that if a strap gave way while they were fighting it would be worse than nothing at all.

Rai's head turned toward them. *I won't let him fall,* he said, and Kormir's eyes widened. Vidarian was grateful that Rai's mind seemed to be settling down enough for speech again.

At last Kormir stood back, a thick needle held between his teeth and the other two stuck through a pad on his arm-wrap, surveying his work with a furrowed brow. "That's the best I can do."

"It's excellent work," Vidarian said, extending his hand. And it was. Kormir looked at him in puzzlement, then awkwardly clasped his forearm. "I must admit, I have so many questions about your childhood . . ."

Kormir caught his meaning at once. "Brannon is a good lad. He'll be just fine. When one is meant for this life, there can be no other."

"I believe it," Vidarian said. "Thank you for this," he said, gesturing to the harness. "I will repay you."

"We have no notion of your 'payment' here," Kormir replied. "You are chosen of my *akrinha*. We are brothers."

Vidarian stood straighter, surprised at his words, and surprised again at how touching he found them. "I will defend your work, and the camp, with my life."

"Of course," Kormir agreed. *"Charnak; vikktu ari lashuul."*

The gryphon battle-words stirred fire in his heart, and Vidarian tightened his hand on Kormir's, then released it. *"Vikktu,"* he agreed, then turned back to Rai, breathing deeply as he took in the height of his scaled shoulder, which stretched high over his head.

Rai's head came around again on his sinuous neck, and he nosed at Vidarian's right foot. When Vidarian lifted it, he pushed upward, all but tossing him into the air. Scrambling, Vidarian vaulted his right leg over the dragon's shoulder, feeling for the stirrup with his left.

Then he was seated, and hooking straps around his thighs. Rai stood from his crouch, lifting him farther into the air, and he wobbled, leaning left and right to keep himself balanced. There was nothing to compare it to; unlike a horse, Rai's movements tilted him up and down as well as left and right, and his back was tilted when he stood, sloping from his high shoulders down to his lower hind legs. Kormir had built the saddle to account for this, reinforcing its back, while the straps kept his legs forward and clear of Rai's broad, flexible wings, as well as the long, deadly spines that lined his neck and tail.

Rai stretched, getting the feel of the harness, and Vidarian's weight with it. He paced in a circle, first in one direction and then the other, before abruptly leaning up on his hind legs and swiping at the air with his foreclaws. Vidarian's stomach dropped and he was sure he'd be hitting the ground—but the saddle held him, the straps sliding but catching at just the right moment.

Then Rai leapt into the air, powerful hind legs pushing them high enough that the broad downsweep of his wings cleared the ground.

The brush grew smaller beneath them as Rai continued to flap, and Kormir, raising his arms to whoop with delight as he saw them rise, dwindled with it. The rest of the encampment came into view, tent roofs and paths, gryphons and humans hurrying between them. Many carried armor, and most rushed toward the warriors' lairs.

Rai tilted his wings, swinging them toward the command clearing. Above it, the skyships had taken to the air and continued to rise, each striking off and away from the camp. Vidarian turned in the saddle, looking for the approaching forces. Their ships still hung in the air, but as he watched, Ruby—in the impossible golden body Oneira had given her?—turned, easily visible at this distance, and struck out with another line of water energy.

Toward the *Luminous*.

Of all of the ships, Vidarian had been sure that the *Luminous* could not be the culprit, being even less likely than the *Viere d'Inar*. Malloray and the relay sphere aboard the ship should have been more than capable of dampening or at least confusing its location. And it was least likely to have had any kind of signal device hidden aboard.

"Iridan," he realized, and Rai's ears flicked back toward him curiously. "He's an automaton—and Justinian spent all of that time with him." He cursed roundly, then pointed. "Can you get us over to them?"

In answer, Rai flared his wings, lifting their leading edges and catching the wind. They shot toward the *Luminous*, and Vidarian worked hard not to look down at the terrain that raced by beneath them. After several moments of tension, it was not so difficult; Rai's presence, the warmth of his body, the strength of his long wings, were more reassuring than a gryphon basket, and even a skyship.

Once he had let go of his fear, he was struck by the spectacular view. The desert had deepened into the shadows of evening before them, the red stone steppes darkening to dark cerulean and amethyst while the sand glowed silver in counterpoint to the searing corals and crimson of the sky. Here above the world there was a kind of peace, a quiet—until it was rocked by the boom of cannonfire from the approaching ship line.

They drew upon the *Luminous*, and spaced around it were Sky Knights, who, of all the Aloreans, had been hit hardest by the emperor's death. It tightened Vidarian's chest to see them here, still protecting the *Luminous*, drawn and grim but determined.

One of them, a woman Vidarian didn't recognize, pointed her lance at the skyline.

Arrayed around the enemy ships were lines and formations she would have found familiar: Sky Knights, those who had knowingly joined the Company's cause, or did not yet know whom they opposed. Vidarian thought of the brutish monster that would have killed the young royal rather than seeing her imprint to a servant, and guessed that most fell into the former. Rai, picking up on his thoughts, lashed his tail at the air, his neck-spines sparking.

Caladan was drawing his reluctant steed closer, and Vidarian called to him. "Sir Orrin-Smyth, can you dispatch your misguided brethren?"

"I should think so," Caladan said, loosening his sword in its scabbard. "I trained more than half of them." He drew the sword, then struck its pommel soundly against the shield strapped to his mount. "Ironharts, to me!"

The knights gave a cheer, steel beneath their spirit, and formed up behind Caladan, who advanced toward the lines, his flight steady and swift.

Just below, Malloray and Yerune had come to the bow, looking to him for orders. That they did so naturally both warmed and stung Vidarian's heart; he had led them time and again into danger, yet still they followed.

"I must fly to Ruby," he said, pointing down to the horizon. "There may yet be a hope she will negotiate."

"Ruby?" Malloray shouted, incredulous. Then, for lack of a better description—"*Your* Ruby?"

"The Company promised her a body," Vidarian replied.

"We will go with you," Yerune said. "If you must confront them, we will witness it."

"The *Luminous* is our small fleet's only relay ship," Vidarian argued. "It can't be risked on the front line."

"Then we will hang back, but be your point of retreat nonetheless, should it be needed."

Vidarian didn't like it, but knew they would have need of the relay ship's instant communication with the ground and sky forces. "Tell the other ships to rally around you," he said. "Now that we know the source of their bearing, there's no need to separate them."

Malloray and Yerune exchanged a glance, startled.

"They draw on Iridan," Vidarian said. "I'm sure of it."

He half expected them to advocate abandoning the automaton, but both of their faces hardened. "All the more reason for us to come with you," Yerune said. "Let us draw the battle to them."

Vidarian touched his forehead in a salute, filled with pride for counting them as friends. "It is an honor to fight alongside you again."

"Enough of that," Malloray said, waving an arm. "Let's show these arrogant bastards how a true imperial ship acquits herself."

He smiled in spite of himself. "As you will."

Rai turned toward the line of ships in the sky, banking in a long arc that first swept them over Gryphonslair. Below, wings of gryphons were taking to the air, light from the setting sun glittering off of their armor. It was not anything Vidarian ever thought to see in his lifetime. The armor was not the heavy barding of the Sky Knights, but lighter, made of a bright metal he didn't recognize, and limited to key weak points: the base of the skull, the throat, the keelbone, wrists and ankles. Thus the small pieces arrayed over the hundred creatures taking to the air formed a glittering battalion, itself divided into small groups of five to ten individuals.

After the gryphons, the smaller bands of seridi were taking flight also, moving in groups behind or even onto the four skyships to perch and rest for precision strikes.

Rai leveled out, gliding fast toward the approaching forces. Streaks of cloud obscured the sun, staining it pink, and dimming the horizon enough that another cloud could be seen: land forces, spread out behind Ruby, three regiments of three hundred fighters each, mixed cavalry and foot soldiers. The Company was not emptying its war chest, but it must be a near thing.

From the air, he could also now see the prison camp that had so occupied Ariadel's thoughts, and the sight of it sickened him. Gryphonslair looked luxurious and rigidly organized by comparison; dark-haired prisoners in drab clothing huddled around black-smoked fires, moving slow. Few even raised their heads to the sounds of cannonfire in the sky, though a handful, children he thought, gathered at the western fence line to watch.

They were drawing fast upon the enemy lines, and just as he was about to direct Rai downward to meet Ruby, a searing blast of fire energy split the air to their right, only narrowly missing them. Rai bellowed a challenge, tipping left and instinctively falling into an evasive dive; when he straightened, he was snarling, flickers of demi-lightning arcing between the spines of his neck.

The strike had come from the front ship, a titan flagship, imperial Alorean and one of the most formidable war machines ever designed.

A cry of surprise from behind them drew Vidarian's attention back to the following *Luminous*, where Iridan stood at the bow.

The automaton had no facial features with which to manage it, but the slack way that he stared across at the other ship was disbelieving, haunted. He was staring at the flagship and the two figures that stood at its bow— Justinian, porcelain-masked; the other an automaton, graphite-armored, taller than Iridan, crowned with a circlet of knifelike curls of steel and striped feathers.

CHAPTER THIRTY
WHAT IS NECESSARY

"*V*eda*,*" Iridan cried, and the wave of misery that echoed with his word nearly made the gorge rise in Vidarian's throat. "*No one was supposed to know about her . . .*"

Vidarian touched Rai's shoulder, and he swooped closer to Iridan.

"*Parvidian swore us to silence,*" the automaton said miserably. "*More than that. We are all under a geis and cannot speak her name unless we see her.*"

"What is she?"

"*The sorcerous automaton. The only one of us endowed with elemental ability. But it made her dark and volatile, angry. Parvidian wanted to destroy her, but the emperor would not permit him. So he put her into a sleep long before the rest of us succumbed to the Dwindling.*"

Another spear of fire sizzled past, and he urged Rai back toward the flagship, now with trepidation. The dragon growled, sharing his desire for destruction, but Vidarian put a hand on his shoulder, asking for patience.

When Rai drew up before the ship, Vidarian expected them to open fire again, but instead Justinian raised his hand in greeting. "Good evening, Captain! It seems our paths are destined to interweave."

"You dare suggest that this is not your intent?" Vidarian said, gesturing to the gryphons lifting from the ground below.

"Hardly," Justinian shouted, and even across that distance managed dryness. "There have been rumors, as you know, of a so-called resistance movement—a destructive group of renegades bent on throwing the empire into chaos. We have come once and for all to quell it. I certainly did not expect *you* to be a part of it."

"You expect to be able to murder the emperor without answer?" Rage rattled his voice, and Rai growled beneath him.

"An outrageous and hurtful accusation! You cast us as villains, Vidarian,"

Justinian said. "But we do only what we must for the benefit of the new world. And when that new world arrives, you will not refuse it your leadership. If we must bear the onus of the ugly task that purchases it, we will."

"Turn back," Vidarian said. "Turn back and gather your pennies while you may, or I will kill you, and destroy every ship in your fleet."

"Veda," Justinian said, quite as if he had not heard Vidarian. "Perhaps we should demonstrate the strength of the resources we bring to bear."

"*We should not*," Veda said, her voice an echoing labyrinth, twisting and unnerving where Iridan's had been harmonizing and light. "*Let Ruby end this.*"

Justinian's shoulders tensed, clearly not pleased with this idea, and his head turned just fractionally toward Veda before straightening. "Of course. Go and speak with her, Vidarian. See what she makes of your plea."

The satisfaction in Justinian's voice made him want to destroy the ship with his bare hands, and Rai's growling increased, but Vidarian forced himself to restraint. If they attacked now, there would never be an opportunity to dissuade Ruby, and whatever catastrophic power they had endowed her with, from attacking the resistance. For surely she was the weapon that had been so rumored to be in the Company's possession.

At his direction, Rai dove, plummeting toward the ground. He swooped up at the last second, backwinging to a hover just in front of the giant golden automaton.

Her metal body was five times the height she had been in life, half again as tall as Rai had he been on the ground. It glittered with elemental gems, larger ones than he had ever seen, an unbelievable amount of wealth that made Iridan's body look shabby and sparse by comparison. In her face there was not even a token gesture of humanity; the prism key rested at its center, framed by two glowing amethyst gems, giving her a three-eyed visage with no hint of the Ruby he had known. Only her presence, the proximity of her mind, was unmistakable.

"*Your little pest has quite grown,*" Ruby said. Her voice was familiar and unfamiliar at the same time—half the Ruby that was, half something else, something alien and cold.

"He's turned out to be quite useful." At this Rai snorted, a flash of lightning arcing toward Ruby. It struck her chest, but without effect, and she chuckled, a hollow sound. "Why are you doing this, Ruby? Do you know what the Company has done? What the resistance is defending?"

"What I know is that Oneira and the Company have done what you could not: restored me to a body."

"I can hear it in your voice, Ruby. You aren't complete. You never will be."

"When the Company has completed its errands and returned stability to this continent and others, the rise in magical resources will allow them to return me to all that I was—and more. Oneira has sworn it."

Vidarian hesitated. From all that Khalesh had said, what Ruby was describing sounded impossible. But her current shape before him seemed equally so. "And what are you willing to pay for that? You know that they intend to kill millions of people?"

"And when the Imperial Armada would have wiped out all of my people, what then? Living innocent lives miles away from any imperial shore, they would die—was that justice? Or is it the strong seizing what they can? There is no justice in this world, Vidarian. Justice is a poor illusion to salve the pride of the weak."

"The flaw in your sentiment, Ruby, is that your people are fighting with me, and with the Imperial Armada. They fight for their families and what they hold dear."

"Then they are as foolish as you are."

"And so you'll kill them? Innocent people, your own kindred, you'll destroy them for the sake of a Company your mother fought every day of her life?"

"You've always lacked the stomach for what is necessary."

With that she unleashed a lash of water energy, and Vidarian shouted to Rai with his mind as the ripples of it warned him. Rai dropped his right wing and fell through the air, narrowly avoiding the strike, and then flattened out, skimming just above the ground and pumping his wings to regain altitude.

Vidarian, you've got to help me, the Starhunter said. She was in his mind as abruptly as she had ever been, and some far-off corner of Vidarian was surprised she was sticking to the same bit for such a long time. She usually became bored much more quickly.

"I'm a trifle occupied just now," Vidarian muttered, leaning to one side to throw his weight in Rai's favor as he sliced downward in the air to avoid another bolt of thundering water.

Siiiiiiigh.

"This really isn't the time!" Rai's mouth opened, and a blinding flash of lightning arced from his teeth to Ruby, this time knocking her backwards for half a step.

Here, have some more gryphons. Then will you help me?

The air around them compressed, and suddenly the giant gryphon he had seen with the Starhunter was hovering in the air to his right, and another to his left. Both of them looked heartily confused, even with their strange pupilless eyes, until one of the human foot soldiers was foolish enough to loose an arrow in their direction.

The two gryphons screamed challenges and dove down over the army, peppering the ground with bolts of flesh-eating energy that unmade soldiers—or pieces of soldiers—wherever it touched. The gorge crept up Vidarian's throat, and he had to avert his eyes.

Well, look at the mess you've made. It's going to take me hours to get their attention back.

"*I* made!" he shouted, then clamped down on it. "I'll help you after all this is over," Vidarian grunted, and Rai angled upward, fighting again for height.

Yay!

Cannons boomed overhead, and the Company's fleet began unleashing fireshot toward the advancing resistance fighters. The gryphon wings had closed the distance, and half now joined the two giant celestial gryphons in harrying the army, while the other half circled around the fleet, grouping together and picking individual ships to dive onto and attack. Many were powerful magicians, and unleashed tornadoes of wind or lances of fire that struck decks and sails. But the Company mercenaries were battle-hardened and not dissuaded even by their onslaught, firing back with muskets and arrows, fireshot and cannon.

Ruby was the variable. She had not yet displayed the fullness of her ability, Vidarian knew; from her pauses between strikes, he suspected she might be still learning those capabilities. In her inexperience should be his advantage; if he could use her own magic against her, draw her into overextending herself—

A shadow passed over them, and Vidarian looked up, shocked to see the imperial flagship descending toward the ground. Its topmast was wreathed in flame that burned too hot to be natural. Far above it, there were three gryphon baskets, each containing several fire priestesses; Endera had settled on a method of attack, it would seem.

Bringing down the flagship could only be a good thing. Vidarian urged Rai toward it.

Rai roared, an echoing sound that thundered in his chest beneath Vidarian's legs, and lightning crackled out from his clawed wingtips, striking the sails of the ship over and over. Wherever it touched, it blackened the silk, which fell away in powdered char moments after the lightning passed.

The ship crashed to the ground, its bow cracking under the weight of the burning wreckage above it. Sailors—those who had survived the crash— streamed out of it, fleeing for the ranks of the army.

As the gryphons continued to harry the land troops and the seridi dove amidst the remaining imperial skyships, the three resistance skyships, with the *Luminous* at their rear, closed in. Cannons fired, raining down on the army, and elemental magic flashed from the resistance ships, and back again from weapons aboard the Company's.

Ruby turned her attention to the resistance ships, releasing hammer after hammer of water that battered at their hulls. One of her assaults snapped a forward mast on the *Argentium*, sending it and the sailors beneath it pitching to their deaths, and another soaked the lowest gundeck of the *Viere d'Inar*, disabling it. If Ruby recognized her own ship, she gave no sign, and attacked it as viciously as any of the others. In that moment, Vidarian finally realized that whatever Ruby had become had no connection to the friend he had known most of his life. His chest caved inward, and he grieved.

Below, a black-grey figure was struggling from the wreckage of the imperial titan ship. Veda blew out a piece of the hull with a sear of fire, then turned, helping Justinian through the fissure. She made a high-pitched whistling call, and three of the cavalry separated from the land force, galloping to them.

Vidarian drew into himself, using his grief to harden his resolve, and reached out with water drawn from all around them. He formed a twisting vortex of it, and then, when its strength had peaked, drew his fire through it, turning them until they locked together in a lance of white energy. He released it, and it hurtled down toward Justinian.

Veda looked up, then sliced at the air with her hand, bringing first a cut of fire and then another of water to deflect the lance.

"*Lovely trick*," Veda said. "*I think I'll borrow it.*" Then, stunningly fast, she repeated his hard-won feat, twisting water into a coil and infusing it with fire, releasing the blast back at him. He rushed through another summoning of the energy, managing it just in time to deflect hers, and then the cavalry reached them, swinging Justinian behind them and dashing back for the land forces. Rai screamed a battle challenge and struck after them with lightning, but only managed to catch the last one, missing Justinian.

Now Ruby and Veda turned toward Vidarian, preparing more lethal strikes. The air dried as they drew the water from it.

A golden sear of fire struck the ground near Veda's foot, interrupting her. It came from high above, and Vidarian squinted against the black smoke still pouring from the fallen skyship.

An old gryphon hovered above them, near skeletal, missing several of his primaries and working to keep himself in the air.

// *Dance with me,* // Malinai said.

Veda looked up, her violet eyes flaring bright, and hissed, a hybrid of animal and machine sound. She turned her attack upward.

Malinai's wings arced above him, and a torrent of fire, the largest and brightest Vidarian had ever felt, hurtled down toward the automaton. It engulfed her, but not in time to stop her own attack, which blistered white-hot toward him, a boiling fusion of water and fire.

"Malinai!" Vidarian cried, and Rai roared, electricity arcing from his wings.

// *It is an honorable death!* // Malinai called back, sun-bright exultation in his voice. // *I go to Ele'cherath!* // And he dove, wings furled, talons extended, straight into the attack, and with him went a ball of white-hot fire that grew stronger the closer he came to the ground.

Veda visibly panicked, her arms flying to her sides—but then her hands came up, the world warped—

And a hole in the universe opened up before her.

Time seemed to still, all save Malinai, who still hurtled toward that point. He engulfed Veda, burning his heat so strong it began to melt her body before he even struck her. The fire sphere around him grew so bright that it flared into explosion, setting afire the very air, too bright to see.

When it faded, they both were gone.

Vidarian and Rai turned back to Ruby, hardly comprehending what they had just seen, but unable to put aside her very real threat. Her metal arms were uplifted, pointing at the sky, releasing a two-handed strike of water, a hurricane blast that tore into the hull of the *Skyfalcon*.

At first Vidarian couldn't see why she would waste such a huge attack on the smaller skyship while he and the *Viere* remained in the air—and then he saw Ariadel, a dimming halo of fire wreathing her hands, falling from the broken bow.

Rai read his thoughts before he spoke them, bellowing a protest, buffeting the air with his wings in a desperate bid for speed.

They tore after her, and the spiral of water from Ruby caught Rai's side, only a glancing blow, but one that sent him spinning through the air. Vidarian clung to his back as the world spun around them, and Rai shrieked with rage as he finally righted himself and continued the pursuit.

Ariadel was plummeting toward the ground, still hundreds of lengths away—they weren't going to make it—

A plume of fire opened up beneath her, engulfing her, and Vidarian howled, reaching out with water, knowing it was too far—

The fire stretched, formed wings, then a head, a long neck with a slender beak at the end of it, shockingly blue eyes. It beat its wings, stopping their descent, then lifted, turning, five long plumes of a flaming tail streaming out behind it.

The bird was huge, nearly as large as Rai. At first Vidarian thought Ariadel had somehow created it with her own elemental ability, but that didn't seem possible. It was clearly alive, with its own consciousness, and at any rate he had never heard of elemental magic being shaped into a creature and flown.

It saw Rai and flew toward him, whistling a greeting. The two creatures touched noses, and Vidarian jumped in his seat. "Is that . . . ?"

Ariadel was clinging to the bird's neck, gripping its feathers. "I might . . ." she panted, " . . . have to change her name!"

The shapechanger, like Rai, had displayed a third and outrageous form: first cat, then spider, and now . . . firebird?

A bolt of water shot between them, sending both creatures winging backwards, trying to regain control of their motion.

"We have to destroy her!" Ariadel called.

"How?" Vidarian shouted back, holding tight to his harness as Rai dove again to evade another strike of water from Ruby. "She has some kind of defensive enchantment—we can move her, but nothing we have is big enough to do any damage!"

"Then maybe we can move her—somewhere far." She gripped a pendant around her neck and shouted. "Arikaar! Khellan! I need Chayim, quickly! And Altair! Send them to the dragon!" It took him a moment to realize what she meant by "to the dragon," and then he saw that, for miles around, he and the skyships were the two most visible objects—with names they would recognize, at any rate, excluding Raven—in the sky.

The gryphons closed quickly, Altair from high above, and the other, a black-plumaged gryphon, from behind the *Argentium*. Below, and spread across the field, fallen foot soldiers and cavalry lay everywhere, and five more of the dozen imperial skyships had been brought down by fire. The air now was thick with smoke, though as Altair arrived, a circle of breathable air arrived with him, a relief.

"We need to open a gate," Ariadel said to them. Altair looked startled, and the other, which must be Chayim, nodded. He looked something like Arikaree in his long, gawky neck and irregular feathers, but his face was a vulture's, bald to pink skin and complete with a long wattle that draped from his nares. He was, by a significant margin, the most hideous gryphon Vidarian had ever seen.

But he was also the one who knew how to be the primary conduit for a gate-opening.

The magic was similar to what had opened the Great Gate, though without the frame for the energy, it was significantly more difficult. On top of this, they would have to open a very large portal, enough for Ruby's entire massive body. And it required energy from all four elements, as well as one, like Vidarian, that could bridge multiple elements.

Chayim clacked his talons together, creating a rough rhythm. A strange feeling clawed at the pit of Vidarian's stomach, and he realized it was the indirect way he was sensing the manifestation of Chayim's earth. Altair's joined him, detectable only as an increase in the breeze, and Chayim's cluck of approval.

Ariadel pulled fire from herself and from the wreckage of the titan ship, siphoning it over to Chayim. And Vidarian pulled forth his own, forcing his nearly exhausted mind to lock the elements together into a single force. This he passed to the vulture-gryphon, who tipped his beak in thanks.

"Hold it!" Ariadel cried. "Steady!"

Another attack opened from below, and Rai squealed, sidling into its path. He lashed at the arc of water with his tail, disrupting it—taking some of its damage onto himself, and shaking away as much of it as he could. Beneath his knees Vidarian could feel the dragon's torso contorting with pain.

"There!" Ariadel shouted.

And indeed, below, the hole in the world was opening beneath Ruby's feet. She made a terrible, shrieking noise of negation, thrashing in an attempt to escape—but her hands and feet found only air, and she vanished.

The portal remained for several moments, pulling at the base of Vidarian's gut, and then Chayim let it go, snapping it shut and returning the brush and grass to their rightful arrangement.

// *That was very well done,* // Altair said, addressing both Ariadel and Chayim, and Ariadel smiled.

"Where did we send her?" Vidarian asked.

"I don't know!" Ariadel replied. "It opened too quickly! She could be anywhere! Malu, Shen Ti, the bottom of the ocean!"

But Ruby's sudden disappearance rippled through the remaining imperial forces, a wave of shock and horror. Bells rang out from the front skyship, and those behind it quickly took up the toll.

The army began to turn around, and the remaining skyships with them. From all around, the victory cries of gryphons filled the sky.

CHAPTER THIRTY-ONE

EARTH AND SKY

The camouflage spell on Gryphonslair came down, and humans, gryphons, and seridi streamed from the tents there toward the Qui-Alorean prison camp. They carried food, blankets, clothing, casks of water—and before them rode Ariadel, Vidarian beside her, Raven's firebird shape revealing long, jewel-taloned legs that made her almost as fast on the ground as in the air.

Prison guards, grizzled mercenaries in Alorean Import Company uniforms, took one look at Rai and Raven and quickly abandoned any heroism they might have been considering. There was no Company official present, and so none to be the wiser when they went so far as to open the gates before them.

Even with the gates open, Rai went one better: he brought his spiked tail around in a punishing lash, crushing the gate to splinters. Behind them, the Gryphonslair resistance raised up a cheer.

The imprisoned Qui-descended—and not just Qui, but those of mixed blood alongside Rikani, pale Ishmanti, and even Maresh unfortunate enough to have been mistaken for Qui by the Aloreans—looked at the gate blankly, thoughts hidden behind masks of suffering. They turned to each other, waiting for someone to emerge; waiting to see if their release was another kind of trap.

Raven crouched, and Ariadel slid down from her back, rubbing the bird's dark beak as she descended. As soon as she had touched down and steadied herself, Raven melted down into her cat shape and leapt into Ariadel's arms, then climbed up to her shoulder, all of which sent murmurs through the gathering Qui. She walked toward them, searching their faces, and Vidarian watched her, his heart in his throat. As quietly as he could, he slid down from Rai's shoulder, dropping to the ground.

"Aloreans," Ariadel called, stridently calling them by their nationality, not their descent; her voice cracked once, then came through stronger. "You have been imprisoned here by the Alorean Import Company, which acted without the authority of the emperor." At this another murmur passed through the group, and more than one face was streaked with tears. "There will be justice for your capture! I promise you this!" Her voice rose, shaking but strong. "We will return you to your homes, and bring food and supplies so that you might recover for the journey. Heal, and be free."

Healers and gryphon-wards bearing water, food, and blankets filtered into the crowd, distributing their goods to first hesitant and then grateful prisoners. Children materialized, brought from hiding places and pushed forward toward the food and water, their faces hollow and smudged with dirt.

It was a familiar voice that turned his head toward faces that at first were unrecognizable. A thin woman was nudging a younger girl before her toward a gryphon-ward laden with baskets of bread, and it wasn't until she spoke again, encouraging the child, that Vidarian recognized her.

"Ellara!" he called, running toward them. When their faces turned, blank and uncomprehending, he thought he'd been mistaken, but then they lit with recognition. Lifan and Ellara ran to meet him, and he knelt so that the young windreader could throw her arms around his neck. He embraced her, his heart sinking as his hands touched protruding shoulder-blades, a prominent spine; his teeth clenched, fury so raw that it misted his eyes with blackness in waves.

Carefully, Vidarian stood, wrapping his arm around Ellara as well, though with more surprise. "Ellara, how . . . ?"

Lifan was half Qui, her heritage written on her black glossy hair and fine cheekbones, but Ellara was not. They were cousins, and, though Ellara was also dark of hair, even the most ignorant Company-man could not have mistaken her blue eyes and faintly freckled skin for Qui. Her jaw firmed, standing out against her cheeks in her thinness. "I told them they could take me with her or they could answer a blade, and we all would die." She spat, but weakly. "Bloody cowards."

"Did you know about this place?" A healer shuffled by them, and he touched her arm, then took an herbal tincture from the tray she carried, a health tonic, and gave it to Lifan.

"No," Ellara said, and her eyebrows contracted with the memory. "I thought we'd be detained in Val Harlon for a day, perhaps two . . . and then they loaded us all on carts bound for the desert. I would have attempted escape, but we saw them behead a young man who tried." When Vidarian's eyes widened, she added quietly, "I've seen things, Captain, that'll turn your stomach more than that. We 'scaped the worst of it, but plenty didn't."

"I've never known a braver soul," Vidarian said, gripping her shoulder, and meant it. He wanted to stay with her, but Ariadel was weaving through the crowd, searching. A stream of refugees were now being led back toward Gryphonslair, and he pointed in their direction. "Go to the camp, they'll have hot food and more clothing. I'll find you there." Ellara nodded, first following his glance to Ariadel, then looking back at him with a surprised smile, before pressing her hand to Lifan's back to guide her toward the line.

When he touched Ariadel's arm, she turned quickly, hope in her eyes that dimmed when she saw him, though the swiftness of her embrace took any sting out of it. Once more he carefully drew his arms around her, careful both of her body and Raven, who still curled protectively around her shoulders. She turned again, searching, and he followed her, one hand on her shoulder.

Beneath his fingers, her muscles tensed almost immediately, and she dashed ahead.

The crowd parted before her, giving way to a grey-haired woman whose eyes and oval face were nearly a mirror for Ariadel's. Like her companions, she was also terribly thin, her skin darkened to leather by the desert sun, but it dissolved into a welcome smile and no few tears as she caught sight of Ariadel.

The two women embraced, the elder exclaiming over Ariadel's condition, and Ariadel in turn interrogated her mother over her own health, stopping a passing healer for a restorative draught and pressing it into her hands. The older woman tried to wave it off, but Ariadel would not be deterred, and demanded she drink the entire vial then and there. She did so stubbornly, and as Ariadel explained what they had done, turned to Vidarian with an expression full of welcome.

"Lady Whitehammer," Vidarian said, offering his hand to her. He'd learned her proper name this time, aiming not to repeat the embarrassing assumption with which he'd introduced himself to Ariadel's father assuming he bore Ariadel's surname.

"Len Tsai was my family's name," the woman smiled, and Vidarian's heart sunk at the correction. "I called myself Whitehammer in Alorea in deference to Alorean culture. I will be using my Qui name from today."

"It's a great honor to meet you," Vidarian said. "Your daughter has moved heaven and earth to find you."

She smiled even more widely, her eyes disappearing into wrinkles. "I am unsurprised."

Back beyond the gate, Rai's head was peeking into the camp as he craned his long neck. He caught sight of Vidarian and gave a tiny yip of greeting that turned heads in his direction. *Brother*, he said, and Vidarian jumped, surprised he could hear the dragon's voice from so far away. *There is a man here looking for you.*

Vidarian turned back to Ariadel, who shooed him. "We'll manage," she said. He thought of insisting on staying with her, but Rai yipped again, and she pushed at him. "Go! Don't be ridiculous!"

Reluctantly, he bowed over both of their hands, then turned to slip back through the crowd and to the gate. Rai's ears were down with apology, and he reminded himself not to be annoyed; the shapechanger could be terribly sensitive.

"I'm sorry to ask for you, Captain," the messenger who awaited him said—a lean man, one of Marielle's sailors. "But we've captured an officer of the Alorean Import Company. Queen Marielle thought you should be present."

Rai became his wolf self and followed, padding along at Vidarian's heels. And halfway to the *Luminous*, his tail started to wag.

It's over now, right? the Starhunter said. *You're ready to help me?*

"Still a bit busy," Vidarian murmured, trying to avoid the attention of the messenger. Eventually, they reached the ship, and the sailor saluted and took his leave. Vidarian climbed down the main ladder and deliberately took a wrong turn, then two more, navigating to a remote part of the ship.

"All right," he said, sighing. "I said I would help you."

Great! It's about the other goddesses.

Vidarian's stomach sank. Chances were even she was about to ask for something proximate to a high mortality rate. "The other goddesses?" he asked. "They don't much like you. The two I've met, anyway."

We-ell, that's the thing. I think the others might be gone.

"Siane?"

And Anake.

Of all of the elemental artifacts, the fire and water ones had been the easiest to recover. In fact, he wasn't even sure he'd *seen* a single earth artifact. It was distressing, now that he thought about it, in fact it made the skin on the back of his neck squirm, but he was hardly the one to investigate such a thing. "Why are you asking me this now?"

Because you can find them now, silly.

"What? How?"

Because of him, duh! She manifested a shadowy hand and waved it at Rai.

"Rai? How is he supposed to find the goddesses?"

You're impossible. She filled his head with another sigh, then twirled in a circle. When she stopped, her head was a pelican-gryphon's, specifically Arikaree's. '*Being a lance of earth and sky,*' she said in the gryphon's voice.

Vidarian stared.

Oops, gotta go, she said. *Those icy bastards never know when to quit.*

And before he could ask what *that* meant, she was gone.

⌇⌇⌇

The relay room of the *Luminous* was full to bursting again, this time with two gryphons—Thalnarra and Meleaar—in addition to Marielle, Iridan, Khalesh, Isri, and Endera. It was an unlikely council, gryphons and fire priestess and sea queen and miraculous machine—but Vidarian was surprised at the swelling of pride and gratitude he felt upon seeing them there around the glowing relay sphere. The captured officer sat bound in an ornate chair at the front of the room, an empty wall behind him. Despite the expensive scented oil in his hair and the fine weave of his white shirt and black coat, he was naturally young, not one of the merchant princes who extended their lives with healing magic. With a spark of disgust Vidarian realized that no one even close to the directors would have risked themselves on the front line—save Justinian, who had trusted his safety to the automaton Veda and escaped.

Meleaar, however, was an unexpected addition, and when Vidarian took his seat and looked between the eagle-gryphon and Thalnarra, the latter explained:

// *Meleaar is one of seven currently known gryphons in the world to be possessed of what our ancestors called a 'mindlink.' He is an exceptionally powerful telepath, but beyond that, mindlinks can speak with any other gryphon bearing the mindlink no matter where they are located. Through our mindlinks, gryphon societies have been able to keep a single connected mother culture for thousands of years. Gryphonslair is deeply fortunate to have him.* //

At her words, Meleaar gave an almost sheepish nod of his beak, and Vidarian looked closely at him, reevaluating all of their conversations.

// *Obnoxious, isn't it?* // Thalnarra continued, when stunned silence answered her, // *Brawn, beauty, and an exceptionally rare talent.* // Then, privately to Vidarian: // *You didn't think we kept him around just because he's pretty, did you?* //

Actually, I did, he thought back at her, not knowing if she would hear, but she, Meleaar, and Malloray all chuckled.

"Continue with your story, sirrah," Marielle said, idly spinning a curved sharkskin-handled knife by its pointed tip on the table. The lacquer would be the worse for it, but it had the desired effect on the officer, who swallowed.

"I've never seen the device myself, obviously," he said, stretching for arrogance and reaching only awkwardness with his wrists bound behind him. "I've seen diagrams. If you bring me parchment . . . ?" He eyed the stack of paper at the empty secretary's place at the table.

"Why should we believe you?"

The officer sputtered, a single hopeless note that ended in a shake of his head. "Why not? They won't come back for me. I'm as good as a fugitive now." He tilted his head to one side. "And if I give you what you want, you'll remember and reward me."

"Don't be so sure," Marielle said dryly, spinning the knife again.

The rest of them exchanged looks, and Isri leaned forward, staring at the man. She stood and approached him, picking up a sheet of the paper and a wrapped stick of charcoal beside it. The officer beamed, twisting in his chair to bring his wrists toward her, but she gently shook her head. When she reached him, she placed her left hand on his forehead and took up the stylus with her right. "Imagine it," she said.

Flummoxed and flushing from it, the man looked about to reply, then took a deep breath. "Fine," he said.

They both closed their eyes, and Isri's charcoal began to move, tracing a diagram of an elemental device onto the parchment. Gradually it began to emerge: tubes and crystal spheres and elemental gems, as well as a marking that indicated placing a strap from it around the arm of a seated human. Isri drew for several minutes, setting down one line and then another, erasing yet another line and redrawing it with a swipe of her pencil.

At last the charcoal stopped, and Isri set it aside, nudging the parchment across the table to Khalesh. The big man accepted the parchment, then turned it around twice, looking at it from one angle after another.

"Mothers protect us," Khalesh whispered. Vidarian wanted to ask him what on earth he meant, but his eyes were riveted to the page. "If this is right—these two devices together could be used to wipe out an entire race. Or more than one race."

The table erupted in intense conversation. It went on for several moments before Marielle banged on the table with the lapis pommel of her knife. "Come now!" she chided them. "But aye, Khalesh, I admit I'd like to know what you mean by that. What do you mean by 'race'? Which two devices? And destroy them how?"

Khalesh spun the parchment on the table, pushing it toward them. He indicated two spherelike devices on it, each dotted with holes. "You see these? They're relay spheres." He tapped three more points. "And an elemental triangulation system. They've bridged two known devices." And then the strap. "This connects to a given person's essence."

They all continued to stare at him, and he tapped the parchment hard with a huge forefinger. "This is a location device, a finder, but with this kind of power, it's meant to find not just one other person, but every person who is *like* the person they connect to it. Or," he looked to Isri and then Thalnarra, misery heavy in his eyes. "Species, I think. If the species is nonhuman." Silence fell again, and he jabbed the parchment once more. "Don't you see? The only reason you would have for locating every single member of an entire species is to attach a weapon to this device, which they appear to have modified it to create." He indicated another part of it.

// *And they have this device already?* // Thalnarra said, skeptical. // *Why haven't they used it?* //

"They don't have it yet," the officer said. "But they know how to build it. They're missing some of the parts. I don't know which."

"Ariadel said the rumors were they were going to test a weapon on the prison camp." Marielle said, her voice harsh with dismay.

Vidarian rested his forehead in his hands. "And Tepeki feared something exactly like this. A killing weapon that could annihilate his entire clan." When he raised his head again, he looked around the table, meeting each set of eyes in turn. "We need to get to it before they do."

"How do you propose we do that?" Endera asked.

"We ask the entire empire. Both empires," he added. "We use what they don't have—numbers." Pushing himself to his feet, Vidarian circled the table, taking up a pair of relay glasses. "Malloray, Iridan, Meleaar—can you make this sphere reach every relay sphere on the continent?"

Man, gryphon, and automaton exchanged glances, measuring. They were silent for several long moments, and then Iridan nodded. "*We can.*" He placed a polished brass hand on the relay sphere in the center of the table, and Vidarian's glasses began to glow. Malloray joined him, closing his eyes.

"*At your leisure*," Iridan said at last.

"Citizens of Alorea," Vidarian said, willing strength into his voice, reaching into his memories of Lirien's imperial addresses. "Citizens of the world. Most of you do not know my name. Neither do you know the names of the men and women who have taken it upon themselves to decide the fate of our world in secret, to seize power and destroy entire populations for their own gain, to rule in small numbers over an enslaved people unfortunate enough to be born without wealth. You do not know the names of the imperial citizens that the Alorean Import Company imprisoned against their will, leaving them in the southern desert to die." He paused then, knowing every moment of silence across the sphere would seem an eternity, but needing to gather his thoughts.

"A great shadow is upon us," he continued, looking into the sphere. "We will need every hand, every eye. The time for division is over. A new age is upon us, one in which we must decide whether we choose a life tailored to a chosen few, or a life that can sustain, a life where people across Andovar can live in peace with one another, not as all-powerful bearers of force, but as brothers and sisters, mothers and fathers, human and gryphon and seridi and shapechanger. I ask you to look beyond the barriers that separate us and look to each other, for strength and healing in our changing world.

"Will you join me?"

AUTHOR'S NOTE

What an amazing and strange year this has been.

Sword of Fire and Sea appeared in June 2011, and, like its predecessor, this book owes its existence to a cast of many at Pyr: Lou Anders, editorial director (2011 winner of the Hugo Award for long-form editing!); Catherine Roberts-Abel, Jacqueline Cooke (art department), Jade Zora Ballard, and Bruce Carle in production; Jill Maxick in publicity and Lisa Michalski in marketing. I'd also like to thank Steven L. Mitchell, editor in chief, Jon Kurtz, president, and the rest of the fine folk at Prometheus Books, for continuing to fan the flames. Beyond Pyr, Gabrielle Harbowy lends her eagle-gryphon-like copyediting eye, and Dehong He honors us with yet another amazing cover.

This book is dedicated to my grandparents: Nellie and Harry, whom I did not know but whose influence permeates and sustains my father's family today, and Dorothy Lee and Masato Asakawa. I am incredibly lucky to have grown up knowing grandparents who were not only strong and loving, but truly heroic. My grandfather grew up on a pier (literally on a pier; there are photos) in San Diego, and in 1942 at age sixteen was sent to the Japanese Internment Camp in Poston, Arizona. While it would be easy for the events of the next several years to calcify a person's life, it is my grandparents' reaction in the decades following that define them to me as heroes: an absence of bitterness, a joy in life, and a deep knowledge that we are every day responsible for creating and fighting for the society that we live in. I inherit from them a good part of my overactive sense of justice and a lifetime of inspiration.

Lastly, of course, my husband Jay was instrumental in my surviving the writing of this book. The perils of a second book are many, but that's a story for another time (and another place: say, erinhoffman.com?).

Some of you joined the journey early on, and, as promised, I'd like to thank you here. What follows is the list of the first one hundred members of the World of Andovar page on Facebook (www.facebook.com/andovar.world). As of the writing of this author's note, the page's membership is at 2,135, and by the time you read this hopefully it will have continued to grow. Thank you all for joining the great gryphon cause of 2011 . . . and beyond!

Mandy Heiser	Christy Marx	Devin Hoffman	Frederick V. Wolfe II
Bruce Harlick	Sharon Axline	Allen Varney	Matthew Thomas Scibilia
Ellen Denham	Tracy Seamster	Tina Tyndal	Andrew J. Cooper
Jason Wodicka	Sharon Keir Patry	Jennifer Crow	Jason Ridler
Ronya McCool	Jeremy Nusser	Zoe Zygmunt	Michal Todorovic
Shannon Ridler	Andrew Carroll	Trudy Marie Brutsche	Justin Howe
Sherry Peters	Katie Connell	Mary Rodgers	Michael J. DeLuca
Adria Laycraft	Michael Dore	Lynda E. Rucker	James Hall
Matthew S. Rotundo	Caroline Yim	Fred Kiesche	Marc Destefano
Jamie Ridler	Erik J. Caponi	Kathy Whitlock Slee	Erica Hildebrand
Susan Shell Winston	Shannon Drake	Gabrielle Harbowy	Shara Saunsaucie White
Rita Oakes	Caroline Wong	Bill Spangler	Jamey Stevenson
Julie Miyamoto	Ethan Benanav	Scott Oden	Reg Rozee
Barbara Barnett-Stewart	Lucy Snyder	Mihir Wanchoo	Maggie Della Rocca
Stephen Gallagher	Carolyn Koh	Julia Mary Breidenbach	Greg Johnson
Charles Tan	Karen Jungsun Lee	Rachel Brook	Jonathan Rodgers
Jocelyn Johnson	Melissa MyWorld	Andrew Mayer	Annalise 'Bents' Fahlstrom
Lana McCarthy	Kimberly M. Rosal	Jill Maxick	Brenda Cobbs
Edward Heiland	Melissa Tomney	Susan Griffith	Sean Dumas
Beth Langford	Kate Marshall	Brandon K. Markham	Jane Pinckard
Karen A. Romanko	Emily Mei	David Alastair Hayden	Geoffrey Jacoby
David J. Corwell	Ken Wallace	Jon Sprunk	Kristin Jett
Marty Brown	Burke Trieschmann	Rene Sears	Wes Unruh
Link Hughes	Michael McCormick	Clay Griffith	Douglas Paton
Sheri Rubin	Rod Hannah	Lou Anders	Corvus Elrod

ABOUT THE AUTHOR

Erin Hoffman is a video-game designer, author, and essayist on player rights and modern media ethics. She lives in northern California with her husband, two parrots, and two excessively clever dogs. For more about her work, and the world of Andovar, visit www.erinhoffman.com.